A BITTER JE

COVETED M

A BEAUTIFUL,

WHO ENJOYED [illegible] PAY FOR DOING

WHAT CAME NATURALLY

THE PAMPERED, OVERPRIVILEGED SON OF

THE NEW RUSSIAN ARISTROCRACY

What did this unlikely trio have in common? And why should a government with the vastest armed might and most awesome political apparatus on earth fear them?

The Soviet leadership is about to find out. . . .

SALT MINE

"Expert tension . . . solid suspense . . . uncommonly vivid!"—*Kirkus Reviews*

"The unimaginable is made into a splendid novel . . . exciting from first page to last!"
—*Chattanooga Times*

"The author, who knows Russia and Moscow well, orchestrates the whole affair with smooth credibility!"—*Publishers Weekly*

SALT MINE

David Lippincott

A SIGNET BOOK
NEW AMERICAN LIBRARY
TIMES MIRROR

NAL BOOKS ARE AVAILABLE AT QUANTITY DISCOUNTS WHEN USED TO PROMOTE PRODUCTS OR SERVICES. FOR INFORMATION PLEASE WRITE TO PREMIUM MARKETING DIVISION, THE NEW AMERICAN LIBRARY, INC., 1633 BROADWAY, NEW YORK, NEW YORK 10019.

Acknowledgments

The Entertainment Company: From "Knock Three Times." © 1970 Big Apple Music Company, A Division of 40 West Music Corp. Used by permission.

The Richmond Organization: From "We Shall Overcome." New words and musical arrangement by Zilphia Horton, Frank Hamilton, Guy Carawan & Peter Seeger. TRO-© Copyright 1960 & 1963 Ludlow Music, Inc., New York, New York. Used by permission.

A hardcover edition was published by The Viking Press and simultaneously in Canada by Penguin Books Canada Limited.

SIGNET, SIGNET CLASSICS, MENTOR, PLUME, MERIDIAN AND NAL BOOKS *are published by The New American Library, Inc., 1633 Broadway, New York, New York 10019*

FIRST SIGNET PRINTING, APRIL, 1980

1 2 3 4 5 6 7 8 9

PRINTED IN THE UNITED STATES OF AMERICA

For my son, Christopher

Сыну моему, Кристоферу

Родился он с даром смеха
И с чувством что мир безумен
Зто — его одно наследие.

РАФАЕЛ САБАТИНИ, Скарамуш

AUTHOR'S NOTE

Purists will probably be upset that the patronymics so dear to the Russian soul have been largely omitted from this book. I plead guilty. It has always struck me as confusing for a reader to encounter a character as "Comrade Katov" on one page and as "Ivan Ivanovich" a few pages later, only to have him reappear in the next paragraph as "Vanya." To avoid this, I have resorted to common English usage. The heresy was committed for the sake of clarity.

PART ONE

1

WEDNESDAY, OCTOBER 21

The man Alyosha pulled his coat tight against the night wind and shrank back into the doorway, waiting. In front of him, he could see his breath freeze, an icy cloud the shape of a great, ominous eye. His rendezvous was not far from the corner of Petrovka Street, perhaps fifty meters from Sverdlov Square; opposite loomed the graceful silhouette of the Bolshoi. The setting was appropriate, Alyosha decided: The four rearing horses on the theater's main cornice had been pulling their stone chariot long before anyone had heard of Marx, Lenin, or Engels.

The theater was dark, and had been for the last half hour; the audience had left, the instruments were packed away, and the performers had gone home. From the safety of his doorway, Alyosha had watched them all depart. Farther down the street, there was a taxi stand, empty now, although earlier a long line of cabs had waited there, picking up fares as they left the Bolshoi. Down Petrovka Street, Alyosha saw a taxi coming toward him and wondered; the green light on its windshield showed it was empty. Tentatively, Alyosha stepped out of his doorway and saw the green light flicker briefly. It was his signal. When the taxi slowed down, he waved his hand as any Muscovite hailing a cab might. The taxi stopped. Quickly, Alyosha stepped inside and sank into the rear seat.

The driver never turned around. His thick neck and the back of his black leather cap were all that Alyosha could see—or, for that matter, ever *had* seen. "Alyosha—it goes well?" the Neck asked.

"On schedule."

"*Khorosho.*"

"There was some talk. One of the team perhaps going into business for himself."

The Neck snorted. "Old KGB rule: Always listen to talk." Alyosha made a sour face.

"We listened." For some time, the cab drove on in silence. From long experience, Alyosha knew he was not expected to say very much. This silence made things easier, since Alyosha didn't even know the Neck's name, only that all of the funds for his operation came through him. Alyosha was the leader, the Neck was the banker, and neither of them spoke unless there was something pressing to say. The Neck turned left on Belinsky, and again on Gorky Street, slowing outside the magnificent old Hotel National to yell at a wobbly American tourist; the man refused to accept that the green light was out and therefore the cab was occupied.

On Arbat Street, the Neck finally spoke again. "One reason I asked you to meet me tonight is that I shall be away for a time. Naturally, I wanted to give you the arrival information on the two men we are assigning you myself. The fifteenth. They will arrive at Domodedovo, Flight two-sixteen from Lvov, on the fifteenth. Do you have that?"

Alyosha sat for a second, letting the date, flight number, and place of origin burn themselves into his brain. "Yes. Domodedovo. Flight two-sixteen from Lvov. The fifteenth."

"Good. I should be back before then, but one is never sure."

They drove on in silence again. To Alyosha, it was infuriating that the man would never turn around. After a long pause, the Neck spoke. "Do you have any questions?"

"How do I recognize the—these two men of yours?"

"They will make themselves known to you. And one will carry a cardboard suitcase with a Lvov sticker." Another pause, then: "The other reason, of course," continued the Neck, "is an installment of funds. You run out, tell one of them, and they will get you more." Still without turning, the driver handed Alyosha a wad of bills across the seat.

"Thank you. It will be enough."

"Don't thank me. *You* are the one taking the chances. You, and now Misha and Avraam. They will make very good additions to your team, I think." The faceless cabman drove on awhile in silence before asking, "Where should I leave you off?"

"Any place near the metro."

They had crossed the Moskva River by the ornate Borodinsky Bridge, and the cab now headed south. Spread out on either side, the sprawling masses of buildings, some large, some small, were bathed in the eerie light of street lamps combined with the glow of a late October moon. The cab stopped across from the Fili metro stop, where Alyosha got out. He was annoyed that the Neck didn't at least wish him luck. Perhaps that is the problem with having no face.

THURSDAY, OCTOBER 22

Vasily Klin stood at the rear of the room, leaning against the French windows, and watched the sight with proprietary pleasure. The ballroom of Arkhangelskoye Palace was a vast echoing place, with acoustics that rattled the chandeliers; at one end, the musicians moved their fingers gently across the balalaika strings, gradually picking up speed until finally all that could be seen of their hands was a thin, white blur. To one side men with the tambours and ratchets began their percussive bursts. Suddenly, as if shot onto the floor by demons, the Ukranian dancers somersaulted back into the room, giving high-pitched, birdlike whistles as the lead dancer soared ever higher into the air. Then, with a thunderous "*Hej!*" it was over.

Klin watched his guests as they stamped their feet and shouted for more. But the balalaika orchestra was quickly replaced by the dance band from the Hotel Metropol, which broke into "Take the 'A' Train." Some of the guests began to dance; others drifted back to the many bars.

Until "The 'A' Train," Klin decided, Pushkin would have felt at home here. The writer had frequently stayed in the town of Arkhangelskoye, often visiting the palace when it belonged to the Yusupovs—next to the Romanovs, the wealthiest family in Russia. An enormous building of ocher stucco with a thousand windows and graceful colonnades, it had long ago been dubbed the "Versailles of Moscow." These days, Arkhangelskoye Palace ordinarily served as a public museum, but Vasily Klin was minister of state security, a position of awesome power, and he had commandeered it for this party. Nobody questioned the arrangement; nobody ever questioned much of what a minister of security chose to do. Besides, the party was the wedding feast of his niece, Katyusha, the sort of occasion all Russians relish. In spite of appearances, though, there was nothing generous in Klin's gesture; the feast was an act of pure politics. (The man Katyusha had married earlier that day was the son of Deputy Premier Chaidze; Klin himself had helped engineer the merger. In the world of the Kremlin, this sort of connection could one day be of help.)

Across the room, Klin saw the deputy premier, a squat, bull-necked Georgian, beaming at his new daughter-in-law, at his son, and at his wife. As each member of the Soviet hierarchy came over to be introduced, Chaidze would grab the man and kiss him wetly, first on one cheek, then on the other. Almost always, this would be followed by ritual linking of arms, a shouted *"na zdorovye,"* and a sudden downing of the vodka put in their hands. As a result, Deputy Premier Chaidze was beginning to look frazzled; the entire hierarchy of ministers had shown up. Only Talanin, chief of state, was missing—and he had sent flowers. Gathered here at Arkhangelskoye Palace was the cream of the new Russian aristocracy, holding forth in the halls of the old. The new aristocracy. It fascinated Klin.

Looking at them, Klin found it difficult to separate the men from the sinister dossiers he had the KGB keep on each. Their weaknesses, their deviations from Party norms, the pettiest of their transgressions, all were neatly recorded against the time when the information might be useful.

With a small sigh, Klin turned and gazed briefly through the French window; the last of a pale, autumn sun cast long shadows across the rolling sea of the Arkhangelskoye Palace lawns. Not visible was the small army of KGB men set up on the perimeter of the palace grounds. In the river, KGB frogmen patrolled the shore off the grounds, and above, a helicopter circled lazily; there were too many men from top Kremlin posts here to allow anything but maximum security. Beyond the perimeter, the sweep down to the river was punctuated by heroic statuary; by the river's edge, sticking out like fingers into the water, was a series of teahouses and summer retreats that Prince Yusupov's ladies once filled with polite laughter. In the main building, the prince's priceless collection of Tiepolos, Bouchers, and Van Dycks still hung. Those people, thought Klin, had known how to live; the new aristocracy was just learning.

Shortly, he would have to rejoin his guests, but the idea made him uncomfortable. Indoors, one could not hide inside one's hat. Tall, patrician-nosed, with classical features, Klin would have been considered handsome—*except*. Some years ago, touring a nuclear power plant in Kazan, he had been exposed to a fleeting burst of radiation. The exposure was not fatal; its most serious effect was that one day all his hair fell out. The hair would return, the doctor had promised, and the ugly, red blotches on his scalp would disappear. The doctor had been wrong. A little later, when the hair did grow back, there were only short, crinkly patches of it, like tufted grass on the tundra. Worse, the piebald blotches on his scalp became even more vivid, a series of angry red discolorations that no amount of combing could cover. To an elegant, meticulous man like Klin, his head appeared grotesque and repulsive. Already the most influential security minister since Beria, his appetite for power grew insatiable, the compensating drive, perhaps, of a man determined not to be deterred by his appearance.

Reluctantly, he moved back into the ebb and flow of his guests, clapping a shoulder here, kissing a fellow minister there, then moving on before their wives—many of whom had never met him before—could pretend not to notice his disfigurement. Klin danced with Katyusha; he danced with her mother; he danced with the Deputy Premier Chaidze's wife. But he was relieved when the Metropol's band withdrew again, this time in favor of a Georgian gypsy group, singing the sad folk songs the Russians love.

The voice beside him came to Klin as a surprise; he had not seen the man sidle up to him. "Comrade Minister, a superb party. Such a happy occasion. So beautiful."

The voice belonged to Mikhail Chorniev, head of the KGB, and one of the few men who reported directly to Klin. Klin thoroughly disliked Chorniev, a thin weasel-faced man whose walk seemed to advance him sideways as far as it did forward. With his soft, insidious way of speaking, Chorniev would have appeared equally at home whispering into Richelieu's ear or telling Nixon to burn the tapes. There was a reason, though, why Chorniev had risen as far as he had. Klin made him head of the KGB because Chorniev was so thoroughly disliked by the rest of the ministers he figured he could never threaten Klin's own flank. In response to Chorniev's compliment, Klin only nodded.

"In fact, everything is *so* beautiful, I hate to intrude upon you with business."

"But you will overwhelm your scruples and intrude anyway."

A soft smile flickered across Chorniev's face as he bowed from the waist to acknowledge Klin's thrust. "It is necessary, Vasily. It can't wait."

Never, Klin thought, would Chorniev become part of the new aristocracy. "Very well. What's on fire?"

Chorniev leaned closer to make sure he could not be overheard. "We have a man waiting some distance down the river. To see you. With urgent information, he claims. He wants to be sure you realize his information cannot wait. It is vital to the security of the Soviet, he says—"

Klin was growing irritated but managed to contain himself. "They always say that. Kindly, Chorniev, find out what the man has. If anything. *You* handle it. My party . . ." He let his hand sweep the room in front of Chorniev.

Chorniev sighed. "Vasily, I'm sorry. But he will give the information to no one but you. Personally. He is quite insistent on that point."

Klin laughed. *"Give?* You mean sell. He will give it to no one but me because he thinks I will pay more."

Chorniev appeared flustered, but his voice never rose above its whisper. "It is not a question of selling, Vasily. You know of this man: Volovno. Last year, he led us to the theft of major supplies from Building Cooperative Number Four."

"In exchange for discharging his wife from Belagin Prison."

"Yes. And in that case, his information proved reliable. So we cannot afford to ignore his offer now. He claims the implications are staggering."

"So will be his price."

Uncomfortably, Chorniev shrugged. "If what he has is as spectacular as he claims, his price, Vasily, is modest."

Klin's smile chilled Chorniev visibly. "*He* wants to be head of the KGB instead of you?"

"Exit visas for him and his wife."

Klin exploded. "Does that idiot think that the Soviet government makes such deals? I will not be hijacked. I will not allow the government to be." In his speech, Klin could detect a slight slurring, the result, he supposed, of too many "*na zdorovyes.*" What was this wretched Chorniev doing spoiling the afternoon for him, anyway? He pressed Chorniev back against the wall, turning his own head slightly to avoid the sour smell of the man's breath. "Where *is* Volovno?" Klin hissed.

"Down in one of the teahouses by the river, Vasily. He would not come here. He said it was there or nowhere."

"He did, did he? Well, my dear Chorniev, take the little bastard back to Dzerzhinsky Street and squeeze the information out of him. If it is anything of value, tell me tomorrow." Suddenly Klin laughed. "Exit visas . . ."

He watched a shaken Chorniev scuttle across the ballroom. The musicians were changing once more, and the folk singers were replaced by the Hotel Metropol band. In the silence between the two, Klin heard the blatant sounds of the punk rock being played downstairs for the teenage children of the Soviet ministers. One hand slid unconsciously across his scalp; they would not know him there. Turning, Klin decided to go downstairs and see what it was like.

• The sky was darker now, and Chorniev picked up two KGB agents outside the building. On the way down the long slope between Arkhangelskoye Palace and the river, he spotted the teahouse where Volovno waited. It was an enclosed structure, built on stone piers directly out over the water; because of the fall rains, the river lapped at the bottom of the teahouse itself. Carefully, the three KGB men approached; neither the agent nor Chorniev saw a sallow, Asiatic face watching their progress from behind a screen of evergreen bushes to the right. For a moment, the face studied them intently, then melted away as the men drew closer.

The first agent pushed open the door; Chorniev and the other man followed him in. Chorniev swore. The teahouse was empty. Explaining Volovno's disappearance to Klin was going to be unpleasant; he knew he should have had the place covered while he was at the palace, but Volovno was so important and Chorniev so eager that he had become careless.

Aimlessly, the three of them clumped around the octagon-shaped room, stamping on the floorboards, looking for what they already knew was not there. "Damn!" grunted the first agent, tripping over something. A closer look showed that it was the cover of a trapdoor. Chorniev moved closer; the agent, still cursing at his wounded toe, yanked the door upward.

Below, the river shimmered in the beam of the man's flashlight. The rain-swollen waters, up almost to floor level, suddenly produced Volovno, his upturned face pressed tight against the flooring, his throat cut from one side to the other, rocking gently back and forth in the dimness of Prince Yusupov's lagoon.

When you looked closer, the rip in Volovno's throat appeared so deep it seemed possible his head might tear loose and float away. "Pull him out," ordered Chorniev, staring fascinated. Then it happened. Chorniev and the two agents gasped; the man who was squatting on his haunches beside the trapdoor fell backward. As if Volovno had heard Chorniev's order, his body suddenly rose straight up out of the water with a spectacular splash and crashed partway out onto the floor of the teahouse.

Once again, Volovno's corpse moved upward; it was accompanied by another great splash, followed by the appearance of a KGB frogman pushing the body from below; the patrolling frogman had seen the body underwater, seen the light as Chorniev's agents opened the trapdoor, and come over to help by pushing from below. He had had no idea of the effect it would have on the men above him. To show that they hadn't been really scared, both of the agents laughed nervously, hitting their hearts with their fists and rolling their eyes to prove how much of a joke it had been.

Chorniev wasn't laughing. He was a survivor. He watched the men at the top as they struggled, they fought, they rose, they fell. Chorniev survived. He should never have brought Volovno here; someone had very much not wanted the meeting between him and Klin to take place.

• At eleven forty-five that night, Alyosha Gregarin slipped along the rain-drenched streets of Moscow. The capital of the Soviets goes to bed early, and there were few people to be seen. Crossing Red square, Alyosha watched the nightly army of old women with their twig brooms sweeping the vast area, wretched but uncomplaining as the raw wind tore at their long skirts. Several times on his journey, Alyosha stepped back into doorways and waited to make sure no one was following him. Twice he had gone into nearly empty cafés, once for a coffee, once for a cognac to take the chill out of his blood. Behind him, reflected in the shiny pavements, he could see the brilliant lights on the Kremlin's onion domes; the red flag over the Council of Ministers Building—"the flag that is never lowered"—flapped briskly in the wind, its floodlights making their own set of distorted reflections on the wet street. Detouring all the way to the Square 50-Letiye Oktyabrya, Alyosha took a slow, circuitous route to the Marx Prospekt metro station. Once there, he didn't even pause but shot down the stairs into its ornate mosaic and tile interior.

At eleven fifty-five, he boarded the 12:07 train of the Green Line, made his way to the last car, and sat down to wait. As he had expected, this car was empty; what few passengers the late train was carrying were up in the first two cars. Alyosha barely saw or heard the man get on at the Dynamo stop; his first real awareness was the man's voice. "You need concern yourself no further with Volovno. He is at peace."

Alyosha turned slightly to look at Tbor; his was the Asiatic face that had earlier watched Chorniev and his men arrive at the teahouse. "Are you certain Volovno didn't tell anyone *before* you got there?"

"Positive."

"Did you search him?"

"There was no time. They came for him faster than I expected."

Uneasily, Alyosha accepted Tbor's logic on the second point; the first still bothered him. "He might have talked on his way out with Chorniev. He could have told him without—"

Looking impatient, Tbor stood up. "No. He would wait for Klin. To tell anyone else would be to waste the information. Only Klin." Tbor's face grew a small smile. "I know how these things work."

"Perhaps too well." There was a note of acid to Alyosha's voice. He did not like Tbor, and liked his profession even less.

Shrugging off the insult, Tbor halted at the exit door as the train slowed down. "I have another possible man for your team. You can meet him—perhaps tomorrow." Alyosha said nothing and Tbor stepped off; two stops later, he got off himself and took the next Green Line train back to Moscow Center. Riding along, staring at the odd reflections made in the window by the signal lights in the tunnel, he kept seeing Tbor's face. Alyosha shuddered. Unlike Volovno, Tbor was a paid informant for the KGB, a specialist in dissidents and possible defectors. Volovno had done what he had done only for urgent, personal reasons. That was bad enough. But Tbor turned in people for money. "I used to be a doctor, a surgeon," Tbor had once explained to Alyosha. "There was trouble, but my tastes remain expensive. So whoever will pay, I will sell to." Before Alyosha, Tbor had had only one buyer; now he had two. Some dissenters Tbor sold to the KGB, as always; the choicer—Alyosha paid more—he sold to Alyosha.

"How do I know you won't turn me—the whole operation—over to the KGB?" Alyosha had once asked him.

"You don't. But logic would dictate that I won't. For one thing, I have no idea of what you and your people are really up to. But more important, almost your entire team was recruited through me. Even I would have difficulty explaining that."

The image of Tbor in the glass vanished. The man inhabited Moscow's seamy underground—a network of informers, petty thieves, and men in hiding who were too inconsequential to bother reporting. That Tbor would soon be plucked from that murky world would come to him as a surprise. But in spite of all the logic Tbor offered Alyosha, beyond a certain point, Tbor was not to be trusted.

FRIDAY, OCTOBER 23

"No, I don't know what it means. Maybe it means nothing." Klin stared at Chorniev across his desk. "Isn't it *your* job to know such things?"

They were in Klin's office, and Chorniev had handed him the slip of paper they'd found in Volovno's pants pocket. A slightly blurred handwriting had been discovered on the inside of Volovno's cigarette wrapper, but the message remained cryptic:

Kli
18 XI.
K.
Op. Salt Min

"Volovno's notes for his talk with me," Klin grunted. "It lost a lot in translation."

" 'Eighteen eleven': the date," added Chorniev. "The only thing he did tell me was that he had the exact date. And there it is: the eighteenth of November."

"The 'Kli': me. The 'K'—well, it could be anyone. Or anything. 'Op. Salt Min'—nonsense. Utter nonsense."

Chorniev looked solemn and took a stab at it. "Salt mines make one think of Siberia. In Olenek, there is the Atomic Power Station Number Five-twelve. Perhaps—"

Klin crashed his fist hard on the desk top; his hand rose to his temple. He could feel his face flush, probably, he thought, the same angry red as the piebald blotches on his scalp. The forbidden word—"atomic"—had been uttered, but he struggled and gained control of himself. "Oh, come, Chorniev. Someone is planning to blow up a power station in Siberia, and he comes all the way here to murder a man who knows about it? No. Someone killed Volovno to shut him up.

That involved the taking of great risks. And only someone with strong connections to the KGB could have known Volovno was even at Arkhangelskoye. That makes the risk higher. It is no power station in Siberia. It is something right here. Something important enough to take such risks. 'Op. Salt Min' is a code name."

Klin could see his assault on the desk top had shaken Chorniev badly: His body shifted in the chair with discomfort; his eyes avoided Klin's; his smile was fixed; the small muscles around his mouth quivered. "Of course, Vasily Dmitrovich," whispered Chorniev. "A code name."

"There is no 'of course' about it, Chorniev. This matter is a Priority One. I want all stops pulled to find out what that code name means. Try your stable of informers. All of them. Get men out to the block watchers; one of them may remember having heard someone use those words; they're unusual enough."

Chorniev winced; canvassing the block watchers was always difficult and usually unproductive. There was a block watcher, a Party volunteer, living in every apartment building in Moscow. They spied upon their neighbors, watching, listening, and reporting anything out of line to the KGB. The flow of information from the block watchers was prodigious—and generally useless—but every now and then they turned up something of real value for the KGB. Working the other direction—dunning them for something specific—rarely had produced anything but failure. Chorniev allowed himself a sigh.

Studying him, Klin could guess a little of what was going on in the man's head; he also suspected that Chorniev had had other subjects he wanted to bring up but had decided the time was wrong. With evident relief, Chorniev accepted Klin's directive to "go get busy on it."

After Chorniev scuttled out, Klin wandered over to his windows at the Ministry of Security and gazed out. The people walking on Dzerzhinsky Street seemed to be going about their usual affairs, giving, as always, the Security building a wide berth; the mere sight of it made most Muscovites nervous. The erratic path this made them follow always amused Klin. There was a certain satisfaction to being feared.

He wondered, though, if their patterns would be as predictable the evening of the eighteenth of November. Klin could not explain it, but a hunch was eating away at his calm, some inexplicable feeling that told him Op. Salt Mine was to be of far greater significance than anyone yet had realized.

Someone should have given the man a medal for precognition.

SATURDAY, OCTOBER 24

He stood on the corner for a long time, waiting. Finally, as Tbor had promised, a car pulled to the curb and stopped. Alyosha gaped at it. The car was foreign, American, he thought, a convertible with its top up. Someone wanting to join a covert operation driving a car as conspicuous as *that?* It was hard to figure what Tbor had been thinking. A small bleat from the car's horn gave Alyosha the signal to walk across the pavement and climb in.

What surprised Alyosha even more was that the driver appeared little more than a boy. Tbor had told Alyosha his possible new recruit was young, but he hadn't expected someone who looked fifteen. Nor was he prepared for the boy's clothes: They appeared to be American, from necktie to shoes. In silence, the two of them drove down Arbat Street, took the bridge across the Moskva River, and then drifted south toward the Lenin Hills.

"How old are you?" demanded Alyosha suddenly.

"Enough."

"How *old?*"

"Eighteen. Actually, eighteen and a half."

"Your ID agrees?"

"Of course."

"Good." He twisted in the seat to face the boy squarely. "But I'll be checking it, you know." The boy nodded but said nothing. They drove on several blocks in silence. Alyosha could not have explained it, but something about this young man—his intensity perhaps—made Alyosha want to trust him immediately. He was too young and too offbeat to be a KGB agent. Agonizing over his own impulsiveness, Alyosha decided to take the chance: "I'm told you might be interested in our little venture."

"Tbor whatever-his-name-is didn't tell me much, but yes, I am interested."

"Why?"

"My father."

Studying him, Alyosha tried to make sense of what the boy said, simultaneously searching for a way to lead him naturally from one thought to the next without giving anything more away. Tbor had mentioned that the boy's father was in the government, an angle that had almost made Alyosha reject him out of hand. "Your father? I don't understand."

"He is minister of production and industry."

Alyosha whistled. He had every reason to. To an American, the title sounds bland enough, but in the Soviet, to be minister of production and industry is like simultaneously being chief executive of all three big car companies, as well as of Exxon, Mobil, and Gulf, of DuPont and Allied Chemical, of U.S. Steel, IBM, and the entire aerospace industry. "With such a father, why would you want to get mixed up in a scheme like ours? It is risky. Possibly reckless. You could be sent to prison for life. Or more probably, executed. Shot. You are one of the privileged . . . well, for instance, this car . . . why—?"

"Because I want to destroy my father." The boy paused, as if embarrassed; finally he blurted it out. "I hate him. If your mission succeeds and I am part of it, that destroys him. If it fails and I am killed, it still destroys him. Nothing noble. I just want to destroy him."

Alyosha had been a professional soldier, a combat lieutenant in the Special Tactical Forces, which specialized in everything from assassination to convert infiltration. But something in the way this boy spoke the word "destroy" made him shiver. He seemed so young, the word was incongruous coming out of his mouth, yet there was little question in Alyosha's mind that he felt it deeply. He explored the point. "Could you kill him?"

There was not even an instant's pause. "Yes."

Alyosha usually didn't make decisions on his team quickly, and it was probably unwise to in this case. But what he had at first thought of as a problem—the father high in government—had suddenly become an asset. He glanced at the boy again; he was driving with great concentration, his lips pressed tightly together in grim determination. "I've been looking for someone who would cover the operation from the outside. With your ease in getting around official restrictions . . ."

The car was braked to an abrupt halt. The grim look the boy had worn since he met Alyosha vanished, replaced by a warm, winning smile. "My name's Keer," he said, holding out his hand. "Kyril Gertsen."

Keer obviously was eager to talk, to be as vocal now as he had been silent before. But Alyosha discouraged the attempt by asking Keer to let him off at the nearest metro station. Instead of Alyosha's contacting him through Tbor, the boy suggested that he telephone, and he gave Alyosha his home phone number. "It's all right," Keer explained, reacting to the surprised look on Alyosha's face. "My father's practically never there. The houseman, Dovo, is used to taking messages for me." Alyosha nodded, a little bewildered at Keer's self-possession. Three blocks later, Keer let him off.

A father who was "practically never there." A houseman who took his phone messages. Where, Alyosha wondered, was his mother? Dead? Maybe, Alyosha thought, Keer had not been overly fond of her either. The shiver ran through him again.

2

SUNDAY, OCTOBER 25

Lisenka got off the metro at Rechnoi Vokzal, the end of the line. At the head of the stairs was the Northern River Port Passenger Terminal. Here, she waited in the enclosed roof garden, watching the few remaining hydrofoils of the year skimming up and down the river with breathtaking grace. When the three-decked motor liner *Maria Ulyanova* came into view—it looks a bit like a modernized Mississippi sternwheeler—Lisenka quickly went down the stairs and boarded her.

As she had been instructed, Lisenka first climbed to the top deck. In rapid order, she went up and down two or three times more so that he could be sure she wasn't being followed. The *Maria Ulyanova* was already moving, beginning its leisurely progress up the Moskva-Volga Canal. Standing by the rail, Lisenka felt curious not to be in uniform; she had taken this trip many times before as an Intourist guide, but today her mission was of considerably more importance. Although the river steamer was not very crowded—the boats would run only about a week more, until the first of November—Lisenka was glad to see that there were enough people to provide cover for her meeting. And glad to note that, in or out of her Intourist uniform, she could still attract attention.

Lisenka had turned twenty-five last summer. Like most Intourist guides, she had been chosen for intelligence, personality, and an ability to mix easily with people. Women in uniform are sometimes overwhelming, but Lisenka—a nickname for Elisaveta or Elizabeth—somehow gained femininity from hers; the small, trim figure, the elfin face, the engaging smile appeared completely at home with the blue-green of the Intourist jacket. The Intourist Board of Examiners must have foreseen this; when Lisenka graduated from Moscow University, they placed her in the most coveted of their training programs, eventually assigning her to their toughest but choicest duty: Moscow and the Americans. Unlike that of some Intourist guides, Lisenka's English was perfect.

By Soviet standards, her personal life was not. Until a month ago, Lisenka had lived, unmarried, with Shymon Bryoshov, a young man she supposed she had been in love with since their first meeting at the university. The Party, had they known of it, would have considered this arrangement bourgeois. So they were not allowed to know of it, and Lisenka and Shymon had lived in their private little world, untouched by Soviet puritanism. My God, she thought, but she had loved him. She would come home from her stint at Intourist, throw herself into his arms, and sometimes dinner would be delayed for hours as they rolled and played and laughed in the old-fashioned double bed that Lisenka had carted in from her grandmother's little farm outside Moscow.

Shymon would spend the day writing articles, an endless series of dissident tracts that were privately circulated throughout the *Samizdat*—the underground press. That this was not smart, Lisenka had known all along. But she loved Shymon so completely she dismissed her own sense of logic. "Don't worry, Lisenka," he would tease her. "They can only stand a man up against the wall and shoot him once. It has something to do with his having only one heart."

"Please, Shymon," she would plead. "The chances you take. Nothing's worth it." But Shymon was a stubborn man, a man who felt if you thought something was wrong you had to say it. And in the Soviet, being Jewish might be a cardinal sin, but trying to tell the world you had rights was blatant heresy. Lisenka pleaded, Shymon laughed, Shymon remained firm; Lisenka supposed this stubborn quality was one of the things she loved so much in him.

The KGB had looked at the matter differently. Without warning, they had arrived one day and seized Shymon. Lisenka probably would have been implicated too, except that at the last second, Shymon improvised a brilliant script: "You goddam Party whore," he screamed at her, struggling with the KGB men as if trying to get his hands around her throat. "I have the right to say anything I want. You can't tell me what is right to think. You kiss all the Party asses and try to make me believe they're right and I'm wrong, and then when you can't win that way, you bring in their strong-arm troopers. Whore! Whore! Fucking whore!"

A KGB man grabbed and twisted Shymon's head, while another slapped his face so hard blood began oozing from his upper lip. As they dragged him from the apartment, his oaths at Lisenka began to alternate with screams, and tears streamed down his face. The KGB men thought it was because he had been hit, and because all Jews were crybabies and cowards—everyone knew that, didn't they?—but Lisenka knew it was because Shymon realized he would never see her again; that his last words to her should be so hateful and cruel was more than either could bear.

Her life became a void. Day followed day, filled with tourists and museums and empty palaces. Shymon simply disappeared. She never heard from him again, or *of* him again. Poor Shymon. Standing there on the deck of the *Maria Ulyanova,* Lisenka could feel her eyes fill with tears at the thought of him, wondering if he was still alive, and if he was, which prison he was in and what he was doing this moment.

The voice startled her. "I watched you go up and down the companionway. It is all right. You were not followed." Lisenka turned toward the voice and forced a smile for Alyosha.

"Nor were you."

"Do you have it?"

She indicated her soft brown Gucci carryall, a thank-you present from some departing American tourists the year before. "Yes. And it checks."

Together they walked toward the stern of the *Maria Ulyanova,* where in busier seasons the tables and chairs were filled with people drinking *kvass;* today, they were empty. From her purse, Lisenka pulled a carefully folded piece of ordinary paper on which a faint diagram of a map was visible. To obscure what it was, the lines were incomplete and the locations were indicated only by letters. Alyosha looked around nervously, his greenish eyes searching the decks. Wherever he was, whatever he was doing, the specter of the KGB followed him like a menacing presence. "Very briefly, please," he said. "I can go over it myself later."

"Right. Mostly, it is as the Old One said. I have checked it myself with what I could find at Intourist Central office. At letter B, yes, you could go that way, but the entire area around A is sealed off. Tight."

"Damn." Alyosha studied the map, smoothing it flat in a nervous motion of his fingers. "We'll have to find an alternate route, then. Or some way through the sealed-off area itself. Not easy, but possible."

"I can check the maps at Intourist Central again."

"Good." For a moment, Alyosha appeared to explore an idea, finally letting the tip of one finger wander lower down on the sheet of paper. "What about here? Letter H. Would *it* work?"

"Soldiers. Crack troops. The best in the army."

A grim smile lit Alyosha's boyish face. He shrugged. "Harder to panic, as easy to kill."

Ignoring him, Lisenka leaned across to stab the paper with her finger. "At letter F, everything works fine. Just a question of timing."

"You have the timetables?"

"Yes, but they vary from day to day."

Alyosha grunted, stared at the map a moment, and slipped it into his pocket.

Lisenka felt Alyosha suddenly grip her arm. "We get off here. The Khvoiny Bor. You will go first. Walk about one hundred meters up the main road and wait for me there."

Perhaps ten minutes later Alyosha appeared, walking down the road, hands in pockets, looking a little like a truant schoolboy. His insistence on separate arrivals and departures and his elaborate checking to be sure the KGB was not following sometimes struck Lisenka as a melodramatic game, the schoolboy again. But in something like Salt Mine, she supposed, there was no room for error.

After another couple of hundred meters of walking, the two of them were getting deeper into the pine forests that gave Khvoiny Bor its name. Abruptly, Alyosha turned right, down a small path. "He should be along here somewhere. Number Twelve Cottage, you said."

"Number Twelve," she repeated. The "he" Alyosha was referring to was Oliver Watkins. Finding him had not been easy. But helped by some information Tbor had dug up, Lisenka finally located him in the tiny retirement village of Ziv. Watkins was an old man—somewhere in his mid-eighties—that rare American who could say he had been part of the Russian Revolution. Technically, he was a deserter from the American army. When the Allies sent in troops to help the White Russians fight the Bolsheviks in 1919, Watkins joined the enemy and became a Communist. Since American sympathizers were few in those days and made good propaganda, he was welcomed effusively. As the months went on, though, the leaders of the Bolsheviks quickly discovered him to be an able and talented man. Now, sick, feeble, old, he lived outside Moscow on a small Soviet government pension, holder of one of the lowest Party card numbers still in use.

At the door, Alyosha's knocking was answered by Watkins's Russian-born daughter, a widow of about fifty. She bowed. "I hope you speak American. Mine is no good, and Papa's Russian—well, he forgets with old age."

In the next room, the walls were covered, ceiling to floor, with faded photographs. There, the widow introduced them to her father, Oliver Watkins. The old man sat in a plain wicker chair, wrapped in what looked like layers of knitted blankets to ward off the draft. The blankets came up high enough in the back to form a cowl; his face was almost invisible in the shadow—all they could really see of this very old man's features were the two piercing eyes that gleamed at them out of the darkness. Alyosha handed something to him.

"The package," Watkins said in a cracked whisper, "the package used to be green, I think." He was staring at the five packs of American cigarettes Alyosha had brought as a gift. Lisenka and Alyosha looked at each other in confusion; to them, the white packs of cigarettes with the red bull's-eye lettered "Lucky Strike" seemed perfectly normal, but then, neither of them had ever seen one before. Watkins laughed. "I'm being rude. They must have changed the pack; I haven't had any visitors in so long it could have been done years ago and I wouldn't have known." He paused; the thin, reedy voice laughed again. "Also, at my age, you know, the mind starts playing tricks. Maybe they never *were* green. If you don't mind, I won't smoke any now; I'll save them for after dinner, one a night. And forgive my rudeness; I was just surprised."

With Lisenka translating from his mixture of English and Russian—Watkins had lived in Russia so long and was so old his language was a curious blend of the two—Alyosha got down to business.

"Oh, yes," said Watkins. "I did some of the design on that one. A great honor. I was stunned. But you see, Lenin had a soft spot for young architects. Architects and artists. And he asked me—"

Stunned, Lisenka couldn't contain herself. "You knew Lenin, *personally*?"

"That pitcure. Top row, second from the right. In those early days, I was a rarity: a believing American. He loved young people—my God, but I was young then—and as I said, he was fascinated by architects." Lisenka had walked over to the wall of pictures; there was Lenin, standing beside a young man with a crew cut, their arms thrown over each other's shoulders: Lenin and Oliver Watkins. His voice droned on behind her; she came back to herself and began translating again for Alyosha. "He was such a gentle man. A dreamer, yes. Perhaps he was. He really thought the Marxist government would eventually wither away. He believed everyone should be free to say what they wanted, to do what they could do best." A resigned sigh came from the blankets around Watkins's head. "But everything changed after him. Stalin, Khrushchev, Brezhnev. The Cheka, the KGB. People like Beria. They took his dream and defiled it."

Alyosha cleared his throat and glanced pointedly at his watch. Between them, they began pushing Watkins into a discussion of the building's architecture. "Yes, I did a lot of work on it. No, I don't have the plans; it's all in my head. I don't know what you want to know so much for, but I won't ask. The letter from you that that Mongolian delivered told me enough. Enough so that I can help you without feeling a traitor to the real communism. I read the *Samizdat* papers. By the time I see them, they're falling apart from being passed from hand to hand, but no matter." Watkins paused, seeming to consider something, and then spoke again. "If what you are doing will help the spirit of Lenin, not hurt it, I will do all I can."

For perhaps half an hour, with encyclopedic detail, Watkins went over the architectural plan of the structure, foot by foot. His grasp of Russian might be fading, his sense of dates and times might be disappearing, but his memory of the building he had helped to design was near to total recall, an incredible feat.

Lisenka was just about to translate a few final questions from Alyosha when a gentle snore made her look deeper into the blanket-cowl. Watkins was asleep, a peaceful smile on his face, as if recalling the past had given him great comfort. Noiselessly, the packs of Lucky Strike slid to the floor. Alyosha and Lisenka slipped out, heading back for the boat dock at Khvoiny Bor.

Again boarding separately, they returned downstream on the *Moskva*. For some time, they discussed their session with the old Mr. Watkins. Then they both fell quiet.

To Lisenka, talking of Watkins for some reason made her think of Shymon, and she wondered if Alyosha might not be acting as stubborn in his own way as Shymon had in his. She knew why she was part of Salt Mine—Shymon—but she had never been quite able to fathom why Alyosha was. The man was so deep and self-contained she suspected she never would. At times, she felt drawn to him, but some strange quality made getting close to him impossible. Raising her eyes, she saw him staring at the Moskva's banks. Wordlessly, the two of them walked to the rail; along the embankment they could see the Novodevichy Convent, rundown, but still operating. Beyond the convent you could make out the five golden domes of its Smolensk Cathedral. In the bright sun of midday, the domes shone brilliantly, the three-barred Russian crosses on the domes visible even at this distance.

"Magnificent," noted Alyosha. Squinting his eyes against the light that bounced off the water, he concentrated on the sight with his whole being.

Lisenka was surprised. Alyosha's mind always seemed so totally absorbed in Salt Mine's tactics of destruction that it appeared out of character for him to be affected by beauty. She studied his face, the skin looking darker than it really was because of the glowing, golden hair that crowned his head.

The fact was that Alyosha was a startling-looking man, tall, sinewy, with greenish eyes that reflected his shifting moods the way the sea changes colors with passing clouds. His family was of Azerbaidzhani stock—some of them still practicing Moslems—born with that fierce sense of independence all Central Asians seem to possess. Moscow could tell the Azerbaidzhan Soviet Republic what to do, and a little would seep through to Baku, the republic's capital. A little, but not much. In general, the Azerbaidzhanis, who still spoke their own language, listened to Moscow only indifferently and then went ahead and did what they had been planning to do in the first place. Like Ireland before the First World War, they were part of the mother country, yet not part of it. Perhaps this explained something of the inborn rebel in Alyosha. Lisenka had watched him earlier today. Golden hair flowing from his head, Alyosha moved as effortlessly as the Afghans his Persian forefathers once used to hunt leopards. His smile was infectious, if rarely used; his look, intense; his whole body charged with animal ebullience.

Whether it was because Alyosha felt Lisenka's eyes absorbing him or because the *Moskva* was getting closer to Moscow, he abruptly turned from the rail, the spell broken. "I get off at the Gorky Park dock. Kindly check out those details at Intourist Central and let me know."

Before Lisenka could even nod, Alyosha disappeared into the small crowd on deck. As the *Moskva* pulled alongside the stop to let off passengers, she saw him again briefly, striding quickly along and disappearing in the direction of the metro station.

Their leader, Lisenka decided, was a very complex man indeed.

• The Russians have a proud boast: There are no slums in Moscow. And up to a point, the claim is correct. It should be noted, however, that some of the nonslums are less nonslum than others. For instance, out beyond the Sadovoye Ring, ironically positioned in the triangle formed by the Moscow Television Tower, the Ostankino Serf Art Museum, and the Soviet Economic Achievement Exhibition, the dwellings are run-down and shabby. Sandwiched between the slab-modern office buildings of the late twenties are the sagging shells of the apartment houses built in that era. While not entirely offensive to the eye, the buildings exude a feeling of imminent collapse, of a brief pause on the road toward becoming tenements. Because in Moscow any sort of housing is in short supply, the government does nothing to remove the buildings; rather, it pretends they don't exist.

At Number 31, Dashnovaya, the stairs were unswept, the windows dirty, and the inhabitants in keeping with their surroundings. On the surface, anyway. The two men behind the door of apartment A-12 looked little different from their neighbors. The only reason no one had yet discovered how different they really were was that the old lady who managed the building—doubling as KGB block watcher—was rarely sober. The two men in A-12 encouraged this condition by regular gifts of vodka. The old lady was not stupid; there had been such shadowy tenants here before. But her affection for vodka was greater than her love of Party, and the pair went unreported.

Klemet, for once unsmiling, stared unhappily at some liquid in a beaker. Set in front of him on a plain wooden table was a collection of retorts, flasks, beakers, and sinister, dark colored bottles, each with a black rubber stopper beside it. Two of the retorts were cooking, one over an improvised Bunsen burner, one over a cheap hot-plate. At first glance, the setup looked like a precocious student's home laboratory.

On a hard wooden chair behind Klemet sat Dimmy. His nervous eyes drank in every move of his friend's. Perhaps unconsciously, Dimmy's long face would mimic the slight wincing of Klemet's eyes every time he added one solution to another. Both of them looked as if the smallest sound would shatter them into a thousand pieces.

Gently, Klemet held up a large beaker. "There. That batch is about done."

Dimmy closed his eyes wearily. "Are you sure you got it right?"

"Duck soup. Easy."

"Not if you're the duck."

"Please don't make me laugh, Dimmy. One good jiggle could blow the building halfway to Leningrad."

"Wrong time of year for Leningrad."

Klemet, pulling a bottle toward his side of the table, turned toward Dimmy, his eyes pleading. "Dimmy . . . please . . ."

Dimmy was forty or so. As with many writers of humor, his face was in perpetual mourning, as if he'd just learned of the death of a close friend or faithful dog. Until recently, even the government had considered him a very funny man, and he had earned a good living as a writer of satirical essays for the Soviet magazine *Krokodil*. Someone in government, however, had not been amused. Abruptly, a couple of Dimmy's pieces were pronounced too pointed—pointed enough to draw official warnings. With the recklessness that always seems to plague satirists, Dimmy promptly wrote an additional pair of essays savagely poking fun at the censor's reaction to the first two. A humorless bureaucracy responded: Dimmy was expelled from the Writers' Union, and therefore his job.

Klemet, although a physicist, also brought disaster upon himself through the written word. Certain Soviet experiments in nuclear fusion, Klemet announced, were not only immoral, but of little military potential. The faceless bureaucracy responded again. Klemet was removed from his government laboratory; and because the area he worked in was more sensitive than Dimmy's, there was talk of the KGB putting him in a sanitarium for "reorientation." Through all of this, Klemet remained smiling, his round cheerful face and thick steel-rimmed glasses making him look more than ever like a happy owl.

Today, Klemet's face looked as pessimistic as he felt. "This is very critical, Dimmy. Please don't make a sound." Dimmy nodded, staring at what Klemet was doing.

Taking a thick glass rod, Klemet stuck it down the neck of a dark bottle. Gently, he poured the clear liquid from the beaker onto the glass rod so gradually that the fluid ran down the rod rather than falling to the bottom of the bottle. As added insurance against jarring the liquid, the bottle was held at an extremely low angle. Klemet blinked hard from the concentration, and a small band of sweat grew visible above his eyes. Slowly, the beaker's contents were poured into the bottle.

To both of them, the knock on the door came as the knell of doom. The sudden sound shot Dimmy partway off the chair. Being more accustomed to dangerous chemicals, Klemet allowed only his face to register alarm; his fingers remained rock steady as he continued his pouring. "Hide it, hide it," hissed Dimmy, but Klemet shook his head.

"We shouldn't even jiggle the stuff at this stage," he whispered. "It's still too unstable."

Dimmy slipped over to the door and spoke through it. "Yes? Yes? Who is it?"

"Grazhdane, grazhdane," said the old woman. "Let me in please."

Dimmy turned around; Klemet did not look at him, but silently shook his head. The rod had been removed from the bottle and placed on the table. With an expression of infinite patience, his lower lip biting hard into the upper, Klemet held the bottle with one hand and eased in a rubber stopper with the other. "Comrade Goda," Dimmy yelled back. "I cannot open the door. I have no clothes on."

A grunt came back through the door. "You have not brought my . . . my little gift yet this week. Old Goda is thirsty. And on the next block the KGB are making rounds, talking to the apartment watchers, asking a lot of questions about something. My little gift—"

"Will be with you as soon as I can get my clothes on." Goda's threat about the KGB was pure blackmail, but the old bitch would tell them unless paid. Now Dimmy turned again toward Klemet to see how far he had gotten. Klemet held the bottle in both hands, raised almost to eye level, carrying it across the room as carefully as if it were a priceless icon. As Dimmy watched, the glass rod suddenly rolled off the table and broke against the floor with a loud crash. The sound took Klemet by surprise; he stumbled, and the bottle began slipping out of his hands, the liquid inside sloshing back and forth.

For a second, Dimmy stood where he was. The beating of his heart was so loud he was sure the old lady beyond the door must hear it. Klemet continued his precarious dance step, a man chasing a butterfly. Finally, he got the bottle under control and sagged wearily against the archway into the bedroom.

Shaking his head with exhaustion, Dimmy yanked the apartment door open and stepped quickly out, closing it behind him. His voice reverberated with confidence. "Comrade Goda. I shall be back from the store before you can say Union of Soviet Socialist Republics." Klemet could hear them going down the hall, the old lady complaining, Dimmy reassuring her that the vodka was already as good as in her stomach.

Limp, Klemet tried to make his breath come in a more reasonable rhythm. He stared at the ceiling. "Alyosha, you madman. Your crazy Salt Mine is going to make an old man of me. Or worse, a dead one."

FRIDAY, OCTOBER 30

"The shakedown has turned up nothing, Vasily. Absolutely nothing." Chorniev's soft whine put Klin's nerves on edge; it always did, but today his irritation was compounded by Chorniev's report. Klin swung his desk chair around so that his back faced the KGB chief and reached for the glass paperweight on his desk. Inside was a plastic figure of Father Frost, which you could make disappear in clouds of whirling snow by spinning the glass globe.

"Perhaps you didn't shake hard enough."

"My men are still talking to the block watchers, street by street, apartment by apartment. So far, nothing. The informers have been told there's a lot of money if they turn something up. Again, nothing. It is as if that note in Volovno's pocket was an invention of his mind."

"It was no invention. The words Volovno attached to Salt Mine—'staggering,' 'a threat to Soviet security,' 'frightening in its implications'—well, they're probably exaggerations. But Salt Mine is important enough so that someone risked getting himself killed to shut Volovno up. The fact that they knew where Volovno would be means Salt Mine has an organization behind it. So possibly his description isn't the exaggeration we'd all like it to be. Anyway, we can't wait to find out." A long sigh escaped from Klin. "To me, it's inconceivable none of your sources has come up with anything. They must all be asleep. Or you are."

"They've come up with a lot of odd bits, Vasily, but nothing that ties to that note. The usual number of dissenters. People without passports. Two Westerners without proper visas. Several citizens without ID cards, in town illegally. But on the code name . . ."

"Turn up the pressure. Pull all the stops. Scare your agents. Raise the ante to your informers. Rattle a few skeletons." As always, Klin's voice remained cool. But, as his chair spun suddenly around, the blotches on his head glowed red.

From the expression on Chorniev's face, Klin knew his litmus-test scalp had registered his real mood. "Comrade," Klin said in his calm, steady voice, only the litmus paper revealing the menace behind his words. "I am counting on you to handle the matter. I believe you understand me."

• From behind her, the voice came like the sound of a shot. Lisenka was in the main office at Intourist Central, where she had no business being, looking through a secret file she had no business seeing. The two top drawers of the small cabinet were filled with ordinary files; the bottom two were marked "Secret: Do Not Open Without Clearance." She turned, her hands clutching the folder.

The woman who had walked in on her was Svetlana Talchieva, supervising administrator at Intourist Central. Although she had nothing to go by except the woman's hostile manner in the past, Lisenka had always felt Comrade Talchieva did not like her. "Ohhh! Svetlana," Lisenka said, collapsing back against the file cabinet for support, "you scared me. Don't creep up on me like that. *Please.* Ever again." It was said with a laugh, but Svetlana remained unsmiling.

"What are you doing in those files? They're marked 'secret.' You have no business there."

Lisenka was able to paste together a story with remarkable speed. This morning, coming to work, she'd lost an earring. On the bus, she supposed. It became the focus of her answer. "I was looking for something in the top drawer, Svetlana. And I reached up and found I'd lost an earring and I thought maybe it slipped down behind the top drawer into one of the confidential ones." Wordlessly she let her hand fondle the earlobe with no earring. Svetlana, a large, square-shaped woman with the build of a Dynamo fullback, looked at Lisenka a moment. One ear *with* earring, one without was a reasonably convincing argument. Still, unanswered questions remained.

"Well, this whole room is off-limits. You know that. What were you doing in here? What were you looking for? Tell me that."

"Next Saturday's schedule of guides," Lisenka answered quickly. "A boy asked me to go to Kuskovo Palace with him for lunch."

Kuskovo Palace Museum was doctrinaire enough to appeal to a hard-core Party member like Svetlana, but it had probably been a long time since a boy had asked her to lunch anywhere—if ever. Yet oddly, the remark seemed to mellow her.

"You still shouldn't be in here, Lisenka. I must report you, of course. To the KGB. I'm sorry." A strange, faraway expression crept over Svetlana's face. "But the Kuskovo Palace, lunch . . . it is a beautiful time of year for a trip there." Suddenly she turned toward Lisenka. "I'm sorry about the earring. They're expensive. Just this once we'll overlook the whole matter." With what was almost a smile, she ushered Lisenka to the office door. She did not notice the small slip of paper that Lisenka neatly folded and slipped into her bag.

Outside, Lisenka let loose a long sigh of relief. No KGB. No interrogation. Thank God for earrings. Thank God for Moscow's crowded buses. And even, she supposed, thank God for closet romantics like Svetlana Talchieva.

TUESDAY, NOVEMBER 3

The sudden sound of a hand slapping metal startled both of them.

"Look out. The door on the *right*'s opening. The stupid bastards."

Keer slammed on the Moskvich's brakes; tires screaming, the car missed the truck's tail end by inches as the van made an abrupt right. Anyone who drives in Russia is aware that most trucks do not have turn-indicator lights. Ordinarily, the truck driver slaps the left door loudly with his palm to attract attention, then throws the door open on his side to indicate a left turn. Making a right, the procedure is the same, except when he opens his door, the driver steps partway out onto the running board and points over the truck's roof to the right.

Apparently, the truck in front of Alyosha and Keer had two men in the front seat and they had elected to open the right door to signal a right turn; it was a dangerous innovation for anyone behind them. For several minutes, Keer remained mute, recovering from the near-accident. "I've never seen that before," Keer said finally. "The *right* door."

He glanced nervously at Alyosha, feeling he had to justify himself. The real trouble, he supposed, was that driving the little three-seater Moskvich rattled him. In spite of his protests, Alyosha had ruled out the Chevy. "It's one thing in Moscow," he had said. "But out here, no one's ever seen an American car. It'll be mobbed."

They were driving along the main road to Yaroslavl, about two hundred and fifty kilometers to the northeast. This was Keer's first mission since he had been accepted into Salt Mine, and he was not too happy with it; playing chauffeur was not what he had imagined. Worse, Alyosha would give him no clue as to what they were going to do, or even what their real destination was. The most he'd been able to get from Salt Mine's leader was that it was just short of Yaroslavl.

Out here, in the open country, you could have traveled this same road fifty or a hundred years ago and it wouldn't have looked very different. In the distance, you still glimpsed sprawling monasteries and hulking forts, and the smaller towns were just tiny clusters of whitewashed stone buildings built around small, central squares. On the road, you found fewer cars than horse-drawn wagons, their lone modern touch balloon tires instead of wooden wheels. The women wore the voluminous skirts of another day, reaching down to the heavy work boots they used to protect their feet from the constant mud.

Out here, it was easy to forget you were in a Communist country. To remind you, even the smallest town had the inevitable picture of Lenin hanging outside the town hall, along with painted signs encouraging you to greater service to the state. A stone-gray sky brooded over the bare fields and winter-black trees, ignoring both past and present, unchanging and uncaring.

Glancing at Alyosha, Keer could see a small diagram resting in his lap. Keer again wanted to ask Alyosha where they were going, but restrained himself. Alyosha was looking hard through the windshield, comparing reference points along the road with notations on his map. "Slow down, slow down," he said suddenly.

The urgency in Alyosha's voice made Keer slow the car

down faster than he meant to; the little Moskvich shuddered, and Keer saw a look of displeasure cross Alyosha's face. "There," Alyosha ordered, "that road dead ahead. Turn there."

The little road was barely visible, unpaved and bumpy. Two battered wooden road signs carried place names on their peeling paint, but Keer was too busy adjusting to the new road surface to read them. For perhaps four miles they bounced along, the springs of the Moskvich complaining bitterly. Another cluster of signs, another right turn. The road was narrower and the countryside more barren, typical farm country for this part of Russia. "It should be just ahead." Alyosha, finding something on his map, said it to himself as much as to Keer. Two hundred yards around a sharp bend, they came to where the road widened abruptly; they were entering the farm community of Bordad. Pulling over, they got out of the car and came into the central square on foot. It was deserted. On one side, the town hall and the red flag; on the other, a wood-fronted church and the Bordad People's Cooperative, a sort of general store that served not only Bordad but two other small farm towns. An old man, walking down the muddy strip that was used as a sidewalk, began crossing from the town hall to the cooperative, and Alyosha signaled Keer to follow him in.

Inside, the first thing that struck him was the steamy, sour smell of peasant cooking; the store was small, and only two people were visible. One of these stood behind the counter, and Alyosha walked directly over to her. "Your husband . . . ?"

"Is in the cellar." The old woman looked over this stranger for a moment, then laughed loudly. "Tbor sent you."

Alyosha nodded. "May I see your husband?"

The old woman laughed again, opening her mouth wide in a toothless grimace. "For months, no one outside Bordad knows he is alive. Suddenly, he is popular with the whole world. I should print ration stamps and sell him."

Even Keer got the old lady's message. From his pocket, Alyosha pulled a small package and handed it to her, "for her trouble"; later Keer would learn it was imported chocolate, a rarity. "Downstairs. Go ahead. He expects you."

The man was no citizen of Bordad. He looked like a less-polished edition of Anastas Mikoyan and, like Mikoyan, was an Armenian. He was sitting in a battered wicker chair when Keer and Alyosha came in; nodding, he rose, bowing to them formally before he shook their hands. What he was doing in a backwater like Bordad was a question that Keer suspected—and Alyosha knew—would never be answered.

"Chai?" With a gesture, Alyosha accepted for both of them, taking the glass of steaming aromatic tea and sitting down on the hard bench that the Armenian had indicated with a courtly sweep of his hand. Nothing was said until the glass—you held it by a small silver handle with a frame that fitted under the bottom of the glass—was empty.

Abruptly, business began. "Tbor gave me the material. And a list of what you wanted. I have everything ready. It was more work than I thought, so the price will have to be higher."

Alyosha shrugged. "As you say." Keer knew haggling was part of the Armenian way of life and suspected the man was disappointed at Alyosha's quick collapse. With a sigh, he rose and took an envelope out of a recess in the stone wall. "First, the key. Very difficult. A very unusual lock. All of it had to be done by hand. But the copy is exact and here is"—he held up the original—"your key back."

Keer watched as Alyosha, standing, examined the key, comparing it with the complicated-looking device Tbor had given the Armenian to copy. Finally, Alyosha nodded. The Armenian returned to the recess and came back with a small box. Keer saw Alyosha reach inside and examine something, while the Armenian watched, his eyes riveted on Alyosha. "Not easy to come by," the man complained. "The army is always hard to deal with."

Again, Alyosha nodded and the Armenian returned to his recess, returning with what looked like a clock. "This . . . well, my friend, I don't know. It is as close as I could come to your specifications, but, you understand, I cannot guarantee it. At one point, the timer was used at Yaroslavl Town Hall to control the lights on Lenin's picture. It should work, but I cannot be held accountable . . ."

He stopped, surprised to see Alyosha laughing. Alyosha held up a hand. "It is nothing, my friend," he said. "Nothing." Alyosha laughed again and then turned serious. "The money . . ."

"Another *chai?*" The Armenian still wanted to bargain; Alyosha was in a hurry to be leaving.

"The price you ask is the price you get." Keer watched as the Armenian's face fell and the man lamely named a price. *"Khorosho,"* said Alyosha. "And oh, yes. Tbor mentioned that you liked these. My personal gift to you." From his pocket, Alyosha drew a pack of Camels gotten for him by Keer.

American cigarettes were so hard to come by that the Armenian appeared stunned. Once again he began insisting—practically demanding—they stay. At one point, Keer sat down again, only to have Alyosha turn and tell him they were leaving. Keer watched as the Armenian began struggling with the cellophane wrapper on the Camels and found himself thrust roughly out the door. "Go quickly," commanded Alyosha.

The trip back seemed to take only half as long as the trip out. As they passed through Zagorsk, Keer finally asked a question that had been bothering him for some time. "What if he talks to someone? What if he tells . . . well, even his wife?"

Alyosha shrugged. "He won't."

The conversation was ended, and Keer went back to concentrating on his driving. The threat of a leak from the Armenian to the KGB had worried Alyosha for some time, but he saw no reason to tell Keer that by the time Tbor, the defrocked doctor, had finished doctoring the pack of Camels, you might walk a mile for one, but you would never walk back.

• To a Westerner, the Soviet citizen's preoccupation with the KGB is difficult to understand. Germans old enough to remember the Gestapo are probably the only non-Russians who can fathom their fear fully. The fact is that the KGB is everywhere, a sinister presence permeating every facet of Russian life. This reality leads to curious patterns of evasive behavior.

If possible, a man avoids speaking to strangers at all; his conversation with acquaintances is only superficial; closer, longer-standing friends are treated with a little more openness, but talk is phrased in such a way that there is little that can be quoted. With perhaps only two or three of his most trusted friends and relatives is he completely unguarded—and even then, with an awareness that such frankness could prove disastrous. The telephone is used sparingly and the conversation encoded; mail is assumed to have already been opened and read.

The national paranoia is a sudden knock on the door, the national nightmare a trip to Lubyanka, the national gesture a quick glance over the shoulder. If you have nothing to feel guilty about, the KGB provides you with a guilt complex; if you *do* have something to hide, the KGB is what you hide it from.

Across Salt Mine, the presence of the KGB hung like a dark shadow. As far as anyone knew, the KGB was so far unaware of Salt Mine, but the operation was always vulnerable to an accidental run-in by one of its members with the KGB. Klemet could lose his head and make another statement about nuclear fusion; Dimmy could share his satirical wit with a passing stranger; Tbor might whisper something to a fellow informer, who, in turn, would inform on him.

And once the KGB had decided someone was suspicious, the secret of Salt Mine would eventually be dragged out of him. The KGB had its methods; there was no defense against its sophisticated brainwashing techniques. Given time, it could make a man admit he was Nicholas II.

This dreaded presence, simultaneously everywhere, was why Alyosha resorted to what appeared schoolboy games of cloak and dagger when meeting other members of Salt Mine. None was ever visited at his home; it might be under surveillance. Meetings took place in subway trains, riverboats, buses, parks, museums, and—occasionally—in the Neck's taxicab.

The KGB was why the Neck had chosen to drive a taxi in the first place. He was deputy leader of the World Jewish Alliance for the Moscow area, and the taxi gave him an excellent operating base for his frequent meetings with people having business with the WJA. Today, however, the Neck was not driving his taxi.

He stood in the hallway of the Borilano Hospital, on the outer ring of Moscow, looking odd in hospital technician's whites. The door to the X-ray room opened and a doctor left; the Neck pretended not to know him, although the doctor was also with the WJA, practicing here with false papers and using a phony identity. As soon as the doctor left, Tbor went in, pretending to adjust the heavy equipment hanging over the emaciated figure streched out on the X-ray table.

For some time he and the man talked. In case anyone should look through the small double-glass window from the hall, the Neck would occasionally press the buttons that raised or lowered the X-ray machine's huge cathode tube.

"I cannot, my friend," said Wiejecki, the man on the table. "Earlier, perhaps, yes. These days, no. The KGB here, the Kobos at home, all are looking for me."

The Neck grimaced. Wiejecki was a Polish leader of the

WJA. The Neck's trip back to Lvov had provided him with very explicit instructions on what to tell Wiejecki, and what answer to hold out for. "How close, Meiciu? How close do you think the KGB is?"

"Very." The man laughed dryly. "They are also too late. My stomach . . . well. I would help you with your precious Salt Mine, the escape route through Poland, all of it, but I cannot go back to Poland. Even to die. That's how close. I will try to make it to West Germany. Or Finland."

The control buttons were again pressed and the giant machine slowly lowered itself with a loud whirring followed by a pneumatic hiss. A new look of concern was clouding the Neck's swarthy face. "If the KGB is that close . . ."

"The growth in my stomach is closer. It is a race." Wiejecki noticed the Neck's expression. "Do not worry, my friend. Your Salt Mine secret is safe with me. I think, if you can carry it off, you will have accomplished the biggest coup of our whole operation. The world will know, then. They will know what it is really like here. That is no small thing. So believe me, Salt Mine's secret is safe. And the growth makes it certain."

The trouble, the Neck knew, was that no secret was ever safe from the KGB. The cancer in Meiciu Wiejecki's stomach would eventually kill him, but if the KGB got to him first, Wiejecki could be made to tell everything he knew. The Neck's instructions from Lvov covered that possibility, too. Looking at the thin, dying man stretched on the table, it seemed suddenly sad. In his younger days, Wiejecki had done much good for the cause. But now, some night soon, he would have to receive a visit from the WJA. One that would render the growth superfluous. Perhaps, the Neck rationalized, it would be more merciful than the death nature had planned for him; certainly, it would be kinder than what would happen if the KGB found him.

A sudden noise made the Neck turn. It was the doctor, his face ashen. "Downstairs. The KGB. They are asking questions. About the forged papers Wiejecki's using. I think they know he is here." He spun toward the Neck. "You had better leave. Quickly." The doctor turned and slipped out of the room without waiting for an answer. On the table, Wiejecki tried to sit up, but he was too weak to maneuver much and was hampered by the machine's pressing hard against his midsection. With a groan, he sank back.

"It is safe. The secret is safe with me. Good luck."

The Neck had little time. There was nothing in the room he could use. Quietly, he locked the door into the hall, then slipped into the viewing room where the X-ray technicians took cover when the machine was on. The Neck locked this room's door into the hall, too, searched for a moment, and found what he was looking for. On one wall, to the right of the window into the X-ray room, was a panel marked "Remote." Below this were two buttons, one red, one black. Ignoring a hammering on the door to the X-ray room, the Neck pushed one of the buttons. With the same whir and the same pneumatic hisses as before, the X-ray head ground slowly into Wiejecki's middle. For a moment, the Neck watched as Wiejecki became aware of what was happening to him; his spindly, puckered legs and pale white buttocks, suddenly visible below the short hospital nightgown, flailed in the air as he struggled to pull himself out from beneath the machine but could not. A piercing shriek rose from him, and the hammering on the door grew louder. *"Shalom,"* whispered the Neck.

Casually, the Neck stepped out into the hall and locked the door from the outside, slipping the key into his pocket. As he walked away, he could hear shouting from the far hall and the sound of running feet. Even through the lead lining of the X-ray room and the double-thick glass, Wiejecki's agonized screams remained audible.

In his taxi, the Neck shot out of the parking lot and lost himself quickly in the traffic of the Sadovoye Ring. He was surprised to discover his hands were shaking. In his years with the WJA, he had ordered much violence; this was one of the few times that circumstances called upon him to commit it himself. He would never be able to erase the sound of Wiejecki's shrieks as the X-ray head bore relentlessly into his stomach, finally bursting through the skin and entering his body. Wiejecki, he assumed, had been mercifully dead by the time the X-ray head came out through his backbone. Damn. It was so incredibly cruel. But he had looked around the room, he kept telling himself, and there had been no other way.

What troubled the Neck most was the realization that his own desperate action to keep the secret of Salt Mine safe from the KGB was just as brutal as the methods the KGB would have used to drag the secret from Wiejecki.

Somewhere in that was a moral.

3

FRIDAY, NOVEMBER 6

Aeroflot Flight 101 hummed steadily through the Soviet sky, the stewards aware by the subtle changes in sound that they were getting close to set-down. In the first-class cabin, Mr. and Mrs. Blaine Decatur did not have such finely tuned ears. They were from Minneapolis, where Mr. Decatur was president of DataCon, one of the largest of international computer complexes. His wife, Lisa Decatur, read a guidebook, while Blaine stared ahead of him, sulking.

It was Lisa who had insisted on the trip to Moscow, and while the idea was one Blaine Decatur disliked, he had little choice. The Arrangement. Nothing much was ever said about the Arrangement with Lisa; nothing had to be. In what was almost a cliché for men his age, Blaine had two years earlier fallen hopelessly in love with a girl twenty years his junior. A PR girl who worked for DataCon, Chessie Davenport. Chessie seemed then, and still seemed today, everything Blaine could ever want.

"If it wasn't for the kids . . ." he'd told her, stepping into another time-honored cliché, in this case one that may actually have been true. "But, hell, Chessie. We can fix up an apartment here in Minneapolis. Lisa, me, the kids—everybody we know lives out in Wayzata. No one's ever going to find out. . . ."

Chessie had laughed, but there was a note of fatalism to it. "They'll find out, Blaine. You know damned well they always do." Chessie's appraisal of the world was more accurate than her boss's. People did find out. People including Lisa.

"I'm hurt, Blaine, of course," Lisa had said, by which she meant her pride was hurt; the appearance of perfection had been violated. "Maybe we were never as close as we should have been. I don't know. Maybe it's just a symptom of male menopause; I don't know that either. Maybe you don't yourself. But that girl . . . it's all over town . . . people . . . you have to think of the children."

The children, invoked by Blaine to Chessie as the reason he couldn't divorce Lisa and by Lisa as the reason Blaine had to get rid of Chessie, had known all about their father's affair for months. Christy shrugged it off; Gary was almost enthusiastic. "Hell, it's good to know the old man can still get it up."

Out of all this had grown the Arrangement. As Lisa pointed out, there had never been very much between them anyway. Appearances were what had to be preserved. So with little said, the ground rules began to take shape. Chessie was transferred to the Paris office of DataCon; Wayzata was silenced; the children were protected from learning what they already knew.

In return, Lisa closed her eyes. Blaine's frequent visits to the Paris office were ignored. But not forgotten. They frequently gave her additional leverage. The Moscow trip was an example. To her husband, being a tourist anywhere was an agony. But slowly, this trip had materialized. In deference to the Arrangement, Lisa and the kids would fly directly back home from Moscow, while Blaine would stop over at some of DataCon's European offices. Such as Paris. This thought was all that made Moscow bearable to Blaine.

The Arrangement. Fooling no one, satisfying no one, but viable for all of them. For the moment, all Blaine had to do was survive the combination of Lisa and Moscow.

Sourly, he rattled his empty glass at the stewardess coming down the aisle. With what attempted to be a compassionate smile, the stewardess shook her head. "Is not possible to serve drinks now; we shall be landing in thirty minutes."

"I'll drink it very fast."

The head shook again. "I am sorry. No cabin service during descent. It is forbidden."

Blaine Decatur grunted. That word "forbidden" bothered him. He liked to think he had nothing either for or against the Russians, but their use of that word was troubling. From behind him, Gary, eighteen, laughed.

"Shut off, Dad?"

"What did you do, Daddy? Goose the hostess?" Christy, his seventeen-year-old daughter, threw in.

Irritated, Blaine Decatur turned around to stare at his two children. In spite of their good looks, good grades, and usually good dispositions, there were times when they could be a royal pain in the ass. "Very funny."

He spun back, ignoring Lisa's inquisitive stare. It was her fault they were on Aeroflot—"I want to *feel* we're in Russia the moment we leave Kennedy," she had said. Well, the way the stewardess said "forbidden" made you feel you were *somewhere,* all right. Pan Am served drinks endlessly any time during any flight. Nothing was "forbidden." Ever. Hell, barely eight hours out of Kennedy and the trip had already filled Blaine with a vague uneasiness. Or was it, he wondered, merely impatience to get to Paris?

He had just pulled out his lighter and put a cigarette in his mouth when the cabin's "No Smoking" sign blinked on. Down the aisle, the stewardess seemed to head directly for him to make sure the sign was obeyed. Appeals, he had already learned, did no good. Sulking again, Blaine Decatur went back to staring out his window.

• Heading toward Moscow from the opposite direction—from Istanbul—Andrew Jax had none of Blaine's vague uneasiness about Moscow. If he affected uneasiness in his syndicated column, it was only because his readers liked to feel that he was constantly threatened, and to share the experience vicariously.

Flying Air France, this trip to Moscow made it twenty-two for Jax, not counting the war. He had no special reason for coming this time, and his arrival would not be cheered by the Soviet government. They were well aware of what he wrote about them in the American papers.

That he would be shadowed by the KGB was certain. To Jax, it was a game. The KGB would follow him; he would lose them. For Jax, this was easy; he knew Moscow better than many Muscovites. Eventually, they would find him again but be unable to berate him for his disappearance without admitting they had been following him in the first place. This was the sort of shadow-boxing Jax reveled in. So did the readers of three hundred and twelve American papers.

Jax signaled the hostess for another drink. She smiled. He smiled back. It was not forbidden.

WEDNESDAY, NOVEMBER 11

Lisenka looked at the people hurrying in and out of the glass front doors and wished they had agreed to meet at some smaller, less exhausting place. The choice had not been hers. Taking a deep breath, she fought her way inside. GUM is Moscow's largest department store. When it was built in the eighteen-eighties, the building was a vast trading hall where merchants could rent space to sell their goods; it hasn't changed much, except that the private traders have been replaced by government monopolies. Lisenka fought her way to the escalator—GUM was always crowded, but today it seemed worse than usual—and rode to the top floor, stepping off into the pale light under the arched glass roof. Walking over to a counter, she shoved her way through a knot of Russians picking over scarves, held one to the light, and pretended to examine it. Beside her, a woman complained about Lisenka's shoving, at the same time heaping a stream of compliments on Lisenka's apparent selection.

The lady's simultaneous complaints and compliments were part of a national need to pry into the affairs of strangers, and Lisenka ignored them. Across the counter, she saw a man's back, and for a moment her heart stopped. It was Shymon, it had to be Shymon. But then the man turned slightly, and Lisenka could see it was not Shymon, but Alyosha. Even for that fleeting, incredible second, the thought that it was Shymon had been ridiculous, and Lisenka swore at herself. Shymon was gone. To some distant prison. Or dead. Almost a year, and she could not shake her sense of loss. Damn.

Throwing down the scarf, Lisenka watched Alyosha walk over to the almost empty canned-delicacies counter and stop there. He must have felt the stare burning into his back, for he turned partway toward her, pretending to read a small brochure listing the prices of various food items. From past experience, Lisenka knew none were available. With seeming aimlessness, Lisenka drifted over to the counter and picked up a copy of the same brochure, leaning on the counter as she read it, her back almost directly to Alyosha.

"Did you get it?" Alyosha asked softly. "We are running out of time."

Still appearing to ignore Alyosha, Lisenka stared hard at the brochure and worked from memory. "Point T has very thick walls. But they are to impress, not protect. Therefore, the doors are of standard weight—and not too thick. Point N was built for protection. So, thick walls *and* thick doors."

"I understand the facts; your reasoning is less clear."

"Think of it this way. Lubyanka was built as a prison. For protection: thick walls, thick doors. The KGB headquarters next door was built as an insurance company, back before the Revolution. The protective doors were added later. So: *thin* walls, thick doors."

"Very well. We must begin to move very quickly now. It is only next Wednesday."

"What time next Wednesday?"

"That depends on you."

"The schedule is not made up until two nights before. I can't tell you until then."

"As early as you can. Let me know."

"How?"

"Keer. You know where to find him."

Lisenka sighed; she did not like Keer. "Very well."

"And, extremely important: Give him this." Alyosha slid a small envelope out of his sketch pad onto the countertop, then slipped it into the brochure Lisenka had left on the counter. Lisenka started to reach for the brochure, but stopped, puzzled by the strange, distant expression on his face and the fact that his hand still held the envelope. She had no way of knowing that merely to hold the envelope, with the thick outline of the key inside hard against his fingertips, made Alyosha's blood surge. Wednesday it would be placed in the lock. Wednesday the lock would be turned. Wednesday the door would open. Wednesday—he shook himself free and got back to business. "It is for Dimmy. Be sure Keer understands; he must get it to him."

Quickly, Lisenka swept the envelope into her purse. For a second, her eyes met Alyosha's, questioning if there was more. He moved his head imperceptibly to indicate there was not. "Until Wednesday," he said softly. *"Do svidanya."* He turned around and went back to studying the brochure, looking as if the word "Wednesday" was repeating itself again and again in his mind.

Behind him, Lisenka walked briskly toward the steep winding staircase in the center of the room. A different set of words was echoing through her head. "Shymon," it said, "Shymon, I do this for you."

• Scuttling down the main hall of his headquarters, Mikhail Chorniev spoke in his soft voice to the KGB men who flattened themselves against the wall to let him pass. With effort, he forced a smile for them; he knew that no one ever likes the head of the KGB—even the men who work for it.

From the outside, the KGB building on Dzerzhinsky Square is almost benign-looking. The neat, white curtains at the windows and the highly polished brass doorknobs give an impression of well-ordered serenity. As Lisenka had mentioned, before the Revolution the building served as the office of an insurance company; the structure's clean, mustard-yellow walls and white exterior trim still look the part.

Inside, it is something else. A short tunnel attaches the building to Lubyanka, where suspects are held for interrogation in the pressure cooker of the KGB. Every day, people are taken to KGB headquarters; some are held, some are released, some disappear.

Unlike the insignia of Hitler's SS, the KGB's symbol is not particularly sinister: the letters "GB," small and gold, on a blue field. There are no epaulets with interlocking bolts of lightning or death's-head insignia. The KGB needs none. Its grip on daily life is awesome, combining the functions of the CIA—espionage, counterintelligence, and foreign political manipulation—with the FBI's internal spy system and police powers. Very simple, extraordinarily powerful, and consummately deceptive. Even the name—KGB—is deceptive. KGB stands for Komitet Gosudarstvennoi Bezopasnosti: Committee of State Security of the USSR.

As Chorniev started up the stairs, he saw two guards trying to hide some slips of paper. He knew what the strips were and could have demanded to see them and then have disciplined the guards, but he decided to let it pass. The guards were only engaging in a time-honored game played at KGB headquarters: a drawing among them as to which of the current prisoners would be released, which sent to prison, which made to disappear. Each guard would pick a slip; the winner won a bottle of vodka. Looked at from Chorniev's standpoint, the game was no more sinister than an American office pool.

At the top of the stairs, Chorniev heard groans floating up from below, then laughter. The drawing had been held, and he could hear that someone had drawn a "release" slip for a prisoner who would probably be held in Lubyanka forever. In his office, Chorniev riffled through the daily action report file for the morning. Something there, marked in red by his secretary, made him pick up his phone and call his deputy.

"Jax. Andrew Jax is coming in this afternoon on Flight Twelve, Air France. From Istanbul," Chorniev said in his usual whisper. "You know the routine for Jax. Class-one surveillance. Yes, it's terrible." With a muted grunt, Chorniev replaced the phone, picked up the file again. Almost immediately his own phone rang. It was Klin.

"You saw that Jax is due in today?" Chorniev smiled thinly; all of the action reports must have been delivered at the same moment.

"Yes, Vasily. And I don't understand why the Foreign Office keeps letting the man in. Anyway, I have already taken the usual steps. Class-one surveillance."

"Cancel it. Token surveillance only."

Chorniev sighed. "Of course, Vasily." There was a considerable pause while Chorniev wrestled with himself; then: "May I ask why?"

"For the same reason the Foreign Office keeps letting him in. To avoid giving him ammunition for his damned column. Last time he was here, he made a big splash in his columns telling how easy it was to get away from the men following him. To lose his surveillance. He got publicity; we got laughed at. This time, we leave him alone."

Unlike Klin, Chorniev was no hunch player. He went by the book, and Klin's order did not. His superior's strategy made him uncomfortable. Still.

"Very well. Token surveillance. Done."

In the new silence that followed, Chorniev could hear Klin breathing. Finally, the man spoke: "Anything on Salt Mine?"

"Nothing. I'm sorry, Vasily, but nothing."

"Damn."

A second later, Chorniev heard the phone hung up. It always irritated him that Klin kept such a tight rein on KGB operations. Worse, Klin, merely by existing, blocked any chance of another rise up the Kremlin ladder. For this reason, Volovno's sudden appearance at KGB headquarters had seemed an act of providence. Klin down was Chorniev up, and Volovno's information might help that progression. Carefully, Chorniev plotted. It was Chorniev who had persuaded Volovno he must talk to no one but Klin—*no one,* including himself. It was Chorniev who played to Klin's paranoia, exaggerating the importance of what Volovno might know—without even knowing himself. It was Chorniev who slyly disagreed when Klin proclaimed Volovno's murder proved a vast conspiracy, knowing this would only feed Klin's belief. For himself, Chorniev felt that Volovno and "Op. Salt Min" were probably nothing more than a black-market ring or a group of dissidents planning to flee the Soviet. For his scheme to work, however, Klin must believe it something far bigger.

Chorniev sighed again, hearing the magic words "Klin down, Chorniev up" whispering in his ear. His eyes went back to the report in his hand. Methodically, he was numbering each item, ranking them and assigning priorities for his deputy. One intrigued him by its outrageousness: Item Number Fourteen, Area Moscow One. Word from a government worker in Fish Lane—at the Ministry of Urban Building Supply, the report said—that someone might be living illegally in the converted town house where the ministry was located. Twice, the worker said, he had met a man leaving the building when he himself arrived early for work. The man was furtive and refused conversation, the worker noted. Chorniev gave it a priority two. It still intrigued him but didn't sound very promising. Still, it was something that should be checked out, and a priority two would get an agent to Fish Lane sometime early next week. Possibly Monday, but more probably Tuesday. Chorniev sighed and continued down the page.

Alyosha would have more than sighed. Tuesday was one day before Salt Mine. And the building in Fish Lane was where he lived. Illegally.

• From the moment Aeroflot 101 set down at Sheremetyevo Airport, Blaine Decatur lost what remained of his usual calm. He was irritated with Lisa for the fact that he was here; he was annoyed that Gary and Christy should choose this moment to act like children; he was impatient to get through with Moscow so he could go on to Paris. Beyond all of these things, some undefinable nervousness about Moscow bothered him; Blaine was not given to paranoia, but he couldn't shake an odd sensation that he was being watched. There seemed to be soldiers everywhere, standing in their scooped-back helmets that looked like inexpert gray haircuts. But they couldn't be watching him; they were merely there to protect the airport. Still, the effect on him was unsettling—like the stewardess's word "forbidden."

The Decaturs were traveling first class deluxe suite—five times the cost of first class—but it still took time before their Intourist guide, Irina, could find them; she finally caught up as they came through the gate. Efficiently she whisked them through Customs and the green-hatted Border Police—more soldiers, thought Blaine—and then handed them the forms. And more forms. More soldiers. Still more forms. Outside the airport, Irina herded them into their Chaika—it looked like a prewar Packard—and introduced them to their driver, who would be at their disposal from 8:00 A.M. to midnight daily. She herself, Irina explained, would be with them for eight hours a day, and should more time be required, arrangements could be made.

"Which hotel?" asked Blaine. It seemed a stupid question, but Intourist would not guarantee in advance where you would be staying. He had asked for the Metropol and had told Chessie she could write him there.

Irina smiled. "The Intourist. On Gorky Street. It is very American. You will like it."

Blaine tried to laugh, staring at Irina and wondering if her remark was a statement or a crack. Damn. There went Chessie's letter. His eyes continued to study Irina. She was a pretty little thing, he admitted to himself. A bit fleshy, perhaps, but still pretty.

While Mr. Decatur was studying her, Irina was studying them. Mr. Decatur was not fat, as the cartoons in *Krokodil* always pictured capitalists. In fact, he was tall and surprisingly trim for his age, with gray hair cut short enough to make him look younger than he probably was. The wife, Irina could tell, was going to ask for help with her Russian, which she would speak absolutely terribly. And want to see too much of everything. And try to have long, serious discussions about peace and human rights and the Soviet system. Evasion would be both difficult and trying.

The children—well, they were typical American teenagers, and Irina could not resist their exuberance. Bright, funny, impudent. The boy, in particular, was devilish—with those perfect white teeth no one in Russia ever seemed to have. Irreverent with his mother and father, with officials, and Irina suspected, with *anyone*. Charming, yes, but he could get himself into trouble. Her eyes went back to Mr. Decatur.

He had it. There was no question about it. She had seen his eyes narrow when he looked at the soldiers at the airport; she had heard it when he asked about the hotel; she could feel his uneasiness in everything he said. The disease was particularly prevalent among American tourists, and every Intourist guide gradually grew used to coping with it—a malady they referred to among themselves as the "salt mine syndrome." The symptoms were a vague, disquieting aura of uneasiness, followed by a shadowy, illogical fear, and complicated by a conviction that one's every step in Russia was being watched by hidden eyes.

Neither guides nor tourists could entirely explain the illness, although many of the guides felt its roots lay in the Westerners' carefully nurtured fear of anything Communist.

To Irina, Mr. Decatur appeared an almost classic victim, and she braced herself for the side effects: He would complain about the Hotel Intourist, he would complain about the car, but these were only minor symptoms. It would be the way he kept looking over his shoulder that would clinch the diagnosis. Traveling on the extravagant deluxe suite plan was probably an effort to insulate himself from his phobias, but it wouldn't work. Nothing she could do would help. Only time.

"Why are we at the Hotel Intourist?" Blaine asked suddenly, still provoked that he would never receive the letter from Chessie.

"Most deluxe suite travelers like it best, Mr. Decatur. And the accommodations you asked for: four bedrooms and a parlor. There are not too many hotels in Moscow—even now, in off-season—that can provide that. You will like it, believe me."

There. It had already started. And now Mr. Decatur was staring out the window of the Chaika as if he wished he were anywhere but where he was. Americans. *Chort.*

• In the basement of the Intourist Hotel is perhaps the bleakest-looking, noisiest nightclub in the world: the Labirynt. The decor has been variously described as Russian modern, as bridge-support antique, or—perhaps most accurately—as a waiting room in Hitler's Berlin bunker. Even this early in the evening, everyone, including the staff, seemed partially drunk; the miniskirted waitresses were struggling to keep up with the orders and charging the foreigners whimsical prices. The Labirynt is a hard-currency establishment, with rubles not accepted, and Keer, as a Russian, technically had no business in such a place. It was for foreigners. But with a father who was minister of production and industry, Keer would not be challenged on the point; he had grown up belonging to the "privileged ones," by right of birth a member of the new aristocracy that so fascinated Vasily Klin.

Besides, to look at Keer, the last thing anyone would think was that he *was* Russian. He looked American. This appearance was not by accident. Keer was crazy to the point of addiction about all things American: He listened to illegal American rock records, read illegal American novels, and pored over illegal American newspapers. He dressed in American clothes, drove an American car—the Chevy—and spoke the latest American slang.

That Keer's father did not approve of his affectations Keer

ignored; his father was busy and rarely home, and Keer's mother had died when he was very young, so he was left pretty much to do as he pleased. Besides, as he had explained to Alyosha, much of what Keer did was done deliberately—out of contempt for his father.

Keer saw her the second she walked in. Lisenka was still wearing her Intourist uniform, which surprised him; usually she wore street clothes or waited outside the Labirynt when she had a message for him. But she walked directly over to him tonight, an envelope in her hand. Keer could see it was an Aeroflot ticket holder. As soon as she handed it to him, Keer felt the key inside. Key to what? he wondered. But if Lisenka knew, she was not prepared to tell him. "Wednesday," she announced loudly in English. "The flight has been changed to Wednesday, sir. We will learn the exact time soon. I am trying to make sure everyone on the tour knows." It was a clever maneuver, Keer thought. There was nothing odd-appearing in an Intourist guide, the organizer of a tour perhaps, coming into the Labirynt to hand a foreigner an Aeroflot travel envelope.

"Wednesday," he repeated. "Flight time still uncertain. All right. Thank you." He paused and considered. "Could I buy you a drink?" he asked in his most casual American manner.

"Thank you, but no. I have much to do." She leaned toward him. "The envelope. Get it to Dimmy. Alyosha said tonight." She straightened up and shook Keer's hand formally, then turned on her heel and walked quickly out of the place, covering her ears against the rock-and-roll blast coming from the bandstand.

Keer sighed and ordered himself another Scotch. Wednesday suddenly seemed terribly close. And he would have to take the damned metro all the way out to where Dimmy and Klemet could be found; his own car was too conspicuous for nighttime travel. He sighed again. Almost beside him, he saw an American roughly his own age take a place at the bar. Keer's eyes grew wide. His watch. Keer had to have that boy's watch. The leather strap must have been three or four inches wide, while the watch itself was anchored somewhere in the middle of this vast expanse of pigskin. It was not hard to start a conversation, and Keer learned the boy's name was Gary Decatur, that he and his family were staying upstairs in the Intourist, and that, no, he wouldn't be interested in trading his watch.

Conversation with this pleasant young man came easily,

but Keer noticed that Gary was a little baffled by him. "Something I don't quite understand," Gary finally blurted out. "You don't sound Russian, you don't look Russian. The clothes . . ."

Keer laughed. "Thank you. About the clothes. I pick up what I can on the black market, but that isn't a hell of a lot. For the rest—I barter." He fingered his houndstooth jacket. "This—with a young American—for a gold Fabergé Easter egg." He paused, then added with a smile. "I didn't point out that the egg was a phony. I should feel guilty about it, I guess, but I suspected he was just going to rip off someone in the States with it." Pointing down, Keer showed Gary his highly polished Peel's Brothers shoes. "These were tougher. Series of swaps with a desperate Englishman who'd run out of cash. Very thoughtful guy. Desperate people don't always have the same shoe size. . . ." A pained look came over Keer's face. "The gray flannels, well, I *do* feel a little guilty about them, I guess. West German kid. I swiped them from the public dressing room while he was sunbathing on the beach at Serebryany Bor." The pained look was quickly replaced by Keer's infectious grin. "I've always wondered how the poor Kraut got home with no pants."

They laughed and they talked and Gary explained that he was here alone because his whole family had crumped out on him. Jet lag, they said. So Keer and he had dinner together at the Arbat, probably the best restaurant in Moscow.

The watch was discussed again, but Gary was immovable. At ten-thirty, Keer suddenly remembered Dimmy and the grim prospect of the metro and the evening went sour. In the end, though, he didn't take the metro; he took a taxi. Alyosha had forbidden Keer conspicuous spending—displays of money inevitably drew official curiosity, and the KGB was known to have subagents among Moscow's taxi drivers—but with Wednesday coming up so fast, Keer said the hell with it. If the taxi driver was a KGB man, Keer told himself, it was his own funeral, not Alyosha's.

SUNDAY, NOVEMBER 15

The man with the cardboard suitcase and Lvov sticker had nodded almost imperceptibly but had kept on walking. Behind him scurried a second man, trying to keep up with the first; he too glanced briefly at Alyosha but, like the first, pretended not to see him. Alyosha had spent an uncomfortable hour, not far from the arrival gates of Domodedovo Airport, waiting for these two to show up, and found himself growing angry. The Neck, driving Alyosha around Moscow in his taxi, had not mentioned that the pair would pretend not to see him. Alyosha swore softly. To get here on a Sunday, Alyosha knew, the men must have traveled to Lvov on their sabbath, something Alyosha had never known any of his contacts in the WJA to do before. He should feel sorry for them but didn't. If he was to follow them onto the bus, unacknowledged until they felt safe, the Neck should have told him.

They were a curious-looking pair, squat and dark, part Georgian, Alyosha suspected. But Georgia was an area with not too many Jews, so he didn't know. He took a seat behind them on the bus and, following their lead, ignored them. At the junction of Prospekt Mira and Kirov Street, the two men got off and began walking across Dzerzhinsky Square. A small coffeehouse loomed into view and the pair went inside. Alyosha followed. The place was empty. Suddenly, as he came through the door, the two men threw themselves at Alyosha, embracing him, kissing him, and thumping him on the back as if Alyosha were someone they had known all their lives.

Alyosha's reaction was immediate and frightening. He wrenched himself free of them, tearing their hands from his body, yelling at them for Christ's sake to get their paws off him, and then brushed himself off furiously, as though their touch might have infected him with some disease.

In bewilderment, the two men backed away a few steps, staring. Still trembling, Alyosha realized he had to say something. His green eyes rose to meet theirs, embarrassed by his burst of fury. "I'm sorry. It's just—it's just that—well, I have this thing. For some time now. I can't stand anyone to touch me. *Anyone.*" He stammered to a halt, paused, and repeated, "I'm sorry."

The two WJA men exchanged a glance, smiled weakly, and shrugged, throwing their hands upward in a gesture of "it's nothing." But the smaller of the two, a man with curious eyes, seemed less convinced. Turning partway around, Alyosha saw a chance to remove the focus from himself and took it.

"The girl . . ." whispered Alyosha, indicating the woman behind the counter, who was openly staring at the three of them. "That girl—"

"—is why we come here," announced the smaller of the two men, going over and shaking the woman's hand formally.

"Zionist," explained the larger man, whose name was Avraam. "We always use this place when we are in Moscow. She is with us." He paused, then saw alarm growing in Alyosha's face. "Not with Salt Mine, of course. With us *philosophically*. She knows nothing."

The smaller of the two returned and waved Alyosha to a table. Halfway into a cross-examination of Alyosha's plans, he remembered to give him his name: Misha. Misha Gordinov. Studying him, Alyosha realized that Misha made him nervous. He had the dark eyes of a Georgian but their color had been mixed with some other strain that gave them a steely, flintlike color. His eyelashes either were very thin or had no color at all, and at one point Alyosha had a feeling Misha's eyes might close from the bottom up instead of the top down, like a lizard's. From Misha came an endless probing. Had Alyosha received the items in good shape? Had he and his team learned to assemble them with extreme speed? Were they well concealed? Avraam said far less; his only questions were about the number of soldiers Salt Mine would have to contend with. When he learned how few men Alyosha had, Avraam became glum, although Misha remained unconcerned.

"The three of us alone," Misha pointed out, "could probably handle most of it between us. Experience. At least,

Avraam and *I* have had experience." His lizard's eyes rose to lock with Alyosha's. They said you . . ."

"Lieutenant, Tactical Forces, Cuba. Angola. Mongolia. Ulangom. The Cubans die quietly; the Chinese are always blowing trumpets. In the end it is all the same, I suppose."

"Enough," noted Avraam. "Ulangom alone is enough."

The invoking of this fierce battle with the Chinese—largely unknown to the world—appeared to impress Misha in spite of himself. The hostility subsided a little. "Good. It was made clear you are in charge of Salt Mine. By our headquarters. But I was unsure if you had the right experience. It sounds more than adequate. What is the time to be?"

"The time cannot be fixed yet. The day, of course, is still Wednesday. *This* Wednesday, the eighteenth."

Misha and Avraam exchanged a look. "Good. Three days. We have to meet with some people, someone from WJA Moscow. Only two or three there know of Salt Mine. I shall keep it that way." He began to get to his feet, as did Avraam, but Misha suddenly sat back down. Quickly, Avraam followed suit. "There is no chance," Misha asked, "to see the place? Before?"

"It is open to anyone. But stay only briefly. To spend much time there would not be wise. I have full plans which I will go over with you." Misha nodded glumly. Alyosha, after all, was the leader. Obviously, the fact still rankled.

After settling when they would meet next, the two new additions from the WJA left the café. Alyosha remained at the table, watching them board their bus. The resentment Misha felt about his being the leader of Salt Mine had been negated, at least on the surface, by the recital of his own experience. But Alyosha suspected it still simmered inside Misha and could come back to haunt him later. Obviously, Misha was used to running things and could not be expected to accept second position easily. Why, then, had the WJA chosen to send *him?* They had their reasons, he supposed. Still.

Everyone had their reasons, he thought once again. The WJA. Misha and Avraam. The Old One. Lisenka. Keer. Dimmy. Klemet. Tbor. It sometimes troubled Alyosha that his own reasons were so deep; no one knew what they were but him. And *he* wasn't really sure.

MONDAY, NOVEMBER 16

Tbor squinted in the unaccustomed light filtering through the giant palm trees. Ahead of him, tall ferns moved back and forth gracefully, stirred by a breeze from an unseen source. Some yellow birds flitted among the branches of the smaller trees, calling to each other and staying still only long enough to groom their brilliant feathers. Tbor's pale, city face looked out of place in this tropical setting, and Tbor himself felt odd surrounded by so much greenery; he was a creature of Moscow's dark, hostile back streets, not of nature.

One of the yellow birds lost its bearings and crashed into the glass wall separating it from Tbor; for several moments it thrashed in the long grass, wobbling uncertainly before regaining its equilibrium and flying back to a branch. There, scolding the world with its small voice for deceiving it in such a manner, the bird rested. Tbor could sympathize.

He was waiting in the Botanical Gardens of the Academy of Sciences. This place, one of Moscow's wonders, is the world's largest greenhouse—890 acres under glass. *So* large it boasts full-sized palm trees and over fifteen thousand other tropical plants, all growing under one roof. On a bright day such as this one, the sun coming through its glass roof can be blinding, even at this latitude. Leaning on the railing in front of the enormous glassed-in bird cage, Tbor kept one eye on the door; Dimmy was late.

He and Dimmy were to exchange messages from and to Alyosha. Tbor's message to Alyosha was a strident one: He had not yet been paid for Keer; he had not yet been paid for the three "foot soldiers" he'd delivered to Alyosha the day before yesterday. Dimmy would kindly tell Alyosha that he, Tbor, demanded payment immediately. Or else. That had been their agreement, hadn't it? Cash on delivery.

Turning partway around, Tbor used the railing as a back rest. His plans for what happened after that were spectacular. Once paid by Alyosha, Tbor would be free to go to the KGB. They would pay him a second time. He had no knowledge of the actual date of Salt Mine, or even that that was what Alyosha called it. But the small, seamy world of informers had been full of those strange words recently, and Tbor suspected Alyosha's team was involved. The KGB would pay handsomely, he had heard. And he believed it. For all across Moscow, word in the informers' underground had it that the KGB was extremely anxious to track this mysterious Operation Salt Mine down. *So* anxious, Tbor knew his own involvement in the recruiting could be overlooked. That was the way the KGB worked.

"I am sorry to be late," said the voice beside him. It was

Dimmy, and Tbor prepared himself to spell out his demands for payment. He never got that far.

"Alyosha says he owes you some money. He will give it to you this afternoon."

"Good. Where?"

"You are to meet him in the basement of the Oruzheinaya Palata. The Old One will be there and show you how to reach the cellar."

Tbor was at first incredulous. "The Oruzheinaya Palata? *Inside* the Kremlin walls? He is crazy."

"Think of a less likely place for the KGB to look for him. The Palata is open to the public; anyone can go in. Be there at two."

Before Tbor could say anything, Dimmy was gone. He could see him far across the hall, turning his back on the tropics and going into the rosarium. Although stunned at first, Tbor had to admire the simple brilliance of choosing the Oruzheinaya. There *was* no less likely place for the KGB to look for Alyosha than in a public museum inside the Kremlin itself. This brilliance almost made Tbor feel bad about turning Alyosha over to the KGB. But business was business.

Looking up to locate the source of a small *thunk,* Tbor saw that the same small yellow bird had crashed once again into its glass prison. This time, it lay in the grass, unmoving.

• Tbor's meeting at the Oruzheinaya Palata was very brief. As he walked in through the ornate doors of what had once been the tsar's armory and was now a museum, the Old One met him. As usual, he said nothing. They went into the Hall of Armor and through a small door in one wall; since there was nothing stealable in the hall, there was only one attendant, and the Old One had waited until the man stepped back toward the Hall of Silver.

The door led to a dusty flight of stairs. Twice, Tbor tried to ask the Old One a question but got no response. He was, thought Tbor, the ideal man to have working in a museum: silent as the painted horses in their armor. As he reached the bottom of the stairs, Tbor heard someone and called out Alyosha's name. There was no answer. A sudden coldness swept over him.

The only sound was a soft *thunk,* very like the one the bird made crashing into the glass wall. Tbor never knew what hit him. To deal with Tbor was to learn not to trust him, and Alyosha had learned quickly. There was to be no chance for

Tbor to try to collect payment both from him and from the KGB.

• At about midnight, Alyosha returned to his tiny room on Fish Lane in Moscow's old Kitai-Gorod section. In theory, no one lived in this maze of tiny lanes and crooked streets, formerly Moscow's main trading center. In other days, wholesale traders of glass, fish, poultry, and so forth had their stands on the cobblestones, living in the small houses set off the street behind them. Today, the trading and the merchants have gone, and the houses are used for minor government offices and ministries. During the day, the streets are jammed; at night the area is as deserted as Wall Street after the banks close. Only a handful of people still live there—the janitor-caretakers of the buildings, given their lodgings free to keep them close to the buildings they tend. It was from one of these men—Strelitz, an old widower—that Alyosha had gotten his room. He felt safe there. One ruble a day for room money was expensive, but he had little choice. Obviously, he could count on Strelitz not to report the arrangement to anyone; it was as illegal for Strelitz to rent out space in the building as it was for Alyosha to live in it.

As a base of operations, the location was ideal for Alyosha; only six short blocks down, Kuibyshev Street emptied into Red Square, roughly opposite the Spasskaya Tower of the Kremlin. At night in summer, he could lean out his window and, by craning his neck, see a fragment of the brightly lit Cathedral of the Twelve Apostles, its Russian cross fighting a losing battle with the red star atop the Spasskaya Tower. Pulling out the old-fashioned key, Alyosha slipped it into a large lock that seemed far too big for the tiny door and stepped inside. At the top of the stairs, he turned down a dim hallway lit only by the street light coming through the hall window and started for his room. Simultaneously, there was a cough and a man stepped out of the shadows. "Tserkhov," the voice said sharply. A flashlight flicked on and was shone directly into his eyes. "Comrade Bleisky. KGB." Mikhail Chorniev's shot in the dark was in the process of paying off. Some effort was made to wave an identifying badge in front of him, but Alyosha barely saw it. He was startled that someone should be here, stunned at the words "KGB," and initially confused by the sound of the phony name he had given his landlord.

The voice continued. "You have no business living here,

my friend. As you well know. We had a report that someone was; I questioned that old fool Strelitz about you, but he was too terrified for himself to tell me much. Come, let us go inside and see what you have to say."

A panic sprang to life inside Alyosha. There were papers in his room. Plans. Lists. Hidden, but not very elaborately. If this man Bleisky had not already found them, he soon would. His own presence as a boarder here was in itself incriminating; Alyosha could see almost a year's work on Salt Mine dissolving before his eyes. "Come," repeated the KGB man, waving the flashlight toward Alyosha's door. It was open, swinging reproachfully from the pressure of the KGB man's hand; the room, then, had already been searched, but if anything important had been found, the KGB would have been there in force—and sounding far less reasonable than Comrade Bleisky.

Still, Alyosha felt he had no choice. Comrade Bleisky's eyes bugged and his mouth drooped open as it hit him. Alyosha had pulled the knife from his pocket—it was a long, round-bladed affair, with so little flat surface it was more like an ice pick than a knife—and drove it home just below the KGB man's breastbone, then rocked the handle up and down and back and forth until he could feel it rip and tear something inside. A bubbling, frothing sound came from Bleisky; a thin red stream of blood ran from one nostril; his eyes widened farther, as if still unable to believe Alyosha had done what he had done; for a moment, the eyes stared at him, glazing slowly, before suddenly rolling upward into his head until only the whites were visible. Quickly, Alyosha reached forward and grabbed the man under his arms; gently, he lowered him to the floor and pulled him into his room.

With a resigned sigh, Alyosha closed the door softly behind him, stepping over Bleisky and sinking into the room's lone chair. Bleisky was the first man he'd killed since the army, and even there, in the special tactical unit on the Chinese border, the killing had been masked in the anonymity of army orders and had never been on so personal a level as with Bleisky. (The Armenian he did not consider killed by himself; the cigarettes that would produce the symptoms of heart attack had been prepared by Tbor. Ergo: Tbor had killed the Armenian.) As for the killing of Bleisky, Alyosha considered it something circumstances required. His rationalization was not satisfactory; the killing continued to upset Alyosha more than he cared to admit.

The faint bubbling that was coming from Bleisky stopped, and a final sigh rose from him. A story would have to be prepared for the already terrified Strelitz; that would be easy. More difficult would be disposing of Bleisky. Even in a half a day's time, the smell would be noticeable. Someone—anyone he could reach by phone—had just gained another job. Alyosha himself would be busy tomorrow: First, there was his daily stint with the sketch pad, a device he used to cover what he was really doing, and then, perhaps three hours later, a meeting with Misha and Avraam to go over plans.

He did not like the idea of these two, nor did he feel that they should be part of Salt Mine. But the WJA had provided funds for over a year—not only for himself, but also for the supplies and materials he had to buy—and then had demanded not only a partnership, but a presence.

Walking over to the window, he opened the *fortochka*—a small window set into the larger one—and craned his neck to see the lights of the Kremlin. They were still there. Like the cold feeling of fear in his stomach about the KGB. Did they know where Bleisky was going? Was a record kept?

He began pacing the room in his long strides, torturing himself with the fragility of Salt Mine. So few against so many. Wonderfully bold, or stupidly reckless? The light coming from the street silhouetted him against the window, dramatizing his lean shape and wiry frame. Alyosha sighed. For the moment, his immediate problem was covering up Bleisky's sudden disappearance.

Abruptly, Alyosha strode to the door and went downstairs, making as much noise as possible, a torrent of words pouring from him as he disappeared down the empty stairway. As he had expected, his landlord, Strelitz, pressed his door shut just as Alyosha rounded the stairs; the man had been listening to see how Alyosha fared at Bleisky's hands. It would give him some indication of his own fate. Continuing to laugh noisily, Alyosha opened the front door, called a loud good night, and slammed it shut again.

Strelitz's door flew open and he stared out at him. As if for the first time, Alyosha pretended to see him. "Oh, Comrade Strelitz, it's you. There is nothing to concern yourself with. Sometimes the KGB's right hand doesn't know what its left is doing. Comrade Bleisky sends his apologies if he frightened you. But understand, please, it was not his fault. Central Bureau had not told him of my assignment here, and he was only doing his duty. I will continue to stay here, but no one must know of it. Even other KGB men. I will be away for a few weeks, but I will continue to pay you room money, of course. If I am to be away longer, Comrade Bleisky—since he already knows of my being headquartered here—will come by with it for you."

Strelitz's eyes were bugging. That a KGB man—Bleisky—should invade his house, question him on Alyosha's living here, and threaten him for allowing Alyosha to circumvent the Soviet habitation laws was unsettling enough for one day. He could end up in Lubyanka. But that his illegal tenant should then turn out to be yet another KGB man on some sort of supersecret mission, that Bleisky and he should come down the stairs talking and laughing together, and that the frightening KGB operative Bleisky might be the one to come back and pay Alyosha's room money—Strelitz's head swam.

"Understood?" Alyosha had one hand on the banister, ready to retreat upstairs. Numbly, Strelitz nodded, his mouth opening and closing, on the edge of saying something but unable to think of anything that might not get him into trouble.

"Do svidanya," said Alyosha, putting one finger to his lips to remind him this was a KGB matter.

Strelitz nodded again, smiling, touching his own lips with his fingertips to show he understood the KGB's ways.

Upstairs, Alyosha opened the wardrobe door and studied Bleisky. He hung from a clothes hook far to one side, like a tattered old coat that has outlived its usefulness. Strelitz would have to wait a long time before this man would pay him anything. With an indifferent shrug, Alyosha fell onto the bed and was asleep in less than five minutes.

5

MORNING, TUESDAY, NOVEMBER 17

"Easy," Keer said over the labored breathing of the others. "Easy, dammit."

The small trunk banged into the banister of the narrow stairs, which groaned a complaint at having to carry such unaccustomed weight.

"Easy is one thing to say," noted Dimmy sourly, holding the bottom end of the trunk. "Particularly when someone else is doing the carrying." He paused and looked at Keer. "Does this mission really *need* a traffic director? Couldn't you help?"

"One more flight," Keer said, ignoring him. "Only one more flight."

"That's what the captain of the *Hindenburg* told himself."

"Don't make me laugh, Dimmy, please," said Klemet. "I shall drop my end." As always, it was Klemet who was worried, yet he was the one who began to laugh; while Dimmy, who looked nervous and sour, could not help but comment on the ridiculousness of the situation.

As Klemet's snicker grew into a full laugh—one so hard he and the small trunk began to shake dangerously—Keer was unable not to giggle himself; even Dimmy smiled faintly. There was an element of gallows humor in their performance; inside the trunk was Comrade Bleisky of the KGB, curled up into a tight ball like a bloodied red fist. It was ten o'clock and the streets would be full of the petty officialdom of Moscow; as it was, they had already had to carry the trunk past two offices full of Soviet bureaucrats even to get to the stair landing.

To Keer, the assignment had all the elements of a nightmare, and had had since he was waked at seven-thirty that morning. Dovo, his father's elderly houseman—so old he still wore the traditional high-necked shirt and sash—had been forced to shake him hard to wake him at seven-thirty. In spite of Keer's attempt to burrow back under the pillows, he was unable to wave Dovo away. Someone wanted him on the phone, Dovo growled, and the matter must be of some urgency. The caller, Dovo said, had been rude—well, insistent. Someone named Alyosha.

Groaning, Keer stumbled downstairs in his pajamas and listened; then: "I'm to *what?*"

"To argue the matter on the phone is unwise," Alyosha pointed out. "Do what I tell you. A present. There is a cold present"—Alyosha added the extra word, remembering the code he had set up—"in the wardrobe of my room. Get your car and dispose of it. I have to be someplace else."

There was a silence. Keer doubted if his father's phone was tapped. Still, one had to be careful. "How?"

"Go get Dimmy. He will help. Or Klemet. Or both. They are in town, until tonight anyway." Alyosha resorted to the code again. "The trophy is presented at three."

"I don't know," Keer began, but Alyosha stopped him.

"I don't have time to argue. Meet me at the corner of Ro Place"—code for the corner of Razin and Itapyeusky streets—"in thirty minutes. I will give you the key." There was the sound of swearing and a click as Alyosha hung up.

Later, it was Keer who was doing the swearing. Alyosha had been right in saying that Strelitz would be out having his normal glass of tea from ten to ten-thirty, so Keer had nothing to worry about on that score. But he had not counted on the swarms of people moving along the crooked lanes and streets outside of Alyosha's building. His car—the '67 Chevy—was parked at the curb and, because it was American, attracted attention as always. Usually, Keer reveled in this; to have people gape at him, to wonder at his beautifully polished convertible—perhaps to assume he was American—satisfied some need in him.

Today was a different story. For once, Keer prayed no one would pay attention to the car at all. At the bottom of the stairs, he told Klemet and Dimmy to get the small but unwieldy trunk across the pavement as quickly as possible, in the hope of avoiding too much curiosity. "It shouldn't be tough," he whispered. "The top's down. But for God's sake, get it over with fast. I'll be right with you." Keer hoped it would be as easy as he made it sound, but he had no way of anticipating the series of complications that would turn that short walk into a nightmare.

As they came out the door, Keer was stunned to discover Fish Lane completely jammed with people, all moving in the same direction. The tinkle of a bell made him look to the left. There, pulled over to the curb, was the old lady with the tea and *kvass* wagon. The sudden mob, like Strelitz, were on their morning tea break. The slow pace at which the tightly jammed crowd were moving allowed them to stop and examine the Chevy; a ring of perhaps twenty people were standing around it, pointing, talking, shaking their heads in wonder. Worse, lugging the heavy trunk across the sidewalk blocked what little movement there was; brought to a complete stop, those pedestrians watched every step of Dimmy and Klemet's progress toward the car.

Then, it happened. Halfway across the sidewalk, the handle at Klemet's end broke. The heavy, overloaded trunk crashed to the cement. Keer's heart stopped, waiting to see if the trunk would split open. Several of the onlookers laughed good-naturedly; others shouted suggestions to Dimmy and Klemet, who were having trouble getting a new handhold on the trunk. Muscovites are busybodies, but they are friendly busybodies, and beyond their good-natured laughter and suggestions, several of them quickly pitched in and helped manhandle the trunk across the pavement onto the back seat of the Chevy. The sight of all this made Keer begin to tremble. An air force captain, panting from the effort and brushing the dirt off his hands, turned to Dimmy with a smile. "What have you got in that thing, Comrade? *Gold?*"

Dimmy's response was quick. It was also dangerous. "More valuable than that, Kapitan. Black-market panty hose." The group around the car laughed, but Keer felt his legs turn to water. What if a KGB man was passing, was not amused, and demanded, in spite of all their explanations, that the trunk be opened to prove Dimmy's answer was only a joke? It had happened before; the KGB was not famous for its sense of humor.

Still shaking, Keer quickly collected Dimmy and Klemet, jumped in behind the wheel, and drove off, heading for Prospekt Mira. Once in the outskirts of Moscow, they could dump their cargo unnoticed.

The wheel in his hands reassured him. He no longer worried at the thought of people staring at the Chevy, or of the passing KGB man with no sense of humor. The hard knot in his stomach began to disappear. He felt good. He had been put to the test, and it spite of his worst fears, he had survived. He was supposed to be the "outside man" throughout Salt Mine, someone to make sure that what they heard inside was actually happening outside. Only at the last minute was he to link up with Alyosha and the others. This assignment had appealed to Keer. But while Keer had known there were to be outside missions when Salt Mine got going, he had not counted on things like disposing of bodies. And before Salt Mine even began.

In this morning's brief meeting with Alyosha, Keer had tried to explain the unfairness of this assignment. But Alyosha had merely looked at him as if he were crazy and had gone on giving instructions. Keer checked his watch, and the image of Gary Decatur's four-inch-wide watchband suddenly swam in front of his eyes. He dismissed it as a rumbling sound came from his stomach. Lack of breakfast, on top of a bad case of nerves. He stepped on the accelerator. If he accomplished his mission quickly enough, he could still make luncheon at the Metropol.

A "cold present" didn't necessarily require a cold lunch.

• Alyosha tucked the sketch pad tighter beneath one arm and drew his overcoat against the blast of November wind. Although it was nearly ten o'clock, the sun was still weak, reflecting palely off the Russian crosses of Blagoveshchensky Cathedral; the great red star above the Spasskaya Tower was higher and larger, but looked no warmer.

Along Kuibyshev Street, the wind moaned through the poplars as Alyosha stepped into Red Square; a particularly frigid blast roaring across the vast open space tore at the pages of Alyosha's pad and made him pull his fur hat down tighter on his head. Quickly, he sought out the zebra stripes and crossed the square, almost running to reach the shelter of the gate of the Spasskaya. For a moment, he stood by the outer wall, shivering and cursing; it was, as he had known, still too early for admittance. From above him in the Spasskaya Tower, the bells of the Kremlin clock struck ten, and Alyosha, along with a handful of other early visitors, began moving through the gate toward Kremlin Square. Abruptly, they had to flatten themselves against the stone walls. The guard for Lenin's Tomb changes on the hour—precisely when the chimes ring—and a squad of honor soldiers marched out through the gate, their goosestep sounding hollow and metallic as they brought their boots down hard on the ancient cobblestones.

Once they had passed, the other visitors began dispersing inside the hollow pentagon, most of them in the charge of Intourist guides; Alyosha alone remained standing at the inner doorway of Spasskaya. Free of the biting wind, he pushed the fur hat back up, the other hand trying to resmooth the wrinkled pages of his sketch pad. Alyosha's green eyes darted around the inner courtyard, searching for signs of anything that might spell trouble for him. Briefly, they fixed on the low mustard-and-white building that had once been the tsar's arsenal but now houses a special detachment of honor troops; besides providing the men who stand stiffly at attention along the passage to Lenin's Tomb, these soldiers guard the Kremlin's art treasures and historical collections open to the public. Shivering but patient, Alyosha waited. A few minutes later, his eyes picked up a sudden flurry of activity outside the Arsenal.

The soldiers who had marched past Alyosha in the Spasskaya had been on their way to relieve another squad; this squad had just arrived back outside their building and apparently were getting the order to fall out. For a moment the soldiers milled around outside, stamping their feet and laughing and jostling. Then, chilled by their hour's duty in the raw wind, they quickly moved inside the Arsenal. Alyosha checked his watch. The change of guard had taken just over fourteen and a half minutes. In the two weeks Alyosha had been checking, the time hadn't varied by more than a minute.

With a shrug, Alyosha headed across the inner courtyard, sticking meticulously to the pathways, as required by the rules posted on each gate. The last thing he wanted was to be noticed by anyone, and the guards enforced this particular regulation strictly. His fingers still trying to smooth the pages of the sketch pad, Alyosha fixed a smile and walked briskly into Oruzheinaya Palata—the old Armory that now houses the Kremlin Museum.

Inside, the Old One, Kropotkin, stood in front of the painting, one eye watching the entrance door, the other guiding the brush in his fingers as he touched up little cracks in the gilt frame. At his feet stood a flat box, its wooden handle worn smooth by his fingers; this held the jars of paint, gilt, and gold leaf which were the tools of his trade. Like so many other jobs in Russia, the maintenance of the Oruzheinaya was performed almost entirely by old women; Kropotkin, because he was a specialist of considerable skill, was, along with the museum attendants, one of the few men who actually worked inside the place. Day after day, the Old One moved from room to room, spotting and refinishing small blemishes in the cases and frames that held the art works; the displays were so numerous that one man could barely make the full round of them, repairing and fixing as he went, before new repair work was needed at the place he had started.

No one, including Kropotkin, knew his exact age; that he was old, very old, was obvious. But his hand was still steady and his eyes still clear, of an intense light blue that shone out from under bristling white eyebrows. Nor did anyone use his first name any more; he was addressed as Kropotkin or the Old One, and had been for so many years that Kropotkin sometimes wondered if his first name hadn't somehow gotten lost along with his youth. (Actually, the name was Sasha, but he couldn't remember anyone calling him Sasha since that whore in the Zagorsk bar. What was it, twelve or fifteen years ago now?)

Out of the corner of his eye, the Old One saw Alyosha making his way toward the coatroom, and nodded imperceptibly. He watched as Alyosha slipped his feet into the backless paper slippers that were required of anyone entering the museum. These slippers were to protect not the Oruzheinaya's highly polished floors but the visitors' bones. Every night, the gleaming parquet is brought to a mirrorlike finish by an army of old women, kneeling on the floor and hand-polishing it with pure beeswax; because the slippers are backless and flap loosely around a person's feet, he has to walk more slowly and therefore becomes less vulnerable to slipping. For himself, Kropotkin wore a pair of old-fashioned carpet slippers with feltlike soles; these were worn not to prevent accidents, but to keep his feet from hurting too badly after a long day spent standing.

Alyosha was laughing with the old lady who managed the coatroom; they were discussing the sketch Alyosha had done of her the first day he had come two weeks before. It was an outrageously flattering one, currently tacked to the cloakroom's rear wall. Keeping on the good side of Natalya Sergeyevna, Kropotkin had told Alyosha, was important; she was not only a Party zealot but a "block watcher." She could just as easily report Alyosha, Kropotkin had explained, if she disliked him and decided there was something suspicious in his coming here every day to sketch the collection. Alyosha and the coatroom lady, Natalya, were laughing now, her single gold tooth gleaming among the yellowed stumps in her mouth. He had done this part of his assignment well, Kropotkin admitted. Natalya Sergeyevna he loathed.

The sketch pad was opened and Alyosha walked out of the entrance area into the Hall of Armor. His stride was purposeful, but Kropotkin, the Old One, noticed he was unable to resist slowing down and glancing at the small door through which Tbor had yesterday gone "to get paid."

At the arch between the Hall of Armor and the Hall of Silver, Alyosha passed the Old One, who stared intently in front of him, apparently lost in his work. As he did, Alyosha dropped to one knee, appearing to have difficulty with one of the paper slippers. While Alyosha was adjusting the slipper, pulling it out and smoothing it flat, Kropotkin heard rather than saw him place something in the wooden tray of paints standing at his feet. It would be a small piece of metal, numbered, and sometimes with a cryptic tag attached to it. The tiny clink had been made by the metal hitting one of his jars of paint.

THE KREMLIN

1. Spasskaya Tower
2. Senate Tower
3. Nikolskaya Tower
4. Sobakinaya Tower
5. Middle Arsenal Tower
6. Troitskaya Tower
7. Kutafya Tower
8. Armory Tower
9. Borovitskaya Tower
10. Vodovzvodnaya Tower
11. Annunciation Tower
12. Tainitskaya Tower
13. First Nameless Tower
14. Second Nameless Tower
15. Petrovskaya Tower
16. Beklemishev Tower
17. Tower of Sts. Constantine and Helen
18. Alarm Tower
19. Tsar's Tower
20. Cathedral of the Assumption
21. Cathedral of the Annunciation
22. Church of the Disposition of the Robe
23. Palace of the Facets
24. Cathedral of the Archangel
25. Ivan the Great Bell Tower
26. Terem Palace
27. Upper Savior Cathedral
28. Cathedral of the Twelve Apostles and Patriarch's Palace
29. Poteshney Palace
30. Arsenal
31. Council of Ministers Building
32. Grand Kremlin Palace
33. Oruzheinaya Palata
34. Building of the Supreme Soviet
35. Kremlin Palace of Congresses
36. Tsar Bell
37. Tsar Cannon

I. Red Square
II. Alexandrovsky Gardens
III. Moskva River

Kropotkin kept his eyes on the frame, slowly moving the fine brush across the corner. But, behind him, he knew, Alyosha was once more on his feet, shuffling along more carefully, smiling in embarrassment at the museum guard who stood at the doorway.

Perhaps half an hour later the Old One, letting his brush hang loosely, stood back several feet and studied the frame. It was done. He reached down, putting the brush back into the holder of the tray, and picked up the box. Slowly, he shuffled toward the coatroom, his felt-bottomed slippers making a slapping sound on the parquet. Going behind the coatroom's counter, he forced a smile for his old enemy, Natalya, and pushed his way into the washroom. Quickly, he checked under the booths and went into the stall to the left, locking the door behind him. There, he removed the ceramic top of the toilet tank, reached into his paint tray, and withdrew the piece of metal. It was perhaps three inches long, tubular, and heavy, but small enough so that it would not set off the metal detectors concealed at the main entrance of the museum. Kropotkin detached the tag wired to it, and placed the curious, tubular element carefully down inside the tank, making sure it did not interfere with the flushing mechanism. Gleaming dully from the tank's bottom were dozens of pieces Alyosha and others had given him over the last month; more were in the tank of the right booth, as well as buried in the sand-filled fire buckets, among his own art supplies, and in a variety of other places Kropotkin knew were safe from examination.

The cover back on the tank, the Old One started out into the cloakroom. But not before he read the small tag he had just torn off the curious fragment of metal: "Piece #47-Ø-nR. Note: W18."

So it was to be Wednesday, the eighteenth. Today was the seventeenth. Kropotkin shrugged. He was surprised he had been given so little warning of the date, but he had spent a lifetime being surprised by events determined by others. Only the intense furrowing of his white eyebrows signaled more than passing interest. With the tray once again dangling from his arm, Kropotkin, the Old One, walked out into the display area, throwing a fierce glare at Natalya's back as he passed.

• From his window on the second floor of the old Arsenal, Kapitan Vladimir Mikhailovich Sokolov—Volodya to those who knew him well—looked out into the immaculate Kremlin gardens below. His arms were clasped behind him as he rocked back and forth on the heels of his gleaming boots, an action that struck him as entirely fitting for a man in his position. Unfortunately, the position might well be temporary. The regular company commander had been suddenly assigned to an intelligence unit; just as suddenly, Volodya had been shipped down from Leningrad to fill in for at least a six-month trial period, perhaps longer. There had been certain intimations that if he did a good job, the posting would be permanent. Intimations, but no commitments. Grinding his teeth, Volodya once again reassured himself that his performance would be not only good, but superior.

He had the background, certainly. In Leningrad, Volodya had commanded a similar elite company, very much like the one here, but without the panache of a Moscow assignment. His company there had provided the honor guard for some of the many memorials to the Unknown Soldier that dot Russia, as well as providing ceremonial escorts for all high-level military funerals in the area.

Leningrad had been all right, but it was no Moscow. To a soldier—to any modern Russian—Moscow is the hub, the heart, the starting place and the pulse beat of the Communist dream. Before his assignment here, the kapitan had been to Moscow only a few times—as a tourist. But he could remember the awe he had felt gazing at Lenin's Tomb, at seeing Lenin himself frozen in his plastic sarcophagus, at touring the Kremlin's courtyards and gaping at the onion domes and imperial spires, of walking through the Palace of the Congresses and studying the vast hall where the meetings of the Supreme Soviet are held.

The thought of this last building raised the one discontent Volodya had in his assignment: While he was responsible for the guard on Lenin's Tomb and the soldiers assigned to protect the cathedrals and museums, the functioning areas of the government—the Building of the Supreme Soviet and the Council of Ministers Building—were guarded by an Army unit reporting directly to the KGB. They were even called the "real soldiers," to differentiate them from his own spit-and-polish men. To Volodya this seemed an almost personal affront; the "real soldiers," too, should be reporting to him.

Volodya sighed. It was a small matter. Idly, he watched the tourists crossing the courtyard and disappearing into the various buildings and churches, steered and prodded like so many sheep by their Intourist guides. No longer was he a tourist.

He was a Muscovite. He was part of the Kremlin. And some of those people in the yard below must stare at him with the same awe with which he, years before, had gaped at the privileged gods who stalked this private world inside the Kremlin walls.

For a moment, Volodya stared at the glossy photograph of Lenin that hung opposite his desk. He asked, he pleaded, he *prayed* to it not to let him do anything wrong. Or for anything at all to go wrong in the Kremlin area during his trial period.

"Please," he suddenly heard himself say out loud. Angry for being crazy enough to talk to a photograph, he sat down behind his desk, pulling the chair up roughly. At any minute, the corporal of the guard should call to check in; these reports came at roughly ten-minute intervals as the corporal went from one post to the next. Volodya would then record them on the complicated electronic check board in his office.

Waiting, he scanned yesterday's list of visitors to the Kremlin's museums and other buildings. In the interest of "movement control," each tourist was obliged to sign in by the Moscow Prefecture Police; for the same reason, each citizen was required to produce his identity card. Kapitan Sokolov's eyes ran down the list without interest, but stopped at one name—Alexei Andreyevich Gregarin—Alyosha. He had seen that name once or twice on his list before. He was sure because he had been amused that the last name was the same as his wife's uncle's. Volodya shifted uncomfortably. Perhaps the name he had seen before had been Andrei Alexeyevich Gregarin. He couldn't remember and dismissed the matter. It was nothing. Nothing at all.

His eyes crept up to the picture on the wall again. Nothing will go wrong. Nothing will go wrong and I, Vladimir Mikhailovich Sokolov, will be assigned to Moscow forever.

6

AFTERNOON, TUESDAY, NOVEMBER 17

Like many New Yorkers who have never visited the Statue of Liberty, Chinatown or Grant's Tomb, Keer Gertsen had never toured the Kremlin. Once or twice—at New Year's—he had gone there with his father to the parties given for the children of high officials, but these visits were restricted to the Grand Kremlin Palace, with entry through the gate in the Nikolskaya Tower, usually forbidden to all but government officials. This last afternoon before Salt Mine, Keer was determined to see the rest. A private Intourist guide was engaged, a pert but extended young lady who towered over him; in the course of an hour and a half she gave Keer the typical tourist's once-over of that remarkable complex called the Kremlin. Keer prayed that he would not run into either Alyosha or Lisenka; this visit was entirely his own doing and was without Alyosha's permission.

Many visitors to Moscow—particularly Americans—are initially startled to learn that they can go inside the Kremlin at all, and even more surprised that about eighty per cent of it is open to the public. Largely, this is because there are really *two* Kremlins: the Kremlin of cathedrals, museums, and theaters, and the more ominous Kremlin that houses the nerve center of the Soviet government.

The tall guide—her name was Yekaterina Yusupovna—pointed out this second set of buildings to Keer, who eyed them nervously. The Building of the Supreme Soviet didn't bother him. The Council of Ministers Building did; it was where Keer's father, the Minister of Production, had his offices. He knew his uneasiness was ridiculous; his father was out of the country on business, in Yugoslavia, he thought, leading a delegation at an international trade meeting.

"That area is never, under any circumstances, open to visitors," boomed Yekaterina, "but the remaining four-fifths are available to all who are interested. When you remember that it is the capital of the USSR, as well as of the entire Communist world, the fact is quite remarkable." She did not add, though Keer was well aware of it, that to provide protection for the Soviet leaders who work inside, the entire forbidden area boasts some of the best-trained security troops and most sophisticated electronic equipment known to man. Nor did she point out that during the days of Stalin, the entire Kremlin—cathedrals, museums, theaters, and working areas—was completely sealed off from the outside world; Stalin brooded inside, taking occasional solitary strolls through the immaculate gardens, nursing his paranoia, and feeling that here, at least, he was reasonably safe from personal violence.

Like most visitors, Keer was staggered by the Kremlin's size. From outside, it appeared merely a huge, rambling collection of buildings surrounded by a high wall. But this is deceptive. Yekaterina pointed out that inside its walls are no less than five full-sized cathedrals and four churches. That lost in the Kremlin's vastness is a building—roughly the size of America's Kennedy Center—that can hold an audience of over six thousand, while its stage can accommodate a double symphony orchestra, a one-hundred-voice chorus, and the whole of the Bolshoi Ballet, all at the same time and all without straining a seam. Adding in a variety of other palaces and the two huge squares—Cathedral Square, where the tsars were crowned, and Kremlin Square, where full-scale military parades are mounted to this day—you still have room left over. Yekaterina seemed carried away by her blizzard of statistics, but Keer could sense there was more than this at work; her eyes shone, she had pulled herself even taller than before, and her voice seemed choked with the sheer intensity of her feelings. "Surrounding it all, my friend, is an impenetrable wall graced by twenty mammoth towers and gates, and there is only one word to describe the Kremlin properly: '*giant*.' "

Her fervent eyes suddenly fixed themselves on Keer as if waiting for some reaction. Keer was every bit as impressed as he was supposed to be but was having difficulty separating the vast beauties of the Kremlin from its associations with his father. The only reaction he could produce was a very unsatisfactory "Remarkable."

His exuberance returned—along with his sense of whimsy—as she continued the tour. To Keer, it was impossible to shake the impression that parts of the Kremlin were the product of some sort of private family joke, the Romanovs laughing from their graves. The architecture and buildings of the Kremlin are symbols of Russia itself, yet, as Yekaterina noted without comment, much of it was designed by Italians. Keer stared in awe at the Tsar Cannon, so large it required cannonballs a yard and a half in diameter. It was a magnificent joining of carved-brass workmanship and the gunsmith's art, yet, Yekaterina noted, the Tsar Cannon was never fired. Asked why, she became evasive. Keer didn't press the point; his own reading had provided the answer: There was an understandable fear the cannon would explode, and while it had been built to delight Tsar Ivan the Terrible's feeble-minded son, no one was willing to delight the boy *that* much.

Farther on, Keer began having trouble keeping a straight face; Yekaterina's manner became increasingly more earnest the further she delved into the curious features of some of the Kremlin's early artworks. She rapped authoritatively on the sides of the Tsar Kolokol (Tsar Bell)—"It stands twenty feet high, is twenty-one feet in diameter, and weighs two hundred tons"—although honesty required her to add lamely it had never been rung. Pointing, she indicated another bell hanging in Ivan the Great's bell tower; it weighed over sixty-four tons. It had never been rung either. There were reasons, of course. . . . Only with effort was Keer able to suppress a giggle.

Keer's mood changed abruptly as Yekaterina, standing in the center of Kremlin Square, extended one finger and pointed again at the forbidden areas of the Council of Ministers Building and the Building of the Supreme Soviet. She talked of their graceful architecture and perfect proportions; Keer narrowed his eyes and thought of their more sinister connotations. From inside these buildings had come the orders for the systematic destruction of several million Poles; from these buildings every day flow the instructions coordinating carefully planned pogroms throughout the satellite nations; from behind the delicately beautiful pale yellow stonework, directives are sent to a network of underground agents who can topple many governments as easily as a child collapses a house of cards. Inside those same walls, so feelingly described by Yekaterina as architectural masterpieces, Keer knew the decisions on Hungary and Czechoslovakia had been taken, along with the more routine decisions as to which dissidents should disappear, which be put into prison, which into an asylum, which expelled. Keer, of course, said nothing, but felt a chill run through him. Abruptly, he drew Yekaterina into a discussion of the Kremlin's beginnings and early years.

A little sheepishly, Yekaterina confessed that no one knew the precise date the Kremlin was started. The consensus is that it was started sometime in the twelfth century, originally as a fortified town with high wooden walls (the word "kremlin" means fort). As it grew, various tsars could not resist adding their personal monuments—a palace, a cathedral, a tower, gate, or garden. As the list of tsars grew longer, the Kremlin grew more lavish.

After Peter the Great moved the capital to St. Petersburg, however, the Kremlin was allowed to deteriorate, its magnificent reception rooms and collections of thrones, crowns, and armor gathering dust and mildew. After this, Yekaterina appeared unwilling to go further into the matter. Keer knew why, and silently supplied the rest from his own readings of foreign literature.

Immediately following the Revolution, there was considerable feeling among early Bolsheviks that they should erase all the evidence of a tsarist past the Kremlin represents. And, but for Lenin, they probably would have. But with his professorial mind, Lenin personally oversaw the meticulous restoration of the Kremlin's treasures, giving his time and attention unstintingly. This went on even while the Revolution was still in progress—and when no one was yet sure whether Lenin or the White Russians would end up living in the Kremlin. Correctly, he saw that it was more than a collection of buildings and artifacts; it was the history of Russia itself. And after his death, his perfectly preserved body became a part of that history, lying in a plain red marble tomb that backs up against the outside of the Kremlin wall.

Lenin would probably have been pained to see the Kremlin sealed during the days of Stalin; he would be equally disturbed to know that parts of it are still off-limits today. But the "other Kremlin"—the one where the day-to-day decisions are made that affect the workings of the government not only in its own country but throughout the world—is a "kremlin" in the original meaning of the word: a fortress. The government figures enter through their own gate—in the Nikolskaya Tower—are guarded by their own regiment of specially trained troops, and inhabit a world of electronic sensing devices, scrambler phones, hidden protective machinery, and concealed underground vaults and chambers.

In silence, each lost in his own thoughts, Keer and Yekaterina made their way across the Kremlin Square toward the exit gate. To Yekaterina, the Kremlin she was leaving behind her represented the summit of the Communist dream; to Keer, it was a frightening, sinister place, one where his father labored; to the rest of the people in Salt Mine, it was similarly sinister, a place they hoped the Salt Mine plan could come to terms with.

As they turned near the Spasskaya Tower, the ominous aspect of the Kremlin was symbolized for Keer by one squat building Yekaterina had shown him earlier just outside the Kremlin wall: Lobnoye Mesto, the Place of Skulls. Ivan the Terrible, when he had beheaded a courtier, used to store the man's skull in Lobnoye Mesto as a pointed reminder to others of what disobedience could bring.

Nothing, thought Keer, had changed much. Today, the skulls are still there, reminding.

• The wind blew hard around the telephone booth, making a strange sighing sound as it crept into the cracks offered it by the door. Wincing, Lisenka shivered, partly from the cold, partly from the strangeness of the sound. The sight of someone across the street made Lisenka shrink down; Karl Marx Prospekt and Intourist Central were only two blocks away, and she was convinced someone from the office was sure to see her. Silly, she told herself.

"Hello," she said into the phone. "Tamara Ivanovna Bleisky? Ah, yes. This is Comrade Tournova at KGB headquarters. No, nothing has happened to your husband. He will be away for a few days—an assignment from the director himself—but he had no chance to call you before he left. That job he left to me. Yes, probably by Friday. Yes. Thank you, Tamara Ivanovna."

Lisenka hung up, feeling both a little sad and a little strange. It always surprised her to think that KGB agents *had* wives and children and homes and dogs. Or that, if they weren't going to be able to make dinner, they would call their wives and let them know so they wouldn't worry. Even more startling was the thought of a KGB man having intercourse; obviously they did, but since Shymon, Lisenka could picture it only the way one might imagine Hitler screwing Eva Braun. In spite of the picture's ridiculousness, Lisenka felt a shudder pass through her. With a sigh, she put more coins into the phone and placed the second call. The names were written on a slip of paper Alyosha had given her.

"Hello? Hello? Section K-fifteen, please. Supervisor Denchek." After a pause: "Comrade Denchek? Tamara Ivanovna Bleisky. Ilya is sick. No, no, nothing serious. Just that bug. He is throwing up a lot and I wouldn't let him go out to call you himself. Probably in a couple of days. Ilya said your little boy had it, so you know how it is. No, no, there is nothing he needs; a few days and it goes away. Yes, of course I'll tell him. Thank you, Comrade."

When Alyosha searched Bleisky's body, he discovered the agent's wallet contained a gold mine of information. Even a note to himself to send the supervisor's child a toy because "he had the bug." And more than enough so that Alyosha could head off any curiosity, either from Bleisky's wife or the KGB itself, when Bleisky didn't return from his day's assignments. That kind of curiosity could have turned up Bleisky's assignment to check out an "illegal habitation" on Fish Lane. Tomorrow was too close to take chances. Lisenka was told to make the calls.

Tomorrow. Tomorrow. Lisenka flung open the booth's door and hurried across the street toward Intourist Central. She had a tour beginning at three-thirty. Mostly Americans, as usual. As well as some Germans, she thought. As she pushed her way through the main doors, a question suddenly struck Lisenka.

Had Hitler ever screwed Eva Braun? Someday, she must ask.

• "You should keep your hands off it. Scratching is the worst thing you can do."

"I don't scratch, dammit. It's infected or something."

"Perhaps in your sleep . . ." The doctor, a woman—most doctors in the Soviet are—tried to be sympathetic but was having a hard time making Security Minister Klin accept his problem. A long-time survivor of treating the Soviet hierarchy, she knew that the blunt statements you make to an ordinary patient were dangerous. A comment just a shade too frank and one could wind up treating blisters in Egve Kinot, a frigid seal-hunting village on the Bering Sea, much invoked by Soviet comics.

The doctor squirmed. She was considered the best dermatologist in Moscow; she knew Klin's case intimately, and she knew how his scalp made him suffer. As much, she suspected, psychologically as medically. But in all the years she had been treating him, she had never seen Klin so irritable and tense, or his scalp in worse condition.

"No, not in my sleep, either." Klin fixed the doctor with a glare, one that accused her of thinking him an idiot.

"One can very easily not be aware of it. Some of my patients wear cotton gloves to bed—"

Klin swore loudly. Jumping to his feet, he stormed around her office. She was amazed to see the piebald splotches on his head turn a brilliant scarlet, a symptom, apparently, that Minister Klin was furious; she watched nervously. Of all the ministers, the security minister was not the one to have angry with you.

"I have a very busy schedule, and you are wasting my time. I do not scratch my head in my sleep. I will not wear white cotton gloves to bed. It is an infection, nothing more. And if you can't see . . ."

By now, the doctor was already writing a prescription. It was for a mild tranquilizer, but she disguised it so he would not know. "Very well," she said cheerfully. "We will treat the infection, then. I'll have someone fill this prescription and bring it to your office."

Grumbling, Klin went toward the door; a mumbled "thank you" was offered and accepted. Climbing into his car, Klin found his hand wandering toward his head and snatched it back. He had no explanation for why his scalp was being such a problem today. But as a hunch player, he was not surprised that the next words to come to him were "Salt Mine." That was it. Tomorrow was "18 XI." If Volovno's note was right, Salt Mine was tomorrow.

He swore at Volovno; he swore at Salt Mine; he swore at the world, at Chorniev, and at his driver. The damned thing was itching like crazy.

• A little after three, Alyosha closed his sketchbook and headed toward the coatroom. The daily performance with the sketch pad was a tiresome ritual. Only one more time to go. On his way through the Hall of Armor, he passed Kropotkin, but the Old One turned his back on him, giving himself completely to the display case he was touching with gilt. At the coatroom, Alyosha exchanged his usual banter with Natalya; with the event coming up tomorrow, Alyosha found his smile more difficult to produce than usual. Not only was the woman, as Kropotkin had pointed out, dangerous; when she laughed, she *smelled*—a sour, lingering odor on her breath that was a mixture of half-digested potatoes, *kvass,* and rancid beets.

Outside the Oruzheinaya Palata it was still cold, but the pale, semi-arctic sun had taken some of the sting out of the wind. Blinking, Alyosha looked around the inner square; he would have liked to go out through the Nikolskaya Tower—it was the one key area he personally had not looked over—but everything near the Nikolskaya was off limits. Crossing from Oruzheinaya to the Spasskaya Tower, Alyosha examined the Nikolskaya from a distance as best he could, trying to get a feel of the layout with his eyes. Halfway across, he stopped dead in his tracks. Fascinated, he watched as a maintenance man unlocked a small steel door and entered; it was the inside entrance to Lenin's Tomb. The man reappeared to pick up some tools he had left on the cobblestones outside the door. Then, he re-entered and, closing the door behind him, disappeared for good.

With a start, Alyosha realized he was standing still, staring. Putting his head down, he tucked the sketchbook tighter beneath his arm and walked quickly out through Spasskaya. In Red Square, the wind once again lanced through his clothing and tore at his skin. Alyosha hurried. He planned to check on everyone in Salt Mine, with the exception of Dimmy and Klemet, during the afternoon; Dimmy and Klemet lived too far away, and Keer had pointed out that he himself had seen them only this morning.

Still shivering, Alyosha slipped down the stairs and onto the platform of the Marx Prospekt metro stop. As in most Soviet metro stations, the walls were garishly decorated; the heroic murals, done in different-colored marbles, looked as cold and unfriendly as the mosaic portrait of Lenin which scowled at Alyosha across the tracks. Well executed, but awash with pretension. If Lenin himself had ever seen it, Alyosha decided, the man would have laughed.

• At the Machina Golodnaya—the Hungry Machine—the noise was deafening. It was every bit as loud as the din which kept drawing Keer back to the Labirynt, but the sound was different. For Labirynt was a hard-currency place, filled with tourists and foreigners and high-livers, and the ear-splitting noise came from a rock-and-roll band. By contrast, Machina

Golodnaya was a working man's café. The noise in the smoky, low-beamed rooms came from men shouting and laughing from one table to the next; it was a place where they came to relax after a hard day's work, to drink the cheap Georgian wine, or, if they were feeling expansive, to splurge on an only slightly more expensive bottle of Georgian champagne. A few drank vodka in the old way, with a touch of salt on the back of their hands, but the government monopoly deliberately kept the price of hard liquor too expensive for most. At one table, someone was sighing his way through Pushkin's mournful lyric "Winter Evening"; he accompanied himself on the balalaika, not expertly, but with such depth of feeling that the workers kept pounding their table tops in appreciation. In the darker corners, several patrons were asleep, heads on their arms, the gray color of their skin indicating this sleep was the product not so much of weariness as of wine.

Far to one side, almost obscured in the smoky haze that shrouded the room, Dimmy and Klemet sat eating bread and cheese and drinking the cheap Georgian. As the wine reached him, Klemet kept returning to the KGB's effort to put him in a psychiatric hospital for "reorientation." This was one topic that could remove the perpetual smile from his face. Dimmy would steer his friend away from the subject; Klemet would return to it.

Ordinarily, the two were rarely seen in public, but with the elaborate chemical device Alyosha had had them prepare for tomorrow now completed—they had brought it with them for safe-keeping, sitting at their feet in an ordinary-looking rucksack—Klemet and Dimmy had decided to celebrate at the Machina Golodnaya. Only Russians could be celebrating and still look so unhappy.

Dimmy stuffed a large piece of cheese into his long sad face and washed it down with the wine. With his head, he indicated the rucksack. "*That* thing. Do you think it will really work?"

From Klemet came a cheerful shrug. "*Nichevo,*" he sighed, a peculiarly Russian expression combining all of what "*che sarà*" means to the Italians, "*c'est ça*" means to the French, and "I'm all right, Jack" means to the British. "And whether it does or doesn't," added Klemet, suddenly gloomy, "it's better than a mental hospital. Electroshock. Character modification. They would remake my whole personality."

Dimmy looked at him. "Electricity is too expensive for anyone but scientists. Writers—well, they just take our paper away."

"That's not very reassuring." Klemet shuddered.

"My dear friend, we'll need more than reassurance if *that*"—Dimmy gestured again toward the rucksack—"doesn't work."

For the first time, Klemet's face looked genuinely stricken. "What are we doing in this thing? How did we get ourselves into it? Salt Mine is insane. Sometimes I think I am crazy."

Dimmy threw back his head and drained the wine in his glass. "Crazy. Well, you and the KGB finally agree on *something*."

From behind them came a sudden commotion. One of the workers had shouted at the balalaika player, and he had quickly changed into an accelerating gypsy rhythm. The other men in the place were clapping their hands on the offbeat, while one drunken member of the group, who had sprung to the center of the floor, was attempting the *kazatsky*, that impossible peasant dance that is done squatting on the haunches, arms folded, legs alternately thrown out in front of yourself. To make it more difficult, one of the workers had balanced a full glass of wine on the man's forehead, so that he had to keep his head thrown sharply back to prevent the wine from spilling over his face. The man made perhaps half a dozen tries at it; each time he crashed noisily to the floor on his bottom, spilling the wine, while the rest of the party laughed and whistled. Finally, the man gave up and threw himself flat on the floor, face up, arms outstretched; someone grabbed a bottle of wine and poured it over his face to mark his defeat. Everyone, including Dimmy and Klemet, laughed and cheered and clapped in delight. Even the proprietor, a great bear of a man, yelled happily. He had been chosen to run the Machina Golodnaya because only someone of his hulking size could handle the rugged workers who frequented the place.

Dimmy suddenly felt Klemet grip his arm as if he were drowning. "Dimmy. Look! The rucksack."

Dimmy looked. Their precious rucksack was on its way out the door. They could just see the last of it disappearing into the darkness of the street outside. "My God," Dimmy gasped. "Can it blow?"

"No, but if we lose it . . ."

"Let's go."

The two of them jumped to their feet and started for the door to catch up with whoever had the rucksack, lost now in the blackness of the street. "No," rumbled a sudden, deep voice. "No." The Great Bear towered over them, planting himself between them and the door.

Klemet felt his heart sink. It had all been a trap. A way to disarm them by getting the rucksack away from them, then arrest. He looked up at the Great Bear, waiting for the KGB to come pouring out of hiding. "No?" he repeated.

"No. Three deadbeats tonight already. You two would make five. Out the door without paying. *Chort.* I was not born yesterday." His great paw, palm up, reached toward them. Klemet began trying to explain, pointing toward the door, relieved that it was as simple as a worried proprietor instead of the KGB trap, but terrified that the rucksack would get away. Dimmy cut him off curtly and handed the proprietor the money—and then some—but it seemed to take forever for the Great Bear to find out how much they owed, and then to count out their change. Finally they shot out the door.

The street was empty. They didn't know whose name to try calling, they didn't know in which direction to search. Dimmy thought it was an accident; Klemet believed it was outright theft. Two blocks down the street from the Machina, they found the man and the rucksack; he had collapsed. His back was against the building, his feet were stretched across the pavement. Across his shoulder, the rucksack hung loosely. The man stared at them vacantly, his eyes half closed. When they tried to remove the rucksack, however, the eyes sprang wide open. "Police! Police!" the man yelled. "Thieves! Police!"

Even Dimmy felt a shiver of fear. The police. One look inside the rucksack and the KGB would be on its way. "Sorry, my friend." Dimmy's words were followed by a gentle *thunk.* He hit the man, not very hard, but hard enough so his shouts turned into mumblings. The rucksack was removed. In the distance, they could hear someone running. "The safest place," Dimmy decided out loud, "is the Machina."

Quickly, they slipped back inside, found the Great Bear, and slipped him some money to keep quiet. And, then, because it was getting close to closing time, and tomorrow stretched out ahead of them like some frightening nightmare, and because what money they had would no longer be of any use to them after tomorrow, anyway, Dimmy and Klemet ordered a bottle of vodka and sat in Machina Golodnaya, getting drunk in that special way only Russians can.

7

9:00 A.M., WEDNESDAY

Like a faithful horse returning to its stable without direction, Keer's Chevy returned to the apartment house on the corner of Gorky and Georgievsky, a building graced by many Soviet VIP's. As minister of production and industry, Keer's father had one of the choicer apartments, a duplex, overly large considering that he was rarely there and that his family consisted only of Keer. Although all the apartment houses in this neighborhood look Victorian, they were actually built in 1950. With a fine sense of irony, the polished granite slabs that were used to face them were booty captured from the Nazis toward the end of the war; the Germans had planned to use the slabs to build a monument marking their capture of Moscow.

Inside, Keer checked to make sure his father was not expected home. Dovo told him that the ministry had called to say he would not be back for at least three or four days. Upstairs, Keer luxuriated in a hot shower and sat down to the huge breakfast Dovo prepared for him. Once or twice, Keer thought Dovo looked at him inquisitively, but he dismissed it as imagination. That Keer had been up since an unusual six o'clock would be quite enough to make Dovo curious. One after the other, each member of Salt Mine had been visited by Keer early this morning. To them, he passed on the information Alyosha had given him at about one o'clock this morning: Salt Mine would take place at 3:00 p.m. They had all known the exact day; now they knew the exact time.

He glanced at *Pravda*. Nothing much. The American and English papers could not be bought until the afternoon. They were illegal—only a few copies went to the larger tourist hotels—but Keer got them from his black-market dealer. Yesterday's foreign papers had a lot of interesting items, but nothing spectacular. Keer wondered what tomorrow's would hold. Salt Mine? Probably not that fast.

For a man about to catapult himself into one of the more improbable maneuvers of current history, Keer appeared remarkably relaxed. He was even considering going back to his room and taking a short nap. But that thought brought home to Keer how much of a pose his nonchalance was; he knew there was about as much chance of sleeping as there was of growing an extra thumb on each hand. Nor had he slept much last night. He would doze for a few minutes and spring abruptly awake again. Only toward morning did he seem to slip into real sleep, and it was a sleep punctuated by recurring wild dreams. One was an eerie nightmare in which his father tried to make things up to him, but Keer wouldn't listen and kept beating him over the head with the arm he'd just torn off Alyosha. Finally, just when exhaustion had submerged him in deep and dreamless sleep, the alarm clock rang, and Keer had to get dressed, gobble some coffee from an angry Dovo, and start driving on his mission.

Sitting at the table, he could feel the exhaustion behind his eyes. He tried more coffee. But his was a weariness no amount of coffee could overcome.

• At 10:05 the special phone on his desk rang, and Kapitan Volodya Sokolov picked it up efficiently.

"The population of Omsk is nine hundred and seventy-three thousand." Lance Corporal Fyodor Shtemkin's voice had a caustic tone to it as he gave the password. According to schedule, Shtemkin was calling in his check of guard position number twelve, just outside Lenin's Tomb.

"But growing by the hour," responded Volodya. The passwords and countersigns were, even he had to admit, ridiculous. But regulations called for them.

"Everything all right at number twelve, Kapitan."

"Fine."

The exchange of secret identifying words, Volodya realized, had taken almost as long as their whole conversation. He would have to work out a shorter exchange for tomorrow. What could happen inside the grounds of the Kremlin anyway? Nothing. Looking out his window at the tourists and visitors already spreading across the grounds, Volodya smiled in condescension. Barely after ten, and already they were coming to see the wonders of this private world that he, Kapitan Vladimir Mikhailovich Sokolov, kept safe for them.

His eyes fell on the picture of Lenin on his wall. The world felt good this morning.

• It was precisely 10:22 when Alyosha, sketch pad under his arm, walked through the gate of the Spasskaya Tower and across to the Oruzheinaya. The museum attendant at the door nodded, and he nodded back. Inside, Alyosha gritted his teeth and faced his painful daily exchange with Natalya. She was ebullient today, and Alyosha had a difficult time shutting off her talk long enough to escape.

This visit was to be short; he had to meet Misha and Avraam by 11:15. In the Hall of Armor he saw the Old One, Kropotkin, and remembered a question he had had earlier. It was no moment to ask; Kropotkin and he were elaborately ignoring each other.

In the men's room, he withdrew some items from his pocket and hid them from sight. He also checked out other preparations, to make sure all of his orders had been followed. Everything was in shape, and Alyosha hoped Kropotkin had done as well with the rest of his assignments in other places.

Coming back out, Alyosha stepped into the Hall of Armor and leaned briefly against the wall. His heart was pounding, something which he could only remember happening to him on the Mongolian border, waiting to counterattack. An experienced soldier presumably was totally calm in such moments; Alyosha never had been. He wondered if the mask of coolness wasn't a device soldiers had invented to fool themselves. Automatically, he checked his watch: four and a half hours.

Natalya looked surprised when he collected his hat and coat so soon. "I'll be back," he promised. Natalya smiled; the *kvass*-breath billowed; the gold tooth gleamed.

11:50 A.M., WEDNESDAY

Suite 1206 of the Hotel Intourist was witness to a noisy family argument. So was Intourist guide Irina Aleksandrovna Zhedina. She sat uncomfortably on the hard sofa of the Decaturs' drawing room, listening, occasionally trying to inject a word to smooth things over. With Mr. Decatur, this was not going to be easy. From a telephone call placed for him by the *dezhurnaya,* the floor lady, he had learned a letter was waiting for him at the Metropol. Chessie. All Blaine wanted to do was get lunch out of the way and go pick up the letter. He could even try telephoning her from there. Lisa had her own plans.

"We've been running ourselves ragged, Lisa," he argued. "Dammit, let's just have a quiet lunch and collapse. Trying to tackle something like that today is going to kill us."

"It won't kill *you*, Blaine." She looked at him, then added her gibe. "In Minneapolis you seemed quite capable of more than one thing at a time—both exhausting."

Blaine Decatur spun for help toward the Intourist guide. "Irina, you're an expert on touring. Isn't it stupid to try something as wearing as the Kremlin when you're tired? Too much in one day?"

"You don't have to—in fact, you can't—see all of the Kremlin in one day, Mr. Decatur. I do have a suggestion, though," she added soothingly.

"Yes?"

"Why don't we stroll a bit around the streets near here, and then you can have a pleasant, early lunch in the neighborhood. I can recommend several very attractive places. After that, if you wish, we can go see a little of the Kremlin today. Just a sort of overall introduction. Tomorrow, or the next day, we can go back and start doing one section a day thoroughly." She studied the look on Mr. Decatur's face; her suggestion had seemed mild enough, yet he appeared more irritated than ever. She applied more balm. "You could spend an entire week, Mr. Decatur, just studying Peter the Great's collection of armor."

"God forbid." Blaine couldn't resist laughing as he heard himself say it. The Ugly American. He would make the effort, Blaine told himself, to be more flexible; Chessie could be telephoned later.

A giggle came from Christy, who had heard the exchange as she walked into the room, still in her pajamas. "I don't know why you just don't go on to Paris *now*, Daddy."

Abruptly, the effort at pleasantness drained out of Blaine. He stared at his daughter, usually an ally, and felt abandoned. "Thank you." She felt the acid in his voice and shrugged.

Lisa ignored both Blaine's effort and Christy's crack, turning toward Irina. "It's a very good plan, Irina. Don't let Mr. Decatur upset you. He's always in a foul mood when he's traveling."

"Give in gracefully, Daddy."

Blaine snorted but knew he'd lost. "Where's Gary?"

"Still asleep," Christy suggested. "He was out late, so I suppose he is trying to make up for it."

"Out? Out *where?*"

"I don't know. Just out."

"Wake him up, dammit. It's lunchtime."

"Oh, let him sleep, Blaine. We can leave a note and have him meet us there." Lisa sat down and Christy ran to her room to throw some clothes on. Still muttering, Blaine took his jacket off the back of a chair and began slipping into it. Lisa looked up from the note she was leaving Gary and turned again toward Irina. "What time shall I tell him?"

"About three. I will let the chief attendant know we are expecting someone, and he can tell your son where to find us."

Serenely, Lisa finished her note, while Blaine stamped aimlessly around the room, his irritation at Christy's gibe making him impatient again. "Damned kid," he grumbled, angry that Gary was allowed to do what he wanted and sleep on, while he was not. Standing up, Irina straightened her jacket. She was pleased with herself that she had preserved at least a vestige of harmony in the family. In spite of their peculiarities, she found it impossible not to like them. There was a certain irony in this.

1:20 P.M., WEDNESDAY

For the director of the KGB to be confused by his own agency's information was unusual, but Mikhail Chorniev would have readily admitted that he was baffled (provided no one was listening).

"Comrade Director," his deputy said, "there is something strange here. You say you didn't send this operative Bleisky off on special assignment? You're sure, I suppose."

"Positive."

"Neither did I. Yet, Supervisor Denchek says he got a call from this man Bleisky's wife, and that she said he had been sent out of town on special assignment. By the director, himself, she said. She needed his pay envelope, you see; that's why she was calling here. Denchek became curious because some woman who said *she* was Bleisky's wife had called him and said Bleisky wouldn't be in for a few days because he had the 'bug.' Denchek began checking to see if someone here *had* sent the man out of town. You see, Denchek was already confused himself, because this woman on the phone said his son had had the bug so Denchek would know what it was like. . . . The point is, Denchek doesn't have a son; he has a daughter."

Chorniev looked at his deputy with impatience. "Get to it, get to it. I don't know Bleisky, I don't know Denchek, and I'm quickly beginning to wish I didn't know you. What the hell's your point?"

"Comrade Bleisky. Something's been done to him. He isn't the type to defect."

"Check out his list of assignments. Find where, and when and what he was supposed to be doing the day he vanished." Chorniev sighed, a man put upon by the incompetence of others. "Surely you could have thought of that much yourself."

The deputy knew Chorniev well enough to know arguing was unwise; something was bothering the man. Nodding silently, as if what Chorniev suggested had never occurred to him, the deputy picked up his paper and turned to go.

Chorniev watched him leave and sank deeper into his office chair. For a long time he sat staring, refusing all telephone calls. The art of the survivor involved sticking out one's neck only *after* the fact. Like the jackal, you wait in the shadows while the great beasts fight, content to know that, whichever wins, you will feast.

But the roadblock to his career Klin represented was making Chorniev act recklessly. Klin had played into his hands by his reactions to "Op. Salt Min"; the opportunity was too promising to let pass. To Chorniev, Salt Mine remained little more than some facet of a black-market operation; for Klin, if Chorniev played his hand correctly, it could become the terminal nail in the coffin.

Calling in his secretary, Mikhail Chorniev began to dictate a memorandum addressed to his superior, Minister of State Security Klin. It was already arranged that Klin should never receive this. Instead, a copy would be given to Marshal Borodinsky, Klin's most powerful and vocal enemy on the Council of Ministers. That the memo was a complete reversal of Klin's actual position was of small importance; that many of Chorniev's own suggestions were described as coming from Klin was part of Chorniev's technique. Listening to his secretary read back the memo, Chorniev made a few minor changes and was satisfied. In Borodinsky's hands, the document could form the basis of some very serious charges against Klin.

Comrade Minister:

It is an unpleasant task for someone who has served the KGB and yourself for so long to write as unpleasant a document as this (one which I assure you, Comrade Minister, will never be seen by anyone but yourself), but my sense of duty to the Party, the State, and to you personally does not allow me to remain silent any longer. From the beginning, your overreaction to Salt Mine has puzzled me; in others it could conceivably raise questions as to your motives. Consider the following:

(1) Your order that I offer the informer Volovno exit visas in exchange for information contravenes all existing procedures. Further, the order flies directly in the face of Party ideology; the Soviet Union cannot be put in the position of submitting to extortion.

(2) Later, after Volovno was murdered, you concluded it was only the work of some underground ring trying to silence the man. Yet, Volovno was killed during your party for your niece, and his presence at Archangelskoye was known only to you and myself. It could appear to someone who does not know you as well as I that, having failed to silence Volovno by getting him out of the country, you had him killed to silence him permanently.

(3) At the same time, you have frequently invoked Volovno's death to explain your continuing preoccupation with Salt Mine. These two contrary points of view, Comrade, simply do not mesh. Is there some reason I am not privy to?

(4) The priority you have assigned to the Salt Mine affair has halted many other pressing assignments of the KGB. Worse, your directive sending KGB Agent Bleisky on some secret mission for yourself—without even informing me—has now resulted in Comrade Bleisky's total disappearance. Again, is there something I have not been told?

As I have pointed out to you frequently, the KGB's position is that Salt Mine is little more than some minor black-market operation. To divert the KGB from its essential tasks for the State on personal whim, to offer free exit visas in exchange for information about this mythical threat to the Soviet, to bring about the death of a valued KGB informer—Volovno—and now the disappearance of an actual KGB agent—Bleisky—are all matters which could be seen by others as a misuse of your official position as Minister of State Security.

Only my personal loyalty to you has stopped me from bringing the matter to the attention of other ministers. However, my obligation to the Party, my duty to the Soviet, and my love of the motherland finally compel me to write this memorandum. I beg and implore you, Comrade Minister, to abandon your fixation with Salt Mine and provide me with explanations as to the steps you have taken, so that my mind may rest more easily. Otherwise, I will have no choice but to take up Salt Mine and your curious behavior with the other ministers.

With all respect,
Mikhail Sergeyevich Chorniev
DIRECTOR, KGB

Chorniev leaned back in his chair and let his own words roll around in his head. He was particularly pleased by his constant repetition of the point that Klin's actions could be seen by others—men who did not know him as well as Chorniev did—as a misuse of his office. It made the point while apparently showing his own unswerving loyalty. That and the mention of his own sense of obligation to the Party . . . to the Soviet . . . and his love of the motherland. . . .

It might be a gamble, but the effort was worth it.

8

2:32 P.M., WEDNESDAY
Carrying the inevitable sketch pad under his arm, Alyosha walked through the gate of the Spasskaya at thirty-two minutes after two by the clock. For a second, he paused inside the gate, taking in—perhaps for the last time—the ageless splendor of the Kremlin courtyard. The sky was a dull winter gray with low scudding clouds, wisps of black racing across a neutral background. Now and then, a patch of wan blue would appear and long thin shafts of sunlight would poke their pale fingers into the picture, briefly washing the onion domes of the Cathedral of the Annunciation with gold. Incredibly, Alyosha discovered his eyes smarting from incipient tears; how, if the sight was that moving, could he have contrived Salt Mine? Shaking himself, Alyosha walked quickly toward the Oruzheinaya. The museum guard at the door seemed surprised to see him again so soon but nodded pleasantly enough. Inside, Alyosha headed directly for the coatroom. Natalya saw him coming and welcomed him back with a broad smile, the gold tooth looking for the first time not merely grotesque, but evil. Alyosha stiffened and braced himself for a final effort at civility.

2:43 P.M., WEDNESDAY
"Damn, but it's heavy."
"Like Bleisky's trunk."
Dimmy and Klemet, both in pin-striped coveralls, carried a small evergreen between them, its root ball heavily wrapped in burlap. They had not been wearing the pin-striped uniform of the Kremlin grounds staff when they came through the gate of the Borovitskaya Tower. Dressed in street clothes, they had gone into the one piece of modern architecture inside the Kremlin walls, the cakelike Palace of Congresses, used in summer for the Bolshoi; today, except for a handful

of tourists, it was empty. Slipping into a deserted men's room, they climbed into the coveralls that Kropotkin, the Old One, had promised to leave in a waste bin.

All this elaborate subterfuge was necessary; for two men, unknown by sight, to come through any of the Kremlin gates wearing the Kremlin coveralls was to invite challenge by a guard. They had forged identification papers, but if they were stopped and examined, it could throw off the timing of the whole operation. Once inside, however, no one was apt to question them; the soldiers were used to seeing men in these uniforms go everywhere freely, including areas that were off limits.

From the broom closet Dimmy and Klemet took the rakes which Kropotkin had left there for them and met him outside. Curtly, he told them to pick up the evergreen and follow him. Panting, they watched Kropotkin cross the white line that demarked the out-of-bounds area for tourists. They gave their heavy load an extra heave and followed him. At a small door in the inner wall of the Kremlin, to the right of the Nikolskaya, Kropotkin stopped. As Dimmy and Klemet lowered the evergreen to a spot along the path, Kropotkin placed his key in the lock and, without even looking at them, walked back toward the Oruzheinaya Palata. Half-kneeling behind the shrubbery, Dimmy checked the guards at their stations, peering through the branches to be sure no soldier was looking in their direction. A slit in the side of the burlap was opened and they began drawing objects out of the dirt-filled root ball, slipping them into the oversized pockets of their coveralls. Then, Dimmy and Klemet walked quickly inside the dimly lit outer vestibule. The time was 2:49. Klemet grimaced. The wait would be murderous.

2:43 P.M., WEDNESDAY

Two minutes behind schedule, Lisenka shepherded her flock of tourists out of the old Poteshny Palace, nodded them along the narrow strip between the palace and the Kremlin wall, and finally into the main entrance of the Oruzheinaya Palata. There, she promised them, they would see Tsarina Elizabeth I's famous sled, Peter the Great's priceless collection of armor, the imperial thrones of all the tsars from Boris Godunov onward, and even the solid-gold eating utensils of Ivan the Terrible. They would also get a brief look at the coronation robes of Peter the Great and Catherine the Great, the Siberian Crown, the Kazan Crown, the Imperial Orb, and seven centuries' worth of the tsars' imperial headgear. By special arrangement, they were also to get an unusual close-up look—perhaps even a chance to touch—the world's largest bible, covered in solid gold and encrusted with diamonds. Lisenka's flock appeared impressed.

There were, according to her vouchers, forty-three Americans, two African businessmen, some Cubans, four East Germans, and a small cluster of other nationalities. The Americans, Intourist Central told her, were "doing" Russia on a Yale Club tour; Yale, Intourist explained, was where the ruling clique of Wall Street sent its sons, and these men, students there in their own youth, included some quite important people. She was instructed to give them any extra time they wanted; the other nationalities could be politely ignored.

"I think it would be good to start with the Hall of Silver," Lisenka explained, walking them down toward the museum's rear, "where we can see the Clock of Glory." This, Lisenka knew, was always a favorite with Americans, and watching the intricate Fabergé eagle drop pearls into the beak of its young would mesmerize her charges long enough so she could slip back, unmissed, to the front part of the museum for the actual moment.

By the time she had gotten them all rounded up in the Hall of Silver and staring awestruck at Peter the Great's boots—each as big as a small man—Lisenka's watch read 2:51.

2:47 P.M., WEDNESDAY

Keer had finished lunch, paid the check, and just risen to leave. Service at the old Metropol Hotel had been unusually good today, and in spite of everything, he felt relaxed. The Metropol had a turn-of-the-century way about it that encouraged this feeling. Its exterior stonework had a greenish tinge, although whether this was by design or from old age no one knew. Inside, the decorations clung to the same ambiance: enormous crystal chandeliers, mirrored walls, palm trees, and even a small string orchestra, struggling valiantly to be heard above the clatter of plates. It was as if someone had taken New York's Plaza Hotel, expanded it ten times, and dropped it into the heart of Moscow.

On his way out of the faded but somehow elegant dining room, Keer was struck by something familiar. The person's back was to him, but there was no mistaking the wrist and the wide-banded watch it carried; they could only belong to

Gary Decatur. As he swung wide around the table to be sure, Keer broke into a wide smile. "My dear fellow," he said, so surprised that he momentarily abandoned his usual American slang for courtly English. Keer caught himself, as Gary smiled back at him, but with a slightly bewildered look. "Goddam," Keer began again, "don't you ever do anything but *eat?*"

Gary waved to the chair opposite. "Everybody went to some crazy museum while I was still in the sack. Told me to meet them there, but the hell with it. Who wants to spend the afternoon sniffing Peter the Great's overshoes?" He paused to swallow a morsel of *chebureki*. "Drink?"

A strange look had passed over Keer's face; he nodded to Gary, but a mixture of concern and disbelief clouded his features. "You mean . . . the Kremlin Museum? They're going to Oruzheinaya Palata?"

"That's it."

"What time were you supposed to meet them there?"

Gary glanced at his watch, suddenly flashing a mischievous smile at Keer. "No, and I still won't make a trade for it, Keer. But let's see. About now. I was supposed to meet them just about now. Three, I think it was. Ten minutes or so." He looked up at Keer. "Why?"

"Nothing, nothing. That drink . . ."

"Now, you're with it."

"I'm buying. Okay?"

It was, Keer thought, the very least he could do.

2:46 P.M., WEDNESDAY

For a few minutes, Alyosha pretended to sketch some of the armor in the outer room of the Oruzheinaya Palata. He had seen Lisenka come in with her group and watched her disappear with it into the Hall of Silver. He had noticed Kropotkin's return and knew, from the slight nod the old man gave him, that Dimmy and Klemet were in position. He had watched the two WJA men arrive; Avraam was staying close to the entrance of the Hall of Armor, waiting for his signal, while Misha, for the moment, had disappeared into the back. Two of the three foot soldiers were already in place gaping at the exhibits as Alyosha had instructed them. The third was busy in the basement.

There was a handful of other visitors, some Russian, some foreign visitors sophisticated enough to tour the Oruzheinaya without guides. At 2:49, he spotted a new, small group—

Americans, he thought—coming in with an Intourist guide of their own. For a moment, this threw Alyosha; Lisenka had chosen the three o'clock time because no other guides would be inside. But, looking at these new arrivals, he remembered Lisenka saying the one thing her schedule would not show was tourists on the deluxe suite plan. These would have guides assigned to them permanently and could therefore turn up any time. The Americans looked prosperous enough for deluxe suite; they also appeared harmless enough not to interfere. The guide worried him.

Inclining his head slightly as a signal to Avraam, Alyosha smiled broadly at the hated Natalya and went into the washroom. A few moments later, Avraam followed. Quickly, Alyosha went into the left booth, while Avraam occupied the right. To make a protracted occupancy believable to anyone who came in, each pulled a pair of trousers from under his jacket. The trousers were allowed to drop in a pile on the floor. Shoes, hidden on a shelf above the toilets, were placed with their toes protruding from under each pair of crumpled trousers. To anyone who checked beneath the doors, all would seem natural: lowered trousers, resting on a pair of shoes. Carefully, Alyosha removed the top from the water tank. Reaching inside, he withdrew the numbered pieces of metal and placed them on the closed bowl. Within one minute, drying with toilet paper as he went, he had assembled one Tekel II submachine gun; this remarkable weapon was the latest product of the Israeli weapons industry and was incredibly light. The second and third guns would have gone even faster, but Alyosha had trouble detaching one of the metal tags on the last Tekel. In his room, Alyosha had been practicing this assembly process from the day the WJA first provided him with the Tekels; Avraam, he was told, had been doing it for months.

Peering over the door top, Alyosha confirmed that no one had come in. He stepped out, the three aluminum guns under his arm. A few moments later, Avraam emerged, wearing a surprised expression. "You did it *faster?*"

"I've been practicing. I can do it in the dark. Or with only one hand, although that *does* double my assembly time."

Avraam kept looking at the men's-room door nervously. With a grunt, Alyosha put the three submachine guns, butt down, into a large metal trash container set in the corner; Avraam did the same with his, using the basket in the far corner. Kropotkin had put an unusual quantity of loose, heavy paper in them this morning, and the six guns were quickly out of sight. Signaling Avraam to wait, Alyosha went outside the room into the museum area again.

They were all there. Alyosha waited, the sketchbook tapping against one leg in a nervous tattoo. He could feel—almost hear—the blood pounding in his heart as he watched the seconds crawl by on his watch.

At 2:57, Alyosha gave a final check, making sure that one of the foot soldiers was in position behind the museum attendant who stood just inside the great doors. At 2:58, he nodded to Avraam, and they walked back toward the men's room, striding purposefully across the gleaming parquet floors.

His old enemy, Natalya, seemed confused to see Alyosha return to the men's room so soon, but she tried to produce a smile anyway. For the first time in five weeks of coming to the Oruzheinaya regularly, Alyosha did not return the smile.

Hypocrisy was no longer necessary.

3:00 P.M.

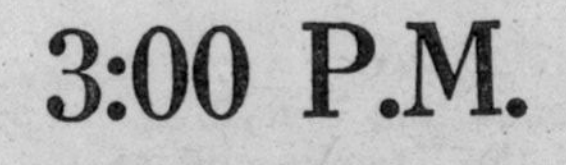

9

3:00 P.M., WEDNESDAY

It seemed to Lisenka that everything happened at once. At the first stroke of the Kremlin chimes, the men's-room door burst open and Alyosha and Avraam ran out into the Hall of Armor. Alyosha carried one Tekel in firing position, with a second dangling from his shoulder. From his mouth came the piercing blasts of a police whistle. He tossed the second gun to Vanya, one of the foot soldiers, who turned to catch it with one hand. With his other hand, he eased the museum attendant at the door to the parquet. Lisenka saw that Vanya had only knocked the man over the head, not stabbed him, as she had first thought. Alyosha's instructions to Vanya were to "take him out of play," and she wasn't sure whether that included knocking him senseless. To Lisenka, the force with which Vanya struck the man seemed unnecessarily brutal. She would learn.

Avraam, she could see, was sweeping the room with his Tekels to keep everyone where they were; the other three Tekels were slung from their short straps over his left arm. Misha ran up and grabbed one, disappearing quickly into the back rooms of the museum, where Lisenka's group of tourists was; another Tekel was handed to a second of the foot soldiers and the third given to Lisenka herself. She felt self-conscious holding the weapon. Days before, Alyosha had briefed her on its use, letting her handle his own to familiarize her with it. It was easy to get the hang of, Lisenka told him. But when she was called upon to hold the Tekel in a real situation, the weapon that had seemed so maneuverable in Alyosha's room suddenly felt awkward. In her mind, one question still burned, now more fiercely than ever: Could she really bring herself to shoot someone?

This, she realized, was no moment for such worries; her post was back in the Hall of Silver with her charges, calming and reassuring them—as much as anyone armed with a submachine gun could. As she turned, Lisenka saw Alyosha over by the door yelling at Vanya; the attendant he had knocked out was to have been used for something later, and now he was useless, a glistening puddle of dark red sending bright fingers of color from beneath his head. Vanya gave some explanation about seeing the attendant reach for the alarm button beside the door, but he said it without conviction and without much evidence he thought anyone would believe it but himself.

As she passed through the doorway into the rear section, Lisenka became aware of the screams coming from the tourists. She realized that others had been screaming in the Hall of Armor from the beginning, but her mind had been so occupied she had not heard them. As she came to her tour group, she saw them stare at her in disbelief, every eye fastened on the Tekel hanging from her shoulder. "You will be all right. Kindly do as you are instructed and none of you will be hurt. Please remain calm and make no sudden moves that might cause misunderstanding with your captors. You will be all right. . . ." As she listened to herself, her years of training made Lisenka want to add: "Intourist regrets any inconvenience you may be experiencing. The difficulty will be quickly corrected and you will be on your way. . . ."

• Clear across the vast expanse of Kremlin Square from the Oruzheinaya, all day long, every day, the reddish marble walls of Lenin's Tomb echo to the sad, shuffling feet of visitors. Slowly, they move past the line of soldiers who stand at attention down the long tunnel from Red Square, and come into the hallowed presence itself. Lenin lies, hands folded, under a sheet of glass or block of plastic—it is impossible to tell which. At either end of what would normally be a coffin, a soldier stands, head bowed, as rigid in his position as Lenin is in his. The state of preservation is remarkable; although pale, the mans looks as if he might sit bolt upright any minute to lecture his heirs on the error of their ways.

For a non-Russian to understand the position Lenin occupies or the reverence with which an ordinary citizen of the Soviet approaches his fleeting glimpse of the "Little Father" is next to impossible. It is as if the entire history of the Russians, rather than one man, were laid out in the sarcophagus. As if not only Lenin lay there, but Peter the Great, Catherine, Ivan the Terrible, Rasputin, and perhaps Father Frost as well. A Soviet, viewing Lenin for the first time, feels in mystic communion with him, almost as if he were actually meeting his nation's founder in person; this sense is heightened by the visitor's opportunity to *see* the demigod's face, rather than just to view the traditional slab of marble or block of limestone. Day after day, month after month, year in, year out, regardless of Moscow's famously savage weather, ordinary Soviet citizens are lined up outside the plain marble mausoleum, waiting their chance to move slowly down the long passage, gaze for a second in awe, and then be moved on. Alyosha had frequently commented on the wonder of this—Lenin's greatest magic.

There were approximately twelve American tourists, one Hungarian, two Saudis, and five Russians viewing Lenin's body when it happened. As the third stroke of the bells in Spasskaya Tower shook the air, Dimmy and Klemet emerged from the shadows of the maintenance man's vestibule into the tomb itself; a short blast from a police whistle in Klemet's mouth made everyone turn to stare at him. The people inside the chamber gasped; the guards seemed frozen in disbelief. In both Dimmy's and Klemet's hands were grenades, held high over their heads. Hanging from their belts were more. With what was almost a bow, Dimmy spoke: "Attention. Attention, please. These are live hand grenades. Their pins have been pulled. If anyone here moves, I shall drop them. Not only will you be killed—two hand grenades in a confined area such as this would destroy us all—but Comrade Vladimir Ilyich Ulyanov over there will be blown out of his little glass case. Understood? Please, soldiers, do not underestimate me and reach for the alarm button; I know this place backwards and forwards. So, comrades, *freeze*."

The soldiers glanced at each other. They had never been trained for a situation such as this; no one had told them what to do or how to react. Their soldier's training told them to resist, with their lives if necessary; their logic told them that not only would they and all the visitors in the room be killed if they did, but the priceless remains of Lenin—what they were there to protect—would be destroyed in the process. They froze.

"Good." Dimmy nodded to Klemet, who reinserted the pins in his grenades and hung them from his belt. "Now then," continued Dimmy, "you soldiers. When my friend walks over to you, kindly surrender your guns. Slowly. Carefully. Hold the muzzle up under your chin until he removes the weapon. Everyone understand? And remember—I still have *my* grenades."

The soldiers appeared in a trancelike state, their movements slow and automatic, their eyes searching each other's for an explanation that was not forthcoming. As one soldier, Private First Class Alexei Alexeyevich Drymko, would later testify during the Soviet High Commission's investigation: "We were paralyzed. We could not believe what was happening. We had the tourists to consider, we had Comrade Lenin's body to preserve. Our own lives were not a factor. I think our first thought—it was mine, anyway—was that somehow this was the work of the capitalists. But the men doing it weren't capitalists, they were Russians, young Russians, like us. Later, one of them said they loved their country, just as we do. They loved Russia, he said, but not the government. I think the fact that it was our own people, our own brothers, rocked us the most. That and the realization they had the power to blow up everything any time they chose to. I don't remember ever feeling so helpless."

Mechanically, the soldiers placed the muzzles of their rifles under their chins, looking embarrassed, like children standing in the corner. Klemet carefully removed the rifles from the three soldiers, emptied the chambers, and stacked the weapons against the wall. From beneath his coveralls, he drew out a four-inch square of what looked like putty and squeezed it onto the glass over Lenin's face. Two wires were stretched from it and connected to something square that Klemet hung on his belt beside the grenades. From this box, more wires stretched to a device held in Klemet's hands; it was a maze of solenoids and contacts that the Armenian would have recognized as parts of the Yaroslavl timer he'd sold Alyosha. Klemet nodded at Dimmy, who began his lecture once more.

"I shall now put the pins back in *my* grenades as well. What my friend has attached to the glass cover is a square of plastic explosive. *Le plastique*. It is connected to a battery on his belt, which in turn is wired to the trigger he holds in his hand. You do not squeeze this particular trigger to make the plastic go off, you *stop* squeezing it. This means if anyone should, for instance, knock him out or shoot him, well, we would all be worse off than if I'd used the grenades. Blown to bits—all of us." Carefully Dimmy lowered his grenades, reinserted the pins, and hung the ugly pineapple shapes back on his belt. A thought struck him. "In case you doubt my friend's competence with the plastic, I should tell you he holds two degrees in chemistry and several more in physics." Dimmy looked at Klemet. "Excuse me, my friend, I am causing you to blush." With another nod, Dimmy took several steps back and after a moment's searching, found the concealed wall phone built into the antechamber he and Klemet had come from. Referring to a slip of paper, he dialed a number. "Kropotkin? *Kropotkin?* Ah, good. Is Alyosha there? Yes, I can imagine how busy he is. Kindly tell him, Old One, that we are secure here. Everyone quiet as lambs. Oh, *my* but they are quiet."

Inside the Oruzheinaya, things were anything but quiet. When Blaine Decatur first heard the police whistles, followed by shouts and screams coming from the Hall of Armor, his initial thought was that someone had gone crazy and was breaking up the place. Automatically, he started toward the doorway of the State Coach Room to see the excitement, but when a small, darkish man with peculiar eyelids—Misha, he would learn later—burst into the room waving a machine gun, Blaine turned around in bewilderment. Their guide, Irina, was gesturing at him wildly; he could see that she and his family were trying to take cover behind the Petersburg sled, which Irina had been showing them when the ruckus began. It wasn't much to hide behind, but Blaine decided it was better than nothing and walked slowly over to where Irina waited with Lisa and Christy.

The din in the room was deafening. The man with the machine gun was yelling orders at them, but they were mostly in Russian, which Blaine could not understand. The man apparently had memorized two English sentences—"Stay where you are" and "No one will get hurt"—but his pronunciation made them almost as hard to understand as his Russian. The man kept repeating them like a litany, interspersing them with shouted commands in his own language.

Decatur's family was a pathetic sight; Lisa's face was white with fear, and she kept clutching Christy. Christy was trying to comfort her, but her eyes signaled to Blaine for help. Decatur spun on their guide, Irina, as if the whole thing was her fault. "What the hell's going on?" he demanded. "What is all this?"

Irina shook her head helplessly. "I don't know. Foreign terrorists of some kind. . . . I don't know. Please get down, Mr. Decatur. Get behind the sled."

Decatur was no hero, but he had no intention of hiding behind any damned sled. Something could be done, some way could be found to get them out of here. Across the room he saw a very old man shuffle along, sliding bolts and slamming the steel shutters across the windows.

Irina saw the man at the same moment. "Kropotkin!" she exclaimed. That one Russian—the man with the machine gun—was involved was bad enough, but a sinking feeling that many more were probably going to turn up as part of the plot was dawning on her.

Decatur looked around. Coming into the room, a machine gun hanging loosely from her shoulder, was another Intourist guide. He heard Irina gasp. "Foreign terrorists, my ass," Blaine exploded. "She's one of *you*. They all are. What the hell is this?"

Numbly, Irina shook her head. That Lisenka should be part of whatever was happening was too much for her to accept. Frustrated and mad, Blaine Decatur listened as Lisenka gave her speech to the prisoners, asking them to be calm, promising that if they followed instructions no one would be harmed. Spoken first in English, it was repeated in German, Spanish, and, finally, Russian.

To Decatur, the situation was unreal—like an airplane accident, something that only happens to other people. Suddenly, DataCon, Minneapolis, Wayzata, and Chessie seemed very far away.

Standing near the outer door, Alyosha pushed up his sleeve under the Tekel's strap and checked his wristwatch: 3:09. To Alyosha, this was nowhere near good enough. On the schedule Alyosha carried around in his head, they were already running about two and a half minutes late. The difference seemed small—nothing in the opening moments of an operation like Salt Mine could be timed with complete precision—but if that difference kept growing, it could become fatal.

Alyosha's green eyes swept the room; things were quiet enough now, and he would try to make up time by starting the next stage ahead of schedule. In his plan, this step had involved the museum attendant who normally stood near the main entrance; Vanya's rashness had cost Alyosha that man. He walked back into the Hall of Armor and grabbed the arm of another attendant, the man who kept an eye on the tourists here. With his head, he nodded toward the dead attendant on the floor. "Quick. Tell me. What was his name?"

Alyosha could see the man's eyes widen with fear and feel

him trembling beneath his grasp. "Borzov. Dmitry Isaakovich Borzov." The man's eyes blinked as he stared at Alyosha. "Please don't—not what you did to him. Please. Children. I have . . ."

With a gentle shove, Alyosha pushed the man toward the main doors. "Here. Say this." Alyosha handed him a scrap of paper. "Say this as if you meant it."

The man swallowed and looked at Alyosha, his face pleading with Alyosha not to get him involved. "They will think that I . . ." His voice faded as Alyosha fixed him with a stare and patted the Tekel. The man crumbled. He pushed open the main door and stuck his head out, turning sideways toward the soldier stationed to the right of the entrance. "Soldier," he called loudly. "Soldier, come quick. It's Borzov. He needs help."

The soldier hesitated, measuring the man's tone of urgency against the rules, which would ordinarily require he call for the corporal of the guard before leaving his post. "I've already called the office. Kapitan Sokolov. He is sending an ambulance. Come quick, please. Borzov needs help."

The mention of Sokolov made the decision easy for the soldier. He ran the few steps to the entrance, his rifle hanging loosely from one hand. Halfway through the door he sensed something was wrong; his eyes took in the strained faces of the tourists and for a moment he hesitated, half in, half out. From one side of the entrance hall suddenly came a woman's voice. "Run! Get help! It's a trap! Run!" Alyosha grabbed the soldier by his gun arm and yanked him into the room, while Misha wrestled him for his rifle. A short burst of automatic fire and Natalya slumped against the coatroom counter, a look of wonder on her face as her hand discovered the blood spreading across her waist. With a strange hissing sound, she fixed her eyes on Alyosha. A second later the hiss became a sigh, like the last air leaving a punctured tire, and she slid down the side of the counter to the floor. Long after Natalya was dead, the pale eyes continued to stare at the spot where Alyosha had been standing, examining the empty air with a mixture of reproach and fury.

Again, Alyosha checked his watch: 3:12. If the changing of the guard followed its usual schedule—and, by observation, Alyosha knew it always did—the soldiers would be outside the Oruzheinaya in two or three minutes. Because Salt Mine was now running four minutes behind schedule, Alyosha realized how little leeway he had before the next move must be made. Quickly, he turned to talk to the captured soldier. "Your name is . . . ?"

"Propechny. But—"

"Propechny. Very well. Propechny, listen to me very carefully. When the guard is changed, when the corporal comes to you, you are to say nothing. Absolutely nothing. Nor are you to make any gesture. You will be more than well covered by a machine gun." Misha poked the soldier in the side with his Tekel to give the point emphasis. "Understood, Propechny?" The soldier stared at Alyosha, his face prepared to refuse.

Alyosha sighed as if he were a disappointed parent. "Ah, Propechny, I know what is going through your mind. You are thinking that you can be a hero. That, yes, those terrible people will shoot me, but while I shall be killed, it is my duty. You are thinking, Propechny, that, well, if I refuse, or pretend to go along and then give the alarm, only I will suffer. You are wrong. All of these people—from this man here to that lady there—will immediately be shot." With his arm Alyosha indicated the nearest group, then walked over, separating the ten or twelve people in an area by themselves along the outer wall. "These. Every one of them. Some are Soviets, more are Americans. Two are children. They will suffer, comrade soldier. The prisoners we have taken in Lenin's Tomb will suffer. The Soviet will suffer. To be a hero with your own life is one thing; to be a hero with someone else's is quite different." Spinning suddenly, Alyosha aimed the Tekel at the now isolated group; a woman screamed; a man flattened himself on the shiny floor; the whole group instinctively shrank against the wall.

The soldier gave up, shrugged, and walked toward the main door, Misha following with his weapon pressed against the man's back. From the window, Alyosha could see, far across the courtyard, the two squads of men who would soon be approaching the Oruzheinaya, a corporal of the guard at the head of each squad.

"Now." On Alyosha's command, Misha nodded to Kropotkin, who reached up beside the window nearest the main entrance and flipped off the alarm switch so that the window could be opened without its registering in the main building; Misha moved toward the slightly open window, leaving Alyosha to cover the soldier. The door was opened, only a crack, and the soldier, again carrying his rifle (the clip had been removed), took up his post. Suddenly, the soldier's stance of "parade rest" stiffened; through the open window, Misha had just poked him in the base of the spine to remind him to follow instructions.

At 3:14 the two squads came to a halt outside the Oruzheinaya. From here, after changing the guard, they would eventually march out through the Spasskaya Tower to relieve the guard at Lenin's Tomb. At each position, so far, the changing of the guard had gone precisely according to the normal schedule; nothing that would happen from this point onward was on anyone's schedule.

Except Alyosha's.

• The changing of the guard was keeping meticulously to its schedule, but the man in charge of it, Lance Corporal Fyodor Shtemkin, was not at all happy with it, his mind on a thousand other things that were troubling him. As they marched up to the Oruzheinaya Palata, Corporal Shtemkin's eyes narrowed. Another petty irritation in a day filled with worries about his own growing dislike of Kapitan Sokolov and unhappiness with his own assignment here. Looking at his guard posted outside the entrance door, he noticed the man was standing about fifteen or twenty feet closer to the door than he should have been. Directly in front of the window. Was it warmer there or what? The guard—Propechny, wasn't it?—would hear about it from him. Kapitan Sokolov was difficult enough, without the soldiers giving him more excuses to be petty. "Squad, halt!" shouted Shtemkin.

"Squad, halt!" echoed the corporal of the relieving squad. As Shtemkin marched over to Propechny, the relieving soldier from "B" Squad trotted up to position behind him.

"What are you doing, Propechny? You're out of position."

The soldier hesitated; if he was ever to escape the terrorists inside the Oruzheinaya, this was the moment. The corporal was directly in front of him, not two feet away. Two steps behind him, was another soldier. And beyond that were two full squads of armed men. Shtemkin saw Propechny tighten in his already rigid "present arms"; he thought it must be the tone of his voice, not knowing that a gun muzzle behind his soldier was grinding hard into the man's backbone.

"Answer me, Propechny," hissed Shtemkin. This soldier was crazy, he told himself. He looked at him hard. "Dammit, what's wrong with you? What's wrong with your eyes?" No answer came. He studied the man's eyes again. Propechny was moving his eyes back and forth violently, trying to let

Shtemkin know something was wrong, without talking or moving his body. A gesture with his head could be seen from inside the window; what he did with his eyes could not.

"You've been drinking, Propechny." The corporal's accusation was sudden and menacing. "That's what's wrong with you. Goddam. Your eyes can't even focus. When I get—"

His tirade, just building up steam, was brought to an abrupt halt by the reappearance of the museum guard at the door. Using this guard had worked a few minutes earlier; Alyosha saw no reason not to use him again. He had told the man what to say, and a gun was pressed against his spine to remind him not to change anything. "Corporal. Corporal, please," called the museum guard. "Kapitan Sokolov wants both of you inside at once. On the double, he says."

Shtemkin's eyes narrowed to near slits. "Propechny, you bastard. Now look what you've done. Sokolov wants to see us. He knows you're drunk. God! You'll be doing extra duty for the rest of your life."

Spinning, furious at Propechny, at Sokolov, and at himself, Shtemkin called to his squad. "At ease! Comrade Private Kazan. Take command of 'A' Squad." He and the corporal from "B" squad conferred briefly; then the soldiers of both squads marched off toward the Spasskaya. Dragging the speechless, unwilling Propechny behind him, Shtemkin marched resolutely inside. Lance Corporal Shtemkin could not believe what he saw. Or what was happening. Or what he would be forced to do in the coming hours.

• America, Keer supposed, would be listed under "United States." China under "People's Republic of." England was easy: Great Britain. But Cuba? What the hell did Cuba call itself? He would come back to that one later. Picking up the receiver, Keer dialed one of the numbers he found in the phone book and told his story.

Although he was dressed for the cold, the outdoor phone kiosks were unexpectedly frigid and the prospect of making each call from a different section of the city had originally annoyed him. But once he'd begun, Keer found that driving from booth to booth gave him a chance to get warm again, the heater in the Chevy wheezing out as much hot air as its ancient machinery could manage. Still, it was a time-consuming process. By the time he was through making the calls, Keer found he was clear out in the Southwestern District of the city, using a booth in the shadow of the old Neskuchny

Castle. If he had gone any farther, he would have been outside the city limits and would have had to resort to toll calls, something Alyosha had expressly forbidden. The KGB could eventually trace such trunk calls.

The calls completed, Keer turned the Chevy back toward Central Moscow—and home. He felt good. The one cloud spoiling his sky was a fear that Gary's family might have chosen the wrong moment to tour the Oruzheinaya or the Tomb. He had called Lisenka—the Oruzheinaya's telephone system was still operating—and she had told him the nationalities of the hostages, but when he'd asked about some Americans named Decatur she seemed more curious than helpful. Finally, she said things were still too confused to know anyone's name, but, yes, otherwise Salt Mine was proceeding smoothly. Their conversation was in one of Alyosha's codes and making themselves clear was not easy.

Gary had promised to come later to Keer's home in the sprawling duplex at Gorky and Georgievsky, and Keer wondered if he'd show up. If his family *had* been caught inside, it would only be a matter of time before Gary heard about it, and he certainly wouldn't be visiting anybody in those circumstances. Unlike Keer, Gary obviously worshipped his father. The two fathers sounded very much alike: completely absorbed by their businesses, plunging into their work with all their energies, and with little time left over for their children. Yet Gary loved his father and felt loved by him in return, while Keer despised his and suspected he was despised in return. It was strange. They had talked a long time about that, trying to understand it, for Gary, like anyone young who is traveling in new places, was open not only to new experiences but to new people.

Keer sighed and studied his American loafers (taken this spring in trade for some old tsarist coins). It was odd, Gary and he. Fathers so alike, yet so different. Themselves so alike, yet so different. Gary so American, Keer so much wanting to be.

The phone rang, and Keer grabbed the receiver before Dovo could pick up an extension. A friend was returning his inquiry. Cuba, he was told, was called the Republic of Cuba. As simple as that.

Lisenka stood, her eyes still wide, her body still trembling, unable to look away from Natalya's body where it lay slumped against the coatroom counter. It had been several minutes since Avraam had loosed his Tekel into her, yet Lisenka had trouble believing it had actually happened. She held nothing against this woman; she could not even hold her attempt to warn the soldier against her. If the woman was a hardcore Party member, she had no choice; warning the soldier was not only to save her own life, but to warn the authorities of a dangerous situation. As a believer, she did her duty. Lisenka pondered. Perhaps, the Party member who had dispatched Shymon to his death was only doing what he considered his duty. Being loyal to the state. And Avraam had only been doing his, Lisenka supposed, when he shot Natalya Sergeyevna.

Looking at the soft heap slumped against the coatroom counter, Lisenka found it difficult to keep thinking in terms of duty or loyalty or the imponderables of what was right and what was wrong. Natalya's mouth sagged open below her staring eyes, and the lone gold tooth glinted in the Oruzheinaya's harsh light like a star of evil. With a sudden shudder, Lisenka returned to the tourists in the State Coach Room, carrying her Tekel with what appeared near to nonchalance. It was not. Inside, Lisenka felt sick.

• Lisenka's attack of nerves was contagious, even in places some distance from the Oruzheinaya Palata. Staring out his window at the Arsenal, Kapitan Volodya Sokolov could not shake the sensation that something he didn't understand was happening. That something was being done to him personally. He glanced again at the check-in board and could see that Corporal Shtemkin was now eight minutes overdue reporting from the call box at guard position number six. His key map confirmed what he thought: number six was outside the Oruzheinaya. Earlier, Volodya had seen the two squads marching toward the Spasskaya, on their way, he assumed, to change the guard at Lenin's Tomb. But that meant Shtemkin should have called in from number six *before* they started.

That stupid corporal—stupid or stubborn, the kapitan didn't know which—had gone on from number six without bothering to call in. Or had forgotten. Volodya was surprised to realize how frequently he repeated this explanation to himself, as if saying it enough might make the uneasy feeling in his stomach go away. Or perhaps Shtemkin had been taken sick. No, Shtemkin would still have called in, if only to report that he had the bug and should be relieved.

The hard knot in Volodya's stomach grew. Throwing on

his coat, the kapitan started out the door. Outside, he looked down toward the Borovitskaya Tower; he could see the guard standing outside the Oruzheinaya, but the sight only upset him further. Even at this distance, the two slanting stripes on the soldier's helmet indicated he was from "B" Squad, showing that Shtemkin had indeed already been there. But while this fact irritated, the same information relieved Volodya. Not too much could be wrong if the guard was being changed as usual. He would, he decided, cross the courtyard and confront Shtemkin and the two squads as they returned from Lenin's tomb. Just as he started walking, he heard his name being shouted. It was Bleimetev, the company sergeant, yelling at him from his office window, something Volodya would have to reprimand the sergeant for later. Within the Kremlin walls, one does not yell at *anybody*. Corporal Shtemkin, the sergeant said, was on the phone. The matter was urgent, apparently. Very urgent. Could the kapitan come back upstairs to the phone quickly, please?

Volodya lowered his head and charged upstairs. Gladly, he would come to the phone quickly to hear what Corporal Shtemkin had to say to his kapitan. But Shtemkin, he thought, would be a little less glad to hear what his kapitan had to say to *him*.

• Inside Lenin's Tomb, the sudden ringing of the phone made everyone jump. For what seemed forever now, both tourists and soldiers had been standing, shifting from one foot to the other, staring warily at Dimmy and Klemet. The unexpected sound jarred their nervous systems, already filed thin. To Dimmy's credit, he allowed no sign of the jolt the sound had given his own nerves but calmly reached over and picked up the phone. It was Lisenka; Alyosha had asked her to call in his place. The message was brief, even in Alyosha's cryptic code: "It is time."

"It is time," repeated Dimmy into the phone. The eyes of the hostages widened. Time for what? Time to blow them all up? Time to shoot them one by one? Time to shoot the soldiers and let the tourists go? Time for *what?*

They watched as Dimmy hung up and held a brief conference with Klemet. Earlier, Klemet had found the switch, precisely where Kropotkin had said it would be, recessed into the wall and hidden by a swinging panel of thin, reddish marble that matched the stone around it.

There was a sound of a distant pneumatic system starting

and the whir of a motor; noiselessly, a large steel door slid across the entrance leading from the tomb into the long passageway up to Red Square. From beyond came the shout of the guard in the passage nearest the door; this sliding steel panel was supposed to be closed only at night, when the tomb was off-limits to everyone but the maintenance staff. The hostages could hear the soldier shouting to other guards in the passageway and even caught a brief glimpse of his hand and foot as he tried to force himself into the tomb before the door closed completely.

Watching, Dimmy shook his head dourly. "He would like to get inside. Everyone inside would like to get outside. How hard people are to please."

• The tourists in the mausoleum had been shaken by what they heard Dimmy say into his phone; Kapitan Sokolov was staggered by what he heard coming out of *his*. "They've *what?*" he roared into the receiver. Corporal Shtemkin's voice seemed distant and rattled, but he patiently began over again. Across the office, the company sergeant, Belimetev, had just picked up another call for Volodya, listened, and was trying desperately to get the kapitan off his present call to take this new one.

Corporal Shtemkin, prompted by Alyosha, while Misha stood behind him with his Tekel, spoke again into the receiver. "They've taken me prisoner. Inside the Oruzheinaya. Along with all the tourists and a soldier. "They say—"

"Identify yourself," bellowed Volodya. Those passwords, he told himself, were going to prove themselves yet. This man on his phone was crazy, even though Volodya did have to admit he gave a very creditable imitation of Corporal Shtemkin. "Identify yourself!" he repeated, his voice crackling with fury.

"Oh, shit," groaned Shtemkin. "The population of Omsk is . . . Kapitan, I can't *remember* the population of Omsk. There's a hooligan behind me with a machine gun in my ribs. . . ."

"And growing every day," answered Volodya wearily. It was as he had feared. Without question, the man on the phone was Shtemkin. The company sergeant was pointing at his own phone, still trying to get the kapitan to the call on the other line.

A new voice jarred Sokolov. "Comrade Kapitan, I don't believe you are being given the message correctly. The corporal is too upset to speak clearly," said Alyosha calmly. "So I shall speak for him. . . ."

"Who is this?" demanded Volodya.

"That is of no significance, Comrade Kapitan. It is not who I am but *where* I am that counts. We have seized the Kremlin. As hostages, we hold—let's see—forty-six American citizens, three Cubans, some Africans, and a scattering of others. Two are children. Oh yes—if your superiors care—we hold fifteen Soviet citizens as well. As additional bargaining tools, we have the crown jewels, the imperial thrones, seven centuries of Russian history, a number of soldiers, and, oh, yes—how could I forget? We have also hijacked Lenin's body. He lies, at the moment, with a charge of plastic explosive stuck on top of his glass case. If anyone does anything they are not supposed to, anything I don't tell them they are allowed to, well, there will always be more tourists and you can buy new jewels, I suppose, but you can't buy a new Vladimir Ilyich."

By now, the company sergeant had written out the message from the other line and was waving it under Volodya's nose. The kapitan merely nodded, something which stunned the sergeant. His note said that guard position number twelve—the one just outside Lenin's Tomb—reported the inner door had mysteriously slid shut, effectively sealing off the tomb. There were people inside. What did the kapitan want done?

The kapitan did what he wanted done for himself. Tucking the phone under one ear, Volodya pressed a series of buttons on the console in front of him, sounding the general alarm. Bells began clanging. Sirens went off. Outside, the courtyard filled with soldiers and attendants, all of them running, scrambling to get to their emergency stations. Bewildered tourists watched in awe as all the gates in the Kremlin walls were slammed shut. From above him, Kapitan Sokolov could hear the crashing and scuffling of feet hitting the floor as the "real" troops scrambled; they would form lines around the buildings where the government functions of the Kremlin were carried out. This term—"real" troops—had always irritated Volodya, but he was suddenly glad they were here. It would make sharing the blame easier.

It occurred to Volodya that the shutting of the gates left his own troops outside the walls; he put his hand over the phone and told the sergeant to stop gawking and tell the KGB office to let them in.

"Good," said Alyosha's voice calmly. "You have sounded

the alarm. Now, when people—the authorities—begin calling you to find out why, outline the situation as I have described it. Tell your superiors kindly not to shut off the electricity, water, or telephones. You can tell them what will happen to the hostages if they do. I realize that under normal circumstances the Party would simply tell the army to blow their way in. They were never much in favor of the individual. However, you may point out to them that, besides the destruction of Lenin himself, the American government would be shocked to learn that forty-six of their citizens could be slaughtered inside the very heart of the Government itself. And the Africans would surely lose respect if the Angolans were to die on Kremlin grounds. And don't you think Fidel Castro would be amused to find his oh-so-powerful ally couldn't even keep order inside his own headquarters? Tell them, your superiors, that we shall make known our conditions for freeing the hostages through the corporal or you. But a little later. First, we have to give them time to appreciate what is happening. *Do svidanya.*"

Ignoring the phones in his office as they all began to ring simultaneously, Volodya sank back into his chair, staring hard. It was impossible. The Kremlin must be the most heavily guarded place in the world. With the most sophisticated detection and alarm systems ever put together. A place where one could barely breathe without the KGB knowing about it. But most of the thought had been devoted to protecting the active seat of government, the nerve centers where the government leaders worked. In the other areas—the museums, the tomb, the galleries, the showplaces—the main concern was protection against vandalism and thievery, in themselves rare inside the Soviet Union. And this skewed concentration had made the entire Kremlin complex vulnerable: No one had imagined someone holding the government itself hostage by seizing buildings full of tourists and visitors. No one had imagined Salt Mine.

Guns, thought Volodya. How were they able to get guns inside the walls? There were hidden metal detectors at every gate, others concealed inside the entrance of every building. Perhaps—but Volodya was suddenly too weary for speculation.

His eyes wandered across his desk to Lenin's photograph. The face appeared to be scowling at him. It had every right to. He had missed somewhere, Volodya admitted to himself. He had overlooked something. He had not followed the regulations precisely enough. And this failure would be the end of him. The kapitan sighed; the man who had prayed nothing would happen during his six-month trial period knew now that everything was going to happen. Regardless of whether it was his fault or not, a shadow would fall across him; he would not be assigned, as he had so fervently hoped, to Moscow forever. He would be lucky if he lasted an hour.

Dreading it, he picked up the phone and dialed the number for Moscow Area One headquarters. He could have saved himself the trouble. They were already on his other line, waiting.

PART TWO

10

THE FIRST DAY, 3:29 P.M.

Vasily Dimitrovich Klin sank into the cushions of the limousine, watching the buildings slip past. Klin was on his way from the Council of Ministers Building to the Ministry of State Security, and the drive took him down Gorky Street, the structures an unsettling mixture of slab modern and gingerbread Victorian.

As they reached a corner, his driver blew the horn and let the ZiL—a Soviet version of the Cadillac limousine—sail across the intersection against the light. Outside his window, Klin could see the pedestrians, jolted by the horn and annoyed at having to get out of his way, staring at him with resentment. He returned the stares without expression. The pose, Klin decided, was fitting for one of the new aristocracy; besides, their resentment fed his feeling of superiority.

On his lap sat the fur hat he usually wore. Today his scalp was itching badly and his head felt better uncovered. A look of irritation crossed his face. That dermatologist. She said her pills were to treat the infection, but Klin wondered. Her turnabout had been so sudden, a flickering suspicion that she might be giving him nothing more than a placebo crossed his mind.

At his elbow, the telephone in the armrest buzzed, a raucous angry sound in the soft hush of the ZiL. With a startled look, Klin rested one hand on it. He had left his office at the Kremlin less than twenty minutes ago, and anyone there would know he hadn't had time to reach the Ministry yet. Klin discouraged people from calling him in his car anyway; a car phone, he always said, can be no more private than a radio because it *is* no more than a radio.

The voice on the other end was his deputy, Pisarev, and although the man struggled to sound calm, the urgency in his voice was unmistakable. Words tumbled out of him in a growing torrent—in spite of Klin's repeated warning to for God's sake remember security precautions. Pisarev didn't even pause to apologize or explain; breathlessly he came to the point of what he was struggling to say.

"They've done *what?*" bellowed Klin, causing his driver to look around uncertainly. Klin's initial disbelief quickly surrendered to the realization that what his forebodings had tried to signal all week had occurred: Salt Mine had happened, and it outdistanced anything his usually reliable hunches had suggested.

"Call the other ministers," began Klin, then corrected himself. "No, don't call them yet. . . ."

"Some of them were there, Comrade Minister. They already *know*."

"Get hold of Chorniev. No, by now, he knows too. See if you can reach—oh hell. I'll be right there. Tell them I'll be right there." The phone was slammed down angrily. Leaning forward, Klin told the driver to get him back to the Kremlin as fast as he could make it. Yes, use the siren. Abruptly, the ZiL made a U-turn on Gorky; the tires screamed as the driver gunned the machine and headed back as if the devil were pursuing them. The high-pitched, two-tone wail cut through the rapidly falling twilight of November like a soul in agony. At the next intersection, Klin noticed the same resentful stares he'd seen when he was going in the opposite direction, only now the expressions were laced with fear as pedestrians jumped to get out of the path of his speeding car.

This time their reaction gave no satisfaction. One of the advantages the old aristocracy had over the new was a sense of permanence. A rank bestowed upon a man by heredity could not be taken away, even by a firing squad.

• Inside the Petersburg sled, Alyosha leaned back against the deep plum plush sofa and let its mystery envelop him. For the moment, he knew, it was safe to sit down; Misha and one of the foot soldiers were posted at the windows that looked out onto the Kremlin courtyard, while Avraam and another of the foot soldiers were in the rear area of the Oruzheinaya, waving their Tekels occasionally to make sure none of the hostage-tourists got out of hand. For the time being, Lisenka had left her weapon with Misha so as not to alarm the hostages further; she was going from group to group with a pad, taking down names, reassuring the hostages that everything was going to be all right.

The Petersburg sled was to be Alyosha's office, his place to be alone, a sanctuary where he could talk to others in privacy. It was so comfortable his biggest problem was going to be fighting off sleep; Alyosha was on his second day now without any, and he felt nearly paralyzed with exhaustion.

Using Tsarina Elizabeth's Petersburg sled was Lisenka's idea, and the suggestion was a good one. When you closed the door, you had the feeling the rest of the world had been shut outside.

Clearly, the tsarina had known how to travel. The interior fascinated him. Besides the chaiselike couch Alyosha was stretched out on, his long feet propped up on the velvet chair facing him, two ornate side chairs were pulled up to a gleaming marquetry table. Apparently, this was where the tsarina took her meals, or played cards, or whatever tsarinas of the time did to amuse themselves while traveling. In the forward corner squatted a woodburning stove, its ormolu decorations still bright in the half-light filtering through the mica windows. In the opposite corner, a chaise percée could be glimpsed, partially hidden by a screen. The entire floor was covered by a handsome oriental, while two smaller ones served as area rugs. Floor to ceiling, the walls of the sled were paneled in light sandalwood and decorated with blue and gold hand-painted designs, giving the interior an airy, sunny feeling. Across the facing wall, the double-headed imperial eagle spread its golden wings.

In spite of squeezing hard on his eyelids, Alyosha could feel them trying to close; the hushed world inside the sled made keeping them open difficult. Occasionally, bizarre images of the afternoon's events—particularly the picture of Natalya's bewildered expression as the bullets ripped into her middle—flew from the ornate stove like errant dreams.

Alyosha slapped his face to bring his eyes open again. Angrily, he cursed himself for not bringing a thermos of coffee. Sleep could come later, not now. Digging into a pocket, he pulled out a list of things that should have been done by this stage of Salt Mine; most of them were crossed out, a couple remained. Leaning forward, he opened the door a crack and waited until he could see Kropotkin, the Old One, whom he had told to stay nearby. When Kropotkin saw him waving, he shuffled over, his face expressionless. "Bring him up now, Old One. But have the foot soldier stay near."

Silently, Kropotkin moved away, saying nothing. Alyosha watched him with wonder; in all of his dealings with Kropotkin, he couldn't remember the old man saying more than half a dozen words.

A few minutes later, he saw the door in the side of the room reopen. Through it, haltingly, came an armed foot soldier and Tbor, rubbing his wrists where they had been tied. Both men's eyes widened as they looked around the room and saw the hostages and the members of the Salt Mine team. Tbor seemed to sag and had to lean against the door. Although the foot soldier knew something of Salt Mine's plans, he had been in the cellar standing guard over Tbor for two days and hadn't expected to find what he saw. Shaking himself, he stuck his Tekel into Tbor's back and followed the Old One over to the Petersburg sled.

Alyosha nodded, pulling Tbor into the sled with him. "Stay right outside," he told the foot soldier. Perched warily on one of the marquetry chairs, Tbor sat rigid, studying Alyosha in amazement. "We meet again," Alyosha noted.

When Tbor spoke, it was a shrill whine. "Why have you done this to me, Alexei Andreyevich? I helped you. I was with you."

"Perhaps. Perhaps not."

"I put you in touch with people—the Armenian. I stole information for you when you asked for it. I helped you get supplies. . . . I—"

"For money, yes."

"I recruited most of your team for you."

"For money. Again, yes. And one of your recruits—Volovno—came close to destroying everything by trading his knowledge of Salt Mine to the KGB."

"I took care of Volovno. You know that."

"For more money."

A sigh of inevitability rose from Tbor. Slowly, his eyes rose to meet Alyosha's. "You think I would have turned you in, don't you? For money."

"Without question."

"You plan to kill me?"

"Possibly. But I have a proposition to make you. We need a doctor. You are one. Or were. These hostages here are in close confinement . . . here and in Lenin's Tomb—"

"Lenin's Tomb!"

A faint smile crossed Alyosha's face. "People in close confinement present a problem. As a doctor, you know that. Two of the hostages are children. It is a situation where a bug could run wild. We could all come down with it. That would be the end of Salt Mine. The proposition I offer: You take care of the hostages. Doctor them. Treat anything that looks a potential danger. That or—"

Tbor exploded. "I will not become one of you. You are all doomed here, don't you realize that? How far do you really think you'll get? What is to stop them from breaking in with soldiers and taking this place back? There is no escape. I won't—"

"A little earlier you asked if I planned to kill you. I said 'possibly.' If you do not feel right about the proposition I'm offering you, that 'possibly' could become 'certainly.' "

Tbor studied the orientals; he squirmed in his fragile chair. Then, lamely: "I have no drugs. No instruments . . ."

"They are here."

Tbor threw up his hands.

"Good. The Old One has the supplies. But I should warn you, my friend, no funny stuff. We will be watching." Pushing open the sled door again, Alyosha waved the foot soldier over, giving him instructions to stay with Tbor at all times. When Tbor had no one to take care of, he was to be locked back in the cellar.

Lying back on the sofa again, Alyosha found his eyes becoming heavier than ever. He must not sleep, he could not sleep. Slowly, though, his eyelids dropped down of their own weight.

A sudden burst of machine-gun fire rocketed Alyosha out of the sled. In the front room, near the entrance, Misha was leaning out of a window, firing toward the ground farther down the side of the building. Uncertainly, he pulled his Tekel back and turned to Alyosha. His look was sheepish. "A shadow. A damned shadow. In this light, it looked like a helmet, like someone crawling along the side of the building." Behind him, in the State Coach Room, the women hostages began to scream. Back there, they could make out nothing of what was happening up near the entrance. All they had seen was Alyosha leaping from his enclosed sled in response to machine-gun fire. In their minds, they pictured the worst: soldiers pouring in, firing their weapons; Salt Mine firing back; they themselves caught in the middle. Quickly, Lisenka, who didn't yet know what had happened herself, tried to calm them down, reassuring them that if anything important was going on, she would be up in front with the rest of Salt Mine.

Suddenly Irina left the Decaturs and walked toward Lisenka. She spun to face the hostages. "Yes. She would be there with the rest of them. With her machine gun. This traitor would be as quick to kill as any of the men. She wants you to stay calm so they can go about whatever criminal act they have in mind. And when they are through, they will kill you. Me. All of us."

Feeling foolish, Lisenka shook her head vigorously, not sure whether it was better to contradict Irina or just convince her to shut up. The matter was resolved for her. Avraam, who had walked to the doorway of the State Coach Room at the sound of firing and had quickly seen it was a false alarm, waved his Tekel at Irina menacingly. "Sit down, you. Sit down, or I will take steps with this that will sit you down very painfully."

"You are all murderers," Irina shouted at Avraam. He began advancing on her; the look in his eye made it impossible to tell how far he would go with his threat. Irina spun back toward the hostages. "If you don't believe me, look at the poor lady lying by the coatroom counter. They killed her, they—"

The slap hit her hard, just below her left ear. With a grim look, Avraam had swung wide and put all of his strength behind one awesome blow of his open hand. Irina staggered backward but appeared ready to go on yelling at the hostages in spite of a trickle of blood that oozed from her mouth. From behind her, two arms suddenly seized her and dragged her back toward the wall. She was surprised to discover that the arms and the sudden, soothing voice in her ear belonged to Mr. Decatur. Patting her shoulders reassuringly, Blaine Decatur led Irina back to Lisa and Christy. Christy produced a handkerchief and began mopping Irina's mouth; Lisa tried to find a comfortable spot against the wall where Irina could sit. Standing back a few feet, Blaine Decatur studied their guide. It struck him as odd that when Irina looked at him, her expression held no glimmer of thanks; rather it was one of lofty contempt. These Russians, he decided, were a peculiar people. Help them, and they hated you for it.

• In a paneled meeting room across Kremlin Square, no one was trying to help anyone. "I agree with you," said Klin. It *is* insane. But from the beginning, everything about Salt Mine has been. On the other hand, the problem we face is cold and rational."

A small sigh rose from the men sitting around the table. Facing this particular problem was something all of them wished they could avoid; Klin's statement put the problem back where they knew it belonged: in their laps. For a moment, nothing was said. The ministers stared, watching the smoke rise from their cigarettes or busying themselves with the pouring of iced mineral water. All of the ministers—except Keer's father, Dmitry Gertsen, who was not in town—were gathered in the meeting room, trying to resolve the unresolvable.

At the head of the table sat the deputy premier, Pyotr Ivanovich Chaidze. He was feared not because his position held much power in itself, but because he was the only man who had daily meetings with Yuri Talanin. As Party secretary (and also, president and premier of the USSR), Talanin worked out of Party headquarters at Number 4 Staraya Square, which also housed the Central Committee. There was nothing unusual in this; Brezhnev had done the same. What did make it different was that no one—with the exception of Deputy Premier Chaidze—had laid eyes on Talanin for six months, giving rise to a host of rumors. Talanin had cancer and was unable even to stand up. Talanin had a mysterious fatal disease, like Pompidou's, which had swollen his face to three times its normal size. And so forth. In one of his meaner moments, Marshal Borodinsky, minister of defense and Klin's highest-placed enemy, stared directly at Klin during one of these bull sessions on Talanin and suddenly laughed. "Or perhaps all of his hair fell out." Remarks such as this were merely symptomatic; Klin and Borodinsky despised each other for a variety of reasons buried in time. Klin loathed the man.

As if reading their minds, Deputy Premier Chaidze cleared his throat and held up a small piece of paper. "In this matter, all personal differences must be put aside. I have talked to the secretary and he gave me a message for you." Clearing his throat again, Chaidze held up the paper and read it in his thin, high voice: " 'Resolve the Salt Mine matter. To our advantage. Forthwith.—Talanin.' " He waved the small piece of paper in the air for a moment, then slapped it on the table. From the group another uncomfortable sigh rose; there was a scraping sound as a dozen chairs were shifted on the polished parquet of the ministers' meeting room.

A deep rumbling sound, a man preparing to speak of important things, made Klin swing toward Borodinsky. The marshal was not of the old school of Soviet marshals, squat and heavy; he was a fragile-looking military technocrat. His spectacled eyes appeared too big for his head and his head too big for his body. The booming actor's voice sounded too resonant for either. About the only thing he shared with, say, a Zhukov, was a quick temper and an ingrained belief that force could solve anything.

The throat rumbled again, and Borodinsky began talking in his window-rattling voice. "I can resolve the matter of Salt Mine. And now." All heads turned to stare at him, the flat marshal's epaulets looking outsized on his tiny shoulders. "A frontal assault. I have Special Tactical Forces and armament on standby. Salt Mine can be terminated in a matter of moments."

Klin looked at Borodinsky in disbelief. "Tanks. Machine guns. Grenades. Why not a hydrogen bomb?"

Bristling, Borodinsky seemed to swell inside his uniform. "Vasily Dmitrovich appears concerned for the hostages. . . ."

"I don't give a bear on a chamber pot about the hostages. But use your head. The hostages are inside the Oruzheinaya Palata. Forty-six of them are Americans. Some Cubans, some Angolans, some French and some East Germans. Two of them are children—a small but emotionally sensitive point. We don't know how many more are locked inside Lenin's Tomb. Harm any of them, and the foreign papers will have a field day. Even ones controlled by the Eurocommunists. And something else. Shoot your way in and the damage will be enormous. The Oruzheinaya's art treasures—objects you cannot even put a price on. Explosives sitting on top of Lenin himself. It is *all* of these things I am worried about." Klin had been toying with a paper clip, bending it between his fingers. Suddenly, it flew across the table, barely missing Borodinsky's head.

Watching, Klin could see Borodinsky's breath coming at shorter intervals; the wide epaulets rose higher and fell farther, as if the marshal might suddenly start to flap them and take off. "If we let Salt Mine get away with this, we become mortgaged to all dissidents. The taking of hostages will roll over us like a tide. We will become the laughingstock of the world."

"Laughed at harder than if we blow up our own capital?"

"It can be repaired—"

"The hostages can't. Their governments will have to be told—"

Barely in control, Borodinsky plowed ahead. "The foreign papers—"

"Are not stupid."

"The hostages' ambassadors—"

"Aren't stupid either."

"Secrecy can be—"

"Forgotten about. There is no such thing as a lasting secret."

Hands whitening around the edge of the table, Borodinsky struggled to remain calm. His violent outbursts, supporters told him, had gotten in his way before. The color rose in Borodinsky's face from the fight raging inside him. "All of you—listen. The face that the Soviet government shows to the world is at stake. We must—I cannot agree—immediate assault—wipe out Salt Mine or—that is to say—"

It was too much for him. With a grunt, Borodinsky shot to his feet, knocking his chair over as he did. Wordless, he stalked out of the room. In the silence that followed, the deputy premier once again cleared his throat and began talking. All of them talked. They argued. They agreed. They disagreed. They talked some more.

It went on this way for another half hour. Finally, Deputy Premier Chaidze called for a vote: Borodinsky's appeal for frontal assault or Klin's plea for waiting events out. One member was to be listed as not voting (Foreign Minister Shtanov), two as absent during the vote (Borodinsky and Gertsen). The vote was a tie.

Cigarettes were lit, a lot of iced mineral water poured, a number of throats cleared nervously. Abruptly, the deputy premier suggested he disqualify himself and called for a new vote. Just as abruptly, Foreign Minister Shtanov—he had abstained from the first vote because he feared Borodinsky almost as much as he feared Klin—began speaking.

"I remained silent because I wished more time to think. But the picture of Soviet soldiers firing on foreign visitors is impossible to accept. The repercussions impossible to handle. In spite of all the good arguments in favor of Marshal Borodinsky's frontal assault"—he stared hard at Blivi, one of Borodinsky's closest supporters—"I have to vote for Vasily's recommendation to wait the events out." Shtanov's commitment tipped the scale in favor of Klin's position—by one vote.

Klin knew he could not yet relax. Soviet leaders are unused to decisions by a majority, and so a vote is never really a vote. Immediately, the argument began all over again. At twelve minutes after five, Deputy Premier Chaidze recessed the meeting, subject to recall any time. He would, he said, consult with Talanin.

Upstairs in his office, Klin brooded, staring out his window. About the only thing the Council of Ministers had agreed upon was absolute secrecy. Even the embassies of the hostages were not to be informed. Twice, Klin's assistant told him Foreign Minister Shtanov was on Klin's line. Urgent. Just as Klin was about to turn away from the window, he saw a large black limousine pull up short beside the building, an American flag flapping arrogantly from its fender. The ambassador stepped out and strode into the building, on his way to confront Shtanov. On his heels, the Cuban and French ambassadors arrived, also to hurry inside the building.

Klin groaned. Keer had felt half-frozen, stamping his feet in one telephone booth after the other all across Moscow, but his calls had just paid off.

• So had Klin's orders for a holding action. Red Square was cordoned off. It is never open to automobiles, but its vast spaces are almost always open to pedestrians. Not only, Keer discovered, was Red Square sealed off from the rest of Moscow by a moving wall of police and soldiers, the entire area around the Kremlin was suddenly off-limits, too. Stretching himself to his full height, Keer could catch a glimpse of the Kremlin walls; two pipe towers had been put up outside the west walls, and he could see men attaching large circular devices—he thought they were searchlights—onto the platform tops.

Oddly, the citizens of Moscow were ignoring this strange activity, although Keer could see them glance furtively in the Kremlin's direction every now and then; Muscovites knew better than to appear too curious about anything that happened in their capital.

As he stood in a side street off the Square, the ground beneath Keer's feet began to tremble. Across Nogin Square, a line of Soviet T-10s—a light Soviet tank—rolled down Razin Street and on into Red Square. Grunting and snorting, the main body of T-10s deployed themselves outside the gates of the Nikolskaya and Spasskaya Towers; others edged along the Kremlin embankment and disappeared in the direction of the Borovitskaya.

From farther away came a deep throaty rumbling and a shaking of the ground so intense the windows in Kitai-Gorod seemed in danger of shattering. A sudden squeaking and clanking of thick metal plates against cobblestones cut through the rumbling sound. As Keer watched, openmouthed, a line of heavy T-55s lurched across Old Square, turned at Nogin, and dispersed themselves, one by one, down the side streets facing Red Square.

Each time a heavy tread crashed down on a time-worn cobble, a shower of electric sparks would be struck; in the foggy light of early winter this cloud of sparks rising through the mist looked as though the devil himself were hammering on the ground, fashioning some new torture rack on which to hang the soul of Salt Mine.

Once the T-55s were parked, their engines sputtered to a halt in a spasm of dying snorts. The drivers leaned back against their tanks, smoking cigarettes and laughing. From them rose a cloud of hoots and catcalls as the Special Tactical Forces appeared. In full combat uniforms, these men trotted down the street, heading purposefully for the Square.

The Council of Ministers had argued. Borodinsky had acted.

11

THE FIRST DAY, 6:23 P.M.

A pad was pulled across the desk on Dzerzhinsky Street. The pencil began doodling on one corner of the top page, drawing a cabalistic design of boxes within boxes. In the center of the innermost box, the pencil wrote one word: "me."

More boxes were drawn. The word "me" stood with increasingly little space around it, a lonely word, looking as trapped as the man who drew it. The pencil was put down and a call made. Whatever was said upset the drawer. "He did *what?*" A sharp grunt, either an oath or an exasperated explosion, came from the pencil's owner. "Please, when you find him, have him call me. Yes. Urgently."

It might seem strange that Mikhail Chorniev, a Soviet official in the midst of a state crisis, should spend more time worrying about himself than he did about the crisis. He chose to ignore this inversion of priorities. Morosely, his hand filled in the square until the word "me" disappeared. It was how Chorniev felt.

As a professional survivor, he had long kept two rules: Never stick your neck out, and always let someone else make any important decision. Now he was suffering from having disregarded the first rule and for hewing too closely to the second. He should never have jeopardized himself by sending the memorandum—addressed (but not delivered) to Klin—along to Borodinsky. The ploy was already backfiring; Borodinsky's secretary had just told him that the marshal had had it copied and sent to several other ministers. Since the memo accused Klin of reckless mismanagement in pursuing a will-o'-the-wisp called "Salt Mine," the "Klin document" could now be fatal.

The second rule—always let someone else make the important decisions—had also backfired. Damn Volovno. When Volovno first turned up, he had seemed to represent an opportunity. But after only a few words of his story, Chorniev had shut him up. He hadn't wanted to hear more, knowing it would require a decision, and that was something that must be shifted elsewhere.

"No, no." Chorniev had held up his hand when Volovno looked as if he were about to continue. "This is something you should tell only to Minister Klin. . . ."

"But, Comrade, there's this group that—"

Again, Chorniev had silenced him. Volovno would be produced that afternoon during Klin's party at Archangelskoye. If, by any chance, Volovno's story *was* important and Klin acted on it, he, Chorniev, would get credit for delivering the man. If the story *wasn't*—and Chorniev had been sure this would be the case—Klin might still be maneuvered into taking action anyway and would have to take the blame. He couldn't lose, Chorniev had decided.

But if he couldn't lose, why was he sitting here sweating? Because Volovno had wound up floating in the lagoon at Archangelskoye and, with him, any advance warning on Salt Mine. And also because of that stupid memo he'd written, trying to scuttle Klin. That was the maneuver not of a survivor, but of a jungle fighter. People got eaten in jungles.

Chorniev groaned, remembering he had government work to do. Klin had demanded an all-out search for Salt Mine's outside man. He picked up the phone, suddenly weary. A manhunt in Moscow is not an easy thing.

• Nothing was easy today. Klin paced uncomfortably back and forth across Kapitan Volodya Sokolov's office, talking as much to himself as to the others there. He knew Volodya didn't like having him in his office, much less being forced to take orders from him. Earlier, he knew, the kapitan had complained to Colonel-General Pskov at Headquarters, Moscow Area One, but nothing had happened. The general was too afraid of Klin himself. A second complaint had produced General Pskov in person, but he had deferred completely to Klin, mostly sitting to one side, observing quietly.

Outside the window, the floodlights set up beyond the Kremlin walls suddenly came on, startling everyone. For a moment, their light wavered, brightening and dimming as the arcs struggled to catch, then settled into an intensive white light. The office was brighter than in daytime, but the light brought an eerie quality with it, lacking color and making those in the room look a washed-out blue.

To Klin, it was apparent the kapitan was concerned about the shambles made of his office. His desk had been pushed flat against one wall, and two large reel-to-reel tape decks occupied most of its surface; a bright red wire connected these directly to the inside phone. The tape deck's operator, a KGB man, would be standing by on a permanent basis. To one side was a small loudspeaker so that everyone in the room could hear the phone conversations; a battery of additional phones squatted on a small table near the desk; more tapes, more tape machines, more men to operate them. Virtually none of Volodya's original furnishings were visible.

"You see," Klin said suddenly, addressing himself to the kapitan, "I want to try and maintain the phone procedure that man in Salt Mine started with your Corporal . . . Corporal . . ."

"Shtemkin."

"Your Corporal Shtemkin. Talking to you, and you, in turn, to me. That way I have more time to consider my answers. They may object, but we should try it; Salt Mine has to give us its demands soon. They should be calling with them shortly."

Volodya nodded, turning as two men in military fatigues entered. They carried folded army cots and began setting them up. The last vestiges of his office disappeared behind a neat row of cots, each with a blanket folded at its foot. It would be like peasants out camping, Klin thought, feeling his earlier sense of superiority return. Abruptly, Klin shouted at everyone in the room to be silent. Something was coming over the loudspeaker from the tapped line to the Oruzheinaya. Smoothly, the tape machines began to turn.

"Alyosha. Alyosha." The man's voice had a sepulchral echo to it, as if it were coming from the bottom of a deep well. "Alyosha, it's Dimmy."

"I didn't think Lenin was calling."

"The air. There's something wrong with the air in here. Klemet thinks the ventilators have been turned off. It's stifling."

"I'll see what I can do."

Over the loudspeaker came a hard click. Almost immediately the phone on Volodya's desk rang. Quickly, Volodya reached for it, only to feel his arm stopped by Klin. He didn't want to appear anxious, so a little time should pass before it was answered.

"Hello?" Volodya made his voice as deep and commanding

as possible. "Kapitan Sokolov," he finally said. To his surprise, it was not Shtemkin on the other end.

"Give me Klin," Alyosha demanded.

Klin shook his head. "He is not here," Volodya answered.

"Klin is there."

"Later. He will be here later. A message—"

"Klin is there. I know he is there, you know he is there. Stop the crap and give me Klin."

Klin waved his arms at Sokolov, his resigned expression telling the kapitan to give in. "He just stepped back into the room."

"I bet."

Warily, Klin took the phone. "Ah, Alyosha. I am sorry I was—"

"You eavesdrop. How else would you know my name? Well, it was to be expected."

"Precisely."

"The air in Lenin's Tomb—"

"Has been turned back on. An oversight. Overzealous underlings."

"Hostages turn just as black when they suffocate from overzealousness as from strangulation. Remember that, Klin."

"Correct." With difficulty, Klin controlled the anger building inside himself. "However, all of this is off the point. Salt Mine's demands. If you give them to me now, I can start working on them."

"You will get them when we decide the time is right. We're in no hurry. We're not going anywhere."

"Definitely not."

"You will be told. When the time is proper."

"Be reasonable. There will be arrangements—"

The click from Oruzheinaya was audible even though Klin slammed down his end of the phone so hard it made Kapitan Sokolov jump. A short time later, the speaker relayed Keer's regular hourly call. Meticulously, Keer described the tanks and soldiers outside the Kremlin walls; the searchlights he assumed they could see.

Alyosha's reply was cryptic. "Avoid Focus One."

"Right," Volodya heard Keer reply. Then there was silence.

Klin's already foul mood grew worse—no one had talked to him as bluntly as Alyosha for years—thinking about Salt Mine's man on the outside. If they could only find him, it would be something tangible to work on. Someone they could get their hands on and squeeze until he talked. Klin felt he had to know quickly what Salt Mine's demands were; it would influence everything they did. This outside man would probably know them.

Vasily Klin stalked over toward his office at the Council of Ministers Building. A replay of Alyosha's conversation was unsettling. Inside Klin, a suspicion that Salt Mine was playing the same waiting game he had sold to the Council of Ministers began to grow. Grimly, he wondered if Salt Mine had its Marshal Borodinsky, too.

• For a long time Alyosha sat outside the Petersburg sled and watched as Lisenka went from group to group of hostages. In Russian, Spanish, English, German, and French she told them that if they had any complaints, a doctor was prepared to treat them.

No one appeared ill, but Tbor discovered they all shared one complaint: hunger. For real food, for cigarettes, for coffee, for something stronger than coffee. Four trays of sandwiches had arrived earlier, but they barely went around. Along with a caldron of thick soup the non-Russians couldn't face. "Tell them I will get the food and whatever else I can," Alyosha told Lisenka, walking over to the phone. It was near the window, and the brightness of the lights along the Kremlin walls hurt his eyes. Just as he reached for the phone, it rang. Keer, with his ten o'clock check-in.

"There is activity, Focus Two."

"A lot?"

"Intensive. Focus is—"

Abruptly, Keer's voice went dead. Without expecting much, Alyosha jiggled the cradle. The phone was dead. From outside, Klin's voice, hard and unfriendly now, could be heard over a loudspeaker. Squinting through the window, Alyosha shielded his eyes and stared. The combination was eerie; the loudspeaker's words boomed across the courtyard, seeming to come from a spot directly between the two huge lights. A spectral *son et lumière*.

"Salt Mine! . . . Salt Mine! . . ." The words reverberated, caroming off the building in a mocking parody of Klin's voice. "We know you have a man on the outside, Salt Mine. We know who he is and where he is. It will not be long. Your phone is cut. To the outside, to Lenin's Tomb. Now, you can talk only to me. I will reconnect the phone to me only to hear what your demands are."

Alyosha nodded to Misha and Avraam, who had moved up from the Hall of Silver to the front area. They were ready. "Lisenka," he called. "Keep them calm back there." The staccato burst of the two Tekels firing simultaneously shattered the sudden silence of the courtyard. Both Misha and Avraam were firing directly at the searchlights. The glass breaking was heard clearly in the Oruzheinaya; in spite of Lisenka's efforts, several women in the rear began to scream. For a second, the lights wavered; then with an incandescent flashing and a sputtering, the arcs fractured, glowing pieces of red-hot charcoal floating lazily downward. Klin had his answer.

Beside Alyosha, the phone rang. It was Klin. "We expected that, of course. They will be fixed in minutes. I hoped you would be more reasonable."

"We are so reasonable we have only two demands for the moment. Food—real food, this time. The hostages are still hungry. Some wine. Cigarettes—American for the foreigners, *papirosi* for our countrymen. That is one of Salt Mine's demands. The other: Reconnect the phones. It's one thing for you to listen in; it's something else to shut them off. Need I add—or else?"

"Since the food, et cetera, is for the hostages, very well. The cigarettes, I can understand that. But the phone, no. If your outside man wants to talk to you, he'll have to buy a carrier pigeon."

"I said 'or else', Klin. I guess you didn't believe me." He turned to Avraam. "Send Lisenka out. I need her."

Alyosha had known it would come to this eventually; Salt Mine's resolve was being tested. And in this running battle of move and countermove, he could not afford to lose. The "or else" was about to be made good.

• Klin hung up the phone with a puzzled expression. "If those hooligans do something stupid . . ." he muttered in the general direction of Sokolov and Colonel-General Pskov. His cold stare focused suddenly on Kapitan Volodya Sokolov. "Call and find out how long the lights will take. They told me minutes when they were putting them up. Well, it's *been* minutes."

Volodya hurried to the battery of phones on the other side of the room. Every time Klin spoke, Pskov jumped, and it struck Volodya as inappropriate that a member of the Soviet Army should respond this way to a civilian's orders. He cast a look at Pskov and could see the man was going to be of no help. He was too frightened of Klin himself.

"If some of them try to break out in this dark, if they try slipping around us to get into some of the other buildings—well, my hands will be tied. There will be nothing to do except move against them. Damn."

Pskov nodded in sympathy, although his expression remained dour. His eyes seemed unable to stay away from the tufted clumps of hair and piebald blotches on Klin's scalp.

The phone from the Oruzheinaya rang. Alyosha's voice sounded hard.

"I said, 'or else.' You are free to listen—and watch."

Over the phone, Klin heard someone—an American apparently—pleading. He didn't know enough English to make it out too well, but the message was clear. A gasp, and the woman began to scream at something she saw about to happen. The short burst of machine-gun fire was so close to the phone it caused Kim to yank the receiver away and hold it at a distance, staring at it, the realization of what he had heard sinking in.

"The front doors are opening," Sokolov shouted at him, relaying what his spotter on the roof told him over the phone.

"The lights, dammit, where the hell are the lights?"

Sokolov shook his head. Another call, and a row of small, weak spotlights came on. Not powerful enough to carry such a distance, they bathed one side of the Oruzheinaya and the courtyard outside it in a shadowy glow; it was inadequate for the spotter to see more than vague shapes and gave only a suggestion of what was going on at the doorway.

According to the spotter, the woman stumbled out, still screaming, and fell to the ground outside the doors, one hand trying to fend off a new burst of gunfire from inside. For a moment, she appeared to twitch, then lay still.

Suddenly aware of the phone in his hand, Klin shakily struggled to find something to say. He had not expected this of Salt Mine, and he realized he was shocked. "Very well," he said finally, "your phone will be reconnected. It is unfair to make the hostages pay further for your depravity."

• The sight at the other end of the phone would have stunned Klin. The reaction of those near the phone was not at all that of people who felt themselves either cruel or unfair. Lisenka was smiling broadly, and Misha, Avraam, and Alyosha were applauding. Even the Russian hostages close enough to hear what Alyosha said on the phone only shrugged, secretly proud, perhaps, of their countryman's ingenuity.

For no hostage had been brutally shot; no hostage had staggered out the door to die, thrashing, on the cobbles of the Kremlin courtyard. What Klin and the others saw, not very clearly because of the dim lights, was Natalya's farewell performance. The voice of the American woman screaming and pleading belonged to Lisenka, starring in a one-time-only appearance. The body was that of Natalya, the coatroom lady. She was propped up, with one hand fastened to a thin wire running from the lintel over the Oruzheinaya's doorway. It was Natalya who appeared to stagger out the door; it was Natalya who stumbled and fell to the ground; it was Natalya whose arm, moved by the wire, had been raised to fend off more bullets. It was Natalya who now lay on the cobbles, as unmoving as a stone, her single gold tooth hidden by her hand.

As Alyosha said, it was probably the only really useful thing Natalya Sergeyevna had ever done.

12

THE SECOND DAY, 7:15 A.M.
Keer hadn't slept very well. And when Dovo shook him awake, Keer thrashed and groaned. Dovo was patient enough, but this made two days in a row he'd struggled to do as he was asked and get Keer up early; he was running out of temper. Blinking himself awake, Keer reconstructed the evening before, having trouble believing any of it. The hourly calls had continued until 1:00 a.m., each one requiring him to find a different phone booth. Earlier, what Keer had been afraid would happen, had. The American Embassy, in checking Intourist's list of who was inside the Oruzheinaya Palata, discovered one of the Decaturs who was not: Gary. And after seeing the ambassador, Gary had telephoned Keer.

"Can I come spend some time with you, Keer? I mean, I don't know anyone in Moscow, and the people at the embassy aren't my type—depressing, you know? I just can't sit here by myself or I'll go bananas." He said all of this in one long breath, apparently wanting to get the whole story out in one piece.

"Dad and Mom and Christy. All of them. Trapped in there with those crazy terrorists. Salt Mine, Christ. The ambassador said there's nothing much he can do, but that Washington's working on it. Anyway, can I come see you?"

Keer tried to be evasive. He'd never thought of himself as a terrorist and the word shook him. He was torn. There were the regular check-in calls to make, and having one of the indirect victims of Salt Mine visiting him in his house was a spooky thought. Still, Gary was a friend and Keer didn't have too many. Although the children of the new aristocracy were used to just about anything, most of the kids Keer's age found his clothes, his American pose, his car, too much of an affectation for them to stomach. "Well," he said finally, "I guess—sure. I'll have to go out to see some people for a little when you're here, but otherwise, hell, sure."

It had been a troubled evening. Gary was so upset about his family, and Keer so nervous, the tension was palpable. Gary frequently seemed near tears with worry. Most of all, he was deathly afraid of being alone; each time Keer left to make one of his reports, Gary looked abandoned. He never asked Keer what his mysterious disappearances were about, but Keer could sense his panic at being left by himself. In the end, Gary asked if he could spend the night, and Keer didn't have the heart to refuse; Gary was installed in a guest room by a disapproving Dovo, who considered all Americans dangerous.

That morning, driving toward a phone booth near Pushkin Square—it was one he hadn't used yet—Keer noticed that there was a lot of curious activity on the street; KGB men were stopping cars and making the drivers produce their identity cards; even buses, he saw, were being halted at random and all of the passengers made to get out and show their papers. Later, having lunch at the Hotel Metropol, he was to discover the KGB had gone over the hotel's rooms one at a time and checked and double-checked the guests.

The KGB was everywhere. People walking down the street were stopped for no apparent reason and made to produce their documents; their names were searched for on master lists the agents carried on clipboards. Occasionally, you would see someone grabbed by the KGB, and after a brief struggle, dragged away. From one of the foreign newspapermen who hung out at the Metropol bar, Keer learned that the small outbuildings in Gorky Park were checked before sunrise that morning; lines of Moscow police spread through the park and poked under bushes and through copses, looking for anyone who could not produce reliable evidence of who he was and what he was doing there. The same correspondent told Keer that he heard every apartment house in Moscow would shortly be given the same treatment.

Although Keer's personal documents were in perfect order, and his father's position would immunize him against anything more than a cursory check, the sight of the KGB turning Moscow on end caused him to shudder. Chorniev's manhunt was a frightening thing to witness, especially if you were the man being hunted.

• Early that morning, Klin had moved his base from Volodya's office to the Vodovzvodnaya Tower. He and two other men stood on the parapet of the tower, all of them struggling to focus their field glasses. The wind tore at the edges of the parapet, making a mournful, moaning sound as it passed across the uneven stones of the old building. Directly opposite the Oruzheinaya, the tower gave the clearest view of the building from anywhere on the Kremlin wall.

The equipment—the telephones and the tape machines—had been installed in the damp chamber just below where the three men stood; Kapitan Sokolov was installed along with them. Probably, Klin suspected, to report everything he did to Pskov.

The wind blew harder, and Klin lowered the field glasses and forced his fur hat farther down; this made his head so hot his scalp began to itch. Swearing, Klin removed the hat entirely. The KGB doctor finally achieved clear focus on his own field glasses and grunted.

"She was not shot here. No blood on the cobblestones. Body put there after she was shot."

"I saw her—the hostage—move her hands," began Klin and then stopped. Something the head museum guard beside him was saying chilled him worse than any wind could.

"That woman is no hostage. I think—no, I'm sure—it is Natalya Sergeyevna. Yes, definitely. Natalya. She is the cloakroom attendant in the Oruzheinaya."

"Damn." Klin headed for the iron stairway, furious with himself. He'd let Salt Mine make an ass of him. The "hostage" was already dead when she appeared to stagger from the Oruzheinaya. Worse, she was no hostage but a Soviet pensioner, an aging cloakroom attendant. Salt Mine had outmaneuvered him to get their phone lines reconnected. For a moment, Klin considered cutting their communications again, but decided listening to the outside man's conversations might provide a clue to where he was. Besides, next time Salt Mine might use a real hostage. Spinning around, he glowered at the doctor and the museum's head attendant. "Not a word of this to anyone, either of you."

Klin clumped down the stairs into the steamy room. Salt Mine. Those bastards.

• Turning the corner onto Prospekt Mira from the Riga Railroad Station, the Neck suddenly found his way blocked by two small sedans. Horn-blowing is not permitted in Moscow except in an emergency, so the Neck leaned out the cab's window and yelled instead.

His swearing ended in the middle of a long, complicated Russian oath. Some sixth sense was whispering in the Neck's ear, warning him; the three men on the sidewalk near where he was stopped had a suspicious look. The Neck had had this feeling of danger—the sounding of some inner alarm—many times, only to be proved wrong. Today, the sense was stronger than usual. He was planning to leave Moscow at the end of the day's tour, staying on that long only to avoid raising questions. Quickly, he began backing the taxi to get around the two stalled cars.

His inner alarm had sounded too late. The door on the driver's side was suddenly yanked open, and a strong hand clamped itself around his left arm, pulling him partway out of the taxi. Like an animal, he responded automatically. His feet were still in the cab and one hand was still on the wheel; jamming down the accelerator, the Neck shot the taxi forward, dragging the KGB man with him as the cab gathered speed. The grip of the hand grew tighter, and the man's feet were scrambling, trying to get a toehold inside the cab. The Neck shot the taxi through spaces in traffic far too small to negotiate safely; a block farther on, he managed to brush the KGB man against a passing bus, at the same time beating the hand around his arm with the heavy club he always kept on the seat beside him.

The man let go and fell to the road; in his rear-view mirror the Neck could see traffic slamming to a halt as cars dodged and swerved to avoid hitting him. For a brief moment the Neck felt safe enough to consider where he could ditch the cab; he barely saw the car that came directly at him from a side street. With a crunching of fenders, he was forced to the curb. Three KGB men jumped out and dragged him from his seat. They had been alerted by radio and were waiting. Without asking questions or even identifying themselves, the men began pounding the Neck with their fists and their truncheons. As the Neck screamed, he saw passersby hurry away, pointedly looking in the opposite direction; no one wanted to be a witness to what the KGB did.

The Neck's vision began blurring as a cloud of red mist lowered itself across his consciousness. The last thing he thought was that the KGB would demand to know things, would ask questions he prayed to God he didn't know the answers to. From somewhere inside himself he heard a groan.

Then the red mist closed in completely and the Neck didn't even feel himself thrown into the back of the car and raced off to Dzerzhinsky Street.

Chorniev's first harvest from the informers' underground had been reaped. Ordinarily, tips from KGB informers come in slowly, but with the kind of money the KGB was offering, leads were pouring into Dzerzhinsky Street. The first human sacrifice: the Neck. But the KGB was already following up other tips in widely separated sections of Moscow.

Across town they were already hard at work at Domodedovo. Domodedovo Airport is where Aeroflot planes take off and land on domestic runs. At five that same afternoon, an old lady, bundled in a heavy cloth coat and wearing the traditional babushka, labored up the stairs of the loading ramp. The flight was Number 412, bound for Yerevan, deep inside Soviet Armenia. Looking up, the lady was relieved to see the door of the plane. To her—the Armenian's widow—it represented escape and safety. Her travel documents were forged but authentic enough to pass muster, done by a friend of her late husband's. She wished Dhigli were here; he would be happy going home. Reaching up, she was helped through the door by an Aeroflot stewardess and for the first time in days felt safe. Until this moment, the rumors of the manhunt in Moscow had her terrified. In the small open area inside the door, she waited while they went through her papers and travel documents. Halfway down the aisle, she thought she saw an open seat. The widow was luxuriating in her new sense of safety when suddenly, behind her, she heard running feet clanging their way up the metal stairs. Years of living outside the law told her it was the KGB; her instincts told her that *she* was why they were here.

In panic, she stepped farther inside, away from the door, although she knew there was no other exit. As the men reached the doorway, they pushed the stewardess to one side. The widow began running down the aisle, screaming for help. No one responded; everybody's head disappeared into a newspaper or magazine. As she fled forward the door to the flight deck opened. In the doorway appeared a KGB man, gun in hand.

The old widow ran back and forth in the aisle, pleading with passengers, screaming at the KGB men. At one point she squeezed herself into the window seat beside a passenger and begged him to do something. Unable to fire in the crowded cabin, the KGB men converged on the spot, trying to drag her bodily across the squirming passenger. Her hands clung to him, to his clothes, to his hair, as they roughly pulled her out into the aisle and dragged her from the plane. Dzerzhinsky Street had just gained another visitor.

The final person scheduled for a trip to Dzerzhinsky Street today did not go gracefully. In her room on the top floor of Number 31, Dashnovaya Street, Comrade Goda sat staring forlornly at the empty vodka bottle. Those shadowy tenants of hers—Dimmy and Klemet, they claimed their names were—had gone, left without a word, disappeared without even the kindness of a farewell bottle. The nerves in her fingertips tingled from a need that only the clear, cold security of vodka could fill. She thought of the daily supply Dimmy and Klemet had provided, and swore. Bastards. She would get even.

Stumbling out into the long dark hall—lit only by one naked bulb hanging on a wire from the ceiling—she struggled to force the right change into the coin phone on the wall. It was no small feat; she dropped as much as she put in. Once she reached the KGB, she asked for the man who took information from block watchers. He made notes as she gave him Dimmy's and Klemet's names and descriptions, portraying the two as "extremely suspicious-looking." Black-market men, she suggested, or possibly spies. There. That would fix them. The KGB would take her revenge for her.

But the KGB man sounded more bored than anything else. The thick slur in her voice made it difficult to take Comrade Goda seriously. And when he asked her why, as a block watcher, she hadn't reported these two highly dangerous-sounding men before now, Comrade Goda felt cold fear tear at her heart. She had blundered. Quickly she backpedaled; the KGB man began laughing. Comrade Goda was not the first block watcher to get drunk and try to settle scores by calling the KGB.

Off the phone, Comrade Goda steered herself downstairs and, pooling all her money, managed to buy another bottle. The pressure on her mounted; the KGB might easily appear in person and ask again why she had delayed so long in reporting Dimmy and Klemet. Other hard questions could be thrown at her. Shaking with fear, she went to work on the vodka.

It was an unnecessary effort. At the KGB, her information had already been dismissed. The man she'd talked to had long since put Comrade Goda out of his mind; the agents were far too busy with their search for the "outside man" to bother with drunken, vengeful landladies.

It was not until late that afternoon, when one of the informers came up with the same two names—Dimmy and Klemet—that the KGB suddenly changed its mind. Perhaps Comrade Goda had made her report out of malice; perhaps she merely wanted to be paid for her information. Or perhaps she had known her tenants were members of Salt Mine all along. There were enough loose ends to warrant digging further.

The pounding on the door and the men outside yelling they were from the KGB panicked the old woman. Shaking free from a paralysis of fear she drained the tumbler of vodka and found she could move again. She bolted. Looking out her window, she stepped out onto the narrow parapet and tried to edge her way along to the window of the next apartment. By the time she got there, she was greeted by a KGB man, waiting inside the window for her. He was smiling, leaning forward in a slight bow, his arms open to her in a macabre gesture of welcome. It was too much for Comrade Goda. Closing her eyes, she calmly stepped backward, as if it were something she did every day. Comrade Goda would not do it again. Her body landed in Dashnovaya Street, a slow stain darkening the pavement around her.

At Dzerzhinsky, Chorniev had been pleased with the manhunt's progress until he heard about Comrade Goda. Earlier, she was of little interest to him, but now, like an unreasonable child, he wanted her more than anything else in the world.

"You stupid bastards," Chorniev hissed, still never raising his voice above its sinister whisper. "She probably knew who Salt Mine's outside man is and where he is hiding. The fact she killed herself to avoid giving information would indicate that. Stupid." The agents looked at each other helplessly.

"Comrade Director," began one of them, "there was nothing we could do. We had no idea she was planning to kill herself. In fact, it probably wasn't suicide at all. One could easily slip. Yes, definitely. She slipped. People in the apartment house said she was usually drunk all day."

"Perhaps. Perhaps not," Chorniev said, borrowing one of Klin's favorite phrases. The thought of Klin made him remember his ill-advised memo about him, and the fact that Borodinsky now wouldn't even return his calls. He turned to the men, his face ugly and accusing. "The second you got a report from that woman you should have followed it up. She would be alive and under interrogation right now."

"There was nothing to connect her with Salt Mine when she called."

"That is no excuse." It was a good excuse, Chorniev conceded to himself, but he was damned if he'd let the agents know it. "Resume interrogation of the others immediately. That taxi driver and the old widow from the airplane. You can't tell me they don't know who the outside man is."

"Yes, sir."

"Authorization is granted for any methods that will produce action quickly. *Any*." Chorniev watched the men scurry out of his office and felt better.

Someone was going to pay for his blunder with the memo. And in the name of the state.

• "No, the time is not right yet. I have told you that before."

"Why? When *will* the time be right?" Klin barked into the phone. "It confounds me why you should be stalling. Surely, when you executed Salt Mine, you had your demands clearly in mind."

"Salt Mine will tell you when it chooses to."

Alyosha heard Klin heave an exasperated sigh. To Klin, the sound expressed only half of what he felt. Dealing with Alyosha was an unfuriating process; the man steadfastly refused to reveal Salt Mine's demands, and this was causing Klin increasing trouble with the other ministers. Talanin was impatient. Borodinsky was using the delay to push for his assault. He had, Klin figured, just so much more time. In his head, a plan was growing that might bring Salt Mine to a bloodless conclusion, but he would have to go through Deputy Premier Chaidze for approval.

To Alyosha, the stalling was important, though the process wearied him almost as much as it did Klin. Standing on one leg in the Oruzheinaya's entrance hall, he leaned against the wall, holding the phone cradled between his shoulder and his ear, trying to light a cigarette with one hand.

Klin's voice again came over the phone, sounding as irritated as its owner. "You are making things awkward for me, my friend. And harder for yourself. There are those, you can imagine, who want to simply blow their way in—hostages or not."

"Remind them of the hostage lying outside the door here. She was the answer to your last power play."

Alyosha was startled to hear Klin laugh. "She was no hostage. Poor old Natalya Sergeyevna—the lady from the cloakroom. She was dead before you staged your little charade. Very clever. But that kind of threat only works once."

"The next dead hostage could be real."

"And the next power play could be, too."

For some minutes, there was a strained silence; both men knew they had reached a standoff, but each was searching for a way to have the last word. Alyosha solved it simply enough; he hung up.

13

THE THIRD DAY, 8:48 A.M.

Keer sat cross-legged on the cushioned window seat in his pajamas, enjoying himself hugely. For a whole day, he had fought with himself because he knew what he wanted to do was both stupid and foolish, but finally he surrendered and let desire overwhelm logic. Down the hall, he could hear Gary taking a shower, so there was no chance that he would walk in.

"Hello? Hello? Oh yes. This is Kyril Gertsen at Number Twelve Georgievsky Street—that's at the corner of Gorky. You probably know of my father, Dmitry Aleksandrovich Gertsen, Minister of Production and Industry. . . ." Keer's credentials had been presented, his address, his father's name and dizzying position in the government. With no hereditary titles, the new aristocracy resorted to this sort of shorthand to position themselves. As always, it worked. The KGB man on the other end of the phone nearly choked in his attempt to be helpful.

"Yes, *sir*, Comrade Gertsen. How can I be of service?"

"I wanted to report a man who—well, let me put it differently. I know about Salt Mine, of course; one of my father's friends, another minister, told me. And of your manhunt. I want to give you something. This man, well, it is probably nothing, of course—"

"Comrade Gertsen. Anything you can tell us will receive—"

"As you say. This man . . . you know the area; we see very few strangers or tourists here. And this man, you see—there is a telephone kiosk down the street I can see from my window—he goes in every hour and calls someone. It would be an unusual thing to do, even a couple of times. But this man was there most of yesterday. This morning, the man was outside the kiosk again. He hasn't called yet, but I know he will."

The voice on the other end had a new electricity to it,

sounding more than just anxious to please. The KGB man knew of the hourly calls to the Oruzheinaya, and making them from a booth in the most exclusive section of town would be a clever maneuver to avoid detection. "What does he look like?" the KGB man asked, trying not to let his excitement show, but waving his supervisor over with his hand. He scribbled a note explaining who was on his phone and what was happening. The supervisor picked up an earphone.

"He looks very suspicious. To me, anyway. But that isn't very objective, is it? He's about medium height, with a sort of wet-looking black mustache. Thick gray overcoat and the usual fur hat. He looks around behind him a lot. And when he's not hanging around the kiosk, he goes down the alley next to Number Eight Georgievsky. I think that's where Minister Klin lives; I haven't seen him in a few days, so I guess he's at his dacha at Kurkin. Anyway, he's not here so he's safe enough for—"

"Yes, yes, yes. Is there anything else about this man to identify him? His suit? His face? His shoes?"

"I can't see that much from here. I could go down and look, but I've been in bed with a cold so—"

"No, no, Comrade Gertsen, don't go near him. Please. But thank you," added the man hurriedly. The mention of Klin's name put the man and his supervisor into a high state of agitation. The minister's safety, along with the possibility that this actually *could* be Salt Mine's outside man, made more than perfunctory politeness impossible. "We'll handle it from here. Our thanks and the thanks of the Party."

Keer smiled and lay back against the wood of the recessed window opening. Drawing attention to himself was unforgivable. Certainly, if Alyosha knew, he would be furious. But the idea had been too delectable.

Perhaps ten minutes later, Keer watched as a small fleet of KGB cars slammed to a halt outside his window and grabbed the man with the wet mustache and gray overcoat. There was a slight scuffle as the man tried to protest, but one of the agents hit him over the head with a hard-rubber truncheon, and the fellow was unconscious by the time they dragged him into a car and drove off.

And this was how on Friday, the twentieth of November, the KGB came to arrest one of its own agents, for doing nothing more sinister than leaning against a telephone kiosk, picking his nose.

• Klin's day did not start at all well. Worse, he had a feeling it was not going to improve with time but, like a snowball rolling downhill, grow bigger and less manageable as it progressed. His bones ached from sleeping on the couch in his office; he suspected the cots in the Vodovzvodnaya Tower were more comfortable, but he couldn't imagine himself sleeping in a room full of snoring serfs like Kapitan Sokolov and the KGB monitoring team.

Blinking himself awake, Klin squirmed uncomfortably, thinking of the meeting with Deputy Premier Chaidze, set for ten o'clock. At this, Klin was to put forward his scheme for a bloodless resolution of Salt Mine. He hoped that Chaidze would then carry it to Talanin for final approval. Working with an invisible head of state like Talanin made things difficult; Chaidze was continually vacillating and deferring, waiting to get the final decisions from the absent secretary general of the Party. The memory of the bridal feast at Archangelskoye passed fleetingly across Klin's mind. He had known marrying Katusha, his niece, to the deputy premier's son would be of value someday; in a distant sense, he and Deputy Premier Chaidze were related.

That man from Salt Mine, Alyosha, had jarred him awake about seven; the men in the tower buzzed him to take the call. At the time, Klin was more than willing to; perhaps Salt Mine was now ready.

"Books," Alyosha had said. "We need books. That means in English, French, German, Russian, and Spanish."

Klin was unable to hide his annoyance. Dragging on the first cigarette of the day, he poured himself some bitter coffee from the thermos flask on his desk; the edge in his voice could not be hidden. "And that's *all*, my friend?"

"No. Playing cards. A chess set. And a checker board. *Regular* checkers. I'll spare you the embarrassment of providing the Chinese variety."

"Very funny. But this doesn't spell much progress for either of us."

Over the phone, Klin heard Alyosha laugh. "It keeps you from sleeping too late, Klin. Bad for the circulation, too much sleep." This time Klin had the pleasure of hanging up.

Now, some two hours later, Klin settled back into the ZiL and tried to enjoy the ride to Number 4, Staraya Square, home of the Central Committee. Here both Talanin and the deputy premier had their offices. It was impossible to take much pleasure in the ride, his first outing in two days. The pedestrians stared as resentfully as ever as his limousine crossed intersections against the lights, but the satisfaction had evaporated. Perhaps it was because Klin felt in the not-too-distant future he might be one of the staring pedestrians himself.

• Standing in Talanin's office, Deputy Premier Chaidze had to lean forward to get the man's words clearly. The voice was thin and fragile, although the brain guiding it was as forceful and dogmatic as ever. "What are our options? We must have options. . . ."

"Not many, Comrade Secretary." Chaidze blinked and stared at the screen of greenery the man hid behind. It was impossible to see much through the protective shield of potted palms and ficus plants surrounding him. Looking his hardest, all Chaidze could really make out of the Soviet's chief of state was his silhouette, sharply outlined by the plant lights against the clouds of steam that rose from the vaporizer. Occasionally, a hand would come into focus, when Talanin coughed and then allowed his hand to hang limply over the arm of his chair.

The room smelled. Something had been added to the vaporizer to help the secretary's breathing, and in the stifling closeness of the steam-filled room Chaidze found it difficult to draw a deep breath. He hated these daily meetings but knew they were necessary. To the Soviet, to his job. The world had not set eyes on Talanin for six months; he himself had seen little more of him for the last three than this ghostly silhouette. Talanin was a vain man and, whatever the disease was, would allow no one, not even Chaidze, to see his face. Only his doctor and nurse, who waited stiffly outside his office, knew what he really looked like.

A minor fit of coughing passed and Talanin spoke. "Nonsense. There are always options."

Chaidze considered, trying to find some; Talanin was being difficult, deliberately, he suspected. "Well, we could blast our way into the Oruzheinaya, but that probably means the end of the hostages."

"So?"

"Most of them are Americans," Chaidze reminded Talanin. "Their government has been very forceful on the subject. They insist we take whatever steps necessary to get their citizens out safely. *Détente*—"

"Was useful as an offset to China. It is something to be considered only when it is to our advantage."

Chaidze pretended not to see the hand, yellowed and shrunken, as it came into focus again after another fit of coughing. "There *are* some advantages, Comrade Secretary. One could almost say necessities. Trade. Industrial expertise. Computers. Wheat. The agreement to appear uninvolved in each other's spheres of influence. World sentiment. This damned human rights thing."

"Their president doesn't believe in it any more than I do. A pose. A gesture. A political maneuver."

Rubbing his forehead, Chaidze hesitated. They were touching on an area where they had long had difficulty finding common ground. "Comrade Secretary, are you completely certain of that?"

The voice grew petulant. "Absolutely. If he really believed in human rights, do you think he'd be trying to normalize relations with Cuba? Even with *China?* Or with Torrijos of Panama or Stroessner of Paraguay? Nonsense. He supports Idi Amin—who would like to eat him for dinner—for the American Negro vote. He smiles on that crazy man—Bokassa, is it?—who claims he is emperor of Africa. For the Negro vote. He condemns Rhodesia and South Africa—for the Negro vote. What does he want—those two countries run by Amin and Bokassa? It's all politics—he criticizes countries like that because they are small and far away. Safe enough. He criticizes *us*. Not so safe. But politically popular. So, yes, Chaidze, I am sure." Talanin attempted to laugh, but it brought on another fit of coughing. The dim silhouette turned to stare at Chaidze through the palms, swaying from the flailing of Talanin's hand. "Don't bother me with your childish questions. It brings on my cough."

Shaken by the sudden snappishness, Chaidze waited for Talanin's wheezing spasm to end. He would try the other extreme. "Another option, Comrade Secretary, is, of course, to negotiate Salt Mine's demands."

"What *are* the demands?"

"We don't know yet. Money, perhaps. Freedom for themselves, certainly. A public statement of some sort, possibly—"

"Never. In a million years, never."

"We are left then with only the option of attack."

Talanin began to say something but was apparently so outraged the cough took over. His shadow was racked by it; at the end of the seizure, Chaidze could hear him breathing hard. "You are dense, Chaidze. That is why you are deputy premier and I am secretary general. Of course there are other options—options within options. Get hold of Shtanov. Have him contact the American secretary of state. If they believe so strongly in human rights, they should start with their own citizens inside the Oruzheinaya Palata. A plan, make a plan. To appear that we have given in, but build into it a device that allows the hostages to be freed, while eliminating the terrorists. The secretary of state will object. Do not be bothered. Face to face with a crisis, both he and the American president are weak . . . unable to make up their minds. They will agree, even if they have to resort to a little deceit. . . . They have had enough practice in it. . . . Tell no one, Chaidze. Let our own people carry on here in their usual, ineffective way."

Something behind the palms crashed as the coughing became so violent the silhouette could be seen to thrash in its attempt to get a clear breath of air. The spasm lasted perhaps four minutes, during which Chaidze became terrified. Then, the voice returned, hoarse and wheezy. "Send in the doctor. It is time for oxygen."

Chaidze left quickly, stopping in the hall to relay Talanin's message to the doctor, still sitting stiffly in the straight-backed chair. Nodding to the nurse, the doctor got slowly to his feet and put his hand on the knob of Talanin's door. He paused and stared at Chaidze, apparently to counter the look of alarm on the deputy premier's face. "It is nothing to be concerned about, Comrade. He needs the oxygen at regular intervals." His eyes bore into Chaidze. "Particularly if he is annoyed. . . ."

As the door opened, the smell from Talanin's room swept out into the hall. The silhouette was still visible behind the screen of greenery, the hands beating the air for breath. Chaidze fled.

• At quarter before eleven, Alyosha heard Avraam shout from the front area of the Oruzheinaya. Running up, he joined the man in staring open-mouthed at what was happening. "*Sobaka*," he grunted. "Tell everyone to get to their emergency stations. The foot soldiers up here, too. Have Lisenka keep the hostages as calm as she can."

The sounds of snorting and clanking were clearly audible now, and Alyosha knew they would produce another wave of hysteria among their captives. He looked back out the window, trying to figure whether his time was best spent studying this new, frightening situation, or yelling at Klin on the phone. Simultaneously, the gates of the Kremlin down by the Council of Ministers Buildings, the Building of the Supreme Soviet, and the Arsenal, swung open. The Nikolskaya, the Spasskaya, the Troitskaya. Through the gates rolled the T-10s, pennants flapping arrogantly from their aerials. Behind them in semicrouching position, came the Special Tactical Forces, their automatic rifles hanging loosely from their hands, their heads slowly swinging back and forth—automatons on attack—as they checked for snipers.

Alyosha felt a coldness grip his stomach. In spite of everything, the authorities were going ahead with their threatened assault. When he tried Klin, a panicked Kapitan Sokolov said he wasn't there. He was at the Central Committee Building, and no one could get to him. And that he and Colonel-General Pskov were as confused as Salt Mine was. "Nobody knows what is going on. . . ."

"Alyosha," called Avraam. "Come. Quick."

Instead of continuing toward the Oruzheinaya, the tanks and the tactical forces had pulled themselves up short. They formed a line that ran from the Arsenal—where Kapitan Sokolov's headquarters had been—across the cobblestone court to the Tsar's Tower. Awkwardly, the T-10s turned on their tracks so that their guns pointed toward the Oruzheinaya.

Alyosha had no way of knowing it, but the fact that the forces advanced no farther than the perimeter of the government buildings was the result of a compromise in the Council of Ministers. With both Klin and the deputy premier absent—at their ten o'clock meeting at Central Committee headquarters—Marshal Borodinsky had made his move. He had called the meeting, he had chaired the meeting, and the first item he had raised at the meeting was an immediate all-out assault against Salt Mine. The arguing was ferocious but futile; the way power was lined up in the Council of Ministers meant that, with Klin and Chaidze absent, the outcome was inevitable.

Once again, it was Foreign Minister Shtanov who changed the course of things. Because they were unable to reach Deputy Minister Chaidze—Shtanov tried the Central Committee offices twice and was rebuffed each time—a lot of arguing hammered out a compromise that left everyone unsatisfied. Marshal Borodinsky could take his tanks and soldiers inside the gates, yes, but he had to stop once he'd established a line of defense around the government buildings themselves. No assault on the Oruzheinaya. No firing. The equipment and men would be in position if the deputy premier, after checking with Talanin, wanted to go farther.

But the compromise was something Alyosha knew nothing about. It wouldn't have been acceptable to him anyway. A line of soldiers around the Council of Ministers Building and the Supreme Soviet meant men could take up position near the rear entrance to Lenin's Tomb. In fact, when the advancing task force suddenly halted, that was Alyosha's first assumption. Dimmy, Klemet, the hostages inside, and Lenin's body would be Klin's for the taking.

"What's happening?" said Lisenka from beside him; he had not seen her join him at the window, and her voice made him jump.

"I don't know. But it's not good. I tried to get Klin, but they said he was at the Central Committee building. That kapitan said they were as surprised as we were. He may be telling the truth, but how do I know?"

Alyosha was surprised to feel her hand squeeze his arm. He was almost as surprised that he didn't yank it away. Instead, he felt a series of shudders run through his body and a sudden warm trembling, but did not pull his arm back. The fact mystified him. "Don't worry, Alyosha," Lisenka said softly. "They won't do anything, not with all these Americans in here. . . ."

On the wall of the outer hall, the telephone rang, its strident sound shattering the hush that had fallen over the room. It was Klin.

At the other end, waiting for Salt Mine's phone to be answered, a rattled Vasily Klin ran his hand over his head without thinking. The rough, scaly skin made him yank his hand down angrily. Deputy Premier Chaidze was almost as furious as Klin when they got back to the Kremlin and saw what Borodinsky had done. But once the soldiers were there, it would be an impossible loss of face to pull the force back. Finally, Klin heard Alyosha pick up his phone.

"Get those damned soldiers out of there," roared Alyosha. "Pull them back outside the gates or accept the consequences."

"I cannot do that."

"Very well." Alyosha hung up the phone with a plastic

crunch. Swearing, he hit the stone wall of the entrance hall with his fist. It was time.

• Although it was cold as only November in Moscow can be, the sun offered a certain pale warmth, provided you could find a protected place to enjoy it. The booth on the south side of Kalinin Prospekt was bathed in sunshine, which is why Keer chose it. It was also not far from the Arbat Restaurant, where he planned to meet Gary for lunch. One of the problems with Gary as a house guest was that Keer's plans had to be tailored around him. In ordinary circumstances, Keer would have loved it; Gary was good company, even in the situation he found himself in now. But Keer's hourly disappearances to make his calls grew increasingly difficult to explain.

His conversation with Alyosha consisted of a single sentence from Salt Mine's leader:

"Listen carefully. It is time. Let the cock crow."

A surge of excitement raced through Keer. He checked his watch and did some figuring. Lunch with Gary would have to be abandoned. At the Arbat, there was time only to tell Gary and to apologize. Then, very nearly running, Keer raced for his car. The moment for him to take center stage had arrived.

• Alyosha's curious order on the phone brought action from people other than Keer. With misgivings, Chorniev studied Klin. Klin's visit to KGB headquarters, brief as it was, left Chorniev shaken. Klin paced back and forth across his office, the splotches on his scalp glowing ominously.

" 'Let the cock crow.' What the hell's *that* mean?" Klin stopped pacing and spun to face Chorniev. "Dammit, Chorniev, find that bastard outside man or you'll be—outside yourself. By now your interrogations—"

"They all keep claiming they don't know who he is," Chorniev whined, trying to keep his eyes away from Klin's head.

"Did you expect anything else?"

"Of course not. But maybe they *don't* know. We've gotten a certain amount out of the cab driver—he's a member of the WJA, the WJA put up the money, things like that—but nothing on the outside man. Every device has been tried. We have one final pressure tactic to try, and if that doesn't work, I guess we must assume the driver's telling the truth."

"Squeeze him," Klin ordered. "Dammit, Chorniev, squeeeeeeze him." Chorniev watched nervously as the minister of State security lowered his head and stalked out of the office, slamming the door hard behind him.

With a sigh, Chorniev walked out of his office and down the gloomy tunnel that linked KGB headquarters with Lubyanka. Unlike many KGB men, Chorniev genuinely loathed the primitive forms of interrogation. But there was no time for the subtler methods. No time for the use of psychology, brainwashing, mindbending drugs, or disorientation techniques. Their only recourse was simple brutality. Physical torture to extract some piece of information. And like a victim on the medieval rack, whether the man knew anything or not, he either talked or was pulled apart. The thought always made Chorniev shudder. This came from no sensitivity on Chorniev's part; he could all too easily imagine finding himself in the same position. It had happened to KGB chiefs before.

As he walked down the tunnel with his strange scuttling movement, his heels echoed off the concrete; Chorniev, as he always did, counted the number of lights overhead. He had never known why; it was like a little boy counting the cracks in the pavement. There were forty-seven bulbs between the KGB building and the cellar interrogation rooms of Lubyanka, the pristine, onetime insurance building. As he got to forty, his steps grew slower, a vain effort to postpone what was ahead of him.

Outside the main interrogation room, a guard came stiffly to attention as Chorniev arrived. Leaning over, the guard knocked on the door, then swung its heavy metal weight open for Chorniev. The room stank. They always did. Of sweat and urine and screaming. The head interrogator, Yuri Pyotrovich Kuznetsov, saw who it was and hurried over to Chorniev. Instinctively, Chorniev felt himself back away. Kuznetsov was a huge man, deathly pale, without a single hair on his unevenly shaped skull. His face wore a fixed smile, as fixed as the smile pasted on a corpse. Interrogation was his lifework, and he enjoyed his job thoroughly. "Nothing more yet, Comrade. But this schedule . . ."

Chorniev winced as the man pulled out a chair for him, the smile still unmoving, and suggested a cup of coffee. Chorniev refused. In front of him, slumped in a chair, sat the Neck. His face was swollen and bloody, and both of his eyes were puffed shut. There were ugly welts all across his body, even on the tops of his feet. Wires stuck out from behind him, one running, Chorniev knew, up his rectum. The probe at its end would be pressed against the hypersensitive prostate. The other lead ran to his genitals, completing the circuit. Kuznetsov nodded and the current was sent through the Neck again; his eyes bulged open; a wavering groan came from the discolored lips. Around him, a faint wisp of smoke arose, and the air seemed foul with the smell of burning hair.

"Who is the outside man? Tell me, who is Salt Mine's outside man?" shouted Kuznetsov into the Neck's ear.

There was no answer but another groan and a mumbled invocation to God that he didn't know. Kuznetsov turned to Chorniev. "It could be true. Either that or he has great courage. Of course, he's a powerful brute . . . an ox."

To Chorniev, the timing of the last jolt seemed too neat. He suspected Kuznetsov had given the man this shock mostly to prove his diligence.

"I think," said Kuznetsov, "it is time to play our last card. That, or write the man off."

The next half hour Chorniev spent wishing he were somewhere else. Psychological brainwashing sessions he always found fascinating, conducted by doctors with whom Chorniev could talk as to fellow professionals. But this . . . Kuznetsov was a brutal pig. Only the knowledge that Klin would pose detailed questions, should the interrogation fail, made Chorniev stay.

A KGB man poured water over the Neck. Another agent stood behind him and held his eyes open. A small metal door to the right flew open and a girl of about twelve was shoved in by a matron; the girl was terrified and stood trembling in her nightgown. The second she saw the Neck she screamed, "Poppa!" and tried to run to him but was yanked back by the matron, whose expression of grimness was as fixed as Kuznetsov's smile.

The Neck, seeing and hearing his daughter, groaned. The groan was not of pain, but of realization. Dimly, through the waves of red that filled his head, he wondered how they had ever found her—or even knew she existed.

He was unaware he had provided the information himself. During one of the sessions, so painful he no longer remembered it, he had told them his real name—Zelinsky. His work papers—using a false name—were quickly exposed as fraudulent, but in filling them out, the Neck had resorted to a familiar name to put down as his birthplace: Kreshatik, a Jewish community not far from Lvov in the Ukraine. It was where he had lived before Moscow. Investigations there revealed that Zelinsky—the Neck—had no wife; she had died five years earlier. But they also revealed he had a twelve-year-old daughter, Serafima, being raised by her grandmother, the Neck's mother. In the middle of the night, the KGB dragged Sera from her bed and flew her to Moscow, not even giving her time to get into her clothes.

To Chorniev, what happened next was a nightmare blur. Kuznetsov yelling in Zelinsky's ear that if he didn't tell them of Salt Mine's outside man, they would use his daughter as a lever to get it out of him. The child crying "Poppa, Poppa" over and over again. Zelinsky repeating his ritual answer that he didn't know. Someone ripping off Sera's nightgown and forcing her backward. Kuznetsov roaring at Zelinsky. Zelinsky mumbling his litany and pleading with them to leave Sera alone. The child crying "Poppa, Poppa!" as her body was explored by one of the KGB men. And suddenly the pleadings of the child turned to shrieks of pain as she was raped. Repeatedly. Each time, Kuznetsov repeating his question. From Zelinsky, there were no longer any answers or denials. He was sobbing, the tears streaming down his face and leaving two broad white tracks under his eyes where the blood was washed away.

Chorniev left, suddenly pale. This was the way of the KGB and always had been. Chorniev was neither a gentle man nor a kind one, but this was too much to accept.

Behind him, he heard the metal door open and saw Kuznetsov stick his head into the hall, the frozen smile unchanged. "Still nothing. I don't know. Shall we continue?"

"No," Chorniev heard himself say. "He doesn't know." Turning, he walked the forty-seven light bulbs from Lubyanka back to the KGB building, its white lace curtains and shiny brass fixtures a disturbing mockery. Swearing to himself, he wondered why he had given such a reckless order. It was not the act of a survivor.

14

THE THIRD DAY, 12:05 P.M.

The tie was not right. Looking at himself in the faded mirror of the equally faded Metropol, Andrew Jax yanked it off and walked over to the closet to find another. When it was tied, patted, and the shirt buttoned, he surveyed himself again. Not bad. For his age, not bad at all. Like many short men, Jax substituted aggressiveness for height; this same effort to compensate also made him an extremely vain man. The year before, when Jax noticed the first sprinkling of gray, he panicked; by now, Jax rationalized the increasing grayness as distinguished.

Outside his door, he heard a muted cough followed by a light knock. Standing there was a bellboy—like everything else in the Metropol, ancient—holding a message in his hand. With a slight bow, the man handed Jax an Intourist envelope. Typed on the cover was Jax's name and the words: "CIRCUS TICKETS. THIS AFT'S PERFORMANCE. PLS DELIVER IMMED." To make sure, the message was typed in both English and Russian.

"I didn't order tickets for the circus," he told the bellboy in bewilderment.

"Yes, yes! Tickets for the circus," agreed the man, nodding with a broad smile. Slowly, Jax realized the man could speak a little English but didn't understand any at all. "Happy circus," continued the bellboy.

Exasperated, Jax tried to get his message across. "I . . . do not . . . have . . . tickets . . . to the circus." The bellboy continued to smile and nod. Jax tried his taxicab Russian. "*Ne menye billet . . .*" The effort collapsed when he was unable to produce the word for circus; it was right there on the envelope, of course, but the Cyrillic alphabet had always been unfathomable to him.

Just as Jax was about to hand the envelope back to the

bellboy and yell something at him—with non-English-speaking Russians, yelling works wonders—the telephone in his room rang. "Just a minute," he said to the bellboy, stepping inside his room to answer it. The telephone message was short and cryptic, as unfathomable as the Cyrillic lettering.

"Take the envelope, Mr. Jax. What is inside is not tickets." The phone began buzzing; the caller had hung up.

The bellboy was tipped—the Soviets claim no tips are accepted in the USSR, but no one has ever been known to refuse one—and Jax sat in his chair studying the note inside the Intourist envelope.

> Dear Mr. Jax:
> If you want to know what all the excitement at the Kremlin is, I can give you the whole scoop on Salt Mine. . . .

Jax's brow furrowed as he stared into space. The entire community of foreign correspondents in Moscow were scrambling to find out what was going on inside the Kremlin. The day before, he went to see the soldiers and tanks surrounding the walls for himself. But *Salt Mine?* No one had mentioned a word about anything called Salt Mine.

> You are already famous. But this story could cop you a Pulitzer. . . .

As he read, Jax tried to form some picture of the writer. From the slang used, he sounded American. And young. But there was something wrong with the language: It was *too* American. A Russian? Christ, who knew what he was? Jax skipped quickly through the details of how to make contact with the writer; what fascinated him was the last paragraph.

> If you don't show, I'll know you're not interested. Well, there's plenty of other correspondents in Moscow. (If your KGB tails are still on you when you get there, take off the sunglasses you should wear for identification. Later, I'll set up another time to meet.) Hope to see you at one-thirty. DESTROY AFTER READING.
>
> K.
> for Salt Mine

Jax was supposed to leave for Chicago tomorrow. Well, whether this turned out to be something or not, it sounded like fun. Adolescent John le Carré. And in the unlikely event it *did* show itself important, he'd call Chicago and change plans.

Next problem: Where the hell did you buy a pair of sunglasses this time of year in Moscow? A solution came to him. He smiled and walked back to study himself again in the mirror. Plenty of other correspondents in Moscow, hell.

• When the Russians decide to build something—a store, a stadium, a greenhouse, a theater—they tend to think on a gigantic scale. There is something about their approach to life that reflects the size of their country, immediately reminding one of Texans, as fond of big buildings, big spaces, and big noises as the Russians.

This colossus complex extends to something as basic as the swimming pool. The Moskva Swimming Pool is of indeterminate size, but you get some idea of its scale when you consider the pool holds twenty-five hundred people at a time, enough to make any Texan groan with envy. The pool, on the Kropotkin Embankment of the Moskva River, is surrounded by a spotless man-made beach and is so well heated that even in the dead of winter the water and air around the pool are invitingly warm. As a result, Muscovites use it year round.

One-thirty gave Jax little time. He'd finally found a bathing suit at the Beriozka Shop at the Intourist. The Beriozka shops are open only to foreigners. They are used to tourists and generally have just about anything. Even here, though, the dark glasses were unavailable. It was then Jax remembered the manager of the Chase Manhattan. Its offices, fittingly enough, are in the transplanted Plaza, the Hotel Metropol. The man wore dark glasses for some sort of eye condition, even in midwinter. He knew Jax, as the columnist frequently went to the bank to draw on his letter of credit. Walking in, Jax strode over to the manager, leaned across his desk, and snatched the dark glasses off his head. "I'll explain later" was all he told the startled banker before stalking out.

At the pool Jax felt self-conscious in his dark glasses; no one else there found the sun as bright as he apparently did. The pool was like any public pool in the world: noisy, loud with the sounds of children splashing, children laughing, children crying. The air was so thick with chlorine your eyes smarted. Glancing around, Jax could see he was still free of his KGB tail; he'd shaken the man by a quick changing of taxis shortly after he left his hotel.

Gingerly, he lowered himself into the water; it was so overheated it was almost uncomfortable, a giant bathtub filled with playful Russians enjoying the benefits of socialism. About halfway down the pool, out toward one of the shallow areas, Jax saw the man he'd come to meet. Man, hell; he was more a boy. He wore the red-and-white striped bathing suit the letter had described, along with snorkling goggles pushed high up on his forehead. As soon as he saw Jax, he began swimming to a deeper section; with no children, these areas were far less crowded. Jax swam toward him. "Circus?" he whispered softly.

"Mr. Jax."

"This story of yours . . ."

"Swim over to the right. There's nobody there."

Treading water in the middle of the pool, the steam rising off the water as the warm air met the frigid winds of Moscow above, Keer gave Jax a complete rundown on Salt Mine. At first, Jax found the story impossible to believe, but the boy was persuasive. "Call your embassy. Mention the name of 'Salt Mine.' Their reaction alone should prove it's true. Or, if you have the contacts, try the name at the Ministry of Information. Be careful there, though. They could lock you up for just knowing about it. To keep you quiet."

Jax felt his disbelief weakening, but was instinctively careful. "How many Americans did you say were inside?"

"Forty-six." The boy was treading water and seemed to be reaching for something below the surface. "Forty-six in the Oruzheinaya, twelve more being held inside Lenin's Tomb."

The Lenin's Tomb thing was the part of Salt Mine that tickled Jax the most. The sheer irreverence of it, the neatness with which it punctured the myth of the USSR's unshakability, the poke in the eye it gave the grim-visaged Soviet pomposity, delighted Jax's sense of humor. For some reason, at first it was also the hardest part of Salt Mine to believe. Yet, Jax realized, the tomb backed up against the Kremlin's walls, and if you could seize one, you could seize the other.

"Reach into the back of my bathing suit," said Keer. "There's a plastic envelope with the names, addresses, and nationalities of all the hostages. Excuse the typing; I did it myself."

Jax did as he was told. When the boy turned his back

toward him, Jax reached under water and slipped one hand down the back of his trunks; the thin, plastic envelope came out easily. "Now," said the boy, "put it into your own trunks and when you get home, try some of those names out. The hotels they're staying at are all there. The hotels, of course, will try to give you some story—the person you're asking for suddenly went on a tour to the Black Sea or something like that. Anyway, you'll find not one of them can be reached." Keer seemed to have forgotten to keep swimming and swallowed a mouthful of water. Without pausing, he resurfaced and began talking again. "Or try some of the names out at their embassies. Just mention the hostage's name and Salt Mine; the embassy will fall apart. Everybody's trying desperately to keep it quiet—to protect their nationals."

"I shall. But now, about you . . ."

"Later. We'll meet somewhere again tomorrow. I'll have more on what's happening inside by then. I talk to Salt Mine on the phone several times a—"

The boy stopped. He'd seen Jax suddenly remove his dark glasses and hold them up to the sun as if he couldn't see well. The boy got the message. Ignoring him now, the boy—Keer, he'd said his name was?—trod water sideways for a little, then turned and swam into a crowd near one of the shallower parts of the pool.

Jax didn't know how the KGB man had found him there, but it was the same man he thought he'd shaken earlier. Probably through one of the cab drivers. In any case, the man caught up with him so late that Jax's business with Keer was completed; their conversation earlier had apparently gone unnoticed. Jax found his heart still pounding. He knew this meant he believed the boy's story, although he would still check the name "Salt Mine" at the embassies. And double-check it by calling the hotels.

In spite of his earlier reservations, Jax knew the story was real; the checking was no more than newsman's insurance. One thing the boy said was going to make things difficult: "The story has to be out by early this evening. If it isn't, well, I'll find myself another correspondent."

The hell he would. This could be the biggest story of his career. And one that belonged to him alone—him, Andrew Jax. The news would hit the streets by early evening or he'd find a new profession.

• Between Moscow and New York, once daylight savings is

out of the way, there is an eight-hour time difference. This bothered Jax. Ideally, his first story should hit the States an hour before the evening news; instead, it would arrive on the East Coast at around ten in the morning. For a brief moment or two, Jax considered delaying his transmission, but dismissed the thought; Keer had been very explicit on the timing, and there was more to be lost than gained by breaking his promise to him—more background, more hard news. Assuming he and the boy could stay out of the KGB's hands.

Jax had never written a story as speedily as he wrote this one. Given time, he could have done better, but time was the one thing he didn't have. "Kept secret from the world," it began, "a group of dissidents known as Salt Mine two days ago hijacked the mighty Kremlin itself. Lenin's Tomb, where the founder of Communism lies frozen in plastic, was also seized. The hostages held in the Oruzheinaya Palata (Kremlin Museum) and the tomb include fifty-eight American tourists, whose names and home addresses are below. . . ."

Originally, Jax planned to sign the article with his by-line. At the last minute, he decided against it, using a pseudonym, Ambrose Jackson, instead. It would fool no one, but it would at least give the Soviets an excuse to pretend they didn't know who wrote the story. Otherwise, to save face, Jax would be thrown either out of the country or into Lubyanka.

Earlier, he had made arrangements for his story to be flown out by UPI courier to Finland; filing it in Moscow would run afoul of the censor. From Finland, the news would be telexed to the States and to his syndicate's offices across Europe.

By 4:00 p.m., Moscow time, the news flash was in an envelope and on its way. By five, it was on the Helsinki ticker. And by six, the whole waking world knew about Salt Mine. A certain number could even guess who'd filed the story.

Getting dressed for a reception at the French Embassy, the diminutive figure of Andrew Jax stopped again in front of the mirror. So he was short; a damned fighting rooster, he decided. He felt good, which frequently even made him feel tall. As Keer had promised, Salt Mine was providing him with the story of a lifetime. Exclusive.

• For a long time, Alyosha stood staring out the window of the Oruzheinaya with Misha. Out in the courtyard, the tank drivers and soldiers of the Special Tactical Forces were struggling to keep warm in the cold wind. Both Alyosha and

Misha knew that the soldiers they saw were only the tip of the iceberg. Occasionally, from the roof, they had spotted others at the windows of the Building of the Supreme Soviet, the Council of Ministers Building, and the former Arsenal, now the barracks of Kapitan Sokolov's 319th Infantry. Soldiers could also be seen near all of the Kremlin towers, particularly those close to the Oruzheinaya. Shooting out the searchlights now would be no easy matter: Instead of the mere two visible yesterday, additional lights could be glimpsed clustered around each of the twenty towers as well as stretched out along the entire length of the Kremlin walls. Someone, Alyosha conceded grudgingly, was being extremely thorough.

"What do you make of them?" Alyosha asked Misha, watching the half-frozen soldiers in the courtyard. A sergeant had organized calisthenics to warm his troops up; they were jumping up and down, clapping their hands over their heads in rhythm, the submachine guns clanking heavily against their backs.

"It's as if someone stopped them halfway here. You were in the Special Task Forces. Would you ever allow your men to line up the way those poor bastards are? Never. Like toy soldiers. Two bursts, and you nail the whole bunch of them."

"Probably. But our own emergency stations could stand a lot of improvement, too. Move the hostages to the second floor, possibly. Less chance of getting caught in cross fire. And, dammit, we've got to get those soldiers and tanks back outside the gates."

Misha nodded but didn't appear very hopeful.

At about three, Lisenka told Alyosha that the two German children were sick. Tbor could not say with what, but they were throwing up and running high fevers. An hour later, one of the adults came down with the same thing. "Can't you figure out what the hell it is?" Alyosha demanded of Tbor.

"It could be anything. I have supplies, but no lab. The fevers are extraordinary; I've rarely seen any that high."

"Keep trying. If there's a drug that'll help, Klin will send it in. At least, I think he will. But we can't get it until we know what to ask for."

"I'll try. But without a lab . . ." Tbor's voice trailed off into nothingness. For Tbor, a moment of decision had arrived. His efforts at diagnosing the sickness were futile. There was only one thing of which he was sure: Whatever it was, more would come down with it. If Alyosha had another doctor sent in—he'd muttered something about that twice now—his own usefulness to Salt Mine was over. There would no longer be any reason for them to keep him alive. As Tbor struggled to find a possible way around his problem, Lisenka came over and told him two more hostages were sick. Grimly, Tbor's hands went about their poking, prodding, searching. His mind, however, had already found what he was looking for.

• Lenin's Tomb was not without its share of desperate men. When Alyosha had demanded books of Klin, he was thinking more of Dimmy and Klemet than of Blaine Decatur, who originally made the request. In one of their frequent telephone exchanges, Dimmy explained they were beginning to go crazy in the tight confines of the tomb. Unlike the Oruzheinaya, the tomb was windowless and airless; a sense of entrapment was making everyone claustrophobic. "My friend," Dimmy said to Alyosha, "I would even settle for a technical journal. Anything." There was a pause before Dimmy added, "Of course, a technical journal would make Klemet delirious; to him that *is* great literature."

Alyosha laughed but worried too. Boredom was dangerous; it made a man groggy and lethargic. The reading matter was delivered, but neither Dimmy nor Klemet found it dissipated their torpor much.

It was a torpor that was not unnoticed by one of their prisoners, a Hungarian hostage named Janos Bognar. Joining forces with a captured soldier who spoke his language, Bognar began to plan and watch and plan some more.

One fact emerged from their observations: the two Salt Mine men took turns standing watch; one would sleep, one would sit, usually with his back against the wall, his hand holding the "deadman's throttle" trigger for the plastique. Roughly every hour, the man on duty would dial a number on the internal phone—presumably checking in with the main Salt Mine force at the Oruzheinaya. Sometimes—particularly when the phoning-in assignment fell to the shorter, round-faced dissident with the rimless glasses—surveillance of the hostages was less than adequate.

The two of them, Bognar, the Hungarian, and the Russian soldier, sat in one corner, fretting impatiently. For the moment, there was little else they could do.

• By four-thirty that afternoon, Tbor knew he was in real

trouble. Three more hostages had come down with whatever the disease was; Alyosha was beginning to talk openly of asking Klin to send in another doctor. Tbor knew his move would have to be made now.

At four-forty-five Lisenka told him an additional hostage was down sick; he told her he would join her at the rear in a moment. For Misha, he had a different story. "It's Avraam," Tbor said. "Lisenka wants you to talk to him. He's got it, but he won't follow my orders." With a worried look, Misha muttered something to the foot soldier and disappeared into the Hall of Silver. Quietly, Tbor prayed that the missing element in his plan would appear quickly. It did. A lady came from the rear and started for the rest room. Tbor grabbed her by the arm and pressed a knife against her back. "Shut up. Don't say a word. We're taking a little trip."

"Please . . . please . . ." Lisa whispered to him, her eyes widening. "Don't hurt me, please." To Lisa, Blaine Decatur's wife, this personal confrontation was the ultimate terror; her whole being began to shake.

Tbor prodded her with the awl-like knife, his Oriental eyes narrowed to knife-thin slits. "Do exactly what I tell you, and you will not be hurt. Do anything I tell you and agree with anything I say. *Anything*. Understood?" He gave her another poke with the knife, and Lisa nodded, her face ashen.

As they neared the vestibule inside the front doors, the foot soldier watched their advance warily. Tbor turned to him. "This lady is nauseated. She will probably vomit any moment. I'm the doctor, and I want to get her into the ladies' room to avoid spreading the infection. All right?" The foot soldier appeared uncertain but was baffled as to what he could do.

He was even more baffled when the pair did not stop at the ladies' room but kept coming toward him and the front doors. "Wait a minute, there—" he finally began, just as they came roughly even with him. The blow caught him on the side of the head; the soldier collapsed on the floor. From Lisa came the beginnings of a scream, but one abruptly stifled when Tbor put the knife back against her side. Working quickly, Tbor threw the bolts on the front door and dragged Lisa silently out into the courtyard. To Lisa, it was a terrifying place, already dark with the brooding black of Moscow at dusk. The searchlights were not on yet, and the yard was lit only by some lower-wattage lights in the nearest tower. The shadows they cast looked grotesque in this strange world of semidark.

Tbor was convinced he had made it. If he could get himself and his hostage to the authorities, he could assume the pose of a man who had escaped from Salt Mine, rather than being branded as a part of it. He had other things to offer: information on the location of the hostages, the number of men in Salt Mine and their meager armament; the fact that they were being stricken, one by one, with some sickness that would shortly make taking the Oruzheinaya easy. Editing out his part in the recruitment, he could say he was forced to do everything he had done. Tbor's own belief was that there would be few survivors to contradict him. The KGB might even reward rather than shoot him.

It was a highly competent plan. Tbor miscalculated on only one major point: Lisa. Stumbling over the cobbles, held onto by Tbor, who kept the knife pressed hard against her spine, Lisa saw something around the base of the Oruzheinaya that threw her into panic. Soldiers. Crouched low to the ground, keeping themselves well below the level of the windows. Russian soldiers. Waiting there, ready to attack. They would think she was part of Salt Mine.

For the moment, Tbor's knife was unimportant. Lisa began to scream. "Don't shoot. Don't shoot! I'm not one of them. I'm a hostage. For Christ's sake, don't shoot!"

The men in the towers were confused. They knew their soldiers were there and why they were there; it was the reason the searchlights were not turned on yet. Marshal Borodinsky's lieutenants were trying a variation on his frontal assault.

Frantic calls were made for instructions; all that the men in the towers knew at the moment was that a man and a woman had come out of the Oruzheinaya, seen their soldiers, and that the woman was screaming. To warn Salt Mine about the soldiers? A few moments later, some of the big lights came on. From inside the Oruzheinaya came a burst of gunfire. Salt Mine had just realized Tbor and some woman were trying to escape.

In the suddenly bright light, the soldiers became confused, and some of them began to fire, too. Tbor started to run, dragging Lisa behind him. If he could get around the corner of the building, he would at least be safe from the firing coming from Salt Mine. Vaguely, he was aware that Lisa had slumped to the ground and lay somewhere behind him.

Both sides were firing at Tbor now—Salt Mine to keep him

from getting across the courtyard to the safety of the government buildings, the Soviets because they didn't know which side Tbor was on but did know his partner's screaming had spoiled their infiltration plan.

From the loudspeaker came a voice ordering the soldiers crouched at the base of the Oruzheinaya back; the element of surprise was lost. The firing grew more intense as Tbor ran, and all of the searchlights finally came on, turning the courtyard a brilliant bluish color. Dodging and weaving in the intense light, Tbor changed direction every few feet, trying to slither away from the hail of gunfire and into the shadows. The repeated changes of light outside the Oruzheinaya, the confusion in the towers and along the wall, and the fact that the searchlights shone directly into the eyes of the men at the Oruzheinaya conspired to help Tbor. The soldiers in the towers were blinded by the lights as well.

"Dammit," grunted Alyosha. "I can't even see him now. If he gets to Klin, we're in trouble. He knows too much."

Misha's lizardlike eyes shone with the reflections from the lights, and he cupped one hand to shade them. "If we keep our fire up, they'll keep firing back. And since they don't know which side Tbor is on—I don't myself—they may shoot him in the confusion."

From the Oruzheinaya, the firing was redoubled. On Alyosha's orders, each man went after one of the lights, adding the sound of breaking glass and the sputtering of fractured arcs to the confusion. Their fire was answered by the soldiers along the wall, as well as those on the roof of the Council of Ministers Building.

Briefly, the great doors of the Oruzheinaya Palata were opened a crack to allow Lisenka and one of the Russian hostages, an enormous peasant woman, to drag in Lisa Decatur, who had crawled back to the building. For a moment she lay on the floor, her head raised to stare at them. Then she collapsed totally from fear and exhaustion.

Tbor sprinted across the courtyard, crouched almost double, and raced past the Palace of Congresses. On top of the wall, the soldiers spotted him again and opened fire. With a sudden dash, Tbor tried to hide behind the Tsar Kolokol, the Tsar Bell. There, he planned to survive long enough for the confusion to clear and then make his way to the authorities. It was not to be. A sharpshooter on the Tower of Sts. Constantine and Helen, posted there since early morning, saw him in the shadow of the bell and fired a rapid succession of dum-dum bullets.

Tbor didn't have a chance. For a second he swayed, frozen in place by a realization that there was no place left to hide. Arms outstretched in appeal, he dropped to his knees, huddling against the stone base the bell stood on. The bullets whined and spat, some of them hitting the bell itself. The sniper finally zeroed in on Tbor and concentrated his fire, nearly cutting the man's body in two. Tbor seemed to hang on the wall of the base for a moment, as if the fact of his death was something his body would not accept. Slowly, it settled to the cobblestones, the hands still raised, held up by the bell's stone platform.

It would probably be small comfort to Tbor, but the bullets hitting the great bell above him had caused it to ring for the first time in Kremlin history.

15

THE THIRD DAY, 6:30 P.M.

Klin was in the Council of Ministers Building when Tbor tried to make his escape. By the time he reached the command post at the Vodovzvodnaya Tower, it was too late; Tbor lay dead at the base of the Kolokol.

"Damn," Klin fumed at Colonel-General Pskov and Kapitan Volodya Sokolov. "You should have let him get to the line of soldiers out there. We needed to capture him, not kill him. I tried you on the phone but nobody answered. That man might have told us a lot. Stupid."

Neither the general nor the kapitan spoke; both stared off into space, as if some object of vast importance lay just beyond reach of their eyes. There was something in Klin's voice that told them he was only speaking for the record. Even if he'd been here at the Vodovzvodnaya instead of in his office, they doubted Klin would have been sure what decision to make either.

They did not know that as Klin talked he was already beginning to see a distinct advantage in Tbor's death, a new and additional facet to the plan Talanin had approved earlier. "We must get the body. For identification," he added hastily, as if he were afraid the men might guess what he was thinking. "Send some soldiers from the Petrovskaya Tower—they can't see it from the Oruzheinaya at all—and recover the body immediately."

Looking at his watch, Klin did some quick figuring. An hour should do. For the first time in days, his scalp was not itching.

• For possibly the only time in his life, Tbor's presence was being missed.

"It's spreading, but I don't think as fast. Some come down with it, others don't—there's nothing to explain the difference. Tbor said . . ." Lisenka stopped. Quietly, she stood beside Alyosha, studying the scene in the Hall of Silver. The glare of the searchlights coming from outside and filtering through the windows tinted everything in the room gray, making it look like an etching of a Boer War hospital. Hostages and Salt Mine members alike were stretched out on the floor under blankets, their foreheads covered with dampened paper towels to ease the pain of their fevers. Almost half the people inside the Oruzheinaya had been stricken, and Lisenka spent her hours going from one person to the next, trying to make them more comfortable. "Alyosha," she began, her hand gripping his arm. Silently, she looked long and hard into his eyes. His eyes closed before he asked the question he dreaded to raise.

"It's that bad?"

"Tbor. Even Tbor was better than nothing. I told you it's not spreading as much, but some of those people look very sick to me. *Very* sick. They could—well, you know. . . ."

Alyosha stared into space. Everything had suddenly gone wrong. Tbor. The sickness attacking at random, flattening some, ignoring others. Salt Mine down to half its strength; it could get worse. If he called Klin and asked for a doctor, the doctor would report back how few men he had left. Everything they had worked for, the whole daring Salt Mine concept, hung by a thread. He could tough it out, but if he did and people died, the world's public opinion, so carefully nurtured by Keer and Jax, would turn against Salt Mine. The sound of one of the German children crying made his decision for him; it was a sound no civilized person could ignore. Klin answered his phone as if he were already holding it in his hand.

"We have some sick people here," Alyosha started. "We need a doctor for the hostages." Instead of the usual sparring—a new request for Salt Mine's demands was what Alyosha had expected—Klin's answer was a long sigh.

"I was afraid of that."

"You were *what?*"

"Afraid of what's happening. That man who tried to escape—Tbor something, his ID card said—the doctors examined his body. Spinal meningitis. With you people all shut up in there, using the same sanitary facilities, others were bound to be exposed. We'll send in a doctor, of course. Not for your sake, but for the hostages."

Alyosha reeled. Meningitis. Unstoppable. Frequently lethal.

Those poor damned people. Killed, in a sense, by him—and for nothing. Because there went Salt Mine, too. Yet, even as he reacted, some inner bell in the rear of his brain sounded a warning. Something was wrong. Something too neat.

"No tricks with this doctor, please," Alyosha said. "We have some sick people, yes, but Salt Mine is still very, very alert."

"I wish you'd give us your demands. Meningitis is nothing to play with."

Alyosha felt gratified, at least, that Klin still performed as expected. His answer was a noncommittal grunt.

• On the opposite side of town, the only apparent concern was the quality of the small talk.

"I don't know why you think it was me."

"I didn't say I did."

"Your face said it for you."

"I cannot help my face, Mr. Jax." For an instant, he paused. "Any more than I can my hair." The statement was unusual; Klin had never been known to make light of what he considered a major calamity in his life.

Jax was surprised to see Klin here—he would have thought the news would send Klin scurrying to the Council of Ministers Building. Klin was just as surprised to see Jax here. It required a certain gall to release a story like his and then show up at a party where the Soviet hierarchy was bound to appear. The two of them stood in the reception room of the French Embassy, drinking the superb champagne—Roederer '69—and nibbling the Malossol. For a correspondent to be invited to such an affair gave some indication of Jax's international standing; ordinarily, newsmen were deliberately excluded from diplomatic receptions.

Perhaps half an hour earlier, at about quarter past seven, an aide had hurried in and handed Klin a transcript of Jax's story, sent from the Soviet Embassy in Helsinki. After a few phone calls, Klin came back in to the party, doing his best to appear unruffled.

The expulsion—even the arrest and interrogation of Jax—was being urged on him by both Chorniev and Foreign Minister Shtanov, but Klin refused. The correspondent might lead them to Salt Mine's outside man, obviously Jax's source.

Leaning against the wall of the French Embassy, Jax studied Klin as he moved from group to group. His was a bravura performance. To anyone who didn't know better, it would be difficult to believe that the Kremlin was under siege only a dozen blocks away. Few of the *corps diplomatique* were gauche enough to raise the subject of Salt Mine with Klin himself, but with those who did, Klin laughed and joked—a man without a care in the world. That, conceded Jax, was class.

He knew, regardless of the seeming coolness Klin exhibited, the Soviets must be in turmoil. His flash had broken at six thirty-five, and from his own conversations with diplomats of non-Communist countries, Jax knew the worldwide reaction was massive and stunned. There was concern for the hostages, of course. But that the mighty Kremlin could be hijacked—and along with it (macabre touch) Lenin's body—was too much for the world to accept without wonder, suppressed admiration, and a faint smile. Jax could see the same smile on the faces of the envoys talking behind Klin's back. At the embassy, his story preempted all other topics of conversation.

Taking a glass of Roederer as a tray went by, Jax gazed deep into its roaring sea of tiny bubbles. How could it be that when he'd stumbled into a newsbreak that was the capstone of his career, he couldn't even sign his own name to it? It was unfair.

• The unfairness of life was also getting to Vasily Klin. The effort of appearing untroubled at the reception left him drained. Being polite, even funny, with Andrew Jax had been even worse. In Klin's mind, the Salt Mine story could be the work of no one else. And unless their shadowing of Jax produced the outside man, there would be more of the same.

When he called Chorniev from the reception, he told him that finding Salt Mine's outside man was now more critical than ever. But about all Chorniev would say was that the interrogations had so far turned up nothing; the outside man was seemingly as much of a mystery to the peripheral figures in Salt Mine as he was to the KGB. Klin fumed. Angrily, he ordered him to double—triple, if necessary—the number of KGB men watching Jax. If they couldn't follow him to the outside man, they could surround Jax with so many agents the outside man wouldn't dare see Jax either. The leak would be sealed.

Racing back to the Kremlin as soon as he could leave without appearing concerned, Klin considered the day's events. From Shtanov, he knew the embassies had reacted.

Washington had reacted. And Talanin had reacted—violently.

One of the items in Jax's release was word that tanks and soldiers were today moved inside the Kremlin gates; an attack against Salt Mine was expected momentarily. Hearing this news made Talanin howl with rage—he had issued highly specific orders to Borodinsky. This led to one of the few small pleasures Klin experienced all day. A direct call from Talanin to Marshal Borodinsky was an unusual event, but in this case it was one Borodinsky would just as soon have skipped.

Through Deputy Premier Chaidze, Klin assured Talanin that his own plan—their new maneuver—was already under way, and that results could be expected shortly. Then, as far as Klin was concerned, Talanin, Borodinsky, Chorniev, Salt Mine, Jax—the whole wretched lot of them—could go drown themselves in the Black Sea.

The thought of drowning brought back a picture of Volovno, his head wobbling loosely as it floated in Prince Yusupov's lagoon. Klin buried himself in a deskful of detail work to erase the image from his mind.

• Lisenka had bummed a cigarette from Misha four minutes earlier and was still struggling to light it. Unlike her, Misha smoked *papirosi,* long cardboardlike tubes with all the tobacco packed at one end. To Lisenka, the shape was awkward and the taste foul, but a few Russians preferred them to the more popular European-style cigarettes.

Exhausted from her rounds of the sick, Lisenka sat down on the bottom step of Tsar Alexei Mikhailovich's diamond-studded throne for a breather. Almost immediately, she stood up again; there was something blasphemous about perching on the second Romanov's throne, no matter what you might think of the tsar's brutal dynasty. Walking slowly through the handsome green halls, their vaulted ceilings soaring above the display of tsarist treasures, Lisenka finally found a less ostentatious spot for herself. It was on a small, thickly carpeted platform; sharing it with her was a display case of Fabergé, including Perkhin's incredible miniature of the cruiser *Pamyati Azova,* each tiny line of its rigging fashioned of spun gold.

No matter what you might think of the tsar's brutal dynasty. Softly, Lisenka repeated the words to herself. The Revolution. How much had it really changed anything? This thought was not new to her. Lenin replaced the tsar, and while he might have been an idealist—a "dreamer," as Oliver Watkins described him—the men who followed him were no less autocratic than the tsars. Something else that was not new: the KGB. It was a linear descendant of the *Okhrana*, the tsarist secret police, with the same household spies, the same network of agents, the same brutality. The people were still the victims, not daring to speak; not strong enough to challenge. *That*, Lisenka told herself, was what Salt Mine was all about. To point out to the world the new prison in which today's Russians were locked. Perhaps, with outside help, the system *could* be changed. Change was why Lisenka joined Salt Mine in the first place.

Across the room, she watched Alyosha climb wearily into the Petersburg sled for a catnap. She knew her own reasons, but what were Alyosha's? No lover had been torn from his arms, as Shymon had been torn from hers. He was not hounded for writing what he thought, as Dimmy had been. Misha and Avraam were serving a cause: the WJA. Even Keer had his reasons for joining Salt Mine, highly personal as they were.

But in the man who had conceived Salt Mine, led it, and was almost solely responsible for its success, the motive was too deep to see readily. Yet, Salt Mine had consumed Alyosha. He lived it, slept it, and breathed it. He had allowed it to take possession of him. And for that, there had to be a reason.

Every time Lisenka tried to uncover Alyosha's secret, she failed. The secret was like Alyosha himself, surrounded by an iron wall. You were allowed to come so close, but no closer.

She imagined him as sleeping dreamlessly inside the Petersburg sled. The secret remained deep inside him, as well guarded as the Kremlin was supposed to be. As she looked down the room toward the sled, she saw Misha gesturing for her. Someone else taken sick. With one final glance toward the sled, Lisenka stood up and ground out the *papirosa* in a paper cup, wondering whether the new victim was prisoner or captor.

16

THE THIRD DAY, 8:10 P.M.

For a long time the doctor stared at the temperature readings he had taken. On the same sheet, he recorded pulse and respiration counts, as well as other notes on each patient he examined. The stricken hostages and members of Salt Mine lay beneath their blankets, occasionally raising their heads to see the doctor's reaction. The room, Alyosha noticed, had begun to smell—the smell of sickness, of fever, possibly of death. Gravely, the doctor shook his head and looked at Alyosha.

"There is no question. It is as we feared. The man from here we did the autopsy on. While there is no known treatment for meningitis—it is a capricious disease—all of these people would at least have a chance if they were in a hospital. We cannot do much, but what we can do is better than nothing. Pack them in ice for the fevers, oxygen to help their breathing, constant care so they can conserve their energy to fight the disease."

A wave of thought raced through Alyosha's mind. He could not have these people here dying because he refused to act, yet the strange, discordant bell still rang in his head. He struggled to make sense of it. The symptoms weren't being faked; these people—including his own men—were genuinely and desperately sick. He had so few choices. If he released the doctor and the sick hostages, Klin would learn how decimated their team was. No one had come down with the disease for several hours, but the doctor explained he felt this was only a temporary remission. Given a few more hours, he said, more would; it was the way with meningitis. He threw up his hands in helplessness.

"Minister Klin assured me no attempt will be made to force entry when we take the sick out," said the doctor. "You have his word on that. To keep them here would be nothing short of murder. If you agree, I can arrange—"

"No."

Alyosha let the word fall like a lead clock-weight. The doctor—he had introduced himself, but Alyosha couldn't remember the name—looked appalled. Apparently, Klin had assured this nameless doctor that Alyosha would release the patients—and him—as soon as his diagnosis confirmed they were suffering from the same thing as Tbor.

When the doctor passed his hand across his forehead, Alyosha noticed the man was sweating. "No?" the doctor repeated.

"No. As you said yourself, meningitis has no known treatment. You talked of packing them in ice, of oxygen, of constant care. Not much, you said, but better than nothing. Very well, we have no choice." Turning, Alyosha walked away from where the doctor was for a moment, analyzing the situation to make sure his decision was a rational one. Then: "We will treat them here."

"*Here!*"

"Here. You, doctor, will call Klin and—no, you will tell me what you need and I will call Klin. Everything you need. Equipment, supplies, and however many nurses you think it will take. Also, any outside medical opinions that would help. . . ."

"That's insane. This place is not equipped—"

"Equip it."

"As a doctor, I cannot endanger—"

"I am doing the endangering. You said there was little you could do. Do it here. I think you will find Klin will agree. For one thing, he has no other choice."

The doctor began to sputter, looking around the room as if trapped. Alyosha suspected he was now regretting not having said there was a lot he could do in a hospital, but *only* in a hospital. The doctor might feel trapped, but he had built the trap, set the bait, and laid the snare himself.

In a sudden effort to reverse his field, the doctor attempted one final maneuver. "I perhaps overemphasized medicine's lack of ability to treat the disease. There *are* things we can do—given proper conditions. Not here, but—"

Alyosha wanted to laugh; the doctor was transparent. "The list, doctor. The number of nurses. Everything. Quickly, please. We are wasting time."

Sinking down onto a platform, the doctor picked up his notebook to start making up his list. Just before he began writing, he looked up at Alyosha as if the man had just sentenced everyone in the room to a terrible death.

Alyosha ignored him. To him, Salt Mine was the most important thing in the world. Even if, in its execution, some innocent people had to fall by the wayside.

• Less than an hour after the doctor's list was read to a protesting Klin, the people and supplies began arriving at the Oruzheinaya Palata. Watching, Lisenka was shocked by Alyosha's haggard expression as he stood near the door, checking the contents of the medical bag each nurse brought inside with her. When they came farther into the room, Lisenka was to frisk the nurses themselves. Behind the three nurses, a small crew of white-clothed attendants carried rolled-up mattresses and a supply of blankets, pillows, and other equipment; since Alyosha would not allow them to come into the museum itself, they piled the stuff neatly outside the doors. Two of the foot soldiers were kept busy moving it all inside. Last to arrive were a half dozen oxygen tanks, each on a wheeled rack, and two large wagonlike affairs that must have held five hundreds pounds of cracked ice apiece.

The nurses were wide-eyed when they first entered the Oruzheinaya; nervously, they eyed the men with machine guns. That their prospective patients were lined up on the floor like cordwood, while the doctor was in a visible frenzy, added to their sense of personal danger. But as more and more equipment followed them into the Hall of Silver, their training took control; fifteen minutes after they arrived, they were bustling through the rooms, directing the healthy hostages where to carry and place the sick, making beds out of floor mattresses, plumping up the pillows, and speaking soothingly to the patients. That many of the hostages did not speak Russian seemed to make no difference; the nurses' efficiency and soft tones spoke some universal language that immediately made the sick feel a little better.

But the look on Alyosha's face still bothered Lisenka. He suddenly seemed old—watching, helping when he could, but mostly just standing to one side and surveying the picture with an intense gloom.

Salt Mine, for which Alyosha—all of them—had risked so much and dreamed such magnificent dreams, seemed on the verge of disappearing behind a surrealistic screen of white starched cloth, oxygen tanks on soundless wheels, and finely crushed ice.

• At around eight-thirty that night, Keer walked down the short flight of heavily carpeted steps into the restaurant. It had struck him that most of the places he'd eaten with Gary—the Metropol, the National, the Intourist, and the inevitable Labirynt—were pale reproductions of European or American spots, Russian attempts at "being with it." Many of them must have struck Gary as ludicrous, and Keer decided to show him someplace tonight with a definite Moscow flavor.

Thinking of it, Keer had to smile, wondering if he'd chosen the Baku—a pure Azerbaidzhani restaurant—in an unwitting salute to Alyosha. The place was determinedly ethnic; its cozy, warm rooms had stained-glass windows of Central Asian design; on almost every wall hung an oriental rug, lit by candles inside the heavy brass lamps that were everywhere. Even the waiters and manager had an oriental flavor, their Azerbaidzhani features hovering over the tables like hybrid ghosts of Tamerlane's horde.

A few minutes later, Keer saw Gary come through the door. The sight shook him. Late this afternoon, Keer knew, Gary had been summoned to the American Embassy; he was, they said, to have a personal meeting with the ambassador. Whatever they told him had apparently left Gary drained of color, his eyes exhausted, his shoulders slumping. Even though Gary had been under great strain worrying about his family—he talked incessantly to Keer about it—until tonight, he had always managed to stay cheerful. That it was a pose, Keer knew. Now, the pose had disappeared completely. Either Gary's concern for his family had suddenly caught up with him, or he had learned something at the embassy that had knocked him for a loop. When Keer waved to him, the old smile struggled to Gary's face, but it was a forced one, as limp and weak as the rest of Gary looked, and disappeared quickly.

The meal was a bust. Keer's persistent probing produced nothing. Yes, the Baku was charming, just great. No, nothing was bothering him; he was just worried and tired. Yes, the Baku Piti Keer recommended was delicious; the soup was as thick and heavy as the clay bowl it was served in. Great. Right, so was the *golubtsy*—he didn't understand why the meat was wrapped in vine leaves, but what the hell, it tasted good. No, they didn't say a hell of a lot at the embassy. The same old stuff: Be patient; it would all work out.

When Gary abruptly changed the subject and began talking about the rugs hanging from the wall, their origin, their design, and how different they were from the usual oriental, Keer took the hint and dropped the subject. But Gary's underlying despondency was never very far away.

After dinner, Keer hauled a not-very-enthusiastic Gary to another heavily ethnic spot, but Gary responded as woodenly to the Varshava as he had to the Baku. It was a noisy, smoke-filled dive on the top floor of an old Moscow building, filled with middle-level *apparatchiks* pretending to be working men by abandoning themselves to the singing and the vodka. Gary, Keer noticed, began drinking prodigiously, growing more morose with each drink, although still insisting nothing new was wrong.

At eleven, when he made his check-in call to the Oruzheinaya, Keer discovered Alyosha was even glummer than Gary. Alyosha had not told him yet of the meningitis problem; the fewer who knew, the better. Disconsolately, Keer hung up. Perhaps it was a cycle of the moon; everyone seemed filled with despair. The mood was infectious and Keer began to fume himself. At eleven-thirty, something occurred to him that might cheer them both up. Grabbing Gary by the arm, he dragged him away from the Varshava. "I know what you need. If this won't cheer you up, nothing will." Without explaining, Keer half pulled, half pushed Gary down the stairs and into a cab.

• Maria Ivanova Sverdlova stood in the entrance hall of her apartment, staring at him incredulously. "An American here? Keer, you are out of your mind. How could you be so stupid?"

Keer flashed her his most boyish smile, something he was aware rarely left her unmoved. "He's a good friend of mine. And he needs cheering up, Manya. His whole family—well, they're all inside the Oruzheinaya Palata. I *had* to bring him. You're so good at handling people with troubles." She felt his two hands pressing hers together and melted. With Keer, she always did; a small shudder of pleasure ran through her.

Manya was a phenomenon of the new aristocracy. To have a mistress in Russia was unusual—but only outside the circles of power. Virtually all the ministers and members of the Supreme Soviet had one; among these men it was taken for granted. Because of Russian custom reaching back to the Tartar past, the wives of Soviet officials are seldom seen in public. Even in the days of the early tsars, the ladies of the court were kept totally sequestered from the males, virtually confined to their quarters, the *Terems*. They were never heard about or from, shadowy figures moving inside the Kremlin walls, unseen and unknown.

With this tradition in his blood, a member of the new aristocracy leaves his wife at home and feels free to dally as he wishes. At thirty-three, Manya was still highly attractive but was plagued by doubts as to how much longer she would be. She was mistress to Minister of Production Dmitry Gertsen, Keer's father, a highly undemonstrative man who appeared at infrequent intervals, satisfied himself, and left quickly, wearing the look of a man who had just been to a chiropodist and had a vigorous foot massage. That Manya frequently cuckolded him with his own son was dangerous, but Manya disliked Gertsen almost as much as Keer did. Besides, the fact that a good-looking eighteen-year-old boy still found her, at thirty-three, attractive enough to visit—and visit frequently—helped reassure Manya that she had not lost any of the sexual magnetism she was famous for.

Mentally, Manya inspected Gary the way a potential buyer might examine a racehorse; his teeth were examined, his build explored, the most intimate parts of his body measured, weighed, and found desirable. But his being here still troubled Manya; there was always the KGB to consider. Because of Minister Gertsen's importance, they undoubtedly knew of her, and, therefore, of Keer. After a pause, she decided the KGB must be ignoring the situation or they would have blown the whistle on Keer and her long ago. The KGB, she decided, did not choose to involve itself in the lives of powerful men's ladies, except to be sure they were not spies. Besides, just now, Manya knew from the tightly knit circle of ministers' mistresses, the KGB was too busy with this thing called Salt Mine to bother with either Keer or her.

Manya seated herself on a sofa between Keer and Gary and went to work. Her apartment was decorated to set her off to advantage; like her, it was from another day, another world. Every chair, every sofa, every chaise was piled high with small pillows of different sizes and shapes; they were stacked on ottomans, heaped on benches, and even mounded in disorderly piles in the corners of the room. The walls were covered in a rich pink watered silk; framed paintings of a more opulent time gleamed softly beneath portrait lights; brass hangings and candlelit icons were grouped on the wall opposite the couch. Keer was used to this; Gary, quite drunk from the sweet wine at the Baku and the raw Polish vodka at the Varshava, stared glazedly at the wall opposite him as if not quite sure what he was doing here. Quickly, Manya made it quite clear.

Looking up at the pink-mirrored ceiling above her bed half an hour later, she kept finding herself excited by the sight of the two young bodies that lay on either side of her, thrashing against her, crawling over her, moaning softly to her, caressing her, entering her.

There was a pause while the three of them lay there spent. She felt a hand—it was Keer's—begin tentatively to explore her again. Reaching over, she allowed her own hand to wander across Gary's stomach so that he too would grow excited for a second time. Suddenly, both she and Keer gasped. With a soft, strangled wail of anguish, Gary tore himself from the bed and slumped down into a silk overstuffed chair against the wall, his head in his hands, the sound of his sobbing matching the sudden heaving of his chest.

"Darling . . . darling . . ." called Manya, rolling out of the bed and slipping into a robe. "What is wrong, darling?"

Gary looked up and appeared suddenly embarrassed, as if he'd just realized he was sitting in a strange woman's bedroom, absolutely naked, and crying like a little boy. Self-consciously, he pulled a pillow into his lap and tried to cover himself with it. A sudden attack of crying swept over him again and he forgot about the pillow and tried to hide his face. "My whole family. My whole damned family. Christ. My mother. My father, dammit, my father. Those people in Salt Mine. That disease—Christ . . ." The sobbing started once more, and Gary began stumbling around the room, trying to find his clothes.

Maria Ivanovna Sverdlova, by any standards, was not a good woman. She had lied, cheated, schemed, and slept her way to her present place in the world. But Russian women, good or bad, are famous for a motherly streak that transcends all else. The sight of Gary, suddenly transformed from a youth thrashing in her bed into a crying child, was something that tore Manya apart. Within the circle of ministers' mistresses there was an unspoken code that nothing they learned from their lovers was ever mentioned to anyone outside the circle. "*Chort*," exploded Magda, "you have nothing to worry about, little darling." She then proceeded, with devastating completeness, to shatter that unspoken code.

• In the ministry office, Klin's houseman was struggling to make up the rolling cot Klin had ordered set up there. The houseman knew Klin was a particular—almost fussy—person; he also knew that no amount of smoothing of sheets, patting of pillows, or tucking of blankets could make the cot more than passable. Across the room from him, Klin sagged wearily behind his desk, his shirt unbuttoned, his tie down, looking as rumpled as the bed.

"You heard me correctly," he grunted into the phone. "Send all of it over. The counterreagents, the emetics. I don't know how, but they know. They seem to find out everything. Sometimes I think Salt Mine must be run by Talanin himself. I am too tired to argue about it. Just send over the medicines; we'll talk about it in the morning." It was quarter past one, but to Klin it felt later. The telephone call from Salt Mine a little earlier had drained the blood out of him. Explaining to Talanin how a plan so carefully constructed could go so wrong was going to be impossible.

"You filthy bastard," Alyosha had screamed, so loudly Klin held the receiver away from his ear. Until now, Alyosha had never seemed to lose his self-control; he was acid, he was waspish, he was blunt, but he always managed to keep his temper. No longer. Alyosha's voice had crackled with fury. "*Chort*-eater. Pisser of slime. Like all of you strangling this country. Prick of a pig."

"My dear friend," Klin had begun, taken aback and bewildered.

"Don't 'my dear friend' me, Klin. I don't like you. I never liked you. But I thought there might be just an ounce of decency in you." Klin remained mute. Inside him grew a terrible suspicion. Over the phone, he could hear Alyosha swallowing, taking deep breaths to get himself under control. "Chemicals in the water, you son of a bitch. Chemicals to make people sick. To produce those fevers. Hostages. Men. Women. Children. You pull that kind of crap on them. The Soviet must be very proud of you, Klin. You call up and say it's meningitis. Very sad, you say. But with meningitis, you'd better give up, you say. The only place for you is in the hospital, you say.

"Well, I'm a suspicious man and made you set up the hospital here. If it wasn't for that . . . damn you, Klin. There must be times when you wonder why Salt Mine despises the government enough to risk their lives fighting it. Trying to show the world what it's like. Well, things like this filthy maneuver are why."

Automatically, Klin had tried to bluff it through. "Look. I

don't know what you're talking about. Chemicals in the water? Never. The doctor is there with you. He agreed it was meningitis. He told you—"

"He told us exactly what you told him to. He's as much of a liar as you are. He also made a mistake and let it slip that there are antidotes that work quickly against those chemicals. Along with emetics, everybody here could make a remarkable recovery from their 'meningitis' in a matter of hours. Very well. Get them here. *FAST.*"

To Klin, the whole conversation still seemed a nightmare. He nodded to his houseman, who brought him a cognac from the cupboard in the office; he could feel his scalp begin to tingle again; it hadn't for two days. Borodinsky would laugh and then probably get his way with Talanin. A frontal assault. Son of a bitch.

Going down, the cognac burned. But it helped neutralize the hollow dread inside him. That damned outside man again. Someone had told him of the meningitis plan—someone who knew the details—and he told Salt Mine. Sitting on the edge of his desk, taking out his cuff links and emptying his pockets while his houseman fussed behind him, Klin wrestled with who that "someone" could be. Only the other ministers knew of the plan.

Klin felt as if he'd run into a stone wall again. The outside man knew so many of the details of the meningitis scheme—Klin's monitoring of his phone calls to the Oruzheinaya had proved that—his information must have come from a top-echelon source. The thought sent a shudder through Klin.

It couldn't be a minister. Or could it? No, not even Borodinsky. A small light flashed behind Klin's eyes. The Americans. The American ambassador had had to be told. Pressure from Washington to know what the Kremlin was doing about the situation. Advance warning about the plan so the Americans wouldn't panic and think the meningitis was real when the world was told. But the American government wouldn't be stupid enough to leak the story; it would be self-defeating. Klin smiled grimly. All governments were stupid. The American as much as the Soviet.

He stood up and let the houseman take his jacket and trousers, watching him hang them up in his office closet. Numbly, Klin listened as the man said he would bring him fresh clothes in the morning. *Morning.* And the damned outside man would still be in Moscow. Pushing them against the wall. Chorniev must be shaken until his teeth rattled to beef up the manhunt.

Klin realized he was sweating. That always made his scalp itch. Damn. But the dim shape of a new way to resolve Salt Mine was forming in Klin's head. This one no one would know about until it was over. This time, no leak. Wearily, he sank onto the edge of the cot. Klin's houseman looked at him and shuddered; Klin's scalp had turned the deep red of thick blood.

17

THE FOURTH DAY, 6:25 A.M.
Coming through the windows of Dzerzhinsky Street, the pale, early morning sun forced Mikhail Chorniev to squint. Torn between the effort of getting up and adjusting the blinds or letting it go and suffering the slight discomfort, he opted for inaction; his conversation on the phone was effort enough. A stream of protest poured from the receiver; the directive he'd given was not being well received.

For the benefit of the three agents who stood in front of him, waiting for him to get off the phone, Chorniev rolled his eyes upward to show what the director of the KGB had to put up with. He shifted uncomfortably in his chair before interrupting the man on the phone, softly, as always, but with unusual firmness. "We shall not discuss it further. I have given you an order. Kindly execute it."

Briefly, he stared at the top of his desk. That was one item out of the way. A bigger, more personally dangerous problem still consumed him, and the three agents, standing uncomfortably on the other side of his desk, were one answer. The solution could turn out to be as dangerous as the problem, but Chorniev knew it was impossible to leave things where they stood.

"You all understand your orders?"

The men nodded, not too happily.

"Regardless of what happens—nothing should, but there is always the possibility—the key instruction is that your orders must never be traced back here. In no case, call this office. Or mention the KGB's name. If you do, we shall deny knowing you. You will be disowned." Chorniev paused, finally softening his remarks to make them less bleak. "In the event of arrest, of course, later, everything will be straightened out for you," he lied. Chorniev let his eyes settle on the tall, thin Ukrainian on the left. "Your assignment, Shevshenko, is probably the most delicate. Borodinsky's office is always under special guard. Not necessarily by the KGB, but by the AFSN. So be particularly on guard."

Without enthusiasm the men nodded. The assignment was murderously dangerous, even for the two men who did not have to contend with Borodinsky's Armed Forces Security Network.

"I have chosen each of you personally because I know I can count on your loyalty to me. It is no easy thing to ask of you. All I can say is that in the end the mission is for the greater good of the Party and the government." The lie was so blatant Chorniev could feel his skin tingle; he wondered if any of these men questioned what they had been volunteered to do. Their expressions never varied from stone-faced grimness.

"Very well. Report back to me as soon as you have completed your mission. Personally."

With brisk, efficient nods the three agents filed from his office. Outside, they were tempted to discuss the matter; Chorniev's orders were highly irregular. But they were aware the building in Dzerzhinsky Street was no place to attempt a private conversation—every inch of the building was bugged—and by the time they reached the street, they would already be setting their mission into motion.

• The clatter of the portable, squatting on an ornate but not very steady writing table, echoed off the walls of his room at the Metropol. The sound seemed out of place in this elegant old hotel, where the scratch of quill pen against vellum would seem more at home than the racket of his Olivetti. Jax rubbed his eyes, pushing himself back from the table while he probed the air for some more colorful phrase; his eyes were beginning to smart from trying to work by the feeble light that came from the desk lamp. Very decorative, not very effective. Beyond the heavy lace curtains, Jax could see the dark squares of the windows and wondered why in predawn Moscow the darkness always seemed so intense.

Jax wore gray flannels and was still in his heavy cardigan; an hour earlier he had had to go out in response to a call from Keer. As always, the message was in code. "Call me at Point D, Focus A," was all Keer said. Translated, this meant to get to the phone booth on Gorky Street and call Keer at the number of a second booth on Lesnaya. Striding through the lobby, Jax saw, seated on uncomfortable couches, his faithful KGB watchdogs eyeing him ominously; they looked as sleepy as he felt. Ensconced in the phone booth at Lesnaya, Keer talked fast, aware that to be on the streets of Moscow at this time of night was asking for trouble. Quickly, he sketched the outline of the meningitis plot for him.

From Jax came a low whistle. It was the kind of treachery his audience would love reading about. His own information from the capitals of the world was that Salt Mine's thumbing of its nose at the Soviet sphinx now had most people rooting for the dissidents. Particularly Americans, with their traditional love of the underdog. Oh, there had been pious editorial comments about the use of innocent tourists as hostages, but Jax offset these with comments Keer supplied from some of the hostages. That both of them to a degree altered what the hostages said was unimportant. Journalistic license.

Jax had made one suggestion: Release the story in two parts—today, report that meningitis was sweeping the Oruzheinaya, tomorrow, that the disease turned out to be a Soviet plot, one that played chemical roulette with the lives of the hostages. This, he told Keer, would add a cliff-hanger element.

Keer agreed, adding one stipulation. The requirement was one Jax was growing used to. "It has to be out," Keer had said, "the first part of that story, by sometime tomorrow morning."

Keer's deadline was why Jax was going blind from the Metropol's dim lighting. He read what he'd written; it was good, and would be finished in time to satisfy Keer's demands. The story lacked one thought, he felt. Pulling himself back to the typewriter, Jax added a few sentences:

> In its embarrassment, the Soviet Union has attempted to fix the blame on the World Jewish Alliance. Those in Salt Mine, the Soviets try to tell the foreign press, are not Russians, but Zionists. Inside the Soviet Union, of course, nothing, officially, is known by the Russian people about the hijacking of the buildings in their capital; the curious are told the gates of the Kremlin were closed because repairs were needed and a specially heavy guard was necessary to protect the priceless art treasures inside. One wonders if the public here really believes this requires heavy tanks and a small army of men outside the wall.

This paragraph was too long, but, looking at his watch, Jax knew he didn't have enough time to fix it and keep to Keer's deadline. The dispatch destroyed the credibility of any further attempts by the Kremlin to link Salt Mine with the WJA. He folded the story into an envelope and began worrying about getting a courier to take it to Finland.

At almost the same moment, the Neck—as much of a Zionist as there ever could be—gave a sudden groan and collapsed to the floor of Lubyanka, pulling the chair he was tied to over with him. Shock, the agony of watching his daughter gang-raped, and electrical torture finally released him from ever being interrogated about Salt Mine again.

• Through his window on Dzerzhinsky Street, Mikhail Chorniev watched two men and a matron hustle the Neck's daughter across the narrow pavement and into the back of a black sedan. The child wore a raincoat provided by someone, but there was no way to know what was beneath it; the girl kept pulling it tightly around herself as if this might prevent a repetition of last night's nightmare. The sight of her made Chorniev squirm uncomfortably, and the fact that it *did* made him even more uncomfortable. He was a professional doing his duty; the Neck was an enemy of the state; that a twelve-year-old like Sera had to suffer to make her father talk was perhaps unfair, but defensible in terms of the greatest good for the greatest number. Chorniev was unable to make the rationalization stick and wondered if he was going soft. Or was he, because of his troubles, already beginning to identify with other KGB vctims? Ridiculous, Chorniev assured himself.

Below, the headlights of the sedan sprang to life, the beams cutting twin paths through the dark, misty predawn. Chorniev saw the door on one side suddenly open, and little Sera Zelinskaya jump partway out, the raincoat flapping apart to reveal her nakedness. For a moment, he could see her struggling and fighting on the sidewalk. Then the matron and one of the men were able to push her back inside.

Chorniev could feel the knot of discomfort in his stomach grip him again; already, early as it was, it had been a bad morning. With a roar, the car with Sera pulled away from the curb and headed out into the still-light traffic. Sera Zelinskaya would not like where she was going. Spinning. Chorniev picked up the phone on his desk and demanded more coffee. Why the hell should he care whether she liked it or not?

• To a twelve-year-old, none of it made sense. There was more logic to the way the windshield wipers moved back and forth across the glass than to what was happening to her. Ever since she was old enough to understand, Sera could remember her father and others in the Jewish community talking of the KGB with dread; she and Katya Blum even used to play a game, hiding behind trees, taking turns, one of them the KGB, one of them the Jew, pretending to do terrible things to each other.

But nothing in any game with Katya anticipated last night. She had never seen her father naked before, and she had no idea of why he was naked then, with a nightmare array of wires running from him. She didn't understand why he would suddenly stiffen until it seemed his bones must crack, groaning, his tongue sticking out of his mouth while he writhed and thrashed in the chair. And then, for no reason Sera could understand, those men had ripped off her nightgown and done things to her that were only whispered about at school by older girls. Lord of Abraham and Moses, it had hurt. A deep excruciating pain that seared her insides and tried to rip her body apart and left her feeling more unclean than she had ever felt before in her life. The men had laughed and stuck their fingers deep inside her and then laughed again as they pulled off their clothes and climbed on her. And they smelled of *kvass* or vodka, and God, oh God, it had hurt so much it was impossible this was the way you made babies because if it was, there would be no children in the world at all.

She could remember her father groaning and cursing and crying as he was made to watch, and it was hard for Sera to know whether she felt the pain more for him or for herself. And then—it can't have been more than half or three-quarters of an hour ago now—two matrons took her into a room and one of them held her down while the other smeared lipstick across her mouth and put rouge on her cheeks and drew great lines over her eyebrows. Why? It didn't make sense; none of it made sense.

From a closet, the bigger of the two matrons had pulled the raincoat and thrown it at Sera, telling her to put it on and to keep her damned mouth shut. They walked down a long hall and she was suddenly shoved into a brightly lit room where a large, thickset woman sat behind a desk with a lot of papers in front of her. The woman wore a uniform of some sort, but Sera couldn't remember ever seeing one like it before. To one side, Sera saw a man she thought she remembered; he had been in the room, standing off to one side, when they—well, when it happened.

"Serafima Pavlovna Zelinskaya," the woman thundered, and shook the papers in her direction. "We have examined your case thoroughly. And the conclusion of the Dispositions Committee of the Committee of State Security of the USSR is that you, Serafima Pavlovna Zelinskaya, a minor, age twelve years, are a promiscuous child, as defined by Section three, Paragraph twelve, General Administrative Code for Civil Order. Do you understand me, Serafima Pavlovna Zelinskaya? Therefore—"

"Promiscuous child," cried Sera, struggling with the pronunciation of this strange new word. "No, I don't understand you. Promisc—promos—I don't know the word—I don't understand—"

The large woman behind the desk seemed annoyed and suddenly impatient. "You should, Serafima Pavlovna. Look at you. Your face—a whore's. Lipstick, rouge, eye pencil. At your age. This committe has evidence that you, Serafima Pavlovna Zelinskaya, in spite of your age, gave or sold your body to—"

The scream that rose from Sera was one of anguish mixed with shame. The fat woman behind the desk took it as some form of denial. Leaning across her desk, she nodded at a slight, bespectacled man and held out her hand. With measured gravity, he walked over to a bored-looking clerk who sat at a stenotype machine and picked up some papers from him. These he handed up to the woman behind the desk.

"Statements, Serafima Pavlovna. Statements from two doctors testifying that you had intercourse with at least three—perhaps more—men, within hours of your apprehension. Smear slides. Report of physical examination. Do you still deny—"

"Yes, yes, yes!" screamed Sera. She was roughly pushed down into a chair by one of the matrons with her. "Shut up," the matron snapped, raising one hand as if to slap her.

"Therefore it is the judgment of this committee—make the accused stand, matron; she is not allowed to be seated during the hearing—it is the judgment of this committee that you, Serafima Pavlovna Zelinskaya, shall be taken hence and incarcerated in the Soviet State Correction House for Wayward and Promiscuous Children at Nelidovo until such time as the authorities there declare you sufficiently rehabilitated to return to a useful and proper lfe." The woman waved Sera into the chair and fumbled through more papers. "As you are an orphan, Serafima Pavlovna, there are no parents to notify." Turning, the woman at the desk spoke to the man with glasses. "Clerk, you will please take note of this fact. The committee stands adjourned."

From behind her, Sera felt someone take her by the arm and pull her forward. She no longer protested or resisted but allowed herself to be moved as they wished, a lump of soft clay, something you could bend any way you wanted. The decision that she be sent to the correction house as yet meant nothing to her; she still did not understand the description of herself as a promiscuous child; but the word "orphan" was something she understood immediately. Her father was dead.

To an outsider, the disposition of Sera might seem extraordinarily cruel. Oddly, no one—except perhaps Kuznetsov, who enjoyed his work—deliberately set out to be cruel. Chorniev knew that it was impossible to allow this child back with the grandmother who had been raising her. She could describe what had happened to her father; she could upset people with the story of what had happened to her. That sentencing Sera for promiscuity was steeped in irony must be overlooked; it was also steeped in necessity.

• The early-morning check-in call he had made from the tomb cheered Dimmy considerably. "Of course, he's awake, Alyosha," said Dimmy into the phone. "Everyone knows his story; Klemet is part owl, part cat, and part mole. He never sleeps. Good for the soul; hard on the eyes."

From Dimmy's end of the phone, Klemet was surprised to hear Alyosha laugh. For the last day or so, Alyosha had seemed terribly glum, as if he were consumed with worry. No one in Lenin's Tomb knew of the meningitis scare; Alyosha had thought it unwise to tell them. From the beginning, though, it struck Alyosha as strange that no one in the tomb came down with the disease, but he had written it off to the separation from those in the Oruzheinaya Palata. The real explanation was simple: Klin didn't add the chemicals to the food and water of those in the tomb because he was afraid that someone might faint while holding the "deadman's trigger" and blow themselves, the hostages, and Comrade Lenin to pieces.

"You sound very pleased with yourself," Dimmy told Alyosha. "Things must be going well."

"Perfect."

"Good. It is time for Klemet's watch now, so I—not being either cat, owl, or mole—can take my sleep without worry."

There was a little more banter and Dimmy hung up. With a pleased expression he sat down on the floor with his back to the wall, smiled at Klemet, and closed his eyes. Less than five minutes later, as Klemet watched, Dimmy's mouth sagged slowly open and a gentle snore rose from him.

Someone else was watching too. Janos Bognar, the Hungarian, nudged his ally, the Russian soldier, and waited. For the last three days they had studied every step in the routine their two captors followed. While one of them read or slept, the other stood guard. Their schedule was based on the classic military formula of two hours on, one hour off. The man on guard sometimes sat, sometimes stood, the trigger that could blow them all up clutched tightly in one hand. Because holding this trigger closed caused the fingers to cramp, the trigger was transferred from one hand to the other roughly every ten minutes. The one on guard also called in their hourly report to the Oruzheinaya over the wall phone.

Janos's eyes narrowed, and holding a book up in front of his face to hide his interest, he watched the one called Dimmy as he fell asleep. From the other, Klemet, came a small sigh of boredom; he lit a cigarette and glanced at a book, checking his watch frequently as if to make the time go faster. Klemet, Janos noticed the day before, was very precise as to how long he would hold the trigger in one hand before shifting it to the other. At the end of the first hour, Janos Bognar watched Klemet walk quietly over to the wall phone to make his report; Dimmy continued to snore slightly. Klemet's stance was awkward. The cord on the phone was not long enough for him to lean across Dimmy's sleeping body and talk into the receiver with any comfort.

Janos held his breath. Beside him, the Russian soldier waited, too, the muscles on his face tightening. Janos felt his own muscles quivering, preparing themselves for what might be their one chance. Janos's book was put down. He saw their opportunity suddenly move closer. In an attempt to make himself more comfortable with the short telephone cord—Klemet was talking to someone named Lisenka—he leaned one hand against the wall. His back was to Janos and the soldier. Janos nodded.

As if on the ends of identical springs, Janos and the soldier sprang forward and grabbed Klemet from behind. The dropped phone clattered loose against the wall. Frantically, both of the hostages tried to get their hands on the trigger to the explosive, but Klemet held it in a death grip. The three of them wrestled for it, their hands high in the air. Blinking his eyes, Dimmy, famous as a heavy sleeper, woke in time to see the trigger elude all of them and suddenly soar into space. From somewhere inside it, came a rasping buzz, the sound of a rattlesnake before it strikes. For one dreadful moment, the still-dazed Dimmy thought they all would be blown up. In what seemed slow motion on a very distant screen, Dimmy saw the trigger turn slowly end over end and float lazily downward. With one hand, he caught it as it fell, staring at it, surprised to discover it in his fingers. Abruptly, the slow motion went to full speed. With a grunt, Dimmy jammed the trigger closed.

"Sit down!" Klemet roared at Janos and the soldier. "Right now, you two. Sit down!" In his embarrassment, Klemet's voice petered out in midsentence. Shaking, he leaned against the wall, the sweat running down his face.

With a faint smile, Dimmy handed the trigger back to him. "I think you dropped this," Dimmy said. And folding his hands on his lap, he let his mouth sag open and pretended to fall fast asleep again.

• The change in the Oruzheinaya's sick—both the hostages and those of Salt Mine who had been stricken—was hard to believe. But the combination of an emetic and the medicines Klin sent in cleared up the "meningitis" symptoms in a little more than four hours. Granted, the patients still felt weak, their stomachs were still uncertain, but the high fevers, the violent cramps, and the vomiting of the night before disappeared. Only two of them—Lisa Decatur and one member of Lisenka's Yale Club tour—appeared still affected; the doctor, thoroughly terrified by now, assured Alyosha these two cases were temporary, too. By nine-fifteen that morning, most of them were complaining of being hungry again, and a call was made to Kapitan Volodya Sokolov for additional food.

The spirits of Salt Mine were riding high. Lisenka noticed that Alyosha was, for him, practically jocose. Something else had been produced by the illness: a total loathing of the Soviet authorities. When you have developed a raging fever and spent hours throwing up at intervals, it is easy to hate the person you hold responsible. All of the afflicted had fully expected to die; this trauma, too, was blamed on the authorities. The doctors and nurses whom the Soviets sent to help had gone along with the deception. To the Americans, particularly, it proved what many of them had felt for years: The Soviets were not to be trusted. The Germans already knew this, from bitter experience. The Cubans suspected it. But now even the Russians who were hostages felt closer to Salt Mine than they did to their own government.

Looking around him, watching the hostages dig into their second breakfast, Alyosha felt an almost parental pride in both the members of Salt Mine and the hostages. They were his children; he was their father. The spell was broken only by a distant voice in his ear that whispered of a time he had been neither. This period was the key to Alyosha; it was a secret so painful he kept it locked away inside himself.

The voice beside him made Alyosha jump. He had been so deep in thought he had not noticed Lisenka walk up to him. "Thank God that's over. I thought everything was going to blow up in our faces. Meningitis. It was a stupid thing for your friend, Klin, to try, but then it almost worked, so how can I say he was dumb? Those two poor children. They had it the worst. What a terrible thing to do to children."

"What a terrible thing to do to anyone." The mood that Alyosha's introspection had put him in left as quickly as it had arrived. He was back to feeling good. So good, he even threw one arm protectively around Lisenka's shoulders. "The whole world—outside Russia, at least—knows about Klin's little treachery. So Klin's plot actually puts us ahead. Keer told me." Keer's call-in had told him a lot more. The second half of the meningitis story—the part about the Soviet plot—was originally due for release tomorrow but had been advanced to later today. Through the press underground, Jax already knew most of the evening papers' reactions. The *New York Post*, the *London Evening Standard* and *France Soir* were all carrying editorials on it. While still not condoning the actions of Salt Mine outright, they were, the editors said, shocked that the Soviet government would try something as dangerous as poisoning the food and water of both hostages and dissidents.

Seeming surprised to find his arm around Lisenka's shoulders, Alyosha quickly let it fall to his side. For a moment, he stood near the door of the Hall of Armor, thinking. "And because by now, the Kremlin knows what the papers are saying, too, I think it is precisely the right moment to present the demands. They'll be on the defensive."

"Good."

"After that—well, after that comes the tricky part. Newspapers and television have done a lot of the work for us already, but we have to get at least some of the demands met. They point up the specifics we want to make. And then, Allah willing, we've got to get ourselves and the hostages out in one piece. It won't be easy. *Chort*, if the government loses its head and pulls something stupid, we *and* the hostages could wind up in pieces. Dead."

"With your plan, I don't see how anything can go wrong."

"Klin will think of something. Or that bastard Chorniev. He's the one who worries me. You don't get to be head of the KGB by being stupid."

His earlier giddiness returned. Stepping over to a fierce-looking figure in gold-ornamented armor guarding the door, he leaned down and read the brass plate naming its original owner and describing the work. "You won't repeat that to anyone, will you, Prince Scherbatow, circa seventeen twenty-one? It would be terrible if anyone heard what I just said."

Patting the armor on the chest, he walked across the Hall of Armor, his step light and springy. Lisenka was amazed. Alyosha was acting almost kittenish, something she'd never seen before. But then, as she had told herself earlier, Alyosha was feeling good.

18

THE FOURTH DAY, 11:35 A.M.

Alyosha might not have been feeling so good if he'd been privy to a telephone exchange between Minister of State Security Klin and Deputy Premier Chaidze. The call arrived on the special phone in Klin's office at the ministry; it was equipped with an electronic scrambling device that allowed ministers to talk to central Party headquarters on Staraya Square with no fear of tapping. To Klin, the small pulsing blue bulb on the scrambler device today looked like the eye of a Nordic demon.

"I saw Talanin this morning."

"Furious?"

"Livid."

Klin sighed. "It was to be expected."

"I have never seen him angrier."

"He has no reason to be. The plan was a good one. The leak—"

"When he heard the meningitis thing hadn't worked, he yelled and cursed. When he read the reaction of the foreign press, he literally screamed. And threw things, too, I understand."

"Well, it proves he's healthy."

Klin's stab at humor was ignored. "You've seen the press reports?"

"Yes. Terrible."

"How does Salt Mine get information to them?"

"The same way they blew up the meningitis scheme. The outside man."

Chaidze's voice took on a probing tone. "This Andrew Jax. Why hasn't he been put under interrogation or at least expelled from the country?"

"I keep thinking he'll lead us to the outside man. He has to talk to him sometime, or he couldn't get the facts. Besides, if we threw out Jax, the outside man would just find himself another correspondent."

"I take your point. I don't think Talanin does; he considers Salt Mine a personal insult."

Klin grunted. For a moment he remained silent; finally he decided it was time to say something reassuring to Chaidze. "I'm sorry to have gotten you into this mess so deep, Pyotr Ivanovich. But there was no one else I could turn to."

"Nonsense, my friend. If the meningitis scheme had worked, we'd both be receiving a 'Hero of the Soviet Union' right now. That it failed—well." His voice suddenly became hard. "Vasily, I have no choice on what is planned now. I disagree with it. Shtanov disagrees with it. Blaveskov disagrees with it. Regardless, Talanin is now determined to follow Borodinsky's proposal. Frontal attack on the Oruzheinaya. I can no longer resist."

"It will be a massacre. The Americans—"

"Will be warned what is planned on the hot line. They will scream. The British will scream. The French will scream. The Africans, well, the Africans will laugh. But Talanin is immovable."

"Dammit, it's insane. We are making progress. Can't you get Talanin to see that? We don't even have Salt Mine's demands yet, so how can we bargain with them? If Borodinsky takes that place with soldiers and tanks, there won't be a hostage left—"

"Vasily, Vasily." Chaidze's voice sounded weary. "I have been through all of this with Talanin. He simply won't accept it any longer." There was a pause, a deathly silence from both ends of the phone, then, from Chaidze: "I *did* buy you a little time. Last night I sent Borodinsky to Prague. To the Eastern Bloc Conference. That gives you until about nine tomorrow morning. After that, Borodinsky has his way. I'm sorry. I think it's a mistake, too."

Klin's eyes came back to the pulsing blue light on the base of the phone. Part of him wanted to keep trying to argue Chaidze out of his position, but he knew it to be futile. "Very well, I guess that settles it. I will try to resolve things bloodlessly by tomorrow, but damn, that isn't much time. Perhaps I—"

"Tomorrow *morning*, Vasily."

"Of course. Tomorrow morning. And thank you, Pyotr, for buying me even that much breathing room. My own opinion is that Borodinsky's assault is a tragic error, but then, you know already I think that."

"*Do svidanya,* Vasily."

The pulsing blue light went off. For some time, Klin sat and stared at the unlit bulb. The night before, a plan had begun to form in his head. He would have to refine it. There was no certainty it would work. But Chaidze had at least given him a chance to try. A sudden random suspicion crossed Klin's mind, and his hand rose automatically to his head. He allowed himself the questionable luxury of scratching.

Standing up, Klin stretched himself and then sat back down to work out his own last effort. For the moment, he would have to set aside Chaidze's possible motives. Time was too valuable to waste it speculating how many demons could dance on Lenin's head.

At eight that morning, three men, each dressed in gray coats, black fur hats, and expressions of self-confidence that bordered on arrogance, had strode through the Nikolskaya toward the Council of Ministers Building. At the door, they produced special KGB passes and, lugging their large boxlike cases, walked inside.

In the lobby, the men stopped again to display their passes to the KGB man on duty. He nodded them through. The building, although under heavy guard, became increasingly empty every day Salt Mine stayed in control of the Oruzheinaya, at the other end of the Kremlin courtyard. On Klin's suggestion, the ministers themselves stayed away, working in their own ministry offices rather than in the Council building. Occasionally, a minister would show up to consult with the skeleton staff left behind, as well as to get a firsthand look at what was going on.

"Pretty quiet, Comrade," noted the tallest of the three, Sergei Shevshenko, to the man behind the KGB desk.

"Like a tomb." The man behind the desk looked over his shoulder, then back at Shevshenko with the expression of a small boy caught saying something dirty. "Not that that's a very popular word around here these days."

Their passes stamped, the three newcomers separated. Perhaps twenty minutes later, Shevshenko opened his case and attached the bug detector to its long pole. This he carefully placed on the carpet in front of Marshal Borodinsky's desk, where he could get at it quickly. Methodically, he began searching the papers on the desk. What he was after was not there. Across the room was a row of filing cabinets set into the wall, and beside it, the copying machine. If necessary, he had electronic equipment to unscramble the combination locks on the file drawers, but the process was time-consuming and Shevshenko loathed every minute he spent in this room. He had locked the door when he came in, but there were several men from the Armed Forces Security Network in offices near the marshal's, and the instinct for self-preservation was pumping adrenaline into his blood. He was well aware that the AFSN teams have as their principal assignment the protection of the armed forces, not only from foreign infiltrators but also from internal ones—particularly the KGB itself.

Shevshenko's assignment here struck him as peculiar. He was to locate a memo from Chorniev and replace it with a new one, bearing a forged date stamp to make it appear that the replacement *was* the original. The first step was to find that original.

On a hunch, Shevshenko leafed through piles of papers on the desk and on a small table beside the copying machine, but the memo wasn't there. The damned combination locks would have to be cracked. Briefly, Shevshenko studied the dials and swore; each row of file drawers had a different lock, and therefore a different combination. Grumbling, Shevshenko rummaged through his equipment until he found the electronic sensors that would guide him to the combinations; he replaced the earphones of the bug detector with the sensor's. A noise made his head snap up and he froze. Outside, he could hear a key being softly inserted into the door. As quietly as he could, Shevshenko crawled quickly across the carpet to the bug detector, getting its earphones on just as the door opened.

In the door stood a slim, erect army kapitan, the blue-green flashes on his lapels identifying him as an officer of the AFSN. He studied Shevshenko through a cloud of cigarette smoke rising from his black *papirosa.* "Enjoying yourself, Comrade?"

Shevshenko turned around in what appeared to be great surprise. By now, he had the small microphone on the end of its long pole suspended a few inches off the carpet, directly beneath Marshal Borodinsky's desk chair. "Just the usual security sweep. Doing all the offices. Looking for bugs."

"Fascinating work, Comrade."

"Pain in the ass, Kapitan. Half the time these things don't work right." He saw the AFSN officer's eyes focus on the extra set of earphones near the files. "The earphones are unreliable. A few minutes ago I just about thought I'd found something under here—very loud pulses from the microphone—when the earphones went dead. With the new set, I pick up a lot of static, but can't get the pulsing back. Maybe the damned micro—"

The kapitan took one step inside the room and another leisurely puff on his *papirosa*. "All these machines work better when they're plugged in." Shevshenko turned and saw the kapitan was holding the plug to the bug detector in his hand; a coldness swept over Shevshenko as he remembered he'd removed it to plug in the sensor for the combination locks. The kapitan followed the sensor's wire and confirmed what he already knew. "Fascinating work, as I said, Comrade. But dangerous." Turning, the kapitan called to someone outside the door. "You were right, Lieutenant. One of our friends from the KGB. Come take him away."

Mikhail Chorniev heard about Shevshenko just as he was leaving for lunch. The KGB man in the lobby called Dzerzhinsky Street when he saw the AFSN men drag the struggling agent through the lobby. "Get the other men out. Fast," Chorniev snapped.

"Already done, Director. Before I called you."

A little later, the other men checked in. Without problems, one agent had located and replaced the letter in Foreign Minister Shtanov's desk. Unlike the armed forces and Marshal Borodinsky, the Foreign Office had no troops of its own and welcomed security sweeps by the KGB. No, he found no other copies, but since the letter was at the bottom of a "To Be Read" box, it was doubtful if Shtanov ever even saw it himself. Chorniev sighed in relief. That was one copy of the Klin document taken care of.

The report from the second man started off badly. He had, he said, practically torn Minister of Production Gertsen's office apart—there was no security there except their own KGB men. At first, he thought the document Director Chorniev wanted was not there. And that the man must have it in his office at the Ministry of Production. Just as he was leaving, though, he told Chorniev, he finally discovered it in a pile of papers labeled "To Take Home." Well, no, he couldn't *guarantee* no other copies had been made, but then, like Shtanov, Minister Gertsen apparently hadn't read it yet himself, so it was doubtful. Chorniev told neither of them about Shevshenko.

Leaning back uncomfortably, Chorniev reviewed things. The original Klin document savagely criticized Klin for sending the KGB on a fool's errand, investigating Salt Mine. Result: a valued KGB informer, Volovno, murdered, a KGB agent killed. Chorniev had expected Borodinsky to add the memo to his dossier on Klin, not copy and distribute it.

The document had backfired badly. For Salt Mine was not the will-o'-the- wisp Chorniev had imagined, but a bombshell; the original Klin document could now, instead of damaging Klin, *destroy* Chorniev. In a desparate maneuver, his KGB men had been supposed to replace the first Klin document with a second, taking exactly the opposite tack from the first. In it, Chorniev accused Klin of not taking Salt Mine seriously enough and predicted Salt Mine would eventually turn out to be of extreme importance. The maneuver turned out to be more complicated than expected; the stealing and replacement had also backfired.

He had two of the copies back in his possession and replaced with new ones. That was good. The third copy was still in circulation. That was bad. And Shevshenko had been caught red-handed in Borodinsky's office, which was worse.

Chorniev was well aware that the AFSN's interrogation techniques were as effective as the KGB's. Like everyone else in the services, Marshal Borodinsky was paranoid on the subject of the KGB, and it would be only a matter of time before he discovered who had sent Shevshenko to his office—and why. The marshal would not be pleased to discover he was being used.

The answer was obvious. The stakes in Chorniev's game continued to grow.

• Blaine Decatur sat against a wall of the Oruzheinaya, his long legs crossed at the ankles, a rolled-up blanket behind his head as a pillow. Watching the interplay between the various contingents of hostages and captors was becoming boring. The Soviet doctor and his nurses, he noticed, were isolated now; because of their part in the meningitis plot, everyone stayed away from them. For a while, he thought about Chessie; the newspaper accounts might convince her he was dead. Perhaps by now she was already on the prowl for a replacement. An angry frown grew on his forehead. At DataCon, the same thing could easily be happening: Behind closed doors, savage politics were being played; secret submeetings were being held; underlings were struggling for his job. And one day, a new president would be presented to the board. Bastards. The frown grew.

Gary. The only reason he wasn't here was his habit of always missing, or being late for, appointments. At least this guaranteed that someone other than his crusty middle-aged sister would inherit his money and stock. The frown changed to a small smile.

"It is good to see you smile, Mr. Decatur," said Irina, trying to smooth her Intourist guide's uniform without much success.

For a moment, Decatur was startled; the woman had materialized in front of him. "Oh. Hi, Irina. It wasn't a very big smile, I'm afraid. I was just thinking how right I was not wanting to come here that day. Maybe it was a premonition."

"Next time, perhaps I shall pay more attention to my Americans' premonitions."

"I only hope you get the chance."

"It will work out, Mr. Decatur." Irina's attempt at reassurance was less than convincing. She appeared to sense this herself and changed the subject. "Tell me, Mr. Decatur, I have mentioned this before. But the closeness between the terrorists—the dissidents—of Salt Mine—and you Americans. It is impossible not to see how it grows every day. Do you really hate us that much?"

"Hate? No. It has nothing to do with that. Somewhere I read about a thing called the 'Stockholm effect.' They call it that because of some bank robbers in Stockholm. See, they held this group of women hostage for several days. The women were scared to death, of course. But when they were finally released, none of them would testify against the bank robbers. Some kind of link had been formed between them. I suppose, in America, the Patty Hearst kidnapping was the same thing. Anyway, one of the women in Stockholm had become so dependent on the bank robbers that later, when the bank robbers were let out, she married one. Crazy, I admit. It's very complicated; psychologists have a field day with the relationship between hostages and their captors."

"I keep hearing that all Americans hate us. Is it the human-rights thing?"

Blaine laughed. "No, *that's* politics." Blaine paused for a moment to consider. "Fear, perhaps, but not hate."

Solemnly, Irina moved around and sat beside Blaine Decatur. For a few moments, she remained quiet, considering what he'd said, her face an expression of wanting to believe but not quite daring to. Blaine saw a small frown form on her face and her mouth open as if to say something more. Both her proximity and the discussion were making him uncomfortable; the last thing he wanted with Irina was a philosophical discussion on politics.

Standing up, Blaine patted her on the shoulder and pretended he was going to the men's room. A little of Irina went a long way.

• The driver of the plain black sedan was not used to coping with traffic on Moscow streets. He swore, ground the gears, and twice stalled the motor as he headed the midsized Volga toward the AFSN interrogation center on Baltiiskaya Street, near the Leningradskoye Highway. Ordinarily, main thoroughfares such as Gorky and Leningradsky Prospekt are easy to navigate, with only the thinnest of traffic; it was not that the roads in Moscow were so wide, but that there were so few private cars.

Today, though, several blocks from the center, traffic suddenly became a snarled mess. The driver turned his head and said something that caused the two AFSN men in the back to laugh; Shevshenko, who sat between them, his wrists in handcuffs, didn't bother to smile. A joke about how much of a hurry their prisoner must be in to get to the interrogation center didn't amuse him.

The driver swore again. The center of the road was torn up, and a crew was busy digging. The right-hand lane was blocked by a truck with a flat tire. To keep some vestige of traffic flowing, a policeman stood in front of the road construction diverting cars onto Pegovsky Prospekt, a winding, narrow street.

Halfway down Pegovsky, the driver could see more road construction; he put the Volga in reverse and found the way blocked by a second truck. With a grunt, the driver moved on up to the construction. Another policeman stood there, planted directly in front of the blinking red lights that commanded traffic to halt. At intervals, he allowed one car at a time to mount the sidewalk and bypass the torn-up road. When it came their turn, however, the policeman held up his hand, craning his head as if to observe something beyond him. "Dammit, tell that stupid policeman who we are," swore the driver. "He can't hear me from over here with all that jackhammering. Tell him so we can get the hell going." He began blowing long blasts on the Volga's horn.

The man on the right of the rear seat rolled down his window and unfolded his ID card, at the same time yelling loudly at the policeman. The policeman appeared deaf; his head didn't turn. Shuffling off the sidewalk, a flower seller leaned in through the open window. "Flowers?" she said.

"Move on, Old One. Go away."

"Pretty flowers, Comrade." The AFSN man became livid.

"I said go on—"

The old woman suddenly shoved the bouquet she was holding in through the window and directly into the man's face. It was only then he saw the revolver in her hand. Shevshenko, too, caught a glimpse of it—just before it exploded in his face. The men in the Volga started to recover and pile out after the woman, but something strange had happened with the bouquet. The inside of the car was filling with acid fumes that made the men choke and cough. They fell out of the car into the street, retching and tearing at their throats, tears streaming down their faces.

Only Shevshenko remained motionless, seated upright in the rear, as if waiting for a light to change. The neat, round hole in his forehead was as pristine and smooth-edged as a newly minted kopeck, so tidy not even a drop of blood appeared.

Why Shevshenko had been sent into Borodinsky's office, what Shevshenko was looking for, and whether or not he had found it could no longer be traced back to Mikhail Chorniev. And because the AFSN wasn't supposed to arrest KGB men, no one would know that Shevshenko had been killed.

Or for that matter, had ever existed.

19

THE FOURTH DAY, 2:00 P.M.

"My dear friend, what you ask is impossible. Be reasonable. I have tried everything to—"

"Trick us, deceive us, destroy us."

Klin's voice began to sputter. His speech stopped making sense, becoming a jumble of syllables, stutterings, and half-finished phrases. Occasionally, a whole sentence would emerge, but it would be something vapid like "You've lost your mind. . . ."

Klin couldn't remember being this shaken since he was eleven and some of his schoolmates held him under the water at Dynamo Beach. He had thought he was drowning then, but no one would listen when he screamed that he was. He felt he was drowning now, but no matter how he yelled or pleaded, Alyosha would not listen, and Klin knew that later, when he repeated Salt Mine's demands to Chaidze, no one in government would listen either. Desperately, Klin tried to explain this, wanting Alyosha to understand, but the man's voice stopped him.

"You're babbling, Klin. Angry, very angry. Bad for the blood pressure, anger. Well, we have a doctor and three nurses in here who might help you; these days, they haven't got much else to do."

The sputtering began again. Forcing himself to regain composure, Klin picked up the small crystal globe he used as a paperweight. It was hollow, and inside was the figure of Father Frost and his sled. When you turned it upside down, a snowlike substance whirled around in the globe. Frequently, Klin used it as a pacifier, but today, although he shook and spun it until Father Frost disappeared, it did nothing for him.

"Klin, are you still there? Klin? Speak to me, Klin," Alyosha hissed. "I want to be sure you haven't come down with meningitis."

Grim-faced, Klin slammed the glass ball hard on his desk top. On his chest, he felt the skin prickle; a damp, cloying feeling was breaking out over his entire body. The sweating made his scalp itch unbearably. Twice, his hand rose to scratch it but was snatched back down; the third time he surrendered and dragged his fingertips across his scalp—a deep, satisfying scratch, but one he knew he would pay for later. Strangely, it brought him a sudden calm. "Look," he said to Alyosha quietly, "what you are asking is beyond anyone's power to grant. I am sorry that—"

"You kept pushing for Salt Mine's demands, Klin. Well, now you have them. Certainly, you didn't expect them to be easy."

"It's not a matter of what is hard or easy. Salt Mine's demands are impossible. I told you a long time ago you are playing right into the hands of those who favor a total attack and the hell with the hostages. They consider my handling of the situation too gentle. . . ."

Alyosha laughed his dry laugh and Klin felt his fury soar. "Oh, my, Klin! You certainly have been gentle. Poisoning children. Soldiers crawling around the foundations of the building. Tanks and troops in the courtyard. Gentle? Definitely. Gentle as the bloodier *suras* of the Koran."

For a moment, Klin was thrown. His image of Alyosha was always jarred when he discovered him to be educated, even erudite. His use of the little-known name for the verses of the Koran—*sura*—made him wonder if Alyosha might not be Muslim. Klin grew furious with himself for being concerned with such a trivial matter at such a key moment. "I should warn you," he noted, "that at this very moment the hard-liners are plumping for immediate action against you. Assault. You have until sometime tomorrow morning and then—"

Alyosha stopped Klin in midsentence. "No, Klin. *You* have until tomorrow morning. Twelve noon. If you have not agreed to Salt Mine's demands by then—or something close to them—we shall start executing the prisoners. As the Kremlin chimes strike one, one hostage. As they strike two, two hostages. As they ring three . . . et cetera. With the number of hostages we have, it needs no genius to see we can continue this process for some time."

The thought of this slow, agonizing carnage—and that the Soviets would, inevitably, be blamed for it—passed through Klin's consciousness. Alyosha seemed to be reading his mind.

"It also requires no genius to predict the effect on world opinion. The name and nationality of each hostage you have forced Salt Mine to execute will be made public. As it takes place. Public outcry rarely affects the Soviet government; this may."

Until this point, Klin had managed to remain reasonably calm-sounding. Inside he was flustered and angered, but his voice had retained its reasonableness. He had sweated; his scalp had itched, but with a high degree of self-control, he had forced himself to listen to Salt Mine's demands—calmly. Klin countered, he argued, he cajoled, he reasoned—calmly. Abruptly, the dam burst.

"Listen, you murdering offspring of a pig, I've had all I shall take." Klin's voice rose to a scream, high-pitched, ranting, his pronunciation disintegrating into what must have been his normal dialect before he cultivated the softer, more urbane accents of Moscow's new aristocracy. "You are a traitor. A hooligan, a kidnapper, a killer of innocents. Spreading a lot of pretentious drivel about government and freedom and human rights. Human rights? You who kill at random? Son of a camel! You try to make your pig-prick Salt Mine a noble cause instead of the self-serving robbery it is. Maybe it makes you feel important; I don't know. I ought to feel sorry for you, but I can't be that dishonest; you make me vomit. Coward. Killer. Eater of horse-droppings." Klin's voice trailed off. There was a pause and Klin was surprised to discover he was breathing so heavily it made a rasping noise over the phone. "And another thing—"

"One hostage will be executed when the Kremlin chimes strike one," repeated Alyosha tonelessly. "As they strike two, two more hostages will be executed. And so forth. Unless you meet Salt Mine's demands—or something reasonably close. Do you understand me?" After Klin's near-hysterical screaming, Alyosha's voice sounded as gentle as a doctor talking to a terminal patient.

"You bastard. Mother-fucker . . . Horse-cocker . . ."

"You should learn some new words, Minister. Yours are as old-fashioned as your politics."

Klin heard Alyosha click off. Possibly he thought Klin would continue screaming into a dead phone—Klin didn't know. He had let his facade crumble in front of the man, and that was not good; to Alyosha, he knew, it was a moment to be savored.

Storming out of the room, Klin climbed the worn stone

steps of the Vodovzvodnaya Tower two at a time, his breath coming in short gasps. On the tower, the raw wind tore at his fur hat and made his coat flap like a loose jib on a windward leg. Even squinting, he could feel the wind-tears gathering in the corners of his eyes, and he rubbed them with the back of his fur mittens. It was good there was something he could rub or scratch without being told he should wear white gloves.

Klin walked to the battlement of the Vodovzvodnaya and let his hands rest on the rough stones. In spite of the cold, he welcomed this moment alone with the wind. Downstairs, the steamy room was filled with equipment and noise and people, and—worst of all—the memories of Alyosha's and Salt Mine's arrogant demands.

Borodinsky would arrive tomorrow morning, early, and would need little time to organize his assault. If his own final attempt was to have any chance at all, it would have to be executed tonight. A volunteer with the right credentials had to be found. KGB men had the wrong kind of training. Soldiers had the right training but reported, however indirectly, to Borodinsky. He kicked the stone of the battlements in frustration. Looking at his watch, Klin took one final breath of the crisp, frigid air and walked slowly down the uneven steps to the office below, thinking.

• In the heart of what has been described as Moscow's St. Germain lies the Bely Gorod, or old white city. Bordered on one side by the Sadovoye Ring, the district was home to Gogol, Chekhov, Pushkin, Gorky, and countless others of the Russian literati. Originally, tradesmen had inhabited the area. Little by little, the nobility pushed them out, building their graceful town houses where small stores and shops once stood. When fashions changed again, the nobility defected elsewhere, and writers, playwrights, and artists moved in. The Soviet planners have allowed their creative imprint to remain and, indeed, have contributed to it: *Izvestia,* the APN (the Soviet Press Agency), and *Trud* (the newspaper of the unions) all have their offices here. Today, it is Moscow's version of Fleet Street.

Keer parked the Chevy around the corner and walked slowly down Markov Street, stopping frequently to gaze in shop windows; this gave him a chance to check behind him.

At Markov Street Number 13, he gave a final backward glance and turned in the doorway. As the door closed behind him, a cloud of dust was stirred up and made him cough; no one could claim that Number 13 had had its original, old-world atmosphere spoiled by the Revolution.

Reaching the top of the stairs, Keer paused at a rippled-glass door; a black-lettered inscription declared a second-hand bookstore lay beyond. The custom of giving stores names as well as addresses is only slowly returning to Moscow, so this fabulous bookstore—something out of Dickens—is known to the world only as Markov Street Number 13 Bookstore.

As Keer opened the door, a distant bell tinkled but produced no reaction from anyone inside. Ceiling to floor, the room was lined by shelves stuffed with books. No attempt had been made to categorize the jumble; a book was simply put on a shelf when a predecessor was sold. To one side were two long tables, each with a glass-covered, boxlike construction on top; confused masses of antique postcards, Russian and foreign—brightly colored scenes from the sentimental to the comic—were piled messily below the glass.

This was always Keer's favorite spot at Number 13. He loved to raise the lids on the cases and thumb his way through the postcards, many of them hand-colored photographs from the turn of the century. In the pictures, the ladies and gentlemen, the minor nobility of the day, were frozen into stiiff, uncomfortable-looking positions, their eyes viewing the camera as you might an enemy, an occasional sad expression indicating the individuals photographed suspected everything in their world would crumble long before the postcards did.

"Fascinating." Andrew Jax's voice materialized behind him. With no further conversation he disappeared into one of the passages between the ceiling-to-floor bookshelves. After pausing to glance at a collection of old etchings, Keer went and stood beside him. In fuller detail than before, he outlined how the hostages had recovered from their government-sponsored sickness, the scenes inside the Oruzheinaya, and how the government had first shot their own doctor, Tbor, and then replaced him with a physician assigned to bring Salt Mine down. (Keer's account was not entirely accurate. Tbor, after all, was no longer a doctor but a government informer shot trying to escape *from* Salt Mine. His own version, Keer felt, would make more damaging newspaper reports.)

His back to Keer, Jax continued to thumb through a dog-eared copy of *The Possessed*, looking straight ahead as he spoke. "It's hard to believe they ever could be stupid enough to get themselves into that mess to begin with. They'll lose the few friends they have with crap like that." He replaced *The Possessed* on its shelf and picked up a dusty edition of Dos Passos. Abruptly, he turned directly to Kerr. "What did you *really* ask me here for today?"

"The big ones. Now the big stories start coming."

"The *big* ones?"

"The demands. The escape. I'll have details for you late this afternoon. Get what I gave you off right away—I know I'm always saying that, but there's a reason—and I'll be ready with the demands."

"Same phone booth, or a different one?"

"Same."

"When?"

"Four-thirty. I won't have all the demand stuff to give you by then, but later I'm going to leave an outline of it in that copy of *Les Misérables* a couple of feet down the shelf." When Jax looked at him questioningly, Keer explained: "That's in case they catch me—there's a regular manhunt on now. At least you'll have the bare bones of the demands to give out. The demands are the heart of Salt Mine; unless the world knows what they are, a lot of people might have died for very little."

Jax was about to ask more, but before he could, Keer walked away. He paused at the desk with a handful of the turn-of-the-century postcards, paid the ancient attendant behind the desk a few kopecks for them, and left.

Jax watched the boy disappear, jaunty, self-possessed. The old-fashioned bell rang as he opened the door to leave. To Jax, the bell sounded sad. Like the people on the postcards, perhaps it had private information about the future.

• Chorniev fretfully paced his office floor at Dzerzhinsky Street. The man who just left—a small, bearded professor from the Institute of Speech at Leningrad—had confounded Chorniev, yet could not be ignored. Chorniev was tempted to write his findings off, but he had had too many profitable sessions with him in the past to close his eyes to what the professor said.

And what the professor said shook Chorniev badly. An analysis of the phone taps from the outside man to the Oruzheinaya, using voiceprint analysis, indicated the outside man was shockingly young. Not over twenty, probably less, the professor said. Further, from computerized word-by-word verbal breakdowns, the professor added that his cultivated, well-educated, upper-class speech patterns indicated he was one of Moscow's "privileged ones."

Certainly, it was not unusual that a young upper-class Soviet citizen—"new aristocracy" was not the sort of expression that Chorniev used—should be in conflict with the Party. It was not new; youth had always challenged the existing order, whether Communist or Tsarist. And the phenomenon was not exclusive to the Soviet. Hadn't rebellious Vietnam protesters—all young, many upper-class—reportedly brought down an American president? French students and their riots. Baader-Meinhof uprisings in Germany. Iran's students. Chorniev sighed; it was something one accepted, he supposed.

What really disturbed Chorniev was where it left his manhunt. If the outside man *was* from Moscow's upper class, it followed that he was the son of some high Soviet official. Chorniev's instincts as a survivor had great difficulty coping with what could grow out of a search among these young people. Perhaps the verbal analysis was not sensitive enough to pick up an impostor, someone who merely affected the accent. No, the professor had already covered that point and said it was impossible. The professor's conclusion, then, was not one that could be taken lightly. In the small, inbred world of Moscow's upper circles, a list of possibles would not be difficult to put together. Wearily, Chorniev reached for the phone.

Something inside made him hesitate. First, he would learn the results of the new interrogation, going on this moment at Lubyanka. It was, as Chorniev himself knew, not much more than an attempt to delay the inevitable.

• "If you had nothing to hide, then why didn't you report the incident to us as required?"

"It seemed so small a thing, Comrade. I planned to, originally, but the more I thought about it, the sillier it seemed."

"It is the rule."

"Yes, but in this case, the rule didn't really seem to apply. It seemed silly."

"If it were silly, it would not be a rule. We don't make rules for you to decide whether they are silly or not."

"But a lost earring. She said she thought it dropped into the secret files from the regular ones, and she was looking for it. . . ."

"Very convenient."

Svetlana Talchiev began to squirm; beneath her Intourist

uniform she could feel small beads of sweat forming between her breasts. She had gone to the KGB when she learned Lisenka was in the Oruzheinaya and was one of the Salt Mine dissidents. She had expected to be praised for her efforts; instead she was being grilled like a common criminal. And the KGB officer doing the grilling—a gray-faced little man in a shiny suit—was all but accusing her of complicity in Salt Mine.

"It remains difficult to understand, Comrade, why you didn't report so clear a violation of rules in your own department"—the shiny suit paused, a mirthless smile pulling the lips away from his teeth—"unless, of course, you had good reason to remain silent. Such as an interest in the outcome. Lisenka something-or-other working inside. You, outside. You as involved as Lisenka. . . ."

There. He had said it. He had come right out and put it into words and hurled them at her. "I am a loyal Party member," Svetlana said urgently, her voice rising as she spoke. "I have always done more than was required. I have given my life for the Party. You make some sort of terrible mistake, Comrade. For you to sit there and suggest—"

The shiny gray suit appeared neither surprised nor affected by Svetlana's growing outburst. He pressed a button on his desk and a matron came in. "Take the suspect, Svetlana Talchieva, to a holding cell until I instruct otherwise." As Svetlana was led away, the suit stood up and left her with one parting thought. "Perhaps, Comrade Talchieva, a cell will give you time to reconsider your statement about a 'terrible mistake.' You describe yourself as a loyal Party member. Well, a loyal Party member is always aware of one thing: The KGB, Comrade, does not make mistakes."

• Farther down the same row of interrogation rooms, Strelitz was having a considerably worse time. He was not a Party member. He had rented a room—a room in a government building—to a private person, which in itself was a crime under the Uniform Residency Act. Worse, that tenant had turned out to be Alyosha Gregarin, the leader of Salt Mine. Forensics had determined that it was in this very room that a KGB man, Comrade Bleisky, had been knifed to death by the same Alyosha Gregarin, shortly before Salt Mine took place.

Did the accused, Strelitz, really expect anyone to believe all of this had gone on under his roof without his knowledge and help? The blows—they were supposed to be slaps but were of such intensity they were really closer to hard punches—sent Stretlitz's head crashing from side to side like a punching bag on a long spring. Yes, he had known what he was doing was illegal. Yes, renting out space in a government building was a crime and he deserved to be punished severely for it. But, no, he had not known about Salt Mine or that Alyosha was part of it. Nor had he known Comrade Bleisky had been murdered there.

"Did you ever see Comrade Bleisky?"

"I saw him come in. I heard him go out. This man Gregarin said Bleisky would pay me the room money—"

"Was that before or after you and Gregarin killed him?"

"I didn't kill him. I knew nothing—"

The punching bag on the end of the spring began snapping back and forth again. The KGB learned nothing. It never occurred to them that this was because there was nothing to learn.

• Each report plunged Chorniev deeper into gloom. His efforts to unearth the outside man seemed stalled, while the pressure from Klin to deliver grew hourly. From his sources, he knew Klin himself was in trouble. In the rapidly shifting kaleidoscope of Kremlin internal alignments, there might be an advantage to be gained out of this somehow. Klin down was Chorniev up, he repeated to himself. Once again he would have to abandon his role of survivor and stick out his neck. Picking up the phone as if it were an enemy, Chorniev set in motion the making-up of lists the professor's conclusion demanded.

He had, Chorniev decided, little to lose.

• "All right," Alyosha shouted, getting the hostages in the Oruzheinaya back into some sort of formation. "Pretty good for a first rehearsal. When you get out of here, you should take up sprinting as a hobby. Out of here and home. I know it's hard, up and down those stairs, but it's necessary in case they keep their promise of an all-out assault. Let's do it again and try to beat our best time. You did it in four and a half minutes. Let's try for four."

"When you get out of here . . ." Alyosha heard himself say the words and wondered if they were hollow. If he abandoned just the right items in Salt Mine's demands, at the same time keeping up the pressure from the foreign press, they might make good their escape.

But Talanin and Klin—the whole Soviet *apparat,* in fact—were a serious lot. They would try every device they could come up with. Against the vastness of their machine, Salt Mine seemed suddenly small and pathetic. He smiled for the benefit of Lisa Decatur, heading toward him, probably to ask for the fourth time today precisely what Salt Mine was demanding for their release. With an apologetic bit of pantomime, he again took refuge in the men's room.

20

THE FOURTH DAY, 2:12 P.M.

"You are pleased to come with us." The man who said it didn't look particularly threatening, but two other men standing behind the first had the look of professional bullies. From his pocket, the first man drew a flat leather case, which he unfolded to show a card with his picture, his fingerprint, and the official stamp of the KGB. These men were playing the arrest by the book.

Jax smiled pleasantly. "I'd say I had another appointment, but I suspect that wouldn't get me very far."

"Please?" The man was confused. Ordinarily, even foreigners turned pale when confronted by the KGB.

"Oh, never mind. Let's go."

The man was so startled by Jax's easygoing reply he even said, "Thank you."

Later, at Klin's office at the ministry, the pose of politeness continued. "Ah, my dear friend, Mr. Jax. I am sure you realize this confrontation was inevitable."

"It crossed my mind."

"Quite frankly, I had hoped you would lead us to Salt Mine's outside man. I underestimated you. However, Secretary General Talanin was quite upset"—Klin laughed; his description of Talanin's reaction was a classic understatement—"at the coverage you gave the 'meningitis' device."

"He should be. It was immoral in the extreme."

"It depends on where one stands. In any case, Secretary Talanin—along with several other members of the Central Committee and the Council of Ministers—feels we cannot afford to have you running around loose any more. Therefore, I have a choice for you."

"Firing squad or hanging."

Klin attempted a smile, but the effect was painful to look at. As if it had a will of its own, his left hand rose to his scalp. Angrily, he snatched it back. "A choice," he repeated. "Either to leave the USSR at once . . ."

"The other choice?"

Ignoring him, Klin poured two small glasses of Armenian cognac and offered one to Jax, who accepted it with a nod. Really fine Armenian cognac has a good deal to be said for it.

"Ah, yes. The other choice. House arrest in your hotel. Under heavy guard. Incommunicado."

"That's not a hell of a lot of choice."

"Well, there are those who feel you should be taken to Lubyanka and interrogated. Fully interrogated. You know who Salt Mine's outside man is. However, Mr. Jax, I have convinced them such a step would only fuel the West's displeasure with us." Klin sipped his cognac, reaching down and picking up a pile of London and Paris papers and brandishing them at Jax. "Really, Mr. Jax. The things you write."

"About the things *you* do."

The phone on Klin's desk rang. It was Chaidze. A précis of Salt Mine's demands had just been read to Talanin; the effect was spectacular. Hanging up, Klin made a face and stared at the phone for some time, then moved his eyes to Jax.

"I must make a correction, Mr. Jax. You no longer have a choice. You are hereby placed under close house arrest at your hotel. Please do not endanger yourself by trying to leave or attempting to talk with anyone. Secretary Talanin is incensed. If it were not for your position in the world . . ."

"And since no one has seen Secretary Talanin for over a year—a stroke, I am told—it is probably unwise for him to become any more incensed. No choice, well, all right. House arrest. Dull as hell."

"Frankly, Mr. Jax, I was against allowing you to leave the country at this time. From the beginning. You could only become a public figure, telling your biased story of Salt Mine. It is better you stay."

"I trust you can arrange for food to be sent in. The Metropol's menu carries a lot of things, but most seem unavailable."

"Of course. Through my office. Merely have one of the guards outside your door call there."

"And that I may have access to foreign papers."

"They will be sent in. But nothing, you understand, will be

allowed to leave your room. Anything else you require, have the guard call me."

"Assuming you're not under arrest yet yourself."

The shudder that accompanied Klin's forced smile told Jax he had struck a raw nerve. Salt Mine's demands had been delivered to Talanin. And Klin was holding the bag. In spite of himself, Jax felt sorry for him. What a terrible way for a man to live. His readers would love it.

• Perhaps an hour later, on his way down Georgievsky Street toward his car, Keer heard a sudden voice behind him. "Don't turn around. Keep walking and I shall please to do the talking."

For a moment, Keer couldn't place the accent. But he thought—no, he was sure—that it was a Frenchman trying to sound English. And not succeeding overly well. Keer continued walking as instructed—but slowly, pausing to stare into the rabbit warren of small shops lining the street.

"Our Monsieur Jax—he had a premonition, a feeling, that is—that he would be arrested soon. It has happened. This morning's story, one presumes. He has given me your Salt Mine demands, but he will write the story. As to how he gets the story out of his incommunicado, well, that is better left unspoken. Along with assuming his other functions for you, I shall take his place at the phone booths." They walked on for several minutes in silence. "The phone numbers, the times, they will remain the same, yes? Do not to speak, please. If the answer is yes, stop and tie your shoelaces.

Leaning down, Keer pretended to have trouble adjusting his shoelaces. It would not have fooled a very observant watcher; Keer was wearing loafers. As he straightened up, he saw the shadow of the Frenchman pass him, and then his back disappearing down the street.

Keer Gertsen was a great lover of James Bond movies, but this was all growing a little too melodramatic for his blood. Suddenly, blood was a word he wished he hadn't used.

• "Where will you go *after?*" Lisenka put the question to Alyosha with some trepidation, knowing how private a person he was. But he only turned to look at her, that smile of his creeping across his face. It was his little-boy smile, a mixture of devilishness, innocence, and blatant deception.

"You mean where will I go *if,* don't you? First, a lot of things have to happen right. Those demands. Leeway for bargaining, yes. But Talanin's an unpredictable man among unpredictable men. They might say the devil with the hostages and come ripping in here with tanks and troops. So, that is one thing that has to go right." Alyosha tapped his lip with the sheaf of papers he held in his hand. "Then, there's the escape plan itself. You can be sure they will try anything and everything to deceive us there. Having us free would be a positive insult to them—"

"You're not answering my question. Where will you go *after?*"

Alyosha suddenly busied himself in the papers again; hers, Lisenka could see, was a question he had no intention of answering. Once more the little-boy smile moved across his face, as if he knew his maneuver with the papers was transparent. "We should start breaking these into two lists, I suppose. Now."

For a moment, Lisenka stood staring at him. His abrupt change in conversation was to let her know she was trespassing inside his private wall; his performance was unsubtle because he wanted it to be.

Infuriating. And yet looking at him as he stood there, Lisenka felt a hot swelling grow inside her, a wave of small shudderings that told her Alyosha had never meant more to her than he did this moment.

"The lists," he repeated, his voice on the edge of sharpness. "No matter what Talanin and Klin have in mind for us, we're going to need those lists, Lisenka."

"Damn." Lisenka snatched the papers out of his hand and, without looking back, walked quickly away.

• The meeting was to be a full-dress one, held in the special room of the Council of Ministers Building. The place at the head of the table was left empty for the perennially absent Talanin. Deputy Premier Chaidze sat to the right of the empty chair, looking uncomfortable and carefully avoiding Klin's eyes.

From the moment he came into the room, Klin knew the skin on his head was changing colors. And as he sat down, he could sense the distance each man there tried to put between Klin and himself. They were civil enough, but none of them could ignore the smell of death that hung around him.

Deputy Premier Chaidze poured himself a glass of mineral water from the bottle set in front of each chair, cleared his throat, and rattled his sheaf of papers to get the members' attention. "Comrades, it would be ridiculous to pretend we don't know why we are here." A soft murmur rose from the ministers, and Klin could feel the walls being built higher.

"This morning," Chaidze continued, "we received Salt Mine's demands. They are impossible. Secretary Talanin then talked to Marshal Borodinsky, and he will undertake an immediate assault on both the Oruzheinaya Palata and Lenin's Tomb sometime tomorrow morning. Preparations are already under way."

This time there was no soft murmur. A chorus of disagreement rose from the ministers who would be most affected.

"Good God," exploded Foreign Minister Shtanov, aware of the chain of reactions their attack would provoke. "The Americans . . . I've talked to their ambassador here . . . Dobrynin has been consulted in Washington . . . assurances were given . . . promises made. . . ."

Deputy Premier Chaidze remained unruffled. He spoke with the firmness of a man who has the chief of state's orders in his pocket. "Talanin is putting himself on the hot line. He will talk to the American president, personally. The Soviet's patience until now will be pointed out, the decision to act explained." Chaidze took a swallow of mineral water. "He will also make clear the decision is unalterable."

For a moment there was silence. Everyone there had expected this decision eventually; no one there was ready for it when it came.

Klin looked Chaidze square in the eye, his voice suddenly soft. "Why?" he asked. *"Why?"*

There was a brief instant when Chaidze appeared thrown, as if he might have to dive into his pile of notes for an answer to Klin's deceptively simple question. The answer came to him as if by osmosis. "Last night. Budapest. A demonstration for Salt Mine, staged by hooligans and dissidents. Warsaw. The same thing there. Closer, the Ukrainian separatist movement is rallying around Salt Mine; so are agitators in the Georgian and Central Asian republics. Salt Mine is an infectious disease; we are being laughed at. In the satellite countries, even in some of the home republics. Given the times, it is exceedingly dangerous."

"With the assault, we will be torn apart by those countries with any number of hostages involved. America . . ." said Shtanov, struggling with the problem of how he could steer the Foreign Office through the incident.

"Without the assault," noted Chaidze, "we will be torn

apart by our own republics." Deputy Premier Chaidze threw up his hands. "Whatever we do, we are damned. It becomes a choice between evils. Secretary Talanin has made that part easier: he has chosen which evil."

Still trying, Foreign Minister Shtanov turned to Klin. "You can think of nothing else to try, Vasily, no way without endangering the hostages?"

"At the moment, no," he lied. "If we just had more time, dammit. If we had more time, we—"

"No." Deputy Premier Chaidze's answer was underlined by the slapping-shut of the leather folder in front of him. "No more time. If we had dealt with this matter more firmly at the beginning, as some urged, there would have been a lot of crying and moaning, of course, but we would not find ourselves in the impossible situation we are in today."

This implied criticism of Klin, stemming from Chaidze's meeting with Talanin earlier today, was missed by no one. Klin could feel his head beginning to ache, a pain so severe it overshadowed the tingling of his scalp. Shoving his chair back, Deputy Premier Chaidze added a note of observation: "People forget incidents quickly; they *don't* forget situations where they have time to choose sides, identify with someone, and then watch them lose. We learned those lessons in Hungary and Czechoslovakia. We should have remembered what we were taught. So—no more time. Secretary Talanin made that quite clear. The assault will take place tomorrow—at an hour chosen by Marshal Borodinsky."

A chorus of voices rose from the table. The clamor quickly became louder and more insistent. Chaidze stood up. "This meeting is herewith adjourned." Looking neither to the right nor to the left, he stalked from the meeting room, strode briskly to his car, and disappeared through the Nikolskaya before anyone at the table fully realized he was gone.

• At the apartment on Georgievsky and Gorky the steaming hot water streamed down Keer's body, calming and relaxing the tightened muscles, massaging the bunched-up nerves beneath his skin with a thousand hot fingers. Inside the glassed-in enclosure, there was so much steam he could barely see his own toes; Keer inhaled the comforting vapor as if it were medicine. Ever since he was a child, Keer Gertsen had loved taking showers; it was where he could be utterly alone, away from the prying eyes of nurses, or even Dovo; it was where he came to think, to wrestle with his problems, emerging later, renewed and ready to face the world again.

Today, as he studied the soap lather following the water across his stomach and down his legs, Keer decided his problems divided into two kinds: one immediate, one future. The key one, of course, was whether tomorrow's make-or-break showdown on Salt Mine worked. That was out of his hands. The future problem was whether Alyosha's escape plan would work or collapse. It seemed even more fragile than Salt Mine itself. No amount of hot water pouring out of the showerhead could make him feel better about that.

And Gary. Gary had to be sent packing. Back to his hotel. The ministry had been unclear whether Keer's father would be arriving tonight or tomorrow morning—they mentioned some important meeting, and Keer couldn't help wondering if it was about Salt Mine—but he was definitely coming. His father, suspicious of all foreigners, would automatically assume Gary was somehow part of it. Anyway, fond as he had grown of Gary, Keer didn't dare have him around during these critical moments of Salt Mine.

Watching the soapsuds swirl around his toes, Keer couldn't resist smiling at the picture of his father assuming it was Gary who was connected with Salt Mine. Quickly the smile vanished. The water was turned off and Keer stepped out of the stall onto the bathroom rug, beginning to towel himself as hard as he could stand it. Dovo, he suddenly reminded himself. Dovo must be told not to mention Gary to his father. He had always kept Keer's secrets from his employer before when asked to; it was an arrangement that went back to Keer's childhood. For, from the time Keer could walk, it was Dovo who really raised him, playing surrogate father and mother to him. Dovo would be silent.

As the steam in the bathroom began to clear, Keer saw his wristwatch on the shelf above the basin. His heart sank. Standing under the shower, he had lost all track of time. Five-fifteen. He was already half an hour late for his check-in call to the Oruzheinaya, and by the time he pulled on some clothes and found a safe telephone booth, he would be almost an hour late. Damn.

Impatiently finishing with the towel, Keer hit upon a solution but promptly dismissed it. A few seconds later, he was back considering the idea as a possibility. It was dangerous. But Dovo was shopping; Keer had talked to the old man earlier. With the endless queues that were always part of shopping in Moscow, Dovo would be gone a long time. Gary, he remembered, was asleep, curled up on his bed down the hall, a small frown marring his face, as troubled dreams of his family intruded into his peace. The cook, Toko, was off today.

For a second, Keer paused, wrapping himself in his towel as he brushed his hair in front of the mirror. Calling the Oruzheinaya from his home was risky, but apparently necessary. If he kept the conversation short—much too short to be traced—it might not be as dangerous as he first thought. Softly, he pushed the door to his bedroom shut. At the phone—an extension he had plugged in because no one else was in the house—he held the towel firmly around his middle with one hand and dialed the number with the other. To Lisenka, he gave assurance that the story of Salt Mine's demands would be on the wire any minute. Please tell Alyosha. He would follow through tomorrow.

Suddenly, Keer stopped; a creaking floorboard outside his room made a sudden and unfamiliar noise. A line of gooseflesh crept across his stomach. "No, no. It is nothing, Lisenka. I said I would follow the Salt Mine story myself and report back. In about half an hour. Yes, it's—"

The board outside his room creaked again. Keer knew this apartment on Georgievsky as he did his own body. He and his father and Dovo had lived here for as long as Keer could remember. No loose board had ever creaked there before; someone was outside. A prowler? A thief? The KGB? Fascinated, as if it were happening to someone else, Keer kept talking, his voice suddenly flat, his eyes unwilling to accept that he could now see the doorknob slowly beginning to turn. Not only was someone making the board outside his door creak, someone was opening that door. He hung up, but continued talking as if still on the phone. Frantically, Keer looked around the room for something to defend himself with; all he could see was the lead paperweight on his desk, a heavy semipyramidal device once used by some minor noble to make sealing-wax impressions on legal papers. There was nothing with a handle that would allow him to keep a distance between himself and the intruder. Grabbing the paperweight, he moved soundlessly on his bare feet toward the door. As he clutched his pathetic weapon, the towel slipped from around him; ordinarily he would have stopped and replaced it; this was no moment for niceties.

Standing directly inside the door, he put one hand gently

on the doorknob, allowing it to continue turning. With a sudden wrench, Keer pulled the door open as hard as he could, the paperweight upraised. For a second he blinked. The hall outside was dim and his room brightly lit, and his eyes had trouble adjusting to the change in light. But the silhouette was impossible not to recognize.

"Jesus, Dovo," Keer laughed in relief, "you scared the shit out of me."

"I am sorry," Dovo muttered, and for the first time Keer saw that he held a revolver in his hand. What had scared *him*, he wondered? In his relief, Keer babbled.

"I heard this noise out here and then I saw the doorknob turning and I didn't know who the hell was wandering around. Wow."

"I am sorry," Dovo repeated. "I am sorry for much, Keer. I tried to pretend that I didn't notice so many things. I raised you since you were a baby. I took care of you when you were sick. I dried your tears when you fell playing some silly game and hurt yourself. It's as if . . ." Dovo stopped, unable to speak. Keer was baffled; the revolver was still in Dovo's hands, still raised.

"Dovo, I don't understand. I . . ."

Dovo straightened himself, throwing back his ancient frame into a braced position. "I know you don't understand, Keer. But I can no longer pretend not to notice what has become obvious even to an old fool like me." From his pocket, Dovo withdrew a thin wallet which he let fall open. Inside was the ID card of the KGB.

"You?" Keer wasn't yet sure whether to run or to laugh. "*You*, Dovo?"

"Yes. Me. Old Dovo. I was assigned to your father when he was still deputy minister of production, but when we already knew he would soon be minister. Every minister has a KGB man assigned to work somewhere around him, keeping track of who he is seeing, what he is saying, how he is thinking. But, Keer, my son, I wasn't assigned to love you as I came to. No one ordered me to replace the mother who died and the father who abandoned you. That just happened. I love you as a son, which makes this duty hard, very hard. I suspected something was happening for a long time. Your strange comings and goings. That American boy suddenly staying with us. And now—that telephone call. I can pretend no longer. It hurts—oh, Keer, it hurts—but I would be a traitor to the Party, I would defile my oath to the Soviet, if I didn't. Please, Keer, don't make it any harder than it already is for me. Put on your clothes and we will go to KGB headquarters. I promise you I will do everything—"

Keer lunged at him. The paperweight slipped from his fingers, moist with sweat, and Keer had to use his bare hands, fastening them around Dovo's neck. The old man was surprisingly strong, and Keer suddenly found that Dovo was sitting on top of him, pinning his arms to the floor.

Keer heard the thud, but at the time, it meant nothing to him.

Looking up as Dovo's body suddenly went limp, he saw Gary standing above the man's head, the heavy Number Nine iron held in his hand. Staring, Keer studied the face that had tended him so many years, his eyes misting as a wave of sadness rolled over him. "Something woke me," Gary began. "I heard someone shouting, then someone falling. I came down the hall and saw the gun in his hand. What . . . ?"

Keer's reaction was odd, causing Gary to stare at him uncertainly. "You shouldn't have done that," Keer said, a plaintive note to his voice.

Gary should have been warned off by Keer's tone, but wasn't. "You helped me when I was in trouble," he said proudly, "so when you were in trouble—I don't know what the hell it is—I helped you. Easy."

"You shouldn't have done that," repeated Keer. He knelt beside Dovo, trying to find some sign of life. There was none.

"Jesus, Keer. I don't know what the scoop is here—something about the KGB—it's none of my business, but—"

"You shouldn't have done that," Keer said again, a stuck needle on a record player. A terrible sinking feeling tore at him.

Gary exploded. "Christ, Keer! The guy's got a gun in his hand. He's kneeling on your chest. You're trying to zonk him with a paperweight, he's trying to strangle you or shoot you, I don't know which. You're both screaming bloody murder. It looked like him or you. So what the hell." Keer watched Gary as he shrugged and stuffed his hands in his pockets, his mouth set in bewilderment. He took several short steps away, then turned to confront Keer again. "I don't get it. You Russians . . . you're all nuts, I think."

The word "Russian" snapped Keer out of his daze. He felt himself coming back to the reality of things. "I'm sorry," he began. "You're right, Gary. Dead right." When Keer stood up, he found himself unsteady. "It's just that—well, Dovo sort of brought me up. He was more of a father than mine ever was. He loved me and I loved him, I guess. Only after all these years I found out he was a KGB plant. So . . ." Keer's voice trailed off.

"Okay, okay. The story's none of my business. Neither's whatever the hell you're mixed up in. And I'm sorry if I did the wrong thing, but . . . Jesus!"

"It should be, but can't be, your business. And you did the right thing, honest, so don't worry about it. You saved my life, really, and I owe you for that. It's just too bad it had to be poor old Dovo. A sweet guy. A good man. Except, well . . ." Keer's voice began to falter.

Gary seemed determined not to let Keer slide back into sadness. He looked at Keer for a long time, then allowed a smile to creep over his face. "Say, is that a Russian custom? I mean, knocking off the KGB buck-naked?"

In spite of things, Keer had to laugh. The towel. He'd forgotten the towel. When he had retrieved it from the floor, he placed it across Dovo's face and went into the bathroom for another to wrap around himself. He looked down at poor old Dovo and sighed heavily. The towel was necessary. Those pale staring eyes had looked at him with trust too long to see him now.

21

THE FOURTH DAY, 7:12 P.M.
Uncomfortably Alyosha shifted from leg to leg, watching them gather. Ahead of him lay his talk to the assembled hostages—they deserved at least that much, he had decided—and Alyosha loathed anything that smacked of making a speech. Grimacing, he saw that Lisenka had the last of the hostages in tow and was trying to settle them into some sort of formation facing him; Alyosha would speak in Russian; she would translate into English, Spanish, and German. Like a performer studying the night's audience, Alyosha watched the hostages form into the natural national groupings you would expect. Considering everything, they were a remarkably cheerful lot, chatting with each other, joking, sometimes laughing. A handful remained sullen.

A hissing sound made Alyosha realize that Lisenka and Misha were hushing the crowd; the chattering and occasional laughter subsided into an expectant silence. "Good evening, my friends," Alyosha began, hoping the slight tremor in his voice didn't show. From Lisenka came the three bursts of translation, sounding silly because he'd paused after so few words.

"I would like to begin by thanking you all personally for bearing with us through such difficult times. I am amazed by the good humor and lack of complaint you have shown. Each of you is a credit to your own country. And it struck me as only fair to tell you at this point what demands we have made to the government for your release.

"To those of you not used to the Russian way of doing business, some of these demands may sound impractical, even bizarre. But ours is a society built upon the art of haggling. Salt Mine will make its price deliberately outrageous; the authorities will counter with suggestions equally outrageous. To receive a crust, we must demand a loaf.

"As for the contents of the demands, kindly remember we are not traitors, we are dissidents. And that the demands of Salt Mine are designed to force the world to see the Soviet government as it really is, not as the Soviet tells the world it is.

"For it is true that we have a constitution. To you Americans, it would read very much like your own. But your constitution is observed as a matter of law; the Soviet constitution is just words on a piece of paper.

"For instance, our constitution, like yours, guarantees freedom of speech. Yet if one says the wrong thing—even to a friend—one may well end in prison. Many who supported Charter Seventy-seven—a Czechoslovakian document—wound up in asylums. That is the Soviet idea of freedom of speech. . . ."

While Lisenka went through the translations, Alyosha again studied the hostages' faces. He was not startled to see the head-nodding among the Russians as he spoke; here, in the Oruzheinaya, was one place they didn't have to fear the KGB. The Americans appeared to grasp what Alyosha was getting at, although here and there he could see traces of irritation that this thing called Salt Mine should involve them in something really not their affair.

Turning around, Lisenka looked at Alyosha expectantly. "And kindly remember also," he continued, "that with these demands we hope to dramatize to the world what we in Salt Mine seek for Russia." Clearing his throat, Alyosha for the first time referred to his notes.

"One: Immediate release from prison of the following eight well-known dissidents. And guarantees that they, and others like them, will not be put in prison again for refusing to silence their dissatisfactions with the present Soviet system."

As Alyosha read the list of eight names—all writers and scientists now in prison for speaking their minds—a stir rose from the Russian hostages; to most of them, the names were awesome and familiar.

"Two: Anyone who wishes to emigrate from Russia is to be guaranteed this privilege. This is not only to apply to Jews—the most oppressed minority—but to anyone anywhere in this country who desires to leave.

"Three: Immediate access to the Soviet public of any foreign publication or television program they wish to see. Also—and more specifically—the government must allow an immediate meeting between Salt Mine and members of the foreign press and television, right here in the Oruzheinaya Palata. The Soviet government must at the same time agree not to interfere with any broadcast coming from here." As the translation reached them, a faint gasp rose from the hostages. You did not have to live in the Soviet Union to imagine the government's reaction to a live, uncensored television program being sent from the heart of the Kremlin by a group of dissidents.

"Four: The delivery to Salt Mine of the following three infamous members of the KGB. While they are enemies of fundamental decency, they will be handled with a scrupulousness they never showed to others. Their disposition is unspecified but will be decided solely by Salt Mine." The names of the three men were read aloud, and the Russian hostages exchanged glances; even to them, the names were obscure.

"Five: Two airplanes from mutually agreed-upon neutral countries to be standing by tomorrow. All hostages will be released upon landing; the members of Salt Mine will take their chances with whatever disposition these foreign countries decide to make of them."

The last item produced general applause; at last, Alyosha had gotten down to the one subject that really concerned them: their own release. Most of the American hostages might agree with Salt Mine's dedication to freedom of the press and its devotion to personal liberties, but the one concept of freedom that was on their minds just now was to get out of this nightmare situation and back to their own lives.

His greenish eyes darting from group to group, Alyosha tried to measure the effects of his outline upon them. He couldn't. "And those, my friends, are what Salt Mine is demanding for your release. I sincerely believe that by this time tomorrow, all of you—not to mention ourselves—will be on the way out of this beloved but tortured country. In just a minute, I shall be pleased to accept any questions you may have, but first, I should like to make an additional announcement. Although, considering what you have been through, it is only a small gesture, we are tonight throwing a small party of appreciation. There will be extra wine, some vodka, and even blinis, a Russian specialty you should enjoy." (When Alyosha had broached this subject to Klin earlier today, he was surprised by the total lack of resistance. "Why not?" Klin asked. "We can always hope you'll be so drunk, you'll come out of your own accord and spare us the assault. Tank ammunition is expensive, my friend.")

The reaction from the hostages to the party—an announcement Alyosha felt a little silly making—was interesting. Lisenka's tour group of Yale graduates applauded, because technically they were still on vacation, and getting drunk was a traditional part of any Yale man's holiday. Irina's charges, the Blaine Decaturs, showed no reaction at all. Lisa didn't believe in alcohol; Christy was too young to care; and Blaine couldn't get over the feeling that he was doomed. God repaying him for Chessie. The Russians cheered wildly, the Cubans remained sullen, and it was impossible to know what the East Germans thought.

Alyosha listened to the excited bantering; the hostages struck him as little children suddenly hearing a grown-up announce a surprise party. His own motives had nothing to do with children, or benevolent parents, or surprise parties. After the nightmare of the meningitis incident, he knew the hostages were feeling the strain badly. The tension was palpable, and they needed an excuse to let off steam. Tomorrow, he wanted them as relaxed and well disposed toward Salt Mine as he could make them.

During the period open to questions from the floor, he even managed to produce the appropriate reaction when one of the Yale Club tour shot to his feet to confront him. "My question, sir," the man said to Alyosha, "is a difficult, complex, but vital one." He stared at Alyosha, his face filled with anxiety. "When the hell," he asked, "do we break out the booze?"

Alyosha laughed.

This particular group might find themselves in desperate straits, but any man who can survive four years of "Bulldog! Bulldog!" Bones, and "Baaa, Baaa, Baaa . . ." is not going to change his habits for anything as transitory as the Union of Soviet Socialist Republics.

• "We should probably add this," suggested Dr. Brezhnietz, holding up a small slip of notepaper. Brezhnietz was the KGB's computer expert, and he had kept the DataCon 101 computer running full tilt all day, absorbing and rejecting information and spitting out hypotheses on Salt Mine's outside man. So far, its only consistent conclusion was that it lacked sufficient information. In front of Brezhnietz lay an enormous stack of paper. Here was collected every shred of evidence or hearsay which the KGB had amassed during their manhunt. Selection of material to be fed the computer was being done by Chorniev personally, because some of it was so highly speculative its inclusion could only throw everything off. Chorniev alone knew what was, and what was not, to some extent reliable. He looked up from his desk, staring at Brezhnietz.

"What is it?"

Leaning forward, Chorniev glanced at the slip Brezhnietz handed him. "Totally uncorroborated," he snapped. "Discard."

With a shrug, Dr. Brezhnietz put the slip on a pile to one side; Chorniev was not an easy man to work with. Chorniev wasn't trying to be. He was consumed by wanting to find the outside man before Borodinsky's assault. Not that he thought it would do any good at this point—he doubted if unearthing the man now would be of any practical value at all. But it would give him credit, at least, for finding him before, rather than after, the fact.

"What about this?" asked Brezhnietz, holding up another KGB report. "It's about some boy from the Georgievsky-Gorkovo area who called the KGB—"

In spite of Chorniev's "no calls" order to his secretary, the phone buzzed angrily at him. Klin. Pushing, cajoling, threatening. By the time the conversation was ended, the slip lay to one side, forgotten. On it was the KGB write-up of Keer's call to the KGB, the call that had resulted in the KGB arrest of one of its own men. The slip included Keer's name, age, and his father's title. If it had been put together with another slip already in the computer—the professor from Leningrad's profile of the person Chorniev was hunting, based on the voiceprint analysis of the Oruzheinaya tapes—and if a voiceprint analysis had been made of Keer's call to the KGB, the computer would not only have indicated Keer as the outside man, but have proved it.

• For what seemed an eternity, Kapitan Volodya Sokolov had been crawling on his stomach, the heavy special equipment strapped to his back making progress difficult. His movement across the Kremlin courtyard was made in the classic army creeping technique, on elbows and knees, the grenade launcher cradled in the crooks of his arms.

Every now and then he could see someone at a window of the Oruzheinaya fire a burst into the courtyard. The firing came frequently; someone must be worried about infiltration teams. Salt Mine tried to frighten these individual soldiers off as soon as they saw them. Often, what they fired at was not a man, but a shadow; still, the irregular bursts kept Volodya's nerves on edge.

He wasn't sure how he had gotten here. "Someone has to at least try it," Klin had said. "My KGB men don't have the training, and the damned soldiers are all under Borodinsky's control." Volodya volunteered. He was as startled as Klin to hear the words come out of his mouth. He stood in front of him, hoping that Klin would remember soldiers *were* under Borodinsky's command and that he, Kapitan Vladimir Mikhailovich Sokolov, was a soldier. Or that Colonel-General Pskov would suddenly materialize again in the Vodovzvodnaya Tower and forbid him to volunteer. Volodya sweated, waiting for Pskov or Borodinsky or somebody to arrive and save him. No one did.

Instead, he had watched aghast as a small smile of appreciation lit up Klin's face. "Good, Sokolov, good," breathed Klin. "You are what the Soviet government needs: men who think for themselves, men who will bend the organizational structure a little to get the job done. Good."

Numbly, Sokolov had nodded. "Come up to the tower roof with me," Klin had said, "and I'll show you how I think you should go about it. Of course, you're the soldier; I am the civilian. I will provide the special equipment, but the exact procedure is up to you."

Crawling along now, Volodya wished to the devil he had surveyed the situation from the Vodovzvodnaya and pronounced Klin's plan impossible. He had not; why he had not remained a mystery. Most probably, it was his instinct for glamour. After all of these years, Sokolov had finally made it to the gilded world of the Kremlin; Moscow was where he wanted to spend the rest of his career, here among the elite corps. Then Salt Mine shattered his dream. If he brought off Klin's plan and became its hero, his dream might be allowed to flourish again.

A burst from the far left window of the Oruzheinaya struck the cobblestones about twenty feet to his right. If they were aiming at him, they were very poor shots. More probably, they were shooting at shadows again.

For a few moments, Volodya froze; he had never been in combat, but this was what the training manual and his refresher courses called for. "A motionless figure is almost impossible to make out clearly in even semidarkness," the manual said. "When endangered, if possible, remain absolutely still."

Volodya remained still, very still. But when he began creeping forward again, each movement of his body made deafening sounds that echoed around the stone courtyard; Volodya felt like the tin cans they tie on lines of barbed wire to let you know the enemy is coming. His helmet hitting the cobblestones, perhaps? No, he was wearing a dark, knitted stocking cap that blended in with his cork-blackened face. Pausing, he looked up; the Oruzheinaya seemed miles away. As he started forward once more, he realized it was the equipment bag of Klin's that made so much racket. The bag was filled with ingenious devices, but to Volodya they seemed unsoldierly, smacking more of the KGB than of the great Red Army. There was a series of special hand grenades for the launcher, filled not with explosive but with narcotic gas; there were strange-looking conical grenades, designed not to kill but to blind temporarily; there were heavy goggles with lenses of thick, dark glass for himself. There was something to take care of everything but his movement across the open space between the Grand Kremlin Palace and the Oruzheinaya. Damn Klin and his crazy ideas.

"You'll have to move right up to the building and stand up, I'm afraid," Klin had told an increasingly dubious Volodya, the equipment bag lying silent and ugly between them. "They've got the steel shutters pulled almost closed on all ground-floor windows. To prevent our using 'stun' grenades the way the German commandos did against the Baader-Meinhof gang, I suppose. You'll damned near have to stick the nose of the launcher right into the room before you fire. Don't forget to use one of the conical-shaped grenades just before you make your run; it should blind them for eight to ten seconds." Klin had paused, trying to remember something. Finally: "And, oh, yes. For God's sake, don't forget to put on those goggles yourself before you fire."

Looking at the distance between the two buildings—a distance that looked much greater now that he was lying on his stomach in the Kremlin courtyard than it had when Klin showed it to him from the Vodovzvodnaya Tower—Volodya swore.

Klin's whole plan had seemed simple when he explained it to him up there. The searchlights around the Kremlin wall were to be extinguished for a forty-five-second period. During this, Sokolov was supposed to start his run from the Kremlin Palace to the Oruzheinaya. Halfway across, if there was still firing from inside, he was to fire a second conical grenade toward the window, blinding those dissidents who were not already affected. With the men at the windows unable to see, Volodya was to race toward the half-closed steel shutters, stick the grenade-launcher's nose through the opening, and, after firing, scramble for cover.

Inside the Oruzheinaya, the special grenades would fracture from their tiny explosive charges and fill the room with fast-acting narcotic gas. And when Salt Mine recovered from the deadening effect of this, they would find that the building had been charged and that they themselves were in custody; the hostages would feel nothing more than a slight, drugged drowsiness. It was a great plan, Volodya conceded—*if* you weren't the man crawling around on the Kremlin cobbles charged with executing it.

Volodya checked his watch. Less than a minute to go. As silently as he could, he pulled one of the conical "glare" grenades from the equipment bag and fitted it into the nose of the launcher; three of the grenades filled with the narcotic gas were stuck into his belt. Across the way on top of the Kremlin wall he saw two of the searchlights go out prematurely and felt his muscles tense. If it all worked as planned, Salt Mine would become a bad memory and his dream of remaining in Moscow forever would become a reality.

• The minute hand of Klin's watch was straight up. "Now," he said into the field phone, then jiggled the cradle for the other line, reaching the "real soldiers" waiting in position below. The lights on the walls of the Kremlin dimmed, came back to full brightness, then went out. It was a reasonably convincing facsimile of a short circuit. From the courtyard, he heard the sound of a man running and assumed it was Kapitan Volodya Sokolov, although the figure was impossible to make out. With a brightness that took one's breath away, the "glare" grenade exploded, and Klin, peeking between his fingers, could dimly make out Volodya's silhouette.

Something was wrong. The kapitan was not running toward the Oruzheinaya but staggering forward in a zigzag pattern. The grenade launcher fell from his hands as he screamed and clutched his eyes. The bastard had loused up everything. Volodya himself was not swearing but crying. His hands groped for his face, trying to reach the terrible pain behind his eyes, a pain made worse by the tears cascading down his cheeks. He was not a fighting soldier, he should have remembered that. If he had been he probably would have remembered Klin's urgent warning, "And for God's sake, don't forget to put on those protective goggles. . . ."

Kapitan Volodya Sokolov was blinder than anyone inside the Oruzheinaya.

• In the courtyard below, the "real soldiers" were having their own problems. Because Colonel-General Pskov had been unwilling to brief them, they were working without knowledge of the whole plan. They had been told by Klin there would be a sudden burst of bright light, but they had not expected anything of the intensity the glare grenade produced. All they could see now was the silhouette of a man in a civilian knitted hat, holding on to a grenade launcher and spinning in their direction. A breakout by Salt Mine? As soldiers, their reaction was instinctive: Three different gunners opened up at the same time. The already blinded Volodya tried to scream who he was, but no one appeared to hear him. He fell backward as the first burst found him, ripping his body apart.

The dream of Kapitan Vladimir Mikhailovich Sokolov—Volodya—had finally come true; he would remain in Moscow forever.

22

THE FOURTH DAY, 9:37 P.M.

Closing the building's front door, Keer slipped upstairs and into the apartment. Without Gary, the place seemed suddenly lonely. Just before Keer had made his check-in call to the Oruzheinaya, Gary had moved quietly, if not exactly happily, back to his hotel. To Keer, the place seemed even lonelier as his eyes strayed down the long hall toward the service area. Down that hall was the sauna. The minister who had preceded the Gertsens in this apartment had been a health buff; on his instructions the sauna went in as the building went up. Just once, Keer's father had tried it, then declared the sauna the work of a madman. Only a couple of years ago, Keer tried it himself and, hating himself for doing it, had agreed with his father. The place had an airtight sealed door, no one ever went near it, and to Keer it seemed an ideal place to stash a body. Disposing of Bleisky with Dimmy and Klemet was one thing; asking Gary to help him with Dovo was something else.

The thought of Dovo made Keer shudder. It had to be done, he supposed, but the man was so much a part of his life the mere thought of him made Keer feel sad. Sad and worried. How often did Dovo check in with the KGB? Once a week, once a day, twice a day?

If his reports were frequent and Dovo began missing his check-ins, the KGB would wonder why and probably come around to find out. Another, equally upsetting thought struck Keer. His father was due back sometime tonight; if *he* found Dovo missing, he might begin wondering what was going on and, good Party man that he was, call the KGB himself. The permutations began to multiply. In a small panic, he tried to think of a place where he could go hide; only Manya Sverdlova's came to mind, and she was off-limits with his father due back any time.

Keer's head began to swim; he had to take some sort of action, but he was damned if he knew what. Defeated, he withdrew mournfully into the place he always did his best thinking: the shower.

• Leaning against the wall, Alyosha struggled to hear what Klin was saying above the growing noise of the hostages' party. To make listening harder, his mind kept wandering, trying to guess whether the threatened assault would really be made tomorrow; Talanin, facing pressure from his military men and concerned about losing face with his own satellites, might feel he had no choice but to act. Alyosha was sure that tomorrow either Salt Mine or the Kremlin would have to give; the game of bluff had been carried about as far as it could go.

"I was only trying to save you from yourselves," he heard Klin say. "It wasn't a matter of treachery on our part; that soldier carried only narcotic gas grenades, which would have freed the hostages without anyone's being hurt."

"Except Salt Mine. By now, the entire team would be dead."

Violence begets, et cetera."

"That's fine—unless you're the et cetera."

"The point I'm trying to make, my dear friend, is that when Marshal Borodinsky storms the Oruzheinaya Palata tomorrow, everybody in Salt Mine will be dead anyway. Along with a lot of innocent hostages, whose only crime was to be visiting a magnificent old museum when you staged your mad action. Your point has been made to the world. And if a point isn't worth dying for, it isn't much of a point. Why take all of those other people—the hostages—to your grave with you?"

"You have the terms for their release—"

"Their release, along with your own."

"If you feel so strongly about the hostages, you would at least be considering Salt Mine's demands. There's a certain give and take to them."

Klin's voice suddenly sounded cold, and Alyosha realized the admission he would negotiate had played into Klin's hands. Klin seized the advantage quickly. "As I've told you, the decision was made not to pay any further attention to your demands."

"Be so kind as to remember, Klin," Alyosha ventured, trying to sound as cold as Klin had a moment earlier, "that you have until noon. Then, one hostage, at the stroke of one on the Kremlin chimes, two hostages at the stroke of two, at the stroke of three—well, I doubt if you have forgotten."

"The assault will take place as scheduled."

"You're a smug bastard, Klin. In this world, nothing has to take place as scheduled. Only the Soviet Union is so unsure of itself as to think that."

Some sort of answer began coming from the other end of the phone, but a burst of laughter from the Hall of Armor, where the party was growing rapidly into full swing, made it hard to hear. And because Alyosha did not really want to hear what else Klin might have to say, he took advantage of the noise to lose the connection.

• On Dzerzhinsky Street, Mikhail Sergeyevich Chorniev was also listening to some things he'd just as soon not hear.

"It's impossible," he argued. "Totally impossible."

"Everything fits. A voiceprint would cinch it, but it appears unnecessary at the moment. Finally, we have your outside man; all you have to do is go pick him up."

Chorniev's battered instincts as a survivor were faced with a dilemma; this new information left him with two directions to go in, both dangerous. Looking up from the DataCon printout in his hand, he studied Dr. Brezhnietz. "How did you arrive at this?"

"Luck. We'd been too selective. I took every scrap of information we had—every item, even the smallest—and fed it into the computer. That is what came out."

"You stand behind such a finding?"

Brezhnietz's face clouded, but recovered. "Absolutely."

"His father is Dmitry Gertsen, minister of production . . ."

"If you remember, Comrade Director, analysis of the telephone tapes described the outside man in very precise terms. 'Well educated . . . a Muscovite . . . teenage . . . one of the privileged ones.' The son of a minister fits that perfectly."

"No motive." Chorniev squirmed with discomfort.

"That we know of. Yet. But kindly remember some other correlations. The boy matches the description given by the Armenian's widow. She remembers him well; he was there with someone from Salt Mine picking up illegal items. That fits." Brezhnietz glanced at his sheaf of cards and papers. "Even more interesting, other reports note that this Kyril Gertsen spends his time almost exclusively with foreigners."

"Still no motive." Chorniev was resisting the evidence. To

arrest—even to accuse—the son of someone as high as minister of production did not suit his survivor role.

Dr. Brezhnietz ignored Chorniev's obvious evasions; his flat, droning voice was an insistent hum against Chorniev's eardrums. "The motives, Comrade Director, I must leave to someone else. But another point of fact." With a flourish, Brezhnietz produced a thick sheaf of papers. "KGB reports on the youth's frequent visits to Manya Sverdlova. They provide the dates of Kyril Gertsen's visits and the lengths of time he stayed. Inevitably, only when his father was out of town. That suggests something, does it not?" Brezhnietz turned partway around, as if not wanting to be seen blushing. "Curious. Manya Sverdlova, after all, *was* his father's mistress." The scientist gave a resigned sigh and turned back to face Chorniev sadly. "Ah, well. Today's youth have no respect for their elders."

"I don't see what . . ." began Chorniev, but Brezhnietz was already forcing the man to see.

"It might explain how the meningitis plan became known to Salt Mine. Those ladies—the mistresses—see a lot of each other. Perhaps Manya Sverdlova told the boy, Kyril. If this Manya woman could be interrogated—"

"By the demons, Brezhnietz. You want me to interrogate a minister's mistress so we can arrest his son? Madness."

"It is what the computer concludes, not I. The Greeks killed a bearer of bad news; what is crueler, Comrade Chorniev, is to ridicule one."

"I cannot take such a step without higher authority. The evidence is all circumstantial."

Ten minutes after Brezhnietz had been sent limping back to his computer, Chorniev made his decision. It was not easy. To interrogate the boy, Kyril, would be reckless; to interrogate Manya Sverdlova useless; to make either suspicious, self-destructive. What was needed, Chorniev decided, was an excuse for a "little talk" with Kyril. The file on Minister Gertsen came out of its locked drawer; Chorniev scanned it to find the name of the KGB man placed in the Gertsen home. Perhaps he would be able to think of some reason.

Dovo. A houseman named Dovo. Calling downstairs to find how he could put himself in touch with this Dovo, Chorniev learned that the man had missed his last two check-ins and must be absent somewhere. This, Chorniev decided, provided his excuse to talk to Kyril: the sudden disappearance of a household servant from a minister's home. It would also give his men a reason to search the apartment, where, if Brezhnietz was right, some hard evidence against the boy might be found.

Before setting the wheels in motion, Chorniev paused. However valid the reason, the searching of a minister's home was perilous. In spite of his misgivings, though, Chorniev sensed some inexplicable thrill of pleasure contemplating what the finding of hard evidence against the boy could lead to. He had suffered mightily at the hands of the Gertsens of this world, and the thought of making the son of one of them struggle and scream satisfied something inside Chorniev. In the fantasy that swept over him, he imagined the boy's father begging for his son's life, unaware that no quarter would be given. Minister Gertsen himself would quietly disappear from the Kremlin, victim of his only son's crimes.

With a grunt, Chorniev picked up the phone. He dialed a number and heard, a few minutes later, the two-toned sirens of the KGB cars heading for Georgievsky Street, a mournful, crying sound, like a child in pain.

• During the course of a normal day on the job, an Intourist guide wanders up and down the labyrinthine workings of many different kinds of minds. With time, she grows used to odd and impossible demands that must be satisfied at awkward and inexplicable hours. Lisenka accepted this. But in her entire experience she had never faced anything as demanding as playing social director to a semidrunken mass of Americans held hostage in a Kremlin museum. That she was one of the people holding them hostage didn't make it any easier.

On this point, however, the Americans no longer seemed to hold any resentment against either her or Salt Mine. To them, this now seemed immaterial: she was expected only to serve as a buoyant interpreter, pouring drinks, listening to stories, and laughing as convincingly as she could when it was clear that she was expected to.

What Blaine Decatur described to Irina as the "Stockholm effect" had completely taken over. The Russians—both those who were hostages and those from Salt Mine not on guard duty—were teaching the Americans the linked-arms way of downing vodka. It is not as easy as it looks. The right arm of one is passed through the right arm of the other, the vodka is held in the right hand of each, and then the heads and arms of both are thrown back as the vodka disappears in one gulp to the accompaniment of a bellowed *"na zdorovye!"*

By way of returning the favor, some of the American women were trying to explain the hustle to their Russian counterparts. Since the only music was provided by a concertina uncertainly played by one of the Russian hostages, the hustle lessons were not entirely a success.

It was not until the singing began that the party hit full stride. No one was sure who started it, but it is rare for any group of Russians, put together with a certain amount of vodka, *not* to break into song. It would have been equally strange if some of the Yale Club group—it contained two members of the Whiffenpoofs of nineteen forty-nine—had not already begun singing also. Quickly, it became song exchanged for song. The Russian hostages hummed, they sang—their rich deep voices making the chandeliers in the Hall of Armor reverberate—the moving, swelling verses of "Volga, Volga." This is not the hackneyed "Volga Boat Song," but an old, old song, telling of the Cossack Rebellion and recounting the soldiers' sad recollections of home after the defeat of Pugachev in the 1700s. The Americans answered with the "Battle Hymn of the Republic." The Russians came back with "Babushka," countered by the Americans singing "The Whiffenpoof Song." The little black sheep were a long way from Mory's and Louis Linder, but the singing, all things considered, was not bad; the lyrics retained their curiously effective sentimentality. Thinking suddenly of Shymon, Lisenka wondered what had happened to her own little black sheep.

During the drinking session that followed this song, one of the Russian hostages—he spoke a little English—approached the American who appeared in charge of the singing. "Please. Am confused. What is Whiffenpoof?"

Told that it was a club whose sole function was drinking and singing, the Russian looked bewildered. "Need *club* for that?" The ridiculousness grew on him; it was the funniest thing he'd ever heard. Leaning against the wall, the Russian, a huge, heavy-set man, began to roar with laughter, bellowing with the insanity of such a thing until the tears ran down his face. "Americans crazy! All Americans crazy!" Watching from one side, Blaine Decatur, sitting against the wall with Irina, was inclined to agree.

The sound made Blaine look up. One of the Americans had started singing "We Shall Overcome" and everyone was joining crossed hands with whoever happened to be closest to them—American, Russian, German, Angolan, or Cuban. Only the Americans knew the words, and most of them were too rich and too white to understand their meaning. But it didn't affect their singing:

> "We shall overcome,
> We shall overcome,
> We shall overcome some day. . . ."

After the first three lines, the words grew uncertain:

> "Deep in my heart,
> This I believe,
> We shall overcome . . .
> Some . . .
> Day."

There was more feeling than assurance, but the idea came across. Blaine Decatur watched and listened, fascinated. Little by little, the Russians were imitating the words, swaying back and forth as the Americans did, completely unaware of what the words meant but knowing the song was intended to be inspirational, an American version of the "International," perhaps.

It was this element of Jax's story—the picture of American and Russian with arms linked, swaying to and fro as they sang—that made the news release in the papers so effective. Smuggled out of Andrew Jax's hotel room by the man from *France Soir*, the story, already on the wire, was jolting midafternoon America with its message. In Europe, where the people were growing sleepy, the song itself had little meaning, but the sense of unity evoked by its picture was clear.

Clear enough so that the Kremlin's reaction was one of fury. At 11:19 p.m., Moscow time, the outside line from the Oruzheinaya was belatedly yanked out. (It had originally been left connected because of Alyosha's threat about the hostages, later because Klin felt he might learn the outside man's identity by eavesdropping on the conversations. It had been a mistake, and the damage was vast. Klin kicked the wall in anger, wondering how he could have been stupid enough not to disconnect the Oruzheinaya's lines days ago.)

Leaning against a wall. Lisenka was trying to explain the *kazatsky* to some of the Americans. Several of the Russian hostages were down on their haunches, balancing wine glasses on their foreheads, while the rest of the party clapped in accelerating rhythm. Lisenka watched them in amazement. In a way, she was as surprised by the degree of bonding between the hostages and their captors as Irina had been.

When their turn came again, the Americans sang "Bright College Years," Yale's alma mater. The Russians grew confused, since the song is set to the music of "Die Wacht am Rhein," a tune with unpleasant wartime memories for the older among them. They grew even more confused when the members of the Yale tour group drew handkerchiefs from their pockets and solemnly waved them back and forth over their heads as they sang. The singing swelled to a climax and the Americans roared their ritual "For God, for cou-n-try . . . and for Yale!" This bit of Americana bewildered even Lisenka.

• "God damn," swore Klin, and threw open a window of the Vodovzvodnaya. It was true. Those crazy people inside the Oruzheinaya were doing what a guard downstairs reported.

"I swear it, Comrade Minister," the guard said, though Klin at first refused to believe him. "I swear they are singing. Sometimes in Russian, sometimes in American."

Having now heard for himself, Klin shook his head. They wouldn't be singing tomorrow morning. Marshal Borodinsky would see to that. Permanently.

23

THE FOURTH DAY, 11:55 P.M.

From beyond, in the Hall of Armor, the die-hards among the Americans and Russians were still singing, but softly now. Softly, sadly, and reminiscently—of home, of other times, of other lives. Most of the hostages had retired to the Hall of Silver, too filled with Minister Klin's best vodka to be annoyed or kept awake.

In one corner of the State Coach Room, almost lost among the dazzling carriages, coaches, and sleds of Russia's imperial past, Lisenka sat quietly in the soft light, wondering. She was perched on the mounting step of Boris Godunov's court carriage, a gift from Elizabeth I of England. The gilded carving was exquisite, the velvet hangings extraordinary, the mounting step uncomfortable. At the moment, Lisenka would have felt uncomfortable anywhere.

Earlier, Alyosha had smiled, yawned, and told her he was going to get some sleep inside his Petersburg sled. Lisenka, though, knew he was still awake. When Alyosha had first disappeared inside, the battery-pak flashlight—found among the emergency equipment in the museum director's office upstairs—was on only briefly before being extinguished. About ten minutes later, Lisenka saw it come back on, glowing through the sled's mica windows. Alyosha, Lisenka could guess, was too tense to sleep and was lying alone, worrying, going over the plans for tomorrow again, trying to think of measures and countermeasures to deal with whatever Klin and/or Borodinsky had in store for them.

Boris Godunov's carriage step finally became too uncomfortable, or Lisenka too restless. She slipped into the next room and fixed herself a little more vodka. Earlier, she had tried to convince Alyosha that a few drinks would relax him and let him sleep, for she knew he'd drunk very little all night. He mumbled something about not caring much for drinking, but Lisenka knew better; he was afraid that something would happen if he really slept, or that his mind wouldn't be clear in the morning, or that Borodinsky would breach his understanding with Klin and attack early, during the night.

Shifting from one foot to the other, Lisenka couldn't help thinking of Alyosha, lying inside the Petersburg sled, alone, sleepless, tortured. The thought sent a wave of shudders through her; a great emptiness crept into her stomach; a burning, swelling inside her met the emptiness and struggled to possess her. Lisenka swore, something unusual for her, and stared again at the soft light coming through the windows of the sled. Almost without realizing it, she reached a decision. Quickly, she walked into the other room, picked up an additional vodka—a stiff one—and marched across the State Coach Room to tap on the door of the Petersburg sled.

"Come," she heard Alyosha say. The sound of his voice sent the small shudders coursing through her again. It was the liquor, she supposed. Alyosha might not have been drinking; Lisenka had.

The door was opened and Lisenka went in, feeling suddenly foolish, a little girl trying to act grown up. "I thought perhaps a drink would relax you." She listened to the hesitation in her own voice and was bewildered. "I saw your light was still on, and . . ."

Alyosha blinked at her for a moment, and Lisenka couldn't tell whether he was pleased with her thoughtfulness or angered by her intrusion. When he finally spoke, his words stunned her. "I was thinking about you—this sled may have suited a tsarina, but I find it very lonesome—and I'm glad you came—and, as I said, I was thinking about you—and you're probably right about a drink or two—and thank you for bringing it—and . . ."

Alyosha stopped suddenly, as if, like Lisenka a few minutes before, he was feeling a little foolish, a small boy trying to act grown up. She stared at him; his greenish eyes were fixed on her, their color deepening as he studied her. For a moment their eyes remained locked; then, as if by mutual consent, they both let them move away at the same moment.

Silently, Lisenka handed him the drink, noticing that her hand was trembling badly. In equal silence, Alyosha accepted the tall tumbler of vodka, tossing it back in one swallow, his expression unchanging. A second later, he blinked, as if in surprise, and a sudden seizure shook his body as the jolt of the alcohol poured into his system. Lisenka saw him blink again; his eyes, deeper now than ever, had a glistening moisture on their surface. "Thank you," he repeated.

Nothing more was said. She was so startled when he threw both of his arms around her she couldn't have spoken if she'd wanted to. Alyosha, the man who could stand the touch of no one, seemed suddenly to want to be touched everywhere and to touch her everywhere. Their mouths came together, hungry people devouring their first food in days, exploring, probing, penetrating, sucking, swallowing. Alyosha's tongue suddenly pushed itself into one ear, darting, caressing. Lisenka was startled and shaken; her whole body began to tremble and an unconscious moaning swelled up inside her. His hand ran across the jacket of her uniform, and loosening the buttons, slipped beneath it, a soft feathery, floating feeling of fingers across smooth skin, sliding gently downward until the fingers penetrated her, kneading the soft lump inside her until she screamed uncontrollably. Each time he rolled the tiny lump between his fingers in just the right way, Lisenka, no matter how hard she tried, was unable to keep her legs from pulling up toward her body as far as they would go, sliding them flat along the upholstery like a frog on its back.

Almost as an afterthought, they let their clothes fall onto the couch, and Alyosha thrust himself into her. In making love, Lisenka would realize later, Alyosha was like a jungle creature. He thrashed and writhed, his legs flailing against the upholstery, his fingers never still. The thrusts grew faster and deeper; Lisenka could barely breathe as wave after wave of shuddering spasms swept over her. Dimly, she heard one of the marquetry chairs splinter, its delicate wood unable to withstand the power of Alyosha's convulsing legs. He made love with the abandon of his Persian ancestors, his whole body an impatient, trembling organ.

From him, when she could hear at all, Lisenka was distantly aware of groans and growls, the music of the blissfully damned. The symbiosis between them grew faster and more frantic, the thrusts so deep she felt she must be dividing in half. At the end, they both screamed simultaneously, his legs and feet quivering tightly into a point, then exploding into a frantic, convulsive tattoo against the defenseless air. For what seemed like hours, they lay motionless, unable to move, listening to each other's labored breathing and pounding heart.

It was only then that Alyosha and Lisenka became aware

of a raucous cheering and clapping outside the sled; there was laughter mixed with catcalls, and two Russians were singing "The Snow Falls Light, My Love," an old lover's serenade. Jarred back to reality but still confused, Alyosha slid back one of the mica windows and looked out. A great cheer rose. Outside were perhaps fifteen of the Russian hostages and a scatttering of the Yale tour group; from the way they laughed and pointed beneath the sled Alyosha immediately realized what was happening. Only when someone shoved Ivan the Terrible's gold goblet in through the window did it make sense to Lisenka.

There is an old Russian custom of tying a string to the springs of the marriage bed; this string extends through the ceiling into the room below, where an apple is tied to its end. There, the wedding guests watch the groom's progress—by watching the apple.

To some, this sounds like a crude peasant tradition, but it was not restricted to the serfs. Even the tsar's wedding chamber was traditionally built directly above one of the Kremlin Palace's ballrooms; the entire court would gather there and cheer and applaud their monarch's vigor, demonstrated by a diamond-encrusted apple suspended from the ceiling.

Alyosha swore, although he had little choice but to accept the goblet, filled to the brim with straight vodka. He hadn't remembered that the Petersburg sled rested on elaborate springs; when one of the Russians saw Lisenka go in—and stay—he had tied an apple beneath the body of the sled and gathered his friends, as tradition demanded.

Now, while the group clapped in unison, Alyosha downed the goblet of vodka and accepted a smaller one for Lisenka. Then, as is the custom, he roared at the group: "To the devil with you! Saint Cecilia begs you to leave us in peace." With a crash, Alyosha slammed the window shut.

He looked at Lisenka and threw up his hands. She giggled. His tired body wanted to seize her and take her again, but the moment he began, he found himself limp with exhaustion.

As suddenly as he began, Alyosha fell asleep, and Lisenka pulled up a blanket against their nakedness, Alyosha asleep in her arms. The distant sound of singing seemed to grow softer and less distinct, and Lisenka was half asleep herself, feeling completely fulfilled for the first time since the seizure of Shymon by the KGB. No, more fulfilled than she had ever been.

She felt the numbness of sleep creeping over her; she lay

there, bathed in the warm glow of contentment, lulled hypnotically by the gentle, reassuring sound of Alyosha's breathing. She had been asleep for—she wasn't sure, but did not believe it very long—when a sudden, violent wrenching beside her was followed by an agonized scream. Instantly, she came fully awake. Her first thought was that someone was trying to escape, or that the assault against the Oruzheinaya had already begun. But as her eyes adjusted to the darkness, she realized that both the sudden movement and the scream had come from Alyosha. He was sitting up, crouched in a corner of the couch, his legs drawn up tightly to his body like a frightened child's. The screams were replaced by a terrified whimpering; even halfway down the sofa from him, Lisenka could feel his whole body shake.

Thinking he'd had some sort of nightmare, Lisenka reached out and tried to take one of his hands between her own. Stunned, she watched his eyes widen in terror at her touch. As if he had seen a reincarnation of the devil, Alyosha began to push himself tighter into the corner, the whimpering sound growing, as if her hands hurt rather than comforted. "Darling," she said, "darling Alyosha. What is it? Wake up, Alyosha. Please, wake up. You are having some sort of crazy dream."

"No, no, no, no. Leave me alone, all of you, leave me alone. The thing was not my fault, I tell you. The trumpets, the damned trumpets. Ilya. Please, Ilya, speak. Tell them, Ilya."

His glazed eyes abruptly turned to her, blinking hard, staring, seeming to see her for the first time. For a long moment, he said nothing. Suddenly, the tears streaming down his face, he put his head in his hands and began sobbing, his whole body shaking. But for the first time, he uncurled from his protective, fetal position in the corner. He allowed Lisenka to fold her arms around him and stroke his head, like someone comforting a little boy with a wound of imaginary awesomeness.

When she dared, she spoke again. "Alyosha. You are all right; everything is all right. It was just a bad dream, a terrible dream."

"It was no dream."

"Tell me, then. To talk about such things always helps. Tell me. It is all locked inside you. Your"—Lisenka groped futilely for an acceptable word—"secret, your fear, whatever it was, is safe with me. You know that."

Lisenka felt Alyosha's body give a convulsive shudder. His teeth clenched. "Ulangom."

"That was a war, Alyosha. A war leaves scars. Injuries, wounds, shattered bodies. And . . . and scars on the mind. People forget that. You are not in Ulangom any longer. That is behind you. You must put it there. There where it belongs. Every soldier, from private to general, carries such scars. Heroes as much as anyone else. You must put it away now; Ulangom is over."

The shudder again. "I was no hero. Can't you understand that? No hero. Ilya was—Ilya . . ." The shuddering grew worse and Alyosha became unable to speak.

To Lisenka, Alyosha seemed close to the edge of collapse. His eyes took on the wild, haunted stare she had seen when he first woke; his body was shaking violently; his hands covered his ears as if to shut out some sound only he could hear. "Ilya, Ilya. They do not understand. The trumpets. Please make them understand, Ilya. Tell them . . ."

Again, slowly, soothed by Lisenka, the stare vanished and Alyosha appeared to return from his private hell. Lisenka was no psychiatrist, but she knew the problem had to be brought to the surface and aired. "This Ilya—" she began. It was as far as she got.

Alyosha whimpered, jumping violently as if stuck with a sharp instrument. Suddenly, with a long, sad sigh, he sat bolt upright; his green eyes were hard, but he was back under control. "Ulangom. The trumpets. They said I was a hero and gave me a medal. But I was a coward. The Chinese kept blowing their damned trumpets. Your teeth rattled with fear when they did, because it meant they were going to attack. They knew the effect; that was why they used them. And before the attack, artillery. Enough artillery to blow Mongolia into the sky.

"Ilya was my best friend. We had been in the line too long, much too long. We were supposed to be relieved the next day. And the night before we were all talking and joking about going to the rear. I was sitting with Ilya—he was my sublieutenant—when God, my God, those fucking trumpets suddenly began blowing like the music of the demons. And then the artillery.

"We were all in our foxholes—they weren't very deep because the ground was too frozen to dig well. Ilya and I were in the same foxhole, waiting for the orders we knew would come: counter-attack. We clutched each other all through the barrage like little children, we were that scared.

"And then the order came. Attack. Ilya climbed out and blew his whistle for the men. I couldn't. I froze. None of my muscles would move. All I could do was sit there in the bottom of the foxhole, crying, listening to those crazy trumpets. And I could hear Ilya shouting at the men, because the barrage had lifted now, and he was trying to form them up to attack before the Chinese did.

"I was a full lieutenant and Ilya was having to do my job for me. And I guess he looked around and saw I wasn't anywhere, and came back to my foxhole and tried to talk me out of my freeze-up. Only he couldn't. He begged and yelled and pleaded and reminded me what the political bastards would do if I didn't get out of there, but I couldn't.

"And finally he held one hand out, Ilya did, and pulled me halfway out of the foxhole. By sheer force. But a grenade—a fucking grenade from a launcher, I guess—blew up damned near on top of us, and we both were knocked down, and I landed on top of Ilya. He didn't have a top to his head any more."

Lisenka didn't dare speak; Alyosha had gone a deathly white and the trembling had started again and his voice had a funny, faraway sound to it. "And that's how the political overseer found us when the soldiers pushed the stupid Chinese back. Their attack, it turned out, hadn't been much. And the overseer sent a message back saying Lieutenant Alyosha Gregarin was a hero because he had fallen on top of his sublieutenant to save his life when he saw a grenade was about to go off.

"But he had it all backwards. And if I hadn't been a complete coward, Ilya wouldn't have been by my foxhole where he was. Trying to save me from the Party overseer. Trying to save my ass and keep me out of political prison or from being shot as a coward."

Alyosha turned his head away. "And they gave me a medal and said I was a Hero of the Soviet Union. And I should have said something, I should have told them what really happened, only I couldn't get my mouth to speak. It was like in the foxhole when I couldn't move." Slowly Alyosha began putting his clothes back on. "That's why I haven't been able to let anyone touch me. Until tonight. Maybe that was wrong, too. Maybe you'll catch whatever it is I've got and be a coward and liar like me."

For a long time, Lisenka said nothing. What Alyosha was talking about was so foreign to her, he could have been describing constellations in another galaxy. That it had come close to destroying him was obvious. A great deal of what lay behind Salt Mine became obvious along with it. It was not, as she had thought, rebellion for rebellion's sake, but his way of avenging the secret war the Soviet waged along its Mongolian border. A silent scream against the government.

Finally: "Alyosha. You can't blame yourself. You froze. So what? So have many men. Marshal Zhukov, in his book, wrote that it once happened to him. Remember? And if Ilya hadn't been killed trying to help you, he might just as easily have been killed leading his men. Not to have told the Party what happened is no shame either. Ilya loved you enough to go back and drag you out of that foxhole to save you from the Party. It would not make him happy to know he did it only to have you tell the authorities yourself. It would be an insult to him. To what he tried to do. For God's sake, Alyosha, you cannot remake the world into something perfect. You are no coward. The man who could conceive and lead Salt Mine is no coward. He is a hero. You are giving Ilya his medal by leading Salt Mine. You are making us all free."

Turning, Alyosha stared at her. And as suddenly as he had put on his clothes, he took them back off. The Petersburg sled shook once again, and it was not the Chinese who blew the trumpets.

• The two teams of men from the KGB went through the apartment at Gorky and Georgievsky with less than enthusiasm. To a KGB man, used to working within the rigid framework of the Soviet hierarchy, searching a minister's home was unsettling. Their instructions were simple: Find Kyril Gertsen. If they couldn't find him, search the apartment until they found evidence against him.

They moved gingerly. Although the search had been commissioned by the head of the KGB himself, Director Chorniev, it was always possible that, if cornered, Chorniev would disavow his orders. Such things happened. Finally, though, reinforced by the arrival of Chorniev's personal deputy, they began tearing the place apart.

One by one, every room in the duplex was searched. The cook, Toko, by then was home from his day off and, eyes wide with fear, led the KGB team through the place, identifying whose room was whose and describing the habits and patterns of father and son, when they rose, when they ate, when they retired.

Minister Gertsen, he explained, was away most of the time. His room was gone over thoroughly, uncovering little except that he appeared a scrupulously tidy man. On his desk, piles of government papers were neatly stacked, each pile arranged alphabetically by category; going through them revealed nothing out of the ordinary. The secret papers, Toko said, were kept in a safe at the rear of one of his closets. After a lot of grunting and cursing, the heavy safe was manhandled onto the elevator and driven off to Dzerzhinsky Street to be opened.

Suddenly from the rear of the apartment a muffled sound startled the KGB men. Guns drawn, they raced to the room, which Toko told them belonged to Keer, the minister's son. From inside, they could now hear music coming from a record player, the Carpenters singing some piece none of the men knew anything about except that it was in English. Illegal. Some other sound could also be heard inside. Two of the men drew back while the rest stood on either side of the door, their guns at the ready. With a sudden rush, the two agents crashed into the door, taking it completely off its hinges. No one was inside. The turntable on the record player spun relentlessly on. The record had changed, and Tony Orlando and Dawn were reciting the details of a poignant American love ritual: "Knock three times on the ceiling if you want me, twice on the pipes if the answer is no. . . ."

The agents were baffled by what could have set the record player in motion. The answer to this question, it turned out, was simple: The player was attached to an electric alarm clock that turned on any appliance plugged into it, instead of ringing a jarring bell. If, however, the "off" button was not pushed in after a certain time, the clock also began emitting buzzing tones. This was the second sound the agents had heard from the room. Searching Keer's quarters produced great quantities of illegal American books and magazines—the KGB men had a difficult time remaining coldly objective face to face with *Hustler* and *Penthouse*. Other illegal items were more American phonograph records, books, and recent copies of *The New York Times* and the London *Times*. Keer's Westernized wardrobe gave the biggest shock of all.

In turn, Dovo's room was searched, but apart from some coded messages from the KGB, it was Spartan. Neat rows of white and black alpaca jackets were lined up alongside the peasantlike blouses Dovo usually wore. All of these hung from one rack; from another hung ten pairs of faultlessly pressed black trousers. On Dovo's bureau was a framed picture of a boy Toko reluctantly identified as Keer. No, the cook said, it was not Dovo's day off, and his absence was unusual. Mr. Keer, well, he spent a good deal of time out. Usually, though, by this hour, he was back home.

Meekly the cook followed the team, making sure they stole nothing; Toko had a distinct feeling the minister was not going to be pleased by this invasion, a point he unsuccessfully made to the KGB men several times. Missing items would only make things worse.

Down the long hall in the rear area, the men followed the path Keer and Gary had dragged Dovo along. It was dark; a light must have blown out, Toko explained. (Keer had removed a fuse, leaving only the weak lights in the hall sconces.) No, the glass window was to the sauna. No one ever used it, explained the cook.

Suspicious, the KGB men warily entered the sauna. The light inside was even dimmer than in the hall, but a hastily produced flashlight showed nothing. The only sound was the heavy drip-drip of a leaking steam pipe; the escaping steam gave the room an eerie atmosphere, redolent with the heavy odor of some kind of aromatic oil. The KGB men swore, switched off their flashlight, and muttering, withdrew to the front of the apartment again. After a brief discussion, they finally called Chorniev at Dzerzhinsky Street to report. Kyril Gertsen was not here; his father, the minister of production and industry, was still out of town, and Dovo, the Gertsens' longtime servant planted in the household as the KGB's agent, still appeared to be missing. Only Toko, the cook, was home.

"Straighten up the apartment," snapped Chorniev. "You had no authority to mess it up. Use their cook, if necessary; we'll send a carpenter and painter to fix the door to the boy's room so it doesn't show. I don't understand how you could exceed your instructions so badly."

It was as the agents had expected. Since their search was fruitless, the damage was their fault. "What about the safe?" Chorniev's deputy asked.

"Return it immediately. Unopened. Replace it so it looks untouched."

"The cook. Toko. He saw us take it."

"The streets are sometimes unsafe, except for the blind."

"Will you handle, or should we?"

"You've done damage enough. We will. In the meantime, leave two men across the street to report when anyone returns. Our man Dovo is important. He must know. Unless he has defected, which I doubt. As for the father, I want to know when Minister Gertsen comes back. Excuses will have to be made. But for the boy, of course, we will continue to turn the town inside out. There are just so many places he can go to cover." The click on the phone was definitive and angry.

Quickly, the men began their cleanup, helped by Toko, the cook with the short life expectancy. A few minutes later, two carpenters and a painter arrived and made short work of the door to Keer's room. Using special paint, they soon made it look as if never touched. While they were hard at work, a team from Dzerzhinsky Street arrived with Minister Gertsen's safe and, grunting and heaving, managed to get it back into the rear of his closet. Undamaged.

The cook, Toko, terrified by Chorniev's direct orders, reluctantly went with the men. There were a few more questions about the Gertsen household the KGB wished to put to him, they said. The cook enjoyed what for him was something unusual, an automobile ride, the car racing through the nearly empty streets of Moscow. Had he known what waited at the other end, his enjoyment might have been considerably dampened.

• Keer sometimes felt that a guardian angel peeked over his shoulder and whispered into his ear what he should and should not do. He had had this sensation tonight as he rounded the corner of Gorky on his way home. To the eye, nothing appeared different. But the voice was whispering to him, cautioning him.

For some moments, Keer stood at the corner and studied the street. At first he saw nothing unusual. But a closer look proved his private angel had better eyes than he did. There were too many cars parked along Georgievsky. Ordinarily, at this time of night, the curbs were almost deserted; the people who lived in this luxe area rarely left their cars out overnight. He could see no one, but this in itself was suspicious; both his building and the one alongside had doormen. Even at this distance, he could usually glimpse them standing inside the heavy glass doors to the lobby. Farther down the street, back a few feet in one of the many building setbacks, Keer suddenly saw the flare of a cigarette, glowing as someone took a deep drag on it. Only the dimmest shape of a face appeared, disembodied as a ghost. The voice whispered again into Keer's ear: Nothing was visible that in itself should cause alarm, but taken together, his observations gave him reason for every caution. Keer could feel the adrenaline surge through him. Walking around the corner, he hailed the first cab he could find. When the driver asked where he wanted to go, Keer hesitated. A moment later, he told him in a firm voice.

• It's me. No, *me*. Bad pennies and all that crap. I'm downstairs in the Labirynt."

Looking disheveled, as if he had been undressing for bed when Keer called, Gary appeared in what seemed only minutes. "Any word?" asked Keer.

"Tomorrow. The embassy said they're going to attack tomorrow morning. The ambassador was sent official notice. It'll be a slaughter. But the ambassador said the president has been on the hot line. Yelling, I guess. And the French premier, and the British prime minister. Even, he thought, Castro. But Talanin sounds like his mind's made up. Of course, the ambassador said that could just be a pose. Nobody knows what's really going to happen. Except I'm scared shitless about my family. My God. A real attack. They could all get it."

This much Keer had already guessed. When he'd tried to call the Oruzheinaya Palata from the lobby, moments before he called upstairs to Gary, he found he could no longer get through. And taking the long way around the Kremlin, he'd seen, even from the distance at which all traffic was kept, that the tanks and special troops—withdrawn outside two days earlier—had moved off the side streets near Red Square back up to the Kremlin gates themselves.

Keer sighed and ordered another drink for each of them. "Don't worry. Everything'll be okay. Talanin's always yelling stuff like that." He tried to give Gary a reassuring smile, but doubted if it was very convincing. The angel's voice had disappeared and he was on his own.

"I don't know what I'd do if something happened . . ." Gary was staring into his glass, as if the answer to his predicament lay deep inside the mixture of Scotch and slightly flat Georgian mineral water.

The two of them talked, ordering drinks steadily and often.

In view of Gary's problems, Keer felt awkward making his request. Finally: "I'm in some trouble myself. Hell, you know that. But I can't go home for a while. There's an extra bed in your room, and if it wouldn't be too much of an inconvenience for you . . ."

There was no reservation at all. "Welcome the company, Keer. And God knows you helped me when I needed it. Letting me stay with you for days and days . . ." Keer ignored the irony produced by his own part in Salt Mine.

One more drink and the two disappeared upstairs.

24

THE FIFTH DAY, 6:35 A.M.

"Dammit, my man Dovo is gone, my cook is gone, and the place is torn up. Someone tried to fix it up—that's how I know it was one of your bunch, not common thieves—but they weren't very efficient. Which makes me think all the more it was the KGB's work. Oh, yes, my son, Keer, is gone, too. Now, listen, Vasily, tell me what's happening and tell it to me straight."

"I'll check, Dimitry Aleksandrovich. It's all news to me. With this Salt Mine mess going on, the left and right hands don't always work together. If it *was* the KGB, my apologies. I'll call Chorniev and—well, what the hell, I'll be seeing you at seven anyway, at the ministers' meeting. If I can reach Chorniev before it starts, I'll have full information for you."

In the pause, a strange and sudden thought appeared to strike Klin. "You said your *son* is gone, too? Keer?"

"Vanished. There's some blood on the rug in his room, but otherwise not a trace. The people who might know—Dovo, Toko, the cook—simply vanished."

"I'll find out what I can for you, Dimitry, but that meeting . . ."

"You damned well better." Klin's phone had a hollow sound after Minister Gertsen hung up.

Pacing the control headquarters set up in the Vodovzvodnaya Tower, Klin considered. He didn't know if it was wise to call Chorniev, because Chorniev could be the man behind whatever had happened in Gertsen's apartment. No, Chorniev was too weak, too dependent, for that. Besides, Chorniev would have nothing to gain. Dovo, Klin knew—he had checked it by phone with Dzerzhinsky Street—was their own KGB plant, so if he was really missing, it was because someone decided to *make* him missing. Like Chorniev, Dovo wasn't resourceful enough to do anything—like run away—on his own.

Keer, well, Klin knew Keer. He was a bright boy, charming, but with a curious fixation on anything American, which drove his father wild. The fact was, just about anything Keer did put his father into a state. As Klin thought about it, he admitted that if he had Dmitry Gertsen as a father, he'd probably go out of the way to upset him himself. A cold, dogmatic, unpleasant man, Klin decided. And definitely not one to cross. Reluctantly, he called up Chorniev. He wasn't there.

• Barely five minutes later, Klin found himself in the middle of a bizarre phone conversation with Alyosha. (While the other lines from the Oruzheinaya had been cut to halt the leak of stories to the papers, the internal lines between Klin and the Oruzheinaya were still intact.) What Alyosha had just said disturbed him.

"Such a rapid move will cause problems," Klin pointed out. "Many different people must be notified." Klin could hear the irritated and impatient sound in his own voice. He was both. At seven-thirty—it had been moved back a half hour so that Marshal Borodinsky could meet first with Deputy Premier Chaidze—there would be a full-scale ministers' meeting. Klin knew he would not fare well. He also had been told by Chaidze that after this meeting, Borodinsky would assume control of the Kremlin area. Klin still did not really believe that Talanin would order the assault this morning, but whether he did or not, Borodinsky in control would mean that Salt Mine wouldn't fare any better than he would.

Klin stalled. "Can I make the arrangements and call you when they are complete? Some of the people I must notify take time to reach. Soldiers, sharpshooters—well, hell, you know what's out there, my friend."

"No, right away," snapped Alyosha. "Given a chance, you gentlemen are fond of treachery. Well, not this time. No interference, no stupid tricks. This stalling of yours is stupid. If you attempt anything—*Chort*, we can always take it out on the hostages."

Klin sighed. "I wish you'd get a new threat. Your old ones are wearing thin."

"This is no game. I will carry them out. Am I understood?" There was a weary boredom in Alyosha's voice. Klin suspected he must feel like a parent who makes the same threat so often it finally loses all effect.

And Klin was convinced Alyosha would never carry his threat out. By now, he felt that he knew the man well, that he could predict how Alyosha's mind worked. Grudgingly, Klin had even come to respect him. Wanton killing was not Alyosha's way. In fact, he had maintained a scrupulous decency in his dealings—not only about the hostages, but about the Russian citizens and soldiers he held.

Wearily, Klin returned to the conversation at hand. "I have to repeat my warning. It will take at least five minutes to notify all the soldiers and so forth; otherwise some Hero of the Soviet Union will, quite by accident, shoot anything that moves."

"Very well," answered Alyosha; Klin's request was reasonable. "Five minutes. No more, no less."

"I shall call you when it is clear. Please hold off."

"Five minutes," Alyosha repeated, and hung up.

Shaking his head, Klin cradled his phone. It was not going to be his day.

• Early that morning, the first snow of winter fell. It was the dry, small-flaked kind that looked as if it might continue all day, but seasoned Muscovites knew it would be light, last little longer than an hour, and only begin to add its miracle brillance to the grayness of this city of stone. Unlike the snow inside Klin's paperweight, it would soften in the mildness of midday and disappear completely by afternoon, only an occasional damp patch lingering in deeply shaded places to remind anyone it had ever been.

Keer watched it fall from a window in the Intourist, marveling as always at the difference its sparkle added to the monochromatic dullness of Moscow. Later, at a telephone booth tucked away in a corner of the Intourist's lobby, Keer was not surprised to hear the howling signal that is Moscow's way of letting you know a line is out of order. The Oruzheinaya's line had been giving this signal since the night before, so it was now a definite fact: He, the outside man, would get no more information. Added to what Gary quoted the embassy as saying and the sudden concentration of T-10s tracing their caterpillar tread marks in the snow just outside the Kremlin, it meant only one thing: The threatened assault on Salt Mine was about to be made good.

Dispiritedly, Keer hung up. He wished there was some way

to talk to Alyosha. Andrew Jax's line was disconnected, too. It left him with no one to talk to but himself. The man from *France Soir* was a possibility, he supposed, but to reach him he would have to use an outside phone booth. This would involve leaving the Intourist, and by now, Keer was sure the KGB had a picture of him in circulation. Even standing in this booth was probably unsafe. Certainly the lobby was. Quickly Keer got into an elevator and went back to Gary's rooms.

So far, the *dezhurnaya* exhibited no curiosity about him; to the old floor lady, Keer was just another of the Americans in the lavish Decatur suite.

How the KGB figured out he was the outside man still baffled Keer. Just as he reached the twentieth floor and turned down the hall toward Gary's room, his original suspicion that Dovo might have regular check-in times with the KGB returned. When Dovo's calls stopped, he supposed, the KGB went to the apartment and found his body.

Keer had no idea that his identity was unearthed by a computer, or that the computer was manufactured by the company—DataCon—of which Gary's father was president. Or that in spite of an exhaustive search of the apartment on Georgievsky Street, Dovo remained undiscovered, lying behind the pile of towels Keer had stacked beneath a bench in the sauna, the stench of decomposition masked by the heavily scented oil of balsam.

Keer nodded to Gary, almost not seeing him because of his absorption in his own problems. "Hi," Gary said, his cheerfulness hiding some deep worries of his own. "Ready to go down for breakfast?"

Keer hesitated. "I don't feel so hot," he lied. "Why don't we have it sent up by room service?"

"Okay." Gary walked over to the phone and dialed. It would take a long time to get an answer. In Moscow, room service is a rarity. It was only because the Decaturs were traveling deluxe suite that the hotel provided it for them at all. Twice, Gary looked over at Keer, his face heavy with concern.

Keer stood staring out the window. The snow was still falling, transforming the earth with its brilliant whiteness; Moscow looked at peace. For the first time, he felt profound doubts about Salt Mine's chances of success. Moscow might look at peace, but the peaceful look was illusory, the peace of snow falling on a new grave.

• Precisely seven and a half minutes after Alyosha's call to Klin, Lisenka saw him return to the phone to answer it. He was acting very mysterious this morning, about everything. The thought of her night with Alyosha still made her whole body quiver. But this morning, he seemed to be avoiding her. Confused and hurt, she kept her distance from him, even if she couldn't keep her eyes off him.

"Not as naive as you think," she heard him say into the phone. "Two Saudis and a Hungarian—hostages—as well as three men from Salt Mine will stay behind to see you don't try that." From where she stood, she could see him continuing to argue with Klin on the phone, but she couldn't make out what he said when he lowered his voice. He hung up, wearing a faint smile of success. Quickly, he ordered men to the Oruzaheinaya's windows and then stood, along with Misha, close to the two great front doors. On some signal, these were suddenly thrown open.

Lisenka gasped. In filed the group from Lenin's Tomb—the hostages, Dimmy and Klemet, and the four soldiers who had been trapped inside with them. The sight of them standing in the doorway, their clothes lightly dusted with snow, brought an unexpected lump to Lisenka's throat. At the same time, Lisenka realized that Alyosha's brave statement to Klin about the men he'd left behind must have been a lie; all were there and accounted for.

Alyosha had good reason to lie. He was convinced the only safe way to engineer their escape was to have all of them together in one place—particularly if the worst happened and Talanin went through with Borodinsky's threatened assault, in which case it would be a matter not of escape, but of survival. Lisenka's nose count was correct. No one had been left behind, and the wires to the plastic explosive were all of Salt Mine that remained in Lenin's Tomb. In case someone should be tempted to cut these, Alyosha had reminded Klin that the trigger to the explosives was of the kind that operated on breaking the circuit, not completing it.

As the hostages moved farther inside, the Americans from the Oruzheinaya laughed and shouted and clapped the shoulders of their compatriots; only the Saudis remained detached, embarrassed, perhaps, by so much blatant emotion. After five days in the dim stuffiness of the tomb, the new arrivals blinked at the light pouring through the huge windows of the Oruzheinaya.

Lisenka began to walk over to where Alyosha stood with

Dimmy and Klemet; halfway over, she stopped. The distance Alyosha was keeping between them this morning still hurt. Embarrassment, she told herself, because he had told her too much about himself and Ulangom last night.

"Ah, Dimmy, Klemet," said Alyosha with a grin. "It is good to have you back with us. How goes it?"

The smile never left Klemet's face. "With us fine. But those soldiers outside the Arsenal and at places along the wall looked as if it was going very well with them, too. Several were even wearing smiles. I think they have something painful up their sleeves. Like blowing us all up."

Dimmy grimaced. "Nonsense. To me, they looked very serious. The way a farmer stares at the chicken he plans for his breakfast." Dimmy made a chopping motion with one hand and a noisy little *klunk*. "Fricassee."

"Please, don't be so colorful, Dimmy." Klemet turned to Alyosha for help. "He has been like that the whole five days."

"Only an attempt to brighten up things," said Dimmy dourly. "You *know* our leaders at the Kremlin are not cannibals. They never eat people. Not for breakfast, anyway." He turned to Alyosha. "Did someone mention breakfast? Ah, yes, *I* did. I'm starved."

Lisenka watched as Alyosha led them back to the corner where the food was kept—slowly, they had been amassing a store of supplies—and saw the three of them sit down. Besides the hurt, she felt something new gripping her insides. She studied the serious expression on Alyosha's face; both Dimmy and Klemet were describing what they had seen on their trip between the tomb and the Oruzheinaya.

Very definitely, all three of them were troubled by something that went beyond hunger.

• At 7:22, Vasily Klin climbed down the uneven stone steps of the Vodovzvodnaya Tower and walked along the embankment side of the Kremlin wall. It would not do to be late for this particular meeting. He walked slowly, having allowed himself plenty of time, scuffing the light snow on the cobblestones with his shoes, sending up puffs of powdery white as he went.

He had no way of knowing whether Alyosha was telling the truth about hostages still being inside Lenin's Tomb; they had never been told how many were there to begin with. The wire two of the men had unrolled behind them as they crossed from the tomb to the Oruzheinaya made him suspect not, but it was a fact that could not be checked without possibly endangering some hostages along with the remains of Lenin. He had given in without argument, aware that Alyosha was as surprised to hear him give in as he was himself.

In the back of Klin's mind was the fact that Borodinsky's arrival would make any further concessions to Salt Mine impossible. He still doubted that the assault would really take place, but one could never be sure.

Klin had just rounded the corner of the wall and headed for the doorway of the Council of Ministers Building when a terrible realization hit him like a hammer. No matter how he tried to avoid facing it, some small foreign part of him was rooting for Salt Mine and was hoping they would get away. The thought was so appalling Klin quickly dismissed it.

Taking his place at the table, Klin should have guessed the ministers' meeting would follow so predetermined a script it was impossible to understand why they bothered to hold it. Talanin, apparently, had laid down the course of action to Deputy Premier Chaidze, and with equal terseness, Chaidze laid it down for them. "The assault definitely takes place on schedule." He checked his watch. "At nine a.m."

Marshal Borodinsky, his head appearing to grow directly out of his shoulders without bothering about a neck, did his best to appear surprised, but his face told you he'd already known he'd won before the meeting started.

From Foreign Minister Shtanov and from the minister of information, Blaveskov, rose a few protests, but they were without feeling. No one flew in the face of Talanin.

Until this moment, Klin had never really believed Talanin would do something so reckless. He repeated his question from the last meeting. "Why?" he asked. *"Why?"* This time, he was ignored.

The arguments of the others were listened to about as enthusiastically as they were raised—for the record. Ten minutes after the meeting started, Chaidze adjourned it.

Walking down the hall with Shtanov, Klin paused, leaned against a wall, and sighed deeply. "I wish they had at least tried to negotiate Salt Mine's demands. They were impossible as they stood, of course, but that may have been only a bargaining position."

Shtanov shrugged unhappily. "I had a long talk with Chaidze last night along the same lines. The international repercussions terrify me." Turning, they continued down the hall.

"I really messed things up. Damn."

This time it was Shtanov who hesitated. Abruptly he stopped walking once more. "You had considerable help. From inside."

Klin looked at him and shook his head to indicate Shtanov's remark left him at sea. Reluctantly, Shtanov withdrew two Xeroxed sheets from his inside pocket and handed them to Klin. "I did not know whether you had seen these or not."

From Klin's expression as he read them, it was clear he had not. He went ashen. "Ordinarily," explained Shtanov, "we wouldn't have a copy of the first. My secretary had it copied by sheer chance. My own copy of the first one disappeared and was replaced by another—a complete reversal—bearing the same date."

"Thank you," Klin grunted. Nodding tersely, he spun on his heel and stormed down the hall toward his office. Clutched angrily in his hand was a copy of the original Klin document, along with a copy of its replacement, both the work of Mikhail Chorniev.

Back in his office, a seething Klin read the new version of the Klin document with disbelief. A portion of the language remained identical, but the tone had been sharpened to the point of accusatory rudeness. Most important of all, the entire thrust of the memorandum had been reversed.

> Comrade!
> As a longtime officer of the KGB and a personal devotee of yours, I am shocked and saddened by your continuing refusal to accept Salt Mine as the threat to the state it clearly is. There are those who could question your motives in the matter. Consider:
>
> (1) When I first outlined to you the informer Volovno's information on Salt Mine, you dismissed it as a black-market operation. This was in spite of mounting evidence that Salt Mine was a danger to the very survival of the Soviet Union.
>
> (2) You refused to see Volovno yourself, but directed me to extract what information I could and then give the man an exit visa out of the country. Some could see this as an effort to silence Volovno.
>
> (3) When, in desperation, I brought Volovno to

Arkhangelskoye, you again refused to see him. Minutes later, he was murdered there. Since only you and I were aware Volovno was even at Archangelskoye, a devious person could assume you had accomplished by murder what your offer of an exit visa had not. Were you so afraid of what he knew about Salt Mine? If so, why?

(4) I was ordered by you to ignore Volovno's death and forget all about Salt Mine once and for all. When I argued the point, you threatened me with false charges.

(5) In spite of your directive, I assigned KGB agent Bleisky to continue rooting for information on Salt Mine. He has now disappeared. Did you, Comrade Minister, engineer a fate for him similar to Volovno's?"

(6) At every step of my investigation into Salt Mine I found you blocking the way. I cannot believe you do not grasp the terrible danger Salt Mine represents for the future of the Party and of our nation. It will be difficult for many of the ministers not to believe some degree of personal involvement on your part was behind your actions.

You may have, Comrade Minister, some perfectly sound explanation for what you are doing. It is possible some higher game to which I am not privy is being played. However, only my personal sense of loyalty to you has prevented me from taking the matter up with some of the other ministers. I can afford the luxury of that loyalty no longer.

Salt Mine is too clearly a savage attack on the Party and the Soviet Union to be ignored further. Unless, Comrade, I have an adequate, documented explanation of your actions by the end of the week, I will have no choice but to take up the matter with Deputy Premier Chaidze.

With regret,
Mikhail Chorniev
DIRECTOR, KGB

For some time, Klin studied the memorandum, shaking his head slowly back and forth. He had always considered Chorniev too conservative a person to take such a chance. He supposed Chorniev would explain why he had *not* gone to Chaidze earlier by describing an imaginary meeting with Klin, supported by documents Chorniev would claim he now knew to be forged, that made Salt Mine appear a Soviet initiative to "flush out dissidents" or some such excuse.

Infighting at the top of the Soviet hierarchy was not unusual; Chorniev's flair for it was.

• At 8:45, the Oruzheinaya's phone rang. Before even lifting the receiver, Alyosha knew it could only be Klin. Klin's voice had a distant, formal sound, laced with stridency and playing the role of Vasily Dmitrovich Klin, firm, unyielding minister of State security. "As you are aware, my dear friend, the assault is scheduled for nine this morning. Marshal Borodinsky, I should tell you, is rarely late. I make this call to give you one final chance to release the hostages; after that is done, we can talk about terms for Salt Mine itself."

The voice was so distant, Alyosha was momentarily thrown. The sudden hardness in it shook his self-confidence, although he attempted to hide this by the banter Klin must by now expect from him. "I am sure the marshal is on schedule in everything. His bowels are a monument to regularity. However, it's been a day since you were given Salt Mine's demands, and I have yet to hear a single word of comment or response. Room was left for negotiation. I am baffled as to why—"

"The Soviet government does not negotiate with terrorists."

"Perhaps some of the other countries involved might feel—"

"Salt Mine is a purely internal affair."

"The hostages of those countries aren't 'purely internal.' I would think you would want to have exhausted every—"

"Ah, my friend. You have struck the right word: exhausted. All civilized nations are exhausted—fed up with hijacks, terrorist attacks, and kidnappings with political motives. The world is drained by the spectacle of South Moluccans, Palestine Liberationists, Hanafi Muslims, Red Guards and Baader-Meinhofs. Certainly, it will be saddened by the death of your hostages. The ruling cliques of countries aligned against us will scream that the deaths were our fault. That we were wrong. That we should have given in. The world will be shocked at what strikes them as a hard, unyielding stance." Alyosha heard Klin pause, as if reviewing the unfair view the world would take of the Soviet Union's role. Then:

"But in the long run, to give in would be the easy decision, but the wrong decision. It would only lead to more terrorism and more minorities using human lives as levers to move the earth. In the long run, the world will realize that in refusing to give in, we made the hard decision, but the right decision: to sacrifice the few for the many."

For a moment, Alyosha stood motionless, staring at the phone as if the receiver were his personal enemy. Klin's words were so unaccustomedly doctrinaire he wondered if the man he'd been talking to for the last five days had just been acting until now, playing the role of sympathetic official to gain Salt Mine's confidence.

Was this the real Klin—ruthless, brutal, determined to destroy Salt Mine, and to the devil with the hostages? For Alyosha, it was impossible to forget Klin's part in the meningitis scheme. On the other hand, the man was in a difficult position; a successful Salt Mine could cost him not only his standing in the Soviet, but possibly his life as well. Alyosha reviewed some of the many small things and minor kindnesses, not strictly necessary, which Klin had done, and struggled helplessly.

For reasons he didn't understand, he *wanted* to like Klin. They had matching senses of dry humor and similar affinities for the ridiculous. In Russia, these were rare qualities. Sitting eye-to-eye over a bottle of vodka, with a moratorium called on politics, Alyosha suspected, he and Klin might easily hit it off.

Oddly, at the other end of the line, a similar confusion was racing through Vasily Klin's mind. Alyosha, by official Soviet proclamation, was an enemy of the people. It was his duty to destroy the man, to rid the people of this evil. Yet Klin knew Alyosha was not evil; his threats about the hostages were hollow. Like Alyosha a minute earlier, Klin wished he could know his opposite number better; this man he'd never met except across a closely monitored phone line seemed suddenly an old friend. But the State was the State, the Party the Party. He had a duty.

Alyosha heard Klin clear his throat as he brought them both back to reality. "My dear Alyosha," Klin said, "you are running out of time. Marshal Borodinsky—"

"Is rarely late. I remember. Very unhealthy. Someday the man will die of an unmet schedule."

In spite of the situation, they both were unable to suppress a small, uncomfortable laugh. During the brief pause that followed the laugh, Alyosha could imagine Klin forcing himself back into his role. "You have one more chance," Alyosha heard. "Then—"

"No, *you* have one more chance," snapped Alyosha, reverting to his own role. "Attack here, kill the hostages, and the weight of world opinion will land on you like the Tsar Bell."

"We have broad shoulders. Good luck, my friend. May we meet in hell."

Alyosha felt a shudder of fear run through him. "It's a large place," he told Klin. "Perhaps we shall be lucky enough not to."

The click from the other end of the phone was Klin's wordless reply.

Quickly, Alyosha rounded up Misha, Avraam, Dimmy, Klemet, and Lisenka. He drew them into a huddle around him and began barking his orders. As rehearsed, all hostages were to be moved upstairs immediately. The ammunition was to be piled near the heavy steel window shutters; some should be taken both to the second floor and to the cellar to make any last-ditch retreat as expensive as possible. Although it would be nearly impossible not to panic the hostages, every effort should be made.

Lisenka looked at him earnestly. "Do we have any chance at all?" For the first time today, Alyosha returned her look, reaching over to touch her left arm. "I don't know."

Klemet, still wearing the smile but beginning to allow his true sense of gloom to show through, sighed. "Chance? But of course. Like a pig coming down the chute of the slaughter house."

Dimmy scowled. "Out of respect for Misha and Avraam, at least, you might have picked a more appropriate analogy."

Alyosha was too impatient for banter. "Let's get them moving. Good luck."

The inside of the Oruzheinaya became pandemonium as the hostages were herded toward the stairs. With them, they carried their mattresses; rolling up inside them would give a vestige of protection from flying glass and stonework. The efforts to keep them calm were useless. Their situation was so vulnerable no amount of reassurance could make any of them believe they weren't about to meet their respective makers. Some of the women were crying; Alyosha saw Lisa Decatur being helped up the stairs by Christy, followed by a grim-looking Blaine Decatur and their Intourist guide, Irina.

Misha and Avraam took up positions at windows on either

side of the door, peering out through the shutters, waiting. In the center of the Hall of Armor, halfway between the outer vestibule and the stairway to the second floor, stood Alyosha, nervously fondling the whistle in his hand.

He glanced at his watch. The minute hand stood straight up. "Oh, God," he whispered to himself. "They wouldn't. They just wouldn't."

25

THE FIFTH DAY, 9:00 A.M.
As the ninth stroke of the great bells in the Spasskaya Tower boomed across the courtyard—so loud the chandeliers in the Oruzheinaya's Hall of Armor shook—Marshal Borodinsky boomed into one of the field phones. "Open."

Beside him on the turret of the Vodovzvodnaya Tower stood Vasily Klin, shivering in the early-morning cold. They were not sharing the Vodovzvodnaya out of friendship but because it offered a complete view of both the Oruzheinaya and the rest of the Kremlin. Across the Kremlin, on the flat roof and in the top windows of the Council of Ministers Building, Klin could see other ministers, unable to resist watching what would probably be the decisive, if bloody, end of Salt Mine. Like Romans watching the Christians prepare themselves for the lions, they half-dreaded, half-anticipated the gore to be produced by the emperor's already downward-pointing thumb.

On Borodinsky's command, there was a hissing sound followed by a gentle creaking. With awesome majesty, the gates of the towers near the government buildings—the Nikolskaya, the Spasskaya, and the Troitskaya—swung smoothly open. At the same moment, the gate of the Borovitskaya Tower also opened.

Across the courtyard, Klin knew, the ugly gray noses of the T-10s were poised outside the gates; the racing of their motors would raise a rasping diesel chatter and send great clouds of condensation billowing into the cold, thin air of Moscow's morning. Borodinsky, Klin noticed, would be able to move his major force toward the Oruzheinaya using the maze of buildings around Cathedral Square as cover. He would also send a second force in from behind the Oruzheinaya. It was a classic pincers movement.

The marshal picked up the field phone again. His voice remained as steady and matter-of-fact as if he were telling a waiter to decant more Georgian. "Enter and hold."

The idling snort of the diesels responded to radio commands coming from somewhere in the courtyard and rose in a shattering crescendo. The slow squeaking and clanking of metal plate upon cobblestone began, picking up speed as the tanks advanced into the gates. For a brief instant, the sound was muffled when the tanks disappeared under the archways over the gates, returning to full volume as they passed through and emerged into the courtyard of the Kremlin complex. Directly behind the tanks, in low, crouching position, came men of the Special Tactical Forces, their submachine guns in front of them. As soon as most of the tanks were inside, these troops began deploying themselves along the buildings of Cathedral Square, the Terem and Poteshny palaces.

The turrets of the tanks were open, and Klin could hear their radios crackling orders to them. When they had ringed the Oruzheinaya Palata, Klin heard an order barked over all of the radios simultaneously. The tanks stopped their forward movement. With a whirring, high-pitched sound, the turrets of the tanks rotated until their guns were aimed directly at the building. Another order, and the roaring from the tanks returned to its former idling sound.

"Speak." Marshal Borodinsky gave the order in his booming, actor's voice but still had to repeat the word; the field phone, apparently, was not easy to understand at best. Again, Klin heard the radio crackling in one of the unbuttoned tanks. A hollow voice from the T-10 directly below the Vodovzvodnaya boomed through the loudspeaker on its turret. At so point-blank a range, the words bounced off the stone interior of the Kremlin courtyard and rattled windows all the way across to the Building of the Supreme Soviet.

"By command of Marshal Borodinsky, Minister of Defense for the Union of Soviet Socialist Republics, I am authorized to offer the terrorists of the so-called Salt Mine group one final opportunity to release their hostages. At that time, we shall also accept the surrender of these dissident enemies of the Soviet state with all assurances of a fair trial under the provisions of the Soviet constitution. This, I am further authorized to tell you, is your final opportunity. If you do not release your hostages immediately and surrender yourselves, the tanks, on my count of twenty, will commence firing and destroy both the terrorists and their hostages. You will indicate your acceptance by displaying a white flag from either a door or window. There will be no further warning." Slowly, the disembodied voice began its countdown. "One . . . two . . ."

With a great crash, the steel shutters of two second-story windows were flung open. Tension was so high that everyone on the Vodovzvodnaya jumped. Even the voice from the loudspeaker hesitated. Behind the two windows, a pair of small figures could be seen preparing to hang out a flag of some sort. Klin heard his own sigh of relief. The folded part of the flag fell open. Beside him, Klin suddenly heard Marshal Borodinsky's *"Chort."* Alyosha's surprise banner had had its desired effect. From somewhere below—from the soldiers, perhaps—a laugh could be heard, loud at first, then stifled. What now hung from the window was a crude drawing of the hammer and sickle crossed with the clenched-fist symbol of the masses. Only the fist wasn't clenched; one finger rudely saluted the Soviet. With a strident clang, the shutters crashed shut again.

For the first time, the carefully controlled marshal let his voice roar. "Resume counting, dammit. Resume counting!"

The incident with the flag—Alyosha had planned it two days earlier and had gotten Lisenka to sew it up—brought a smile to Salt Mine's faces, but only for a moment. The situation was too grim. Through the steel shutters the voice on the loudspeaker came loud and ominous: "Five . . . six . . ." With each number, Alyosha's brightly polished conviction that the Soviet government, in the end, would be unable to accept the international consequences of attack grew dimmer. Perhaps he had overestimated the power of international repercussions on the Kremlin's thinking. Perhaps he should have realized that Moscow could not allow itself to appear weak or foolish in the eyes of the world.

"Nine . . . ten . . ."

"Take cover, take cover," Alyosha yelled at the Salt Mine team clustered around the windows. "Get down behind something thick. . . ."

"Eleven . . . twelve . . ."

A whirring sound below the Vodovzvodnaya made Klin realize the guns on the tank turrets were being lowered as far as they would go to give the shells maximum destructive power. A few moments later came a series of metallic slams, like car doors being shut. One after the other, each giving a small wave to the driver of the tank to his right, the drivers disappeared, slamming their hatch covers as they went. The last man visible was the tank unit commander. With a final look around, he too grabbed his hatch cover and disappeared.

"Thirteen . . . fourteen . . ."

"Give command to fire on count of twenty. . . ." For some reason the voice of Marshal Borodinsky startled Klin. It seemed impossible, but he had forgotten that the minister of defense stood beside him. Amazed, Klin turned and stared at him.

At the bottom of the stairs leading to the second floor, Alyosha blew his whistle. "Everybody upstairs! Roll yourselves in your mattresses. Curl up as much as you can. And good luck."

"Fifteen . . . sixteen . . ."

The sudden ring on the internal phone sitting in front of him jarred Klin's nerves. For a second, he didn't even move, but stood looking at it as if the instrument had suddenly developed a set of arms and legs and were walking over toward him to seize him by the throat and strangle him. Blinking, he picked it up.

"Klin? Talanin here. Tell Borodinsky to hold his fire."

Klin spun with a yelled message. "Talanin: Hold your fire."

Marshal Borodinsky stared at Klin as if he were crazy. Leaning into the phone, he identified himself. Both Borodinsky and Klin pressed their heads against the receiver. Talanin's voice sounded irritated. "I said, hold your fire, Marshal. And that's what I meant."

"Seventeen . . . eighteen . . ."

"Hold all fire!" As Borodinsky roared his command, he raced to the edge of the Vodovzvodnaya, waving his arms frantically and leaning over the edge, as if the movement of his body might help prevent the coming salvo.

From the loudspeaker came a confused argument, the words unclear and indistinguishable. With a clanging thud, the tank commander's hatch opened and his head and shoulders appeared, frustration written across his face.

"Not a shot, Comrade Secretary," assured Klin into the phone. "We were in time."

"I have been on the hot line with the American president. I had to agree to . . ." Talanin groped for more dignified words. "An arrangement has been reached. Make the best deal with Salt Mine you can. No delivery of KGB men or release of dissidents from prison, of course. Just do the best you can. There still may be a way to turn this to our advantage, I don't know. Chaidze has the ground rules we must operate under. Goddammed Americans . . ."

Borodinsky watched Klin hang up, a questioning expression on his face. "We are to make a deal," Klin said. "Chaidze will have the outline."

"*Chort.* It is a terrible show of weakness." Borodinsky spun and spoke into the field phone. One by one the hatches of the tanks opened, and the tanks and soldiers withdrew to the perimeter of the Kremlin walls. There, the tanks noisily backed up to the walls themselves, motors grumbling and snorting as they idled. Standing in front of and between the parked T-10s and 55s, the soldiers of the Tactical Force broke into loose groupings, smoking nervously and exchanging small talk with one another. From the hatchways, the tank commanders studied the situation with superior expressions, gods in their chariots.

For a moment Borodinsky and Klin locked eyes. The temptation for Klin to smile was overwhelming, but he had been in the hierarchy too long to be that crude. The new aristocracy learned its manners slowly but thoroughly. Klin even tried to pretend he didn't hear the noisy clatter as the shutters of the Oruzheinaya were thrown open, and that he didn't notice the cheering and shouting coming from inside. Ignoring the expression of contempt on Borodinsky's face, Klin merely shrugged, taking off his fur hat and mopping the piebald scalp with his handkerchief.

The angry purple shade had disappeared.

• Inside the Oruzheinaya, the noise was deafening. The moment he heard the countdown stop, Alyosha had raced to the windows. "I do not understand. I do not understand," Misha yelled. "They are pulling back. God of Abraham, they are pulling back!"

That, Alyosha understood. Someone—the Americans, probably—had called Talanin's bluff. He knew neither how nor what had been promised in return; possibly, Talanin and the American president had exchanged promises both knew would never be kept. Salt Mine would have to resist any temptation to relax its vigilance. For in the last analysis, the American politicians cared little more for Salt Mine's ideals, or even the lives of their own nationals, than the Soviets did. It was all a game of appearing on the world stage in the right costume.

From upstairs, the hostages came barreling into the Hall of

Armor. They were confused, but ecstatic with the growing realization their lives were spared. They sang, they drank, they cheered. The concertina was produced and the Russian hostages began whirling and leaping in their violent folk dances, now and then grabbing an American woman and whirling her briefly to the music while the other Russians clapped their hands in rhythm.

Except for one fast-spinning whirl around the room with Lisenka, Alyosha stayed to himself, turning away from the excited talk and the drinks shoved in his direction. It was only a matter of time, he knew, before the phone in the outer vestibule would ring, and he needed silence, time, and a clear head to develop counterstrategies to whatever Klim would come back with.

Just now, time, silence, and clear heads were perhaps the rarest commodities of all in the Oruzheinaya.

• At the Decatur suite of the Intourist Hotel, the atmosphere was hardly less subdued. The embassy had called and told Gary that the assault was called off—for different reasons, Keer was as excited by this news as Gary—and that the hostages, including Gary's family, would probably be set free by tomorrow, possibly tonight.

"Isn't that great? Isn't that *something?*" Gary yelled at Keer, staging a fistfight with a couch pillow to use up some of his sudden excess energy. Falling in with it, Keer picked up another pillow and beat Gary over the head. Gradually, Gary's euphoria began having a strange effect on Keer; it was so genuine and honest, contrasted to his own, that a subtle depression began creeping over him.

A few minutes later, Gary, babbling and talking endlessly in his excitement, left for the embassy. It wouldn't take long, he promised Keer, and he'd be back, and maybe they could go downstairs to the bar to celebrate or something. What the hell, sure it was early, but your family doesn't get a last-minute reprieve from being blown up every day. Almost dancing with happiness, Gary shot out the door.

For a long time after he left, Keer sat on the couch trying to explain his gloom to himself. Salt Mine had won. All that was left now was the escape. A faint smile crossed his face as he listened to his mind repeat the phrase "all that was left." It was plenty.

And the escape would involve him far more directly in Salt Mine than anything had yet. Was he afraid? He put the question to himself and decided he was. Checking his watch, he saw he had a little time to kill, but not too much. Worrying about an imponderable future was no way to spend his time. To clear his head, Keer retreated to his womblike security symbol; taking off his clothes as he went, he walked into the bathroom and proceeded to take a long, hot shower.

By the time Gary got back, Keer was dressed again, but not really feeling much more self-confident. The shower had failed him. They had a brief talk on what Gary had learned at the embassy, but it turned out to be very little of anything new. They would call, they assured Gary.

Keer turned suddenly toward Gary and broke into his still-excited chattering. "I have to go. There's no other way. You've got some idea how much trouble I'm in, and Moscow isn't safe for me any more."

Sitting down, Gary stared at him. "Okay, yes. I know you're in trouble. I won't ask what kind because it's none of my business. . . ."

Keer studied Gary's expression. It was strange, the whole thing. Only ten days ago, he'd never even met Gary. Now, with everything that had happened, he felt as if Gary had been part of his life from the beginning of time. It was crazy, he admitted to himself, but he had few close friends and the prospect of not seeing Gary again—possibly forever—made Keer overflow with sadness. Abruptly, Keer shook himself and struggled to get back to business. "Anyway, I've got to go."

Gary forced a smile; it wasn't a very convincing one. "I'm going to miss you, Keer. Who the hell will I do my drinking with?"

"Oh, shit, Gary. You'll be all right. That visit to the embassy. They said probably by tonight. Back with your family. Better than some crazy, mixed-up Russian like me any day."

Usually Keer was the more perceptive of the two; it had been one of the things that had fascinated Gary most about Keer. Today, Gary was gifted with Keer's perception; his friend was feeling sorry for himself. "You look as sad as Chekhov. It's not like you; I'm not used to it."

"You said you were going to miss me, Gary. Well, I hope you'll remember me laughing. Chekhov, for Christ's sake! I wouldn't go, but, dammit, if I don't, the KGB will lock me up for a thousand years."

"Okay, okay, I understand. There's just one question that's been bugging me. This thing you're into. Does it have anything to do with—?" Gary stopped abruptly. It was a question to which he didn't really want to know the answer. "Oh, forget it. The question was stupid anyway. Good luck, Keer. If you come through in one piece, write me."

At the door, they shook hands quite formally, in that shy, seemingly emotionless way that teenage boys reserve for each other. But just as he put one hand on the door, Keer suddenly spun around and, Russian style, kissed Gary on each cheek. They both blushed furiously. *"Do svidanya, Tovarishch,"* said Keer and was gone.

• Alyosha's prediction that Klin would not take long in getting to him was correct. Less than half an hour after the tanks withdrew, Klin was on the phone to begin what he glumly predicted would be "interminable negotiations." Actually, they took only a series of calls, probably totaling not over an hour.

For his part, Alyosha enjoyed the process thoroughly and wished it could last longer. In his blood ran the Central Asian's love of haggling and the sharp bargain. Even more fun, Vasily Dmitrovich Klin, a pure Russian, obviously hated every second of it. No, the government would not release eight dissidents. Not now, anyway. Perhaps later, one by one, if Salt Mine would give its word any connection between their release and Salt Mine would be kept secret.

"Our word? A few minutes ago, your opinion of us was so low that you wanted to blow us all up. Now, you want our *word* on something? Insanity."

"You want the dissidents out. We will not release them from prison unless we can be sure their freedom doesn't become propaganda; you cannot expect us to advertise the effectiveness of dissent."

Alyosha sighed. "So promised."

At opposite ends of the phone line both men smiled. Each had made promises he had no intention of keeping; each knew the other would not keep his part of the bargain either.

Point by point, it went on this way. No, no, and no. Never would the Soviet allow a broadcast about Salt Mine to be televised from the Oruzheinaya. Or a word published about it in the USSR. One reporter, picked by the correspondents' pool, could conceivably be admitted, but that was all. And without any kind of recording equipment, of course.

"You're not bargaining, you're dictating."

"No broadcast, no television. Just one reporter," repeated Klin.

"How about one reporter and two still photographers then?"

"*One* still photographer," Klin snapped back. His voice sounded shrill and tired.

"Done. One pool reporter, one still photographer." Alyosha smiled to himself. That was all he'd wanted in the first place. In Alyosha's home town, Baku, capital of the Azerbaidzhan Republic, Klin would have been despised as much for his lack of trading shrewdness as for being from Moscow.

The emigration of Jews and other minorities was handled in much the same way as the release of the eight dissidents; it was to be done—an official promise—only after time had passed, and with no visible link to Salt Mine. Again, while each man knew the other to be lying, each felt he had won a point.

The issue of whose airplanes would be used to take Salt Mine and the hostages out of Russia provided the longest and toughest battle. With reason. On the hot line, Talanin and the U.S. president had struck a cynical bargain. Its object was to get the hostages to safety, while landing as many of Salt Mine as possible in a country from which they could be extradited to the Soviet. To make it work, the country chosen had to appear above this sort of duplicity.

The American president had suggested Ireland, a country generally considered a bastion of neutrality and freedom. But the president was to apply economic pressure of such weight that the Irish would have to agree to the extradition. The Irish had been approached, and in the end, economics took precedence over morality. They capitulated, secretly hoping world opinion would free them from their part of the bargain.

The catch would come, Klin knew, in getting Alyosha to agree to putting as many of Salt Mine as possible on this Irish plane, and in introducing the idea of Aer Lingus in such a way that Alyosha would not get suspicious. Klin started the bargaining with what he knew was an outrageous suggestion.

"There will be two planes, as agreed. One could carry the hostages, one your Salt Mine team, to land wherever you choose."

Alyosha laughed. Painfully, they bargained their way down to one plane with *mostly* hostages plus a guard force from

Salt Mine, and one plane with *mostly* Salt Mine plus a sprinkling of hostages. Alyosha sighed. It was probably the best he could get.

A little later, a number of countries were discussed and rejected by Alyosha or Klin. Finally, Sweden was suggested and accepted by both for one of the planes. On the second plane, the two of them seemed at an impasse—Klin was holding the Irish plane in abeyance until the right opportunity—and the talks were recessed for half an hour.

Wearily turning away from the Oruzheinaya's wall phone, Alyosha sank into the Hall of Armor's one thronelike chair. Lisenka walked quickly over to him, studying his face. "Trouble?"

"We're all right on everything except the nationality of the second plane. They're up to something."

"But with all those hostages on board . . ."

"Klin's bright on some of his trades, dumb on others. He's got some sort of scheme, I think. It could be just politics, or it could be a trap they're laying."

Lisenka thought for a moment. "Separate us from the hostages somehow, and . . ."

"Something like that. Anyway, in the last couple of days I've worked out a maneuver to avoid that kind of double cross. It's simple."

Lisenka moved closer, adjusting herself on the arm of the thronelike chair Alyosha was sitting in. The ancient piece creaked dangerously, and she remembered that before Salt Mine a velvet rope stretched across the seat to prevent anyone's sitting down. Somewhere on the floor was a card noting that the chair was originally made for the Patriarch Nikon. She ignored the creaking; the hell with the patriarch. Lisenka wanted to be this near to Alyosha forever—to see him, to touch him, to hear his voice.

From the vestibule, they heard the strident ringing of the phone. Probably Klin, with some new twist. With a tired little groan, Alyosha walked out of the Hall of Armor into the vestibule, patting Lisenka lightly on the hand as he left.

On his way, a sound made him turn and he saw Lisenka's expression. She was wondering, he suspected, how a man could be as wild as he had been the night before and so distant the next day.

It was a good question, and one to which Alyosha had no answer.

• In his office at the Council of Ministers Building, Klin leaned back in his chair, cradling the phone in one hand. Opposite him slouched Deputy Premier Chaidze. He was there at Klin's request, in case any sudden, on-the-spot decisions were required, monitoring the conversation through a single earphone. The bait was about to be offered to Alyosha and, they hoped, the hook set. As Klin talked, he fingered the Father Frost paperweight on his desk. A child's toy, Klin thought, and a stupid one for a grown man to play with, although perhaps the world's politics weren't so far from children and their toys at that. "I'm sorry a Yugoslav plane upsets you, my friend," said Klin. "The Yugoslavs hardly take their orders from Moscow these days. On the other hand, I suppose I can see your point."

Over the phone Alyosha's laugh was dry and irritating; Klin was wondering what he would have done if Alyosha had accepted his phony suggestion; the Irish, at least, listened to reason. "Well," Klin continued, "I have already talked to the Italians. They are quite ready."

"No." Alyosha's voice became suddenly firm and hard. "Too Communist-oriented."

Klin leaned forward, nodding at Chaidze to pay careful attention now. Ireland was on the launching pad. "The Irish. There's always the Irish."

For a moment, there was a pause from Alyosha; then: "I hadn't thought of them. I don't know. . . ."

As he waited, Klin gave the crystal paperweight a violent spin, completely burying the beleaguered Father Frost in a blizzard. "If you don't mind inferior food, I should think the Irish would certainly appeal to you. They wrote the book on dissension."

Slowly, painfully, unable to find any grounds for objection that would hold water even for himself, Alyosha agreed. "All right. Ireland."

"Done. That gives us Ireland and Sweden." Klin again nodded at Chaidze to be sure he paid attention. "Sweden has the great advantage of being close. The hostages will surely want the shortest trip possible. In fact, you might consider making the 'mostly hostages' plane the Swedish one, and the 'mostly Salt Mine' the Irish one. The decision, of course, is yours. Not important. Just an idea."

"It sounds all right. I'll think about it."

Klin could guess that the reaction meant Alyosha would accept. He smiled at Chaidze. "About the press," he said into the phone, changing the subject before Alyosha could change his mind. "The pool reporter and his photographer will be there at three sharp." Klin's laugh sounded forced as he listened to Alyosha's question. "No, my friend. Not *Izvestia.* The reporter was chosen by the foreign correspondents here in Moscow."

There was a sprinkling more of talk; Klin wanted to keep it short now that the planes had been agreed upon. As soon as the call was done, Klin and Chaidze looked at each other.

"Very well executed, my dear Klin. Masterful."

Klin smiled happily. He was convinced he'd won. That Alyosha had agreed to have one plane with mostly hostages, one with mostly Salt Mine, was a great step forward. That Alyosha appeared to be going along with his suggestion that the "mostly hostages" plane should be the Swedish one, requiring most of Salt Mine to land in Ireland, was icing on the marzipan. Chaidze congratulated him again and stood up.

As Chaidze left, Klin's secretary came in to remind him that KGB Director Chorniev was still waiting in the anteroom. Klin picked up the spherelike paperweight and spun the snow around so wildly that poor old Father Frost disappeared entirely. "Let him cool his heels a while longer—quite a while longer—and then send him in."

With the tight, small smile of victory—it was to be a day of triumphs—Klin pulled his Xerox of the original Klin document out of his desk drawer. With the palms of his hands, he smoothed it flat on the desk. Even reading upside down from the desk's other side, Chorniev couldn't fail to recognize what it was. Then, it would begin.

He was going to enjoy this.

26

THE FIFTH DAY, 2:55 P.M.
A little before three, Chorniev was still waiting to see Klin. He paced the floor angrily, occasionally going to look out the windows of the anteroom, which overlooked the Kremlin courtyard. At other windows in the Council of Ministers Building, he could see the faces of some of the ministers, unable to keep their eyes away from the courtyard. The sight of the tanks and special troops pulled back to the towers and walls made Chorniev snort with contempt; he wasn't sure who was responsible for calling off the assault on the Oruzheinaya, but he suspected Klin.

Promptly at three, an Intourist limo pulled up to the Nikolskaya. Two men stepped out and strode through the gate, stopping to show their passes to the guard, who halted them while he called someone. The pair was the pool reporter and his photographer; Klin's deputy scurried out of the building to meet them. Like any professional photographer, the cameraman was festooned with black cases, leather sacks, belts and boxes, all attached to various parts of him by a spiderweb of straps and harnesses. Apologetically, Klin's deputy said something to him and peeked inside each of them. The thought of a deputy minister of security—Pisarev, his name was, Chorniev seemed to remember—apologizing before searching a foreign photographer's bags caused Chorniev's blood to curdle.

The reporter, Andrew Jax, carried only a yellow legal pad. Smiling, he offered the pad to Deputy Pisarev to search; once Pisarev realized it was a joke, he smiled too. Pisarev led the pair, the photographer clanking as he walked, across the cobblestones, around the Palace of Congresses, and into the side entrance of the Terem Palace. Presumably, they would emerge on the other side and walk across the smaller courtyard to the outer doors of the Oruzheinaya. Just as Chorniev was called to his feet by Klin's secretary, he saw Pisarev come back out through the Terem Palace, motioning back two soldiers he felt were posted too close to the building.

"Minister Klin wants you. *Now,* Chorniev," announced Klin's secretary, a thin, wisp-bearded *apparatchik.* Apparently he had sensed Chorniev's impending demise and now felt safe to redress old grievances by being rude. He virtually shoved Chorniev, his face stricken, through the door into Klin's office. Chorniev had seen such treatment before.

His abrupt summons into Klin's office meant that Chorniev never got to see a face at another window, also watching Jax and his photographer stride across the Kremlin courtyard. The face belonged to Dmitry Gertsen, Minister of Production and Industry, who thought the photographer looked strangely familiar. At first, the minister assumed it to be no more than a remarkable resemblance, but the powerful field glasses he kept on his desk left no question: the photographer was his son, Kyril.

The minister knew this was the end. Keer had always mystified him. For that, he always blamed the house servant, Dovo, who had done everything but wet-nurse the boy. He would fire Dovo the moment he got home.

As Gertsen considered the satisfaction in getting rid of Dovo, a new thought suddenly flew across his mind. By the time he got home, there probably wouldn't be a Dovo to fire. Or a household to fire him from. Such perks went with position, and his own position would end the moment the government learned that his son was involved in Salt Mine. Many high ministers had troublesome adolescents to explain away; in this, the new aristocracy was no different from the old. But Keer was not just being troublesome; he was caught up in outright treason. Dovo had raised Keer, not he, and yes, he had allowed that to happen. His position almost mandated it. He was so busy and so often away there had been no choice. So if anyone was to blame, it was Dovo. It was Dovo who made Keer a traitor to the Party; it was Dovo who made Keer hate his own father; it was Dovo who ruined Keer—and was now destroying his father.

The thought of his own downfall made Gertsen wonder if he shouldn't salvage what he could, call the KGB, and tell them who the photographer really was. Quickly, he decided against it. Possibly no one would recognize Keer. Possibly, then, he could stay on as minister of production. Keer would be sent somewhere, far away from Moscow. But that could come later.

Wearily the minister turned away from the window. He decided he'd leave early today and go see Manya. To Gertsen, she was far more than a mistress. His underlings at the ministry might hate him, Dovo might hate him, Keer might hate him, but Manya loved him.

She was the one person in this world he could trust.

• Tucked away in a corner far to one side of the Hall of Armor was the museum director's tiny office. Inside, Andrew Jax was settling into the first of his interviews, face to face now with Blaine Decatur.

"No, in general they treated us pretty well. Hell, I tried to make a break for it once"—this was sheer fiction on Decatur's part—"and when you're a hostage that's usually a good way to get shot. These Salt Mine people didn't do anything but laugh at me." Blaine Decatur searched the ceiling of the Oruzheinaya for a second. "Of course, I could think of a lot of things I'd rather spend five days doing than sitting in this place. . . ."

To Jax, the expression on Decatur's face seemed an odd, dreamy one. The chief executives of large corporations such as Decatur's, Jax remembered, frequently acted that way; while talking to an interviewer, they seemed to be dreaming of something else. Jax's instinct was right. Decatur was indeed thinking of something else—a better way to spend five days: five days in Paris with Chessie. Jax brought him back to earth.

"And your wife and daughter . . . how do they feel about—well, their adventure?"

"Ask them yourself," snapped Decatur and walked away from Jax and his yellow legal pad and his microphone. The microphone and recording machine were not part of what Klin and Alyosha had agreed to. The men from CBS and NBC had "wired" Jax with a hidden recording machine, adding the plug-in mike so that Jax could record the voices with complete clarity.

During the sessions, each member of Salt Mine was to be interviewed by Jax. Only Alyosha and Kropotkin, the Old One, refused. Alyosha said he had his reasons; Kropotkin, as usual, said nothing.

Lisenka, her voice sometimes uncertain with emotion, told of how she had loved Shymon. How he had run one of the *samizdat* papers, considered an act of treason in the Soviet Union. And how one day the KGB arrived at their door and tore Shymon out of her arms. "He had to turn against me, to scream terrible things at me, accusing me of everything ugly he could think of. He didn't mean it. It was to make the KGB believe I was a good *apparatchik* and prevent suspicion from falling on me. It was brave, Shymon was very brave. But, oh, what a painful way for lovers to part. I have not heard of him since; I never will. Shymon is probably dead." Lisenka shook her head and paused to gain control of her voice. "You asked me, Mr. Jax, why I joined Salt Mine. It was because of many things, but what brought it all home to me was Shymon and what they did to him."

Lisenka took a chair to one side of the desk so that she could translate for Jax and those in Salt Mine who didn't speak English.

As a writer, discussing freedom of speech came naturally to Dimmy. He did it well and at length, but his statements, coming directly after Lisenka's highly emotional recital, sounded much flatter. "Speech," he noted, "is all that separates a man from the instinctive language of an animal. And that is what the Soviet government would like its citizens to be: obedient animals. We believe too deeply in a man's right to express what he thinks to accept that. . . ."

Klemet, although smiling as always, sounded frail and uncertain during his interview with Jax. Doggedly, he tried to explain the relationship of the scientist to the state in the Soviet Union, but confessed he was not sure whether he was being threatened with assignment to an asylum for his words about nuclear fission, or because he had signed Charter 77.

Jax leaped at this, trying to make Klemet get specific. "Yes," Klemet admitted. "I signed Charter Seventy-seven. Can it be wrong to demand basic freedoms?"

Jax was drawing Klemet into a discussion of the charter—originally Czechoslovakian—when the door to the room burst open with a crash. Framed in the doorway stood Irina, who had pushed past the foot soldier posted outside. She went straight across the room toward where Lisenka sat on the desk, translating. "Traitor! Traitor!" she screamed at Lisenka, and then spun around on Klemet and Dimmy. "All of you are traitors." She turned toward the startled Jax. "These are not the voices of the real Soviet people, Mr. Jax; these are the voices of traitors and terrorists. Kidnappers. Criminals who hold men, women, and children and terrify them for their own ends. How can you use your microphone to take down what these traitors and hooli—"

The slap hit her hard, so hard it made Jax drop the microphone; later, playing the tape back, he admitted that the effect of Irina's screaming, the sharp crack of Lisenka's slap across Irina's cheek, followed by the hollow, thundering crash of the mike hitting the desk captured the drama in a way his best writing never could. Irina was struggling to get back at Lisenka—a lot of unhealed wounds lay behind her attack on her fellow guide—but Dimmy and Klemet stepped in and pinned Irina's arms to her side.

There was no struggle when Alyosha, drawn by the noise, stormed into the director's office. He grabbed Irina by both elbows and lifted her bodily out of the room, dragged her across the vestibule, and dumped her unceremoniously among the Decaturs. Blaine Decatur, in the midst of a rare sustained talk with Lisa, looked at Irina without sympathy. His conversation with Lisa only made things worse; he would have traded his company, his stock options, probably his own children to be with Chessie.

Pulling himself together, Jax continued with the interviewing. Misha and Avraam took turns in the room, one of them always staying outside on guard. In a few short phrases, Misha sketched the picture of what being a Jew in the Soviet was like, concluding on a bitter note: "The Soviet government is attempting nothing less than our annihilation. Like Hitler, the Kremlin has its own 'final solution.' From the gas ovens to something subtler: slow, planned expulsion from society as the new form of genocide. Death by exclusion."

Out in the Hall of Armor, using a small, failure-proof Minox to photograph Salt Mine and its hostages, Keer was enjoying himself. Earlier that morning, the man from *France Soir* had showed him how to work it; even for someone with little background in photography, it was simple.

Keer was laughing and joking as he snapped away, but his face turned serious when Lisenka called for him to come into the director's office for his turn with Jax. Figuring what Keer could say had been an exercise for them all; he could not very well admit his reasons for joining Salt Mine were a loathing of his father and a fascination with all things American. To avoid this, they decided to let Keer summarize for Jax the collective intent behind Salt Mine. He spoke excellent English—a plus—and was an articulate youth with a deep, dramatic speaking voice. What he was to say had been carefully worked out by Alyosha and Lisenka and Misha. Facing Jax, though, Keer felt his knees shake at the thought of the millions who would eventually hear him speak. It did not show.

"A government that believes freedom of speech, freedom of movement, and freedom of thought are dangerous must be a dangerous government. A government that muzzles its best writers, philosophers, and scientists must be a scared government. And a government that systematically represses its minorities must be afraid of being suppressed itself.

"Marx said the government, having set up the socialist state, would eventually wither away. We know now that no government *ever* withers away; it only grows larger and more suffocating.

"All of us in Salt Mine love our country. But we can neither love nor tolerate its government any longer. Our one hope is that the drama of Salt Mine brings home to the world the real conditions inside our country. For to stifle human rights in any country diminishes human rights in *all* countries.

"And so, now, we in Salt Mine must leave our beloved country. Not in anger, but in sadness. With the hope that those we leave behind will someday find, as we have, that glorious soaring of the spirit that comes only with freedom."

Jax was unsure how to take Keer. He appeared too young to be so fervent in his beliefs. And over the years, Keer had become a good enough actor to be unsure how to take himself. Like all good actors, he had difficulty drawing the line between reality and the part he was playing. By the time he had finished his performance for Jax, he was not sure everything he said about his reasons for being in Salt Mine—his entire summary—wasn't precisely what he believed.

• Although Alyosha had refused to take part in the taped interviews, Jax, a little later, was able to pull him to one side in the Hall of Armor. "It seems strange," he pointed out, "that as the leader of Salt Mine you wouldn't want to explain your point of view. I'm not deprecating your feat, you understand, but you did make a lot of people innocent victims; there must have been a reason . . ."

Alyosha stared at him. "Yes, there was a reason. You call the hostages 'victims.' The members of Salt Mine are victims, too." He made a wide sweep of his arm to indicate the entire Kremlin complex. "So are those soldiers outside. So are all citizens of the Soviet, or, for that matter, of the United States."

Jax looked bewildered. "I don't think I get you. . . ."

"Victims. Victims of their own governments. People presumably there to protect and serve them. But actually—American *or* Soviet—cynical, self-serving men. Take the United States and the Soviet Union. One is a socialist dictatorship, one a democracy. But their leaders, their governments, are less interested in what happens to their citizens than in what happens to themselves. Their internal and external policies are designed mainly to perpetuate themselves, whether through the ballot box or the KGB. And this is as true with the cynical dogmatism of a Stalin or a Nixon as with the homespun ineffectiveness of a Khrushchev or a Carter. They do not serve their people; they *use* them. This is the reason I chose not to speak. My beliefs—particularly about America—would only have blurred the picture." And with a nod, Alyosha walked away and disappeared among the hostages.

Jax watched him go. Alyosha's was an interesting point of view, not too different from Max's own fear of suffocating big governments. He could agree with Alyosha and understand why he decided not to speak. The point of view did not fit the world's self-image. His readers, for instance, would loathe it.

America was not yet ready to face this kind of truth.

• From his position on the Vodovzvodnaya Tower, Klin watched the Intourist buses roll through the Spasskaya. To him—to anyone familiar with the workings of the Kremlin—it presented a strange sight: tourist buses inside the Holy of Holies. The buses followed the inside of the Kremlin wall until they slipped past the Cathedral of the Archangel and the Cathedral of the Annunciation, took a wide turn around the Grand Kremlin Palace, and finally pulled up outside the doors of the Oruzheinaya Palata itself.

In all the windows of the ministers' building, Klin could see faces pressed against the glass. The sight made him shudder, a feeling so different from his mood a little earlier. Then, he had enjoyed watching Chorniev strain to see the Klin document on his desk. From Chorniev's expression it was evident he suspected what the piece of paper was but still hoped he was wrong.

"I am not pleased with you, Chorniev," Klin had begun. "I

cannot believe you are pleased with yourself. Somehow, I don't believe you understand why I chose you for your job in the first place."

The statement tore Chorniev's eyes away from the document; Klin's words were as confusing as they were ominous. "I am afraid, Vasily Dmitrovich"—Klin's expression made him rephrase his response—"I am afraid, Comrade Minister, that I don't understand. I believe I have done a good job; I always thought you chose me for the position because you believed I would."

"I thought the job you did would be adequate, and it has been. Adequate, but no more. I chose you, to be frank, because you are so thoroughly despised by most of the ministers I felt I never had to fear you. I underestimated your stupidity. You have tried to sabotage me—with this."

He handed the Klin document to Chorniev, holding it between two fingers as you might a dead fish. "Oh, that," said Chorniev lamely.

"Yes, 'oh, that.' A primitive effort. And you became afraid it was going to backfire on you. Embarrassing to have a document accusing me of wasting the KGB's time on a will-o'-the-wisp like Salt Mine, you decided. Particularly given recent events. So you made a second document, a forgery. A forged document is always stupid."

"Forged?" Chorniev was genuinely confused, although a terrible fear that he *did* understand was growing inside him.

"Forged. I know that your original memo, the first so-called Klin document, was replaced when your debugging team paid their little visit to the ministers' offices. By this." Klin yanked open his drawer and pulled out the second document. Chorniev, who was unaware Klin had, or even knew of, either memo, turned ashen.

"Comrade Minister. The time-and-date stamps showing when the memo was received at each minister's office—"

"Were easy for anyone in the KGB to fake. Please don't insult my intelligence; for some years I ran the KGB myself."

"Someone else must have—"

"Not someone else, *you*. I have the testimony of two of the three agents you sent on the debugging mission. The third was apparently killed by the Armed Forces Security Network. Or by you."

"Comrade Minister," began Chorniev again, grabbing for straws. Klin held up his hand for him to be quiet.

"I would announce your"—Klin paused for effect, pretending to have trouble finding the precise word—"*retirement* immediately, but it would cause too much talk just now. In Salt Mine's waning moments it could even reflect on my ministry. But you may consider yourself relieved from duty as of now. Your deputy, Dzavatisky, can stand in your place. I shall decide what to do with you tomorrow. In the meantime, kindly get yourself out of this building, out of your office, and, most important, Chorniev"—Klin rose to his full height, towering over the diminutive Chorniev—"GET OUT OF MY SIGHT!"

When Chorniev stood up, his stomach seemed to lag behind his body by several seconds, as if he were in a high-speed elevator that was plunging out of control. Blinking, he turned and walked toward the door; it opened before he could reach it. Two solid-looking KGB men filled the doorway, then moved inside to take Chorniev, one grabbing each arm. Chorniev's head spun back toward Klin in surprise.

"Just a pair of your former colleagues, Chorniev, to make sure you reach your home safely. And that you stay there until sent for."

To Klin, staring out the window, that fleeting moment of satisfaction seemed very long ago, even though it had been only a little earlier. Below him, he could see the buses opening their folding doors, one of the drivers blowing his horn loudly as if he thought no one inside the Oruzheinaya realized they had arrived. He watched Salt Mine and the hostages emerging from the Oruzheinaya in single file.

As he had suggested—and a little to his surprise—Alyosha had separated his people into two groups, one mostly hostages, and one mostly members of Salt Mine. Klin suddenly felt he had won. The plane with most of Salt Mine would arrive in Ireland, and Salt Mine's members would promptly be imprisoned and eventually returned. He was almost surprised Alyosha had fallen into the trap, although unless you knew of the arrangement between the American president and the Irish Republic, he supposed it was an easy trap to fall into.

Neither Klin nor anyone else except Talanin knew the strategy behind the deal the secretary-general had struck with the president. Until the last moment, Talanin had insisted on the Soviets' right to storm the Oruzheinaya Palata; what might happen to the American hostages inside was regrettable, but the preservation of Soviet sovereignty was more important. A vacillating American president had changed his direction several times, clearly emerging as the petitioner.

Talanin had expected exactly this. Circuitously, he allowed it to be suggested that a few concessions in the new arms talks, a lifting of present blocks in strategic materials, and withdrawal of American protests about Communist-sponsored "nationalist" groups in South Africa might soothe Russia's sense of ruffled sovereignty. The deal was struck. The Irish were pressured. Salt Mine and its hostages would be allowed to leave.

Observers of the Soviet, of course, suspected that Talanin would not allow the assault on the Oruzheinaya to take place. Relations with too many countries—including Soviet client states—were at stake. But by appearing to accept any deal at all only with the greatest reluctance, the Soviets, at no cost to themselves, had forced the president to make concessions to them for doing what they were going to do all along anyway.

But Klin was ignorant of these specifics, and his mind was far away from such considerations at the moment, anyway. Staring out the window, he wondered which of the Salt Mine men—easy to distinguish from the tourist-hostages by their clothes—was Alyosha. He would like to meet the man. But then, he supposed, watching the last of the two groups climb into the second bus, they would be meeting soon enough.

27

THE FIFTH DAY, 6:15 P.M.

The two buses hummed along the road toward Sheremetyevo International. Although only thirty-two kilometers from Moscow, the airport is in deep countryside, where one can still see an occasional *izba,* the log structure in general use three or four hundred years ago.

Ahead of the buses, two motorcyclists with flashing red lights and sirens split the air behind them, followed by more motorcyclists and an ominous procession of KGB and Moscow Militia cars, their blue lights spinning as they sounded their mournful two-tone sirens.

Inside the buses, the talk was excited—children on a picnic. In the "mostly hostages" vehicle, Alyosha watched the strobe flashes from Keer's camera. (Jax had called Klin from the Oruzheinaya and said he and his photographer would go on the plane to Sweden. He had interviewed Salt Mine at the Oruzheinaya Palata, he said, and now he wanted to get pictures and interviews with the hostages. There was no objection; Klin figured anything said by the hostages about Salt Mine was bound to be negative and therefore make good propaganda for the Soviet.)

"Hold it. Let me get a shot of you like that. Right where you are." Keer aimed the camera at Dimmy and clicked the trigger.

Dimmy was adjusting his tie. Or rather, Blaine Decatur's tie. "I realize the USSR is the land of opportunity," Dimmy announced. "Anyway that's what they say in the Party literature—but I never thought it would give me the opportunity to dress like a card-carrying capitalist."

"It becomes you." Klemet shifted his shoulders inside the unaccustomed clothing. "But most writers are poor, and you look very rich."

"Nonsense. I look American. The American way of being poor is to look rich."

Listening to the hum of the highway, Alyosha noticed an abrupt change in pitch. They were slowing down. Ahead and to one side, he could see the lights of Sheremetyevo; the normal lighting had been augmented for their departure by special floodlights, a hard, flat, glaring illumination that left no dark corners for anyone to hide in. Klin's helicopter was already down and parked to one side of the tarmac; the area where the buses would stop and the two planes load up with passengers was teeming with soldiers, KGB men, and police. The two gleaming jets—one with the brilliant green shamrock of Aer Lingus, the other with the broad blue-and-white markings of Scandinavian Airlines—stood in the center, while maintenance men, mechanics, and security guards crawled over them. As they sighted the procession coming toward the airport, the flight crews of the two planes appeared and began their last-minute checks. When the buses turned into the airport itself, the stewards and stewardesses came out and stood near the old-fashioned rolling boarding steps of the planes, shivering in the cold, damp wind.

Through the window of the bus, Alyosha looked at the planes and saw the surrounding crowd part to make way for their buses. "Everybody follow their instructions now. It's critical. Don't let the guards or the soldiers rattle you. And Salt Mine, for God's sake, keep quiet. No talking outside. We'll be getting off any minute now."

• From outside the circle, standing on a small rolling platform used by mechanics in servicing the hard-to-reach jet pods of planes, Klin watched. In one gloved hand was a walkie-talkie; patched in to the powerful transmitter of a mobile KGB communications truck parked just outside the field, this enabled Klin to reach anyone he needed. Over the portable radio, Klin heard the KGB officer in charge order his men back and away from the boarding area; the two buses pulled into the cleared circle and stopped, their tail pipes sending puffy clouds of exhaust into the frozen air. On some signal, the doors of both buses opened simultaneously.

By advance agreement, both SAS and Aer Lingus were taking the unusual step of allowing armed men to board their planes. Unlike airplane hijackers, Salt Mine had everything to gain by allowing the planes to reach their destinations; they had, after all, selected these themselves and had no reason to try to seize the planes in flight. It made the pilots nervous; it made the hostesses and stewards nervous, but it was the only arrangement that Salt Mine would accept. Sweden went along, taking the risk in the name of a humanitarian gesture, Ireland because of the economic squeeze put on the country.

The line of hostages, guarded by a handful of Salt Mine, their Tekels slung over their shoulders, walked briskly over to the SAS jet and began mounting the boarding steps. The clothes of the hostages and of Salt Mine, seen this way, one next to the other, provided a study in contrasts: the hostages in their trim, expensive topcoats, the Salt Mine guards in heavy sweaters, tattered overcoats, and fur hats.

From the other bus, the members of Salt Mine, mixed with a handful of hostages to provide insurance from attack, climbed onto the Aer Lingus plane.

There was a pause while the last of each group climbed up the stairs and disappeared inside the planes; the buses rolled away through the crowd and parked on the dim periphery beyond the lights. It was easy, too easy, thought Klin, gnawed at by some fear he couldn't define.

• The stewardesses came down the aisle, cautioning everyone to fasten their seat belts and not to smoke until after takeoff. Lisenka was seated next to the window in what would normally be the first class; this was not where she wanted to be—she had planned on an aisle seat in the larger tourist section—but once aboard the plane, she found that the crew, not Salt Mine, was in charge. Twisting, Lisenka craned her neck to find Alyosha but decided he must be seated in tourist.

Through the window, she watched the turmoil outside. A man with odd blotches on his scalp showing through wispy patches of hair stood on a raised device. In his hand was a portable radio. He appeared completely surrounded by KGB men, so many he looked a little uneasy himself.

It was then that she saw Alyosha. Outside. Lisenka's breath left her. A sudden empty, burning realization gripped her: He was not coming. On the outer edge of the crowd, he stood close to the circle of light around the planes, dressed in the uniform of an Intourist bus driver. For a moment the uniform baffled her, but slowly, Lisenka remembered his asking her to get one for him about two weeks before Salt Mine went operational.

The uniform explained how he was planning to get away from Sheremetyevo. Damn him. Alyosha must have hidden on the floor of their bus until the driver parked it and went outside to get further orders. Then Alyosha changed into his own driver's suit and waited until no one was near. A few minutes later, all anyone would have seen was an Intourist driver climbing out of an Intourist bus, hardly enough to arouse curiosity in anyone. Damn him again, not to tell her.

From her window, she saw Alyosha button his coat, turning around to stare at their plane as he did. She waved at him desperately, but if he saw her, he pretended not to. Quietly, he melted into the crowd and disappeared. Part of Lisenka disappeared with him. She kept her face pressed against the window on the chance she might catch one final glimpse of him. It never came.

The jets whined, the 707 strained against the brakes, the wheels began to turn beneath them, and Lisenka felt the plane roll down the runway. With a final sigh, as if reluctant to part from the ground, the giant plane rose slowly into the air. The passengers cheered. As the plane rose higher and banked slightly, the stewardesses began coming down the aisle, pouring champagne into plastic glasses. The passengers cheered again.

Lisenka sat in her seat, unmoving, unsmiling. She was stunned. Alyosha had said it would work and it had, a reality she still had trouble adjusting to. Across the aisle, Mrs. Blaine Decatur tried to make herself comfortable in the woolen peasant dress of a Russian housewife. It was impossible. She stared at Lisenka—Lisenka was wearing *her* mink over *her* favorite Halston—and wondered if she could demand that Lisenka give them back to her now. She decided the idea was an unwise one; there was no telling what these desperate people still might do. For the moment, she settled for unfamiliar, uncomfortable clothes and freedom.

The clothes were at the heart of Alyosha's device for avoiding any last-minute treachery by Klin. It was a simple maneuver. Alyosha knew nothing about the American president's arrangement with Ireland—extortion might be a better word—but he became suspicious when Klin caved in on point after point. Too easy, too good to be true. Particularly when Klin produced a sudden high degree of concern and suggested that the "mostly hostage" group be put on the SAS jet so "the poor hostages can be freed sooner." It was at this point that Alyosha decided Aer Lingus was not safe for Salt Mine. "I don't know what Klin's game is," he told Lisenka. "Whether the Irish plane is going to be forced down over Poland or Rumania or someplace, or whether the Irish—it's hard to believe—are going to enforce their extradition treaty . . . well, anyway, there's something smelly about that Irish flight. I don't want the 'mostly Salt Mine' group on it, yet Klin has to be made to believe that it is. . . ."

"I think it worked," the voice beside her said. It was Misha, the Tekel back in place over his shoulder but looking strange hanging across the pin-striped suit he had borrowed from one of the hostages.

"I hope so." The very simplicity that sometimes confused Lisenka had worked indeed. Most of Salt Mine—with the exception of Kropotkin, the Old One, and one of the foot soldiers—were not, as Klin believed, on Aer Lingus. *Hostages* dressed in the clothes of Salt Mine and carrying empty Tekels were on Aer Lingus instead, kept in line by one foot soldier, whose Tekel was not empty, and by Kropotkin, staggering under the load of grenades he wore beneath his St. Laurent overcoat. Almost all of Salt Mine, dressed in hostages' Western clothing, were on SAS. Kropotkin's decision to go on Aer Lingus and guard the real hostages was his own. "I am too old to care, too near death. Salt Mine has made its point for me: A government, like a man, must keep its promises. At my age, bones ache, joints hurt, movement becomes agony. Death will come as a release."

As the jet reached the upper air, the interior of the plane grew quiet; everyone was lost in his own thoughts. Lisenka could not shake Alyosha's presence. He had refused to be interviewed, he had not allowed himself to be photographed, and now Lisenka realized why. Using one of his forged ID cards, he would make his way home to the Azerbaidzhan Republic and disappear. The Azerbaidzhanis are a clannish lot; even had they known who he was and what he had done, they would never tell anyone from the Party. To them the Party represented a hated Moscow. At first, she had thought Alyosha conceived Salt Mine as rebellion for rebellion's sake. After their night in the Petersburg sled, though, she decided it was his proof to the world—to himself—that he was not the coward Ulangom made him feel. Ilya, the Chinese trumpets, and Ulangom now were made up for.

Again, Lisenka asked herself why, dammit, why hadn't he told her he was staying? She knew he was a loner, but beyond that, he had probably wanted to avoid any suggestion that she stay with him. Not telling her was an act of unselfishness; she felt pretty sure he would have liked her to stay, but he also knew it would not be safe for either of them if she did. Above everything else, he seemed, in those last few hours, to be worrying about her safety, even if it was done in his usual withdrawn way. "It will be safe in Sweden," he had told her. "They have no extradition agreement with the Soviet Union. Sweden has only a four-year sentence for airplane hijacking. And they can't even invoke that. We did not hijack their plane; they came and got us of their own free will and flew us out. You"—he had corrected himself—"*we* will be safe."

Lisenka blinked hard and went back to staring out the window into the dark night. She was not alone. Most of Salt Mine was looking down, seeing the faint spots of light far below that would be their last glimpse of home. Whatever their reasons for leaving, no one in Salt Mine could ever return.

Even Keer, his lifetime dream of someday living in the States now a possibility, found himself saddened by the departure, suddenly so final. He reached into his jacket pocket for his cigarettes and his hand touched something hard. It was Gary's wristwatch, the coveted one with the four-inch-wide band. His question of how much Gary knew was answered.

From the loudspeaker came the pilot's voice, speaking in English. "We are leaving the coast of the Soviet Union now. Our flying time to Stockholm will be approximately one hour, ten minutes. The lights slightly to your right are the lights of the city of Petrozavodsk. After that, we will be flying above the gulfs of Bothnia and Finland, and you will see little until the lights of Stockholm."

The microphone clicked off. This time only a handful of Americans aboard applauded. For the members of Salt Mine, the moment was too emotional. The plane banked steeply to the left, turning toward Sweden and into the safety of a free, clear sky.

L'ENVOI

In less than a week all external signs of Salt Mine had been erased from the Kremlin. A platoon of expert woodcrafters descended upon the Oruzheinaya Palata, replacing the paneling where bullets had been fired into the walls. Other experts were flown in from Leningrad to repair the damage done some of the display cases, and special cabinet makers and painters quickly eliminated the scrapes and scratches from the wainscoting and paneling. They were followed by teams of floor specialists and the usual army of old women to polish the beeswax on the time-smoothed parquet. In Lenin's Tomb, the job was simpler, a matter of cleaning, washing, and polishing the marble.

The only difference a visitor might notice was the number of soldiers posted around the nongovernment buildings; Salt Mine had demonstrated to the Soviets their vulnerability in this area, and they did not intend to allow anything like it to happen again.

By the end of an additional week, both the tomb and the Oruzheinaya were once again open to the public; the Ministry of Public Information urged this step be taken as quickly as possible, since the longer these points of interest remained closed, the more the memory of Salt Mine burned itself into the public consciousness. Nothing, it was realized, was going to erase it—Salt Mine was still the number-one topic of conversation in Moscow—but there was no point in accenting the phenomenon with sealed-off areas and closed-off buildings.

The same effort was made inside the Council of Ministers Building. Although a lot of soul-searching was going on, everything appeared normal. If you walked into Klin's office, nothing appeared changed: You would find his high-backed leather chair swung around, as always, so that its back faced the door. The phone cord disappeared behind the chair;

someone on the other end of the phone was being counseled by the Minister of Security. "It is difficult to contemplate punishing a man for what his son has done. On the other hand, Gertsen should have kept a closer eye on the boy. I should suggest, while he cannot possibly continue as Minister of Production, Gertsen should not just be cast away. He is a valuable man. Perhaps an assignment running a complex of factories somewhere far from Moscow . . ."

There was a pause while the voice on the other end of the phone reacted. The crystal ball was spun in the air as always; Father Frost disappeared into the whirling snow, a lone red figure surrounded by impenetrable white. "Very well. Good. I shall."

Klin's heavy chair swung around. Mikhail Chorniev looked as at home in it as Klin ever had. Chorniev smiled slightly and made Father Frost disappear again. A couple more whirls and the figure became as invisible as its former owner.

Chorniev tilted the chair back and relaxed, luxuriating in the unaccustomed comfort of the new aristocracy. With a slight sigh, he put the crystal back on the desk and reached for the phone to place another call. The new minister of security was as busy as the old one.

A few of the flakes still whirled around Father Frost's feet, but once the snow settled, he appeared again, unchanged.

Like Chorniev, Father Frost was a professional survivor.

About the Author

David Lippincott is the author of VOICE OF ARMAGEDDON, TREMOR VIOLET, BLOOD OF OCTOBER, and SAVAGE RANSOM, all available in Signet editions. He lives in Connecticut with his wife and twelve-year-old son.